Halfway Perfect

Julie Cross & Mark Perini

sourcebooks
fire

Copyright © 2015 by Julie Cross and Mark Perini
Cover and internal design © 2015 by Sourcebooks, Inc.
Cover design by Sourcebooks, Inc.
Cover image © hexvivo/Thinkstock; Glow Images, Inc/Getty Images

Sourcebooks and the colophon are registered trademarks of Sourcebooks, Inc.

Published by Sourcebooks Fire, an imprint of Sourcebooks, Inc.
P.O. Box 4410, Naperville, Illinois 60567-4410
(630) 961-3900
Fax: (630) 961-2168
www.sourcebooks.com

Library of Congress Cataloging-in-Publication Data

Cross, Julie.

 Halfway perfect / Julie Cross and Mark Perini.

   pages cm

 Summary: Eve's time as a fashion model nearly destroyed her and now she is determined to build a career behind the camera after landing a photography internship in New York City, bringing her face to face with her dark past, her ex, and an up-and-coming male model named Alex who is falling for her.

  (trade paper : alk. paper) [1. Fashion--Fiction. 2. Photography--Fiction. 3. Models (Persons)--Fiction. 4. Love--Fiction.] I. Perini, Mark. II. Title.

 PZ7.C88272Hal 2015

 [Fic]--dc23

                                    2014036352

           Printed and bound in the United States of America.
              VP 10 9 8 7 6 5 4 3 2 1

Halfway Perfect

"Imperfection is beauty."
—Marilyn Monroe

Chapter 1: Eve

October 2, 6:45 a.m.

I cut everything in half.

And by everything, I mean everything—buildings, vehicles, trees...*people.*

Through the lens of my camera, I attempt to slice a billboard in half, allowing only Conan's right half into my shot. I shift the camera down lower and zoom in on a man seated at a table across the busy street. He's got a coffee cup in one hand and uses the other to press his cell phone to his ear. On one side he's Wall Street and the other half—the side with his fingers gently wrapped around the paper cup and his eyes staring straight ahead—he's an artist deep in thought. Maybe an author or a musician. Or a journalist who's feeling the emotional impact of a recent devastating story.

I lower my camera and tuck it into my bag as a woman approaches. She's exactly as I pictured her—fortysomething, brown hair in a messy ponytail, khakis cut off at the knee, tan lines in all the wrong places from hours of shooting outdoors, a giant bag of equipment slung gracefully over her shoulder.

I stand up and stick my hand out to shake hers. "I'm such an admirer of your work. I love the—"

"Eve Nowakowski, right? Professor Larson's student?"

I have Professor Larson for three classes this semester as part of the photography program at Columbia.

"Yes, I'm—"

Janessa Fields cuts me off again, waving a hand as if to say she doesn't have time or patience for my fangirl moment. And just like that, we're walking at a brisk New Yorker's pace and I'm stumbling to follow, despite the fact that she's the one lugging fifty pounds of equipment.

"Do you need some help with your bag?" I ask.

"I've got it, thanks." It's clear this is not one of those times where you should insist on helping anyway. "Professor Larson is the only person in the world who can talk me into allowing an eighteen-year-old student from Boston—"

"Actually, I'm from Indiana."

She glares at me, and I bite down on my tongue. "Professor Larson was my mentor years ago, so just try to stay out of the way today, understood?"

"Professor Larson didn't mention what you're working on today."

"That's because I didn't tell him."

She opens the door to a building and my pulse speeds up. I know this building. I've been here before. "Isn't this *Seventeen*?"

"Exactly why I didn't mention the client to Professor Larson." Janessa Fields rolls her eyes. "I was afraid if you knew the client, you might have come with a clan of screaming friends."

No, but I might not have shown up had I known.

"I'm just picking up some equipment for the shoot today. This isn't my usual cup of tea, but we all have to do some editorials now and again."

Not her usual cup of tea? That's like the biggest understatement of the year. I mean, seriously? Capturing third-world poverty on film versus taking photos for editorials on prom makeup or how to get your crush to notice you—the difference is greater than the distance between New York City and Africa.

Walking through this building and toward the elevator, I'm already feeling sick to my stomach, fighting the urge to turn around and run. I'm supposed to be studying photography with a woman who can make tragedy look beautiful in a photo, not someone photographing teen models for an article about how to tell if your boyfriend's cheating on you.

Janessa yells at me to keep up, then she leaves me in the magazine's lobby while she gets her equipment from an intern. I stand at the end of a long, carpeted hallway. The walls are lined with framed covers from dozens of issues.

I stroll slowly past each one, looking at the gorgeous, perfect models, knowing more than I'd like to about what goes into those shots. I pause on an issue from four years ago. The cover features a brown-haired girl from Indiana—*International Model and Only Fifteen Years Old: Eve Castle Tells All in an Exclusive Interview with* Seventeen. She's thin in a Kate Moss way, with gangly limbs and a flat chest. She was nearly six feet tall when she was in middle school, and boys used to stare at that flat chest because her training bra was at eye level for them.

My hair hasn't changed much in four years and neither has my height. But she's different. *Her* eyes are different, and she looks happier than I feel now. I almost want to reach into the picture and shake her, tell her what's going to happen to her. Maybe I can make it so she stays happy.

"Wasn't he just adorable in that issue?" someone says behind me. "Hard to find that blond, youthful, all-American look. That's probably why we've had him on the cover three times."

He? Fifteen-year-old me may have been flat-chested, but I didn't look like a boy.

My gaze drifts to the right. To the guy on the cover of a different issue. His arms are wrapped around the waist of a perky cheerleader-type model with shiny black hair. The headline at the top reads: *How to Win Over Your Crush This Valentine's Day.*

I hear the swish of Janessa's equipment bag against her water-resistant khakis. "Absolutely adorable," she says. "Middle school boys make excellent sex symbols."

My heart pounds as Janessa's gaze slides left, to the cover beside the "middle school boy's" photo. I glance over my shoulder at the perky twentysomething intern. She looks a little red in the face but doesn't respond to Janessa's crude remark. Janessa nods toward the photo of the guy and the girl together. "Actually, I think this kid's in our shoot today. Lucky you. You might get to meet every girl's Valentine's Day crush."

Yeah. Can't wait for that.

Does Janessa recognize me? Does she care? Is anyone else at the job going to recognize me? Surely I'm old news by now. What if I'm wrong and I get thrown into a situation where I have to explain why I left modeling? Might be best to take off now, just in case.

But you don't get into a school like Columbia without putting grades above emotional stability—at least some of the time. And I can't imagine running away and disappointing Professor Larson after he used his connections to set this up for me.

Janessa turns around and launches herself down the hall. I let out a big sigh before following her.

When we get to the studio, Janessa introduces me to the producer, who introduces us to several wardrobe and makeup people. No one gives me a first glance, let alone a second glance. For a moment, I relax. I'm in the clear.

Then I see him. Red hair gelled and spiked to perfection, slim dress pants perfectly pressed, and a button-down shirt half-untucked in that trendy way. He's barking into his cell phone, flashing a tight smile at the producer.

Wes Danes.

The air is sucked out of my lungs, my legs instantly weak.

My first thought hits: What's he doing here?

Followed by the second: I need to stay far away from Wes Danes.

Unfortunately, I've been staring at him like an idiot for a good thirty seconds instead of finding something to hide behind.

Wes gives me a double take. But he plays it cool. He doesn't show any sign of surprise beyond a quick widening of his eyes. He slowly makes his way over, walking past me with a slight nod toward the elevator.

Don't do it, don't follow him.

But I can't stop my feet. He nods and they move. Traitors.

I hold my breath and follow the trail of his designer cologne through the elevator doors. As they close, the walls press in on me from all sides.

"How are you, Evie?" he asks in a quiet voice so different from the commanding assertive voice he'd used on the phone moments ago.

"I…I'm…" The doors open, letting us out on the first floor. I trail Wes down a hall and into a secluded corridor.

He spins around to face me. "What are you doing here?"

"It's just…I have this…" I can't look him in the eye. "It's a long story."

He steps closer—too close—and scrubs his hands over his face. This is Vulnerable Wes. The guy I fell in love with. It'd be much easier to have this chat with arrogant, It's-Not-Personal-It's-Business Wes. "Who are you working with? What agent? And what have they booked for you? Why didn't you call me, Evie? After everything—"

"I'm not working," I say, finally able to look him in the eye. "I'm here for a photography class. My professor—"

His eyebrows lift. "You're in college? In New York?"

"Yeah," I nod. "At Columbia."

The surprise is evident on his face, and I feel the tiniest twinge of satisfaction. *A lot can happen in two years, Wes.*

Suddenly, a memory from two years ago returns. Him yelling at me, his warm breath in my face. The crash of the chair against the china cabinet, glass shattering all over his apartment floor. I remember the panic I fought that day. It was like my brain and body were completely torn in two—half of me ready to bolt out the door, the other half clinging to our yearlong relationship. That night I had walked through his door ready to tell him I wanted out, ready to tell his boss that I needed a new agent, but the second Wes held me and said he was sorry, I caved. It took me two more weeks to leave, and I haven't seen or spoken to Wes since.

Why does a tiny part of me still feel drawn to him? I hate him. I know I hate him. But he made me love him. Apparently two years isn't long enough to make that fade. It should be, but it isn't.

"Yo, Wes!" someone shouts from down the corridor.

Wes springs into action. "We'll talk later," he whispers.

No, we won't. Not if I can help it.

He's already walking away before I can respond. He won't know where to find me, right? Why didn't I lie and say I went to NYU? But I guess Wes knows me better than that. I've had my heart set on going to Columbia since I started modeling in New York City when I was fourteen.

I recognize the guy Wes is talking to. He's the model that Janessa called a middle schooler. Except he looks older now. That cover photo was from a few years ago. On my walk to the elevator, I feel his eyes burning a hole in the side of my face. I just look straight ahead, wishing away the heat flaring on my cheeks.

Does he recognize me? He might. Or maybe he's checking me out. I guess that's possible. Statistics are in favor of him just being a guy and staring at me for guy reasons and not personal ones.

Since I've returned to New York for school, I've been looking for a nice guy to date because that seemed so…I don't know… normal. But this guy would not fit into that mold. Not even close. But I'm still in favor of being ogled rather than being recognized as Eve Castle.

I avoid eye contact and slide into the elevator the second the doors open, but not before I hear Wes giving muffled instructions. Something about impressing Elana or "making nice with her."

I don't even want to know what the hell that means.

Chapter 2: Alex

October 2, 7:30 a.m.

After escaping the hungover intern sleeping in my bedroom, I was hoping for a few minutes of calm on the way to this shoot, but of course my phone rings. Wes. *Before nine in the morning. Can't be good.*

"Finally! I've left you three messages in the last two hours!"

"My phone was in my room—"

"And you weren't?" he asks, then keeps talking before I can answer and explain that I'd left a girl, along with my phone, in my room. And slept on the couch. "Never mind. I don't want details. I'm at the studio. We need to chat before you head up to hair and makeup."

"I'll be there in five," I assure him.

"Good. See you in a few."

He hangs up with no further explanation. He's at the studio? Wes has my schedule, but that doesn't mean he actually shows up at jobs. I don't know any agents who do that.

Weird. Now I'm getting a little nervous. I thought this would be an easy morning. There's not too much on the line for me here.

Unless I somehow managed to get myself fired? That would suck. Majorly. Getting fired from even the smallest jobs can damage your reputation.

When I get to the studio, I spot Wes in the lobby, talking to some brunette.

"Yo, Wes," I say so he knows I'm here.

He breaks away from his conversation. My gaze follows the girl he had been talking to. I know her from somewhere. It's possible I've worked with her before on a job. She's pretty—very pretty. And thin, but not runway-model thin. The girl lights up the button and waits for the elevator. Before I can figure it out, I hear the elevator ding, and my attention snaps back to Wes who looks a little distracted. "What's up?"

He closes his eyes for a second as if to refocus. "One of the agency's newest clients—Elana—is also in the shoot today. She's an import from France. Really green, but huge potential. I need you to make nice with her, all right?"

I scratch the back of my head. Wes and his assignments. Last night it was a *GQ* intern and today it's a new French model. "Okay?"

He leans in closer and lowers his voice. "When you get paired together today, a little chemistry certainly won't hurt you at all. Elana's pretty young, but let's keep that on the DL."

"Got it. No problem."

Wes gives me his best agent grin. "I knew I could count on you. This could be a great opportunity. A lot of doors could swing open after this shoot."

I relax, relieved that I haven't done anything wrong, and then my brain catches up, replaying his words. "Wait… Exactly how young are we talking?"

"Fourteen," Wes says without missing a beat. "But that's between you and me. We're still deciding how to market her, so we're avoiding age labels."

"Great," I grumble. Not that I haven't worked with girls that young before—I have, plenty of times. It's not really a big deal. It's just that faking chemistry with a girl who is the same age as my little sister tends to mess with my muse a bit.

Is Wes trying to get us some couples' campaign? Not likely he'll tell me before the decision is made. He's always got a few tricks up his sleeve—some ethical and some not so much. But I trust him.

I call the elevator, and when it arrives, Wes takes a step inside, then hesitates.

"Are you coming?" I ask, not because I expect him to, but because he looked like he might.

He shakes his head and walks three paces backward. "No, I've got a meeting at the office. Just needed to catch you before things got started. I'm sure it'll be a great shoot."

I shrug and head up to the seventeenth floor, where I'm greeted by Frankie, the producer, and led to the back of the studio, where hair and makeup have set up shop. A familiar high-pitched cackle comes from behind a huge vanity mirror.

"The queen has finally graced us with her presence." Hugo curtsies down to the floor before turning to face me. "Need some Earl Grey, Your Majesty?"

"No thanks. I only drink the good stuff," I say with a grin.

I'm trying not to be too obvious, but I scan the area for Elana. I recognize another girl from my agency, Finley. She's also one of the only agency models that I know of who might actually spend more hours at the gym than me. I see her there all the time. Finley waves when she spots me, and I give her a quick wave in return.

A few more witty comments round out the brief hair and makeup session, then I'm off to set. No matter how many jobs I've done, it's always strange to introduce myself to a girl I've never met and then act like high school sweethearts for the camera. I try and quiet my mind, knowing nerves or apprehension of any kind have no place on set, and greet the photographer, Janessa Fields. Wes mentioned the other day that she's a big deal.

The woman barely acknowledges me, but she doesn't seem rude or anything, just on task. I can deal with that.

"Let's get the two lovebirds together," she says, nudging me on set.

It's immediately clear why Elana was imported from France at fourteen. There's a rawness to her that makes her unique. She stands out. Maybe it's the tan skin and black hair too. I'm so lost in thought that I stumble over some rigging equipment, almost falling flat on my face. I recover with an awkward jog. Unfortunately, no one buys it and there are a lot of laughs at my complete lack of grace.

My near face-plant gets Elana's attention though, and our eyes meet. "I'm Alex."

She looks like she's trying not to laugh. "I'm Elana. Hopefully you can keep your feet on ground."

"Right. Me too."

The accent is heavy, but her English seems good. Not to mention that she's pretty confident for fourteen if she's standing here making jokes rather than shaking with nerves. But she's French. She's probably walked around topless since birth.

Janessa cuts the small talk and starts positioning us, which means Elana is now basically straddling my lap. I shut off the part of my brain that's telling me exactly what I would do to any guy who put his hands on my sister the way I have my hands on Elana. *At least she isn't topless.*

We finish up the first shots quickly, and Elana and I both move on to our first wardrobe change, and Eduardo and Finley, the other model couple, step into the spotlight. While I wait for Janessa to call us back up again, I'm careful to keep out of Frankie's way. He's stomping around like a crazy person grumbling about an intern taking forever to fetch his coffee. It's never a good idea to attempt small talk or try sucking up to producers before they've had their morning coffee.

Hushed voices converse behind me. It's Hugo and the other wardrobe people.

"They look so perfect together," Hugo says.

"How long have they been dating?"

"I heard they met in Paris over the summer."

"That's probably true," Hugo says. "Alex spent June in Paris. He did that show for—"

I glance over my shoulder, knowing it will stop the gossip. I've been here, like, an hour. How did I suddenly end up dating a costar? Don't these people have anything better to do? Like work? That is what we're here for.

I catch Finley's arm before we switch places again. "What's with all the whispering?"

She pretends to adjust her hair while checking out my fan club. "Who knows? I wouldn't get too worked up about stories traveling through the hair and makeup rumor mill."

"That's excellent advice." I raise my voice to a normal volume and proceed to have the typical *how have you been, what jobs are you getting* talk with Finley. "Are you still commuting from Connecticut?"

"Yeah, but as of December I'll be a New York City resident."

"What happens in December?" I ask, but my gaze is on Janessa, waiting for her to wave me over again.

From the corner of my eye, I see Finley nod toward Elana. "That's when the agency decided the foreign exchange student would be 'assimilated' enough to ditch her personal assistant, which leaves an open bed in her room for me."

For the first time today, I notice the older woman watching Elana from the sidelines. With her round body and practical, comfortable clothing choices, she doesn't look like someone in the fashion industry—a babysitter working under the assistant label most likely. And seriously? After less than two months in New York City, a fourteen-year-old girl from a foreign country is expected to take care of herself? Is she going to turn eighteen between now and December? I guess according to Wes that's possible.

I turn back to Finley. "You don't seem too excited about that."

"I'm not really thrilled," she admits. "I like being at home with my family."

I laugh out loud. "Okay, I totally can't relate to that." My parents are cool and all. And my two brothers have been known to stand up for me a time or two, but they aren't exactly accepting of their younger brother—to quote them—"prancing around in underwear with a bunch of other dudes." So my time with my family includes my dad's brooding silence, my mom pushing food, and Jared and Bradley's relentless teasing. Hanging out with Katie is all right, not that I've seen my sister lately. I haven't been home in months.

"My dad's making me move out." Finley rolls her eyes. "He says he wants me to have fun. I don't think he has any clue what he's talking about, but whatever. It makes him happy."

I grin at her. "You mean this isn't fun?"

She glances down at her dress. "The clothes are fun. But the five hundred pins stuck in this outfit are digging into my back and ruining this game of dress-up."

I tug at the collar of the very uncomfortable and similarly prickly shirt that I'm wearing. "Good point."

Janessa calls Elana and me back for more shots in our new outfits. That's when I notice the girl Wes had been talking to in the lobby. She really *does* look familiar. She's standing next to Janessa, watching her work and carting around a professional-grade camera of her own. I catch her staring at me. It's the kind of stare that makes me want to spend a few minutes flirting with her. When we break for a minute so Hugo can fix my makeup, I decide to take advantage of his gossip obsession.

"Hey, do you know who that girl is? The one beside Janessa?" I whisper so she doesn't hear me.

Hugo jabs me in the side with an elbow. "I thought you were taken."

I'm not even dignifying that with a response. "Seriously, do you know her? She looks familiar."

He shrugs, coming at me with a makeup brush and powder. "She's some college student writing a paper on Janessa or something. Eve, I think. Frankie introduced us before you got here."

"Oh. She probably just looks like someone else."

Okay, so maybe I'm a little intimidated by the idea of flirting with a college girl. Not that I couldn't have gone that route myself. I still can. I'm only eighteen. Some people don't go to college until they're, like, forty.

"These shots are going to be so fabulous," Hugo says. "I hope it works out with the two of you because you look gorgeous on camera together. Her dark skin and your light features—it's stunning."

I work hard not to roll my eyes. *Whatever.* Let Hugo tell everyone that I'm hooking up with the new "next big thing." Although, wouldn't that technically be illegal if she's only fourteen? No wonder Wes and the agency didn't want to share her age yet. If she ends up booking a big campaign with some teenybopper guy who's not old enough to drive, then she can be fourteen. But if she books something with me, they'll want her to be what? Sixteen? Seventeen? Please let it be at least sixteen.

Janessa dismisses me and Elana for the second time. After handing my shirt over to wardrobe, I head straight for the opposite side of the room, to avoid more gossip.

I could only assume when Wes said, "make nice with Elana,"

he meant on camera, not off. Or maybe he just meant to make her feel welcome, like, "Check to make sure her Happy Meal includes a toy." God, even that could be twisted into something vulgar. I let out a frustrated breath and keep my back to the watching eyes. I just need to get through this job and then maybe Wes will be kind enough to fill me in on what the hell is going on.

Chapter 3: Eve

October 2, 9:00 a.m.

"You! With the gelled hair," Janessa shouts at one of the male models. "Why do you look constipated?"

Eduardo's face reddens, and he pulls at the back of his shirt. "This shirt's so tight I can barely breathe."

Janessa throws her free hand up in the air as if to say, *Why did you wait so long to say something?* "Can somebody please fix the model's wardrobe before he passes out?"

Several people rush forward, giving Janessa a short break. I laugh under my breath. Everyone seems so afraid of her. I guess I am too, but not in the same way. I've worked with a handful of photographers when I modeled who would have told me to suck it up and quit whining.

And I would have done just that. Thank God Compliant Eve died along with my modeling career.

I've been observing for a little while now, and my legs have finally stopped shaking from my conversation with Wes. He doesn't appear to be returning to the set. Every hour he doesn't show up puts me that much more at ease.

Janessa flips through images on her camera while she waits. "You have some questions for me, I assume? For your paper?"

"Um, sure." I retrieve my notebook from my purse and flip through some of the questions I'd written last night when I couldn't sleep. "What was it like in Africa? Spending all that time there, it just seems so…I don't know, *exotic*."

She laughs and keeps her eyes on the camera in her hands. "Africa? It's lovely. With the worst economic conditions possible, the constant threat of malaria, and the poverty, I can't think of anything more exotic."

"But that isn't how I felt seeing your photos," I say in protest. Maybe exotic wasn't the right word. *Epic*. That's what I'd meant to say. "The spread in *National Geographic* and the piece in *Time*, not to mention your book. I've memorized every image. I could hardly look away long enough to turn the page."

I bite down on my tongue. Janessa Fields doesn't seem the type to enjoy college girls gushing over her work.

"I can tell you exactly how I pulled that off," she says, gracefully ignoring my fangirl moment. "You have to find something uplifting as a focal point. You can find that focus in any situation if you look hard enough. And then let the destruction take over the background of the photo." Janessa says. "It's human nature to want to watch people survive against the odds."

The producer shuffles toward us, interrupting the philosophical lesson.

"Everything looks great so far," he says to Janessa. "Let's get Alex and Elana again."

The couples switch places. Alex takes the floor again. The more

I look at him, the more familiar he seems. Besides the younger version of him on *Seventeen*'s wall, he's probably on a billboard somewhere posing in boxer briefs.

Elana looks really young. So young that I'm sure it took effort to make her appear old enough to pose with Alex. I watch them for several minutes while Janessa gives directions. Alex does everything she asks perfectly. He's not even a little bit intimidated by her or by the dozens of people watching him. His chemistry with Elana is almost immediate. Whether manufactured for this job or real, it's there, and it'll be there in the photo too.

His arrogance is also painfully familiar. So much that I can't watch them anymore. I lift my camera to my face again and start snapping shots of Janessa as she works. Despite her comment about teen fashion magazines not being her "usual cup of tea," she's completely absorbed and on task. It's as if she's never taken a bad picture in her life and she doesn't plan to start now.

By the time my focus returns to the actual photo shoot, Janessa has moved on to a different set of models, and Elana is on the floor punching buttons on her sparkly-pink cell phone.

"Are you supposed to be taking pictures in here?"

I glance at the intern beside me. "I'm writing a paper on Janessa Fields. She said I could include some environmental photographs of her workplace." *Okay, so maybe she didn't say that, but she didn't tell me I couldn't either.*

"Oh. Gotcha," the girl says, backing down so quickly that I almost feel guilty for lying. "It's just that Elana—actually, her *assistant*—would have a fit if we allowed photos that aren't part of the shoot. Especially with all of the reporters. No, we wouldn't want that."

I lower my camera and take in the round Hispanic woman the intern referred to as Elana's assistant. "How old is Elana?"

"Not sure. All I've gotten are mixed answers," the intern says. "What's your guess?"

I shrug, shaking off a flashback of me, four years ago. "Hard to say."

My guess is fourteen or fifteen. Sixteen tops.

The girl leans in to whisper to me, as if we're suddenly BFFs. "She's already hooked up with Alex Evans. I heard they might be doing a big campaign together."

My camera returns to my eye, and I zoom in on Alex, who's clear on the other side of the room. After all his flirting with Elana a few minutes ago, I expected that to continue off camera, but he's moved himself as far from her as possible.

"I wouldn't be surprised if you're right," I say to the girl. This seems to please her, and she leaves me to return to her work.

I zoom in on Alex. His back is to me as he stares out the window. His hands are stuffed in his borrowed jean pockets. He lets out a breath and his shoulders slump forward a tad and the muscles in his back become less defined. A rush of adrenaline zips through my veins and I start snapping a dozen pictures, walking sideways to capture his profile.

Without any warning, his back becomes perfectly erect again and his head snaps in my direction.

Shit.

"What are you doing?" he demands, stalking over and placing his palm over my camera lens.

"Nothing." My heart thuds a little too fast. "Just getting some shots of the skyline. You know…out the window."

His eyebrows lift, challenging me. "Oh yeah? Well don't let me block your view."

He steps aside and now I can clearly see that there isn't anything out that particular window except the side of another building. My face heats up despite telling myself *not* to blush. He's gonna think I'm some obsessive girl trying to sneak pictures of shirtless models. As if I haven't seen enough of them for a lifetime.

I have yet to be caught photographing a human subject. Usually I'm in wide-open spaces like Central Park and no one suspects they're in my shot. And those photos are for my professor or my own walls, not *National Geographic* like Janessa's stuff or even *Seventeen*. If the roles were reversed, I'd be pissed off too.

I flash him my most genuine fake smile. "Sorry. The light captured your profile so well. It's a flattering image, really."

I have to give him credit because he snorts at my bullshit answer and tries to snatch my camera. I jerk it away from him, pressing it against my side. "All right, *Fabio*. So I caught you in a rare moment when you don't look like a pompous asshole trying to feel up a fourteen-year-old girl. You can sue me if you want."

His face fills with anger, then changes as he absorbs all my words. "How did you know her age?" he whispers so softly I can barely hear him.

Okay, apparently I've guessed right.

JULIE CROSS AND MARK PERINI

Before I get a chance to respond, his expression changes again as if realization is hitting hard and fast.

Uh oh.

"Holy hell...you're...you're—" he stammers. I hold my breath, knowing what's coming. "That chick who bailed before that big Gucci campaign. You were with Wes Danes, right? I've been going crazy for the last hour trying to figure out how I knew you!"

With Wes. Does he understand the double meaning in that?

My heart is pounding. My eyes dart around the room, scanning for listening ears. My hand shakes, nearly spilling my camera onto the floor.

"What?" I ask, trying to brush off the accusation in the off chance that Alex is a complete idiot and buys my denial.

No such luck. In fact, he's got out his phone and is typing faster than should be humanly possible. I close my eyes for a second, visualizing what words he typed into the search engine: *model who quit Gucci.* Or maybe, *sixteen-year-old diva who's decided she's too good for Gucci* or possibly, *ways to ruin your modeling career.*

He looks up from his phone. "Eve Castle!" Triumph fills his voice, like it's fucking Final Jeopardy and he's correctly answered the million-dollar question: *This female model mysteriously left the industry at the brink of superstardom.*

Ding, ding! Who is Eve Castle?

I should have faked food poisoning the second I arrived at *Seventeen*'s headquarters.

"Please keep your voice down," I bark at Alex. I lift my camera in front of his face. "Eve Nowakowski. Photography student. Columbia University. Not a model."

He ignores my response. "What happened to you, anyway?" he asks. "Must have been something big for you to take off like that."

"I'm sure you've already got ideas, right?" I can't hide my frustration. There were hundreds of stories claiming to know why I left, but none of them were true. "Which story did you read? Drug rehab? Teen pregnancy? Psychotic episode? It's not like I'm going to be able to pitch a new version to you."

He shrugs and lowers my camera so it's waist high. "Whatever. I never believe that tabloid shit anyway."

And just like that, he walks away, leaving me stunned. A few moments later a voice startles me by saying my name. I turn around to face Janessa. I can't tell how long she's been standing there, but if she heard my conversation with Alex, there's nothing I can do about it now.

She holds out her hand. "Let's see if these photos of yours are worth the shit I'm getting from the producer."

My heart is still racing as I hand over the camera. I don't even stop myself from biting my nails as she looks over my work.

Her eyebrows lift. "I can see why Professor Larson likes you so much. You've actually given him something worth criticizing, unlike most of the students he's forced to pretend are talented."

Did Janessa Fields just call me talented? And wait…my photos are worthy of criticism from my professor—and that is a good thing?

"Thanks," I mumble, not sure how to handle this maybe compliment. "I'll put my camera away now. I don't want to cause any more trouble."

"If anyone asks, I just reprimanded you and forced you to delete every one of those photos." She winks at me before returning to work.

I walk back toward the makeup and hair area. My footsteps seem overly loud. Then I realize most of the crew and models are glaring at me. My face heats up again, but I'm sort of relieved, because I know it's my taking photos that's gotten everyone hot and bothered, not my identity.

There's space to lean against the wall several feet behind Janessa. I set my bag on the floor, holding up my empty hands as if to say, *I'm done, no more pictures.* Then the room is in motion again. Several of the models return to whatever it was they were doing. Janessa and the producer are looking over pictures on the monitor while the intern girl scribbles notes furiously.

I close my eyes for a second, taking in a slow deep breath. Today's emotional roller coaster has already exhausted me and it's only 11:00 a.m.

"So...?"

My eyes fly open. "College Eve, right?" A blond-haired, blue-eyed model who's practically the only person in the room not glaring at me is now in front of me, initiating conversation.

"Yeah, I guess," I say.

"I'm Finley." Her hair is curled perfectly, her makeup a mask over flawless skin. She's shorter than me. Probably only five seven or five eight. Not a runway girl like Elana and me. "I'm not in the least bit concerned about having my picture taken without authorization, but I prefer Instagram. Tumblr tends to add ten pounds."

I laugh. "No tweeting or tumbling, I promise. But I might send them to an old professor who loves to study human subjects in photos for a living."

"Just so long as you split the profits with me." She bends down to smooth the hem of her dress, which has flipped upward. "You're here for a school paper, right?

"Yeah, I'm writing about Janessa. She's a former student of one of my professors."

"That's awesome. I've never heard of Janessa before today, but everyone here has been going on and on about how famous and important she is," Finley says. "I'm just loving the fact that she hasn't yelled at me, made me take my top off, or told me to suck in my gut. It's nice to get direction that I can actually follow."

Unfortunately, I know exactly what she means. "Are you in college? Or high school?"

I shift from one foot to the other, regretting the question. Finley watches me and grins. "It's hard to tell with us girls, isn't it? I just graduated in June, but I'm saving up before college. Hopefully only a year. It's been a little depressing though. All my friends are off at school and call me to tell me about their roommates and dorm food and all that. I wish that's what I was doing too. But you, you're living that life."

"Sure am," I say. "Where do you want to go?"

"I've always loved NYU. My parents met there. Can you imagine taking out four years of student loans for NYU tuition and with no high-paying corporate job planned?"

Actually, I have calculated student loans for Columbia's steep tuition, and I only got to adding five years of interest and payments before nearly passing out. "You'd have to be really passionate about your studies.

She laughs really hard. "Exactly. Which is why I'm here. My dad says he'll get a loan or figure out something, but I don't want to put that burden on him. Not if I have a way to make my own money. What's a year in the long run anyway, right?"

Clearly we have very different families. Her dad wants to bend over backward for her, and my parents prefer to live on their daughter's modeling checks.

"Where's the perky blond girl?" Frankie shouts, turning slowly around the room.

"Finley," Janessa says with her eyes still on the monitor.

Finley nods toward Janessa, flashing me another smile. "See why I like her?"

Finley walks over to set, again pausing by Alex. The two of them chat for a few seconds and he pulls out his phone again and punches in a number. *Her number.*

I let out a breath and then close my eyes, this time getting a full four minutes of calming solitude before being interrupted again.

"They're still talking about you and your paparazzi moves over there." Alex laughs softly. "And I thought today would be boring as hell."

Alex is the only person in the room to recognize me, and he doesn't seem to be in a rush to spread the gossip, so I decide it's safe to talk to him. "Glad I could entertain you with my humiliation."

I smile to myself. It's just like Janessa said, find something good to use as a focal point and leave the destruction in the background. Guess I don't need to go too far to learn that lesson.

"What's so funny?" he asks me.

"Nothing." I shake my head. "Today is royally fucked up. And after a certain level of fucked-upism, it becomes funny."

"Fucked-upism," Alex repeats. "Is that a real word?"

"Yeah, they teach it at Columbia. It's in the Ivy League dictionary."

Alex laughs and our eyes meet for a second before we shift our gaze toward Elana, who is getting a new outfit for the next set of photos.

"You know, I bet Elana is pretty entertaining," I say, just to test him. Maybe I'm flirting. I'm not sure, but it's kind of nice, whatever it is. He's nice and nice to look at too.

He rolls his eyes. "Yeah, totally. I'm thinking about surprising her with One Direction tickets."

"Very age appropriate," I say, surprised by his sarcasm. "It has been quite a day for you, hasn't it? You've been the center of the gossip, got to aid in my humiliation, solved a crucial fashion industry mystery, *and* got digits from the hot blond model."

He scratches the back of his head, confused for a second, before glancing toward set, then back at me. "You mean Finley? I didn't get her number to ask her out or anything."

I have no idea why I even brought this up, but at least we're not talking about Eve Castle. "Why not? She's nice. She might be the only nice person here."

Alex's eyebrows lift and he leans against the wall beside me, lowering his voice. "I know she's nice. I've worked with her before. Plus we run into each other at the gym all the time. But that girl's got a fortress around her. I guess because you're a chick you can't see it."

I look over at Finley, as if expecting to see an actual barrier surrounding her. Does that mean I don't have a fortress? If Alex mentioned hers, then I must not have one. "A fortress, huh?"

"Yeah," he says like it's common knowledge. He's talking about another girl but his eyes are glued to mine. It's the kind of stare that makes me blush. "My guess is she's either Mormon or she's one of those girls who's happily in love. Probably had the same boyfriend since seventh grade or something."

"You've thought about this a lot?" I ask, teasing. Yes, teasing. Which is a type of flirting. My outgoing sophomore roommate, Stephanie, would be proud if she could see me right now. Actually, she'd probably be wedging herself between me and shirtless Alex. Can't say I'd blame her.

He shrugs, completely shameless. "It's always good to analyze people's potential motivations."

"If I were you, I'd be analyzing the reason why everyone here seems to think you and the One Direction lunch-box carrier over there are an item." I wave my hands out in front of him, tracing an imaginary box. "I'm seeing a fortress around you when it comes to Elana."

Alex turns serious again and lowers his voice. "How did you know her age? I'm not even supposed to know."

"Honestly, just a lucky guess. I started modeling at fourteen, and I remember how it was to play it down or up. But she looks fourteen when she doesn't think anyone is watching."

Alex's gaze stays on mine. "Yeah, I think you're right."

I'd rather be wrong. I'd rather Elana be eighteen or even sixteen, but honestly, I'm going to leave here in a couple of hours and, I hope, never see these people again.

Though, now that I know he's nice, I wouldn't object to an occasional billboard sighting of Alex in boxer briefs.

Chapter 4: Alex

October 2, 11:20 a.m.

Okay, so I got totally curious despite my noble declaration to Eve about not believing tabloid lies, and I gave myself sixty seconds to quickly scroll through the search results still open on my phone before I walked over to talk to her. The headlines alone provided a sea of information…

Teen Model Sensation Disappears the Day Before Shooting Huge Gucci Campaign

Design.com

Sixteen-year-old star model Eve Castle must have taken a hard hit to the head or swallowed a handful of crazy pills. After beating veterans and newcomers alike to win over top Gucci designers and execs for a career-launching campaign, she's vanished from New York, and the label is now scrambling to replace her and prep for their shoot tomorrow…

Diva Model Leaves Designers Empty-Handed

Vogueonline.com

Eve Castle is nowhere to be found, and *Vogue* was unable to get a statement from her agency, One Model Management…

Runaway Teen Model Suspected to Have Checked Herself Into Drug Rehab

Fashionreporter.com

Insiders are reporting that the young star who abandoned Gucci earlier this week is, in fact, suffering from addiction and is now residing in an unknown drug rehab facility…

One Model Management Makes Statement on Teen Client's Behalf: Is There Such a Thing as Too Young in the World of Fashion?

New York Times

Wes Danes, the agent who's responsible for launching teen model Eve Castle's career, says he was just as astonished by the sixteen-year-old's disappearance as we all were. "If she was having problems, I wish she would have come to me first," Danes says. The agency's head, Josh Valentine, was not as kind as Danes. "Yes, I'll admit, there were early signs of a breakdown…she'd become unstable and an emotional train wreck but we saw no evidence of drug use or eating disorders…if we had, of course we would have contacted her parents and gotten her help," Valentine says. "None of us want to see a young girl fall like that…the agency takes every precaution to protect these girls."

A One-On-One With Teen Model Sensation Eve Castle

Seventeen.com

She's only fifteen years old, but already she's managed to snag the attention of designers like Prada, Calvin Klein, Ralph Lauren...*Seventeen* editor Jillian Martin sat down to talk to the young star about how she got started and what she's experienced so far in the world of fashion...Jillian even talked her into sharing some of her photos from her summer in Europe, and *Seventeen* was so impressed we've included them in this issue along with Eve Castle's candid and enlightening responses...

The last headline I've actually seen before, and it's the reason Eve looked familiar to me today. A couple of months ago, I was at a cocktail party at *Seventeen*'s office, and I didn't know anyone there except Wes, so when he walked away to talk to someone, I got bored and scanned the cover photos plastered all over the hallways, one of which featured a younger me. Some girl walked up beside me and pointed to the issue next to mine and started rambling on and on about a girl who bailed on Gucci and hasn't been seen since. But I couldn't remember the name of the girl. Plus, the picture I saw of Eve on that cover was a much younger version of the girl at the shoot today, which is why it didn't click instantly.

So, of course, I had to talk to her and see if I could fill in the missing gaps. Now I'm in the middle of a conversation with Eve Castle—correction—Eve Nowakowski. Who I now can label as the last female model Wes Danes ever represented. I bet he lost a bunch of contacts when she bailed, burned some bridges and couldn't make up for it on the girl front and had to switch to repping guys. Good for me, I guess. But they were talking earlier. That must have been tense.

"What exactly are you doing here?" I ask Eve, still deciding if I'm going to turn this conversation into flirting. She's given me tiny hints of it, but nothing obvious and over the top. But solving the mystery is throwing a cloak over any other objectives. "If you're trying to hide, this isn't exactly the best place."

"No shit." She closes her eyes and lets out a breath before opening them again. "It's just the way my life goes, I guess. The second I think I've got everything figured out, I'm at a photo shoot for *Seventeen*. Janessa is a former student of one of my professors, and he thought I might like to observe her for this artist profile paper I'm writing."

"And you had no idea where that observation would take place," I finish for her.

"If I had known, I would have made up a really good excuse."

The conversation is halted when my phone buzzes in my pocket. Even though I don't usually do phone calls on a job, I glance at it quickly and see the name: Katie.

My little sister.

"Hey," I say to Eve. "Can you cover for me for a minute? Just say I'm in the bathroom." I figure she'll go along with it, considering what I know about her.

I dive behind the wall Eve and I had just been leaning against and answer my sister's phone call, though I don't know why she didn't just text me like she usually does. At least five times a day.

"Katie, what's up?"

"I need a favor," she says, almost whispering.

I'm immediately suspicious. "Are you calling from school?"

"Yeah. I need you to get me out of advanced algebra," she says, sounding a little louder and a little more desperate. "It's social suicide, and you know Mom won't listen to me. All you have to do is call my counselor and say you're Dad—"

"No."

"Please, Alex...*please*...I'll write and mail all your birthday and Mother's Day cards for the next four years...*please*."

I feel the tiniest bit of sympathy for her because she must really not want to be in that class, but I'm still not doing it. "Why don't you ask Brad? He's the expert on cheating and forgery."

"Because he's not my favorite brother," Katie says. *Manipulative little suck-up.* "Like Brad and Jared know anything about social suicide. They've never even been in the general vicinity of it."

True. But I'm slightly offended that I don't get the same label. "I'm not even sure you deserve to be in advanced math. You obviously haven't thought this through. All the school phones have caller ID, and don't you think your counselor will be suspicious of your dad calling from a New York City area code? Plus, what are you going to tell Mom and Dad when it's report card time and your grade is for the wrong class?"

"You suck," she says with a groan.

"Sorry." I smile down at the floor, trying to keep it out of my voice. "Go back to your nerd math class. I promise you, in four years the threat of social suicide will be completely dissipated."

"I hate you."

I laugh. I can't help it. "I know. But can we talk about how much I suck later? I'm working right now. I thought someone died. That's the only reason I answered the phone."

"You're working? Where? For who?"

"It's just a shoot for *Seventeen*."

"Oh my God, that's awesome. What issue?" She's temporarily forgotten to hate me for not lying and cheating for her. Honestly, if I actually thought it would have worked, I'd have considered it. It's not like she's dropping out. And in our high school, smart math *is* kind of social suicide. At least for someone like Katie who's already on the cusp of dork status due to being a bit of a shrimp, plus glasses and braces.

"I'm not sure which issue. I'll let you know when I find out. Now go to class and learn something—like how to do my taxes. *That* would be useful."

I hang up before she can call me an asshole. When I walk around the wall to the other side, Eve is still standing in the same spot.

She smiles at me. "Do I even want to know what that was about?"

"Just a distressed high school freshman trying to avoid the nerd label." I don't know why I'm telling her this. Normally I'd make up something, but she probably heard enough anyway. "God, I'm glad I don't have to deal with that shit anymore."

"What? High school?" she asks.

I nod.

"Yeah, me too."

"But you're in college. Is it that different?" I honestly don't know if it's the same or not. Last April, when I turned eighteen, I'd already been going back and forth between Nebraska and New York since the middle of junior year and knew I wanted to model full time and drop out. My parents made me get my GED first, so I studied like crazy from January to April and aced it on the first try. It was probably more studying than I'd ever done in all of high school and middle school combined. I never even looked at colleges like a lot of my friends had been doing junior and senior year.

"College is completely different," Eve says. "Especially if you compare Columbia to my high school, where we're lucky to have a handful of students actually leave the state of Indiana for college."

"So basically everyone at Columbia suffered through the nerd math in high school."

"Everyone," she says with a nod.

"You know, the hiding-out plan might have worked better at Yale or Princeton or… Where else is Ivy League?"

"Harvard, Stanford," she says with a laugh. "And you're totally right, but I saw the campus when I first came to New York, and I knew that's where I wanted to go. It's so worth it."

We get interrupted by Janessa calling her over. When Eve walks off, I glance up for the first time in several minutes and notice a bunch of eyes suddenly diverting their attention from me to something else.

What the hell is going on with these people today?

The weirdness is enough to cause me to pull out my phone and send a text to Wes.

36

ME: Everyone seems to be under the impression that Elana and I are an item?

WES: Just ignore it. Don't deny it either.

ME: Okay??

WES: Let's have a meeting tomorrow morning to discuss your schedule. 9 a.m.

ME: Sure

Something is up. I decide to walk closer to set and see how long until my next turn.

I hear Janessa say to Eve, "If you're really trying for the Mason scholarship—"

"I am," Eve interrupts as if declaring her honorable duty to serve her country at war.

"All right," Janessa says. "Then you'll need an assistantship with someone, and my name might be impressive on that letter of recommendation."

"Oh my God," Eve mumbles. "Seriously? That would be—"

"It's not a paying job, but it will be worth the slave labor if you win a scholarship for next year. And you get to spend the summer studying in Paris," Janessa says with her I-don't-really-care-either-way attitude, such a contrast to Eve's elation.

"When can I start?"

Janessa laughs and shouts out some direction before answering Eve. "How about next Monday morning? I'm still working out some details with the clients I've booked next week, so I'll have someone email you the schedule. It's either a shoot for Calvin Klein or a week of editing lookbook photos."

Eve's face temporarily fills with alarm, but she wipes it clean before Janessa even looks up. Maybe she can't start next week? Or it's the mention of Calvin Klein. And what's the deal with this scholarship, anyway?

Now I'm even more curious. Not so much about Eve Castle but more so about Eve Nowakowski. Though I do see why she went the fake name route. Nowakowski's quite a mouthful.

I get sent back to wardrobe a few minutes later, and then Elana and I spend a good forty-five minutes embracing and looking in love for all those teenyboppers reading *Seventeen*. After those shots are finished, I end up beside Eve again while she sits on the floor taking notes.

For a long time, I watch her pen move in a circular motion as she fills the bottom of a page with tiny slanted cursive. Instead of flipping to the next blank page, she closes her notebook and looks over at me. "So was that your sister on the phone earlier? Or another fourteen-year-old girlfriend?"

My forehead scrunches up, trying to process the questions inside questions. "I don't have a girlfriend."

Shit. Wes told me not to deny it. Too late now. Although I kind of killed that lie when I made the One Direction concert comment.

"I know. I'm just messing with you. I don't have any siblings, so the whole brother/sister thing is pretty fascinating to me." She's now begun the process of taking her camera apart.

"I also have two older brothers."

"How much older?" Eve asks.

"Bradley is twenty, and Jared's twenty-two," I say.

"What do they do?"

No one's ever this curious about my family. "What do you mean? Like are they models too?"

She rolls her eyes. "I mean are they in school? Married? Working? In prison?"

I laugh. "Brad's in school. I have no idea what he's studying, and there's a good chance he doesn't either. I've always got the impression he was just extending his time not being a real grown-up by doing the college thing. And Jared had a football scholarship but lost it after he hurt his knee last spring. He's working for my dad's construction company now. And I can't imagine them being married. Or even dating seriously. Prison is a possibility." I stare at her for a second, weighing my options. "Now that you have enough material to write my biography for the Lifetime Movie channel—"

"Not quite there yet." She flashes me a perfect smile. "Do you get along with them?"

I pick up one of her spare lenses and hold it to my eye. "Yeah, we get along okay. My brothers aren't really into the same things as me. But Katie and I have always been close. She usually calls me first if she needs something. Like today."

"Honors math isn't so bad, you know," Eve says. "Does she do anything else at school? I feel like with high school you have to dive into a club or group or something right away so you don't get lost. Although, I'm kind of a hypocrite, because I hated it so much I bribed a friend's older brother to drive me to an open call in Chicago for an agency and couldn't wait to get the hell out of Indiana."

I laugh. "Yeah, that is so hypocritical of you. Katie's too short for modeling, thank God. She runs cross-country. She's on varsity as a freshman, which is pretty good, but it's cross-country, not football."

"Running is good," Eve says like she's really putting in the effort to contemplate my sister's daily drama. "I started running last spring. I used to hate it. Hated working out in any form, but now I love it. Clears my head. One of the girls in my dorm started a group to train for a half marathon in April and so far we've done three different runs around Central Park and the city. It's awesome."

I've started to forget that I'm working and there are tons of people around, but no one has asked either of us to get up and do something. "I like running too, just haven't done it with people, or off the treadmill," I admit. "I don't like the stop-and-go that comes with running in the city, and I haven't had time to figure out the Central Park routes."

She turns her body to face me, legs folded sideways to keep her skirt down. "You have to come on one of our runs, seriously. Lanie, the girl from my dorm, she's a genius with these routes. It'll change your entire outlook on working out. We're doing a 5K in a month and I need another person for my team."

Okay. This day is taking an interesting turn. "Is it a student thing?"

She shakes her head. "Totally doesn't matter. The more the merrier. We're bound to thin out as midterms approach. Seriously, you'll love it. I can't believe you live in New York City and you run on a treadmill."

"It's pure insanity. I'm a disgrace." I roll my eyes and then finally give in. "All right, is there a website for this group or something? Maybe I will give it a shot."

She opens her notebook and starts scribbling on the corner of a blank page. "There's a Facebook page, but I don't know it off the top of my head. Just send me an email and I can send you the link."

The paper is torn from the notebook and placed in my hand. I glance down and see she's written her email and phone number. I grin at her and make a big show of typing "Eve Nowakowski" into my phone, spelling it aloud. "I just might take you up on that offer. I've been doing the same workouts for a long time now. I go to this indoor climbing facility and I've wanted to give outdoor climbing a try, so I should do the same with running."

"I promise you'll love it." She starts tucking items into her bag, taking the spare lens from my hand, and I feel this sudden urge to lengthen the conversation before it's time to go.

"You know, you were Wes Danes's last female client," I say, trying to steer toward my questions from earlier. I can't help wanting to solve a good mystery.

Her face darkens, and her eyes focus on the windows across the room. "Yeah, that's probably a good thing."

A million different scenarios and theories sift through my head until I decide to shut them off for now. That was Eve Castle, not Eve Nowakowski. "Well, I guess I have you to thank for landing me someone who could make me enough money to pay the bills and keep me far away from college and real jobs."

She forces a smile. "You're welcome." She's standing up before I can stop her or apologize for obviously bringing up a painful subject. "I've got to catch Janessa and finish my interview, but seriously, I really do need another runner for my team. You don't have to be fast or anything."

I hold up the paper she gave me. "Your persuasive skills are well developed. I'll try it once if it works with my schedule."

She seems pleased with herself when she walks off to find Janessa again. I pull up her number, knowing her phone is tucked away in the bag on the floor beside me, and send her a quick text.

> **ME**: There. Now you have my number too, so if you don't hear from me, you can tell me again how I'm a bad New Yorker for running on treadmills

I get another text from Wes while my phone is still in my hand.

> **WES**: Meeting postponed. Need you to go to Buenos Aires tonight.
> **ME**: Tonight? Seriously?
> **WES**: Why? Are you busy? Don't answer that. You're not busy.
> **ME**: I'm not busy.
> **WES**: I'll send you the flight info in a few minutes. I'll need you back in forty-eight hours for a Macy's thing.
> **ME**: Macy's! You rock. Seriously.
> **WES**: Just wait. There's more. We'll talk Friday morning.

If I wasn't pumped up before, I sure as hell am now. This is good. Really good. The only pinch of disappointment I feel at the moment is that I might not be able to take Eve up on her offer to join the Hot College Girls' Running Club.

Maybe next week.

I don't know what Wes did to book me these fairly big last-minute jobs, but I'm not about to ask. Or do anything to ruin this winning streak I seem to be on at the moment.

Chapter 5: Eve

October 2, 6:30 p.m.

I'm still standing in the middle of my dorm room, staring at the letter in my hand, when my roommate Stephanie comes in. I haven't seen her since this morning before the *Seventeen* shoot.

"You look like you're in shock. Are you in shock?" She moves closer, lifting a hand to wave it in front of my face.

I peel my eyes from the paper in my hands and glance down at Steph. She's barely over five feet so I have to look down at her blond head. "I'm a finalist. For the Mason scholarship."

If I could have chosen any way to conclude such a crappy day, it would have been this.

"Seriously?" Steph squeals and then pries the letter from my fingers, reading it quickly. "Oh my God! Do you know how many people enter this competition every year? Like thousands. Holy shit. You have to do an interview with the committee. And get letters of recommendation. Professor Larson likes you, right? He'll help you out."

Breathe. Breathe again. Good job, Eve.

My heart starts to speed up and then slow down again, returning to normal. "Right. Larson. I'll ask him first. We won't even get our interview scheduled until the end of next month. I have time to find more people."

I walk to my desk to tuck my letter carefully back in its envelope so it doesn't fly away. That's when I notice the red business card sitting on the desk. *Wes Danes. Agent. One Model Management Agency.* I spin around to face my roommate and hold up the card. "Where did this come from?"

Steph's face breaks into a smile, such a contrast to my utter panic. "Oh, you mean the much older, extremely well-dressed hottie that stopped by asking for Eve and looking like he might die if he didn't see you right this second?"

Now I need to sit down. "Wes," I mutter under my breath. "How did he find me?"

Steph's eyes are wide with alarm now. "He didn't come to the room. The front desk called me down. He only knew the building. What are you not telling me?"

I take a deep breath, staring at my roommate, trying to decide if I can confide in her and if I even have a choice. "That was Wes. My agent…or he used to be my agent anyway. Until this morning, I hadn't seen him for nearly two years."

"Agent?"

"Modeling agent," I say.

"Modeling agent," she repeats like it's a foreign language. It probably is, considering the Eve she's known for an entire month.

"I moved to New York when I was fourteen to work. But I used a different name—Eve Castle."

Steph's mouth falls open, but it takes her several seconds to say something. "Wow, okay, I can see you modeling for sure, but I totally didn't see that coming. So, you're not still modeling, are you? I've only seen you go to class and study, unless you sneak out in the middle of the night for glamorous photo shoots."

I attempt a smile, but my hands are shaking. I've only ever told one person about me and Wes and it completely backfired. "No, I quit a few months before I turned seventeen. I actually walked away from a huge campaign with Gucci. My agency made up stories about me, and the tabloids came up with their own reasons. Rumors and more rumors—"

"You didn't want to do it anymore?" Steph prompts. "Because of…?"

I blew air out of my cheeks. "Wes."

"Wes," she repeats. "What did Wes do? Take all your money?"

"No, that would be my parents," I say bitterly.

By the time I realized they had been spending all my money, I had already quit and only had a couple of checks still coming in from jobs I'd done six months before returning home. Getting those envelopes in the mail had been like staring at the last candy bar left while stranded on a desert island. And even worse was writing that big fat check to the Columbia bursar's office. I broke out in a cold sweat and nearly had a panic attack.

Steph shifts on her bed, pulling her knees to her chest. "So if Wes didn't take your money, what happened?"

I wring my hands together. I have to tell her something. He might come back here.

"Promise this is just between you and me?" I'm already chewing on a fingernail, my eyes focused on the floor. There's so much shame and a degrading weight that comes with admitting the truth. "When I was fifteen, we started dating—"

"Fifteen?" she says. "How old was he?"

I release the air in my lungs and close my eyes so I don't have to see her reaction. "Twenty-four."

"Wow." She's quiet for way too long and I have to open my eyes and make sure she's still in the room. "So he's how old now?"

"Twenty-seven…I think."

"Okay, right." She nods, faking calm. I'm taking in her expression, taking in the fact that she doesn't look disgusted.

"Honestly, it was okay for a while. I loved him. And he took care of me, which I never wanted to admit that I needed at that age. It's just…he's so intense and he's got a temper that would put drunken trailer-trash men from my town to shame. It took me a long time to decide to leave."

"And you didn't tell anyone?" Steph asks. "The tabloids surely would have loved that story."

My palms are sweaty, and I have to rub them on my teal comforter before answering. "I told Wes's boss. I thought he'd do something. I thought maybe he'd get me a new agent and make sure I didn't have to see Wes anymore."

I close my eyes for a second, remembering that day in Josh Valentine's office. I had gone the nice route. I'd wrapped a scarf around my neck to conceal the stitches I'd gotten after Wes got pissed off at me and threw a chair at a glass china cabinet, causing glass to fly everywhere. "He brought Wes into the office and asked him, right there in front of me, if he was involved with me romantically. And Wes looked right at him and lied. And I knew if I didn't leave right then, the confrontation later would be hell. I was scared, so I left, and part of me figured he'd come after me and it would be better with us, but he didn't. And then my career was in the toilet. It was so stupid. I should have gone to the shoot and gotten my huge check from Gucci. Then I could enjoy being a scholarship finalist instead of thinking about how I'll pay for tuition next year if I don't win."

Steph covers her mouth with one hand. "Oh God. I'm so sorry. If I had known, I would have lied and told him he had the wrong building."

I shake my head. "It's not your fault. I should have been honest with you a long time ago. Besides, he's completely civilized. It's the two of us. We're a mess together. A complete mess. And I didn't tell you because I didn't think I'd have to deal with that world again."

"Wait..." Her hand drops from her face, and her forehead scrunches up. "Did you say you saw him this morning?"

My body is beginning to relax or else it's turned to Jell-O from being tense all day long so I lie back on my bed and give her all the details of this morning's photo shoot. Everything.

· · ◆ · ·

I groan and pull a pillow over my face. "Please don't Google me. The stories will have you convinced I died of an overdose while in a drug rehab. And I got fat. I'm sure somebody has decided that I left and then got fat. For models, that would be worse than drugs."

"That's fucked up," Steph says. "You didn't actually go to rehab, right?"

I roll my eyes. "Of course not. I'm still an addict, can't you tell?"

"You don't look like an addict," she says, laughing. "And I still can't believe you made it into Columbia with all the correspondence courses and working full time."

The truth is, I never stopped wanting to go to college. Modeling was fun at first. It was an escape from everything I hated about my life. But it also felt temporary, like a bridge I'd use to get where I really wanted to be. But there were long stretches of months with Wes when I lost sight of that and when I let myself think he was enough for me.

I hate how weak I got. How stupid.

"Okay, so let's go back to the part where you gave a hot underwear model your email and phone number." Steph is still on her laptop looking for my *Seventeen* cover debut, most likely. I'm not going to try and stop her. She's been supportive enough already. Actually, she's been supportive since the day I moved in. If it weren't for her, I would be all study and no play.

"I never called him an underwear model," I correct. "And I didn't give him my number. Okay, I did, but not the way you're implying. I just thought he might like the running group, and I need someone else for my 5K team." I lean over the bed and raise my eyebrows. "Maybe if you would have agreed to join, I wouldn't need to give my number to strangers."

Her eyes stay focused on the computer. "I already told you, running makes me sweat and then I itch. So, is he hot?"

"He's a model, of course he's hot." I pull out my phone to glance at the text Alex sent me earlier and as I'm saving his number, I catch myself fighting off a smile. Good thing Steph isn't watching me. "He seems nice. Like easy to talk to, you know?"

Steph grins at me, sets her computer aside, and holds out a hand to pull me off the bed. "You just got really awesome news and we're celebrating with ice cream. My treat."

I'm not sure I could eat right now. Too much emotional drama. But it feels good to talk to someone, to not have to hide the ugly parts of my life. "Okay, but I want to hear your pitch for that journalism midterm project thingy."

"Midterm project thingy," Steph repeats, rolling her eyes. "You know, journalism is not that far off from photography. You could stand to take my passion a bit more seriously."

We both laugh. It's an ongoing debate between us—photography versus journalism. Unlike a math or science career, both of our majors include a wide range of talent. You'd be surprised what can pass as a great photograph or a noteworthy story.

I slide my flip-flops on and open the door for Steph. "Promise me you won't work for any tabloids or gossip columns."

The smile drops from her face and a crease forms between her eyebrows. "Your animosity toward journalism is making a lot more sense now."

She's right. I don't think it was even a conscious choice, but I do have a certain level of annoyance with journalism majors. I'm also completely spent and can't do any more talking on this subject today.

"Don't turn into a psych major on me."

Steph gets the message and leads us out of the building, saying, "All right, let's stick with the underwear model topic. I've got so many more questions…"

I try to imagine being behind the camera, in Janessa Fields's place, photographing Alex Evans in a pair of boxer briefs. My face flushes, and I smile down at the ground.

Then I remember Janessa's offer and the potential client for next week. Calvin Klein.

Speaking of underwear models…

Chapter 6: Alex

October 6, 9:00 a.m.

I walk into Wes's office unannounced and plop down on the plush leather chairs, prop my feet up on the desk, and sip my venti cup of coffee. I've had an awesome week, so in my mind, I'm entitled to this luxury. In fact, my week was so amazing this meeting got postponed for three days while I took a trip out of the country, did a swimwear shoot, then rushed back for a Macy's shoot. And now I'm totally beat, and I've forgotten what day it is.

Wes is yakking away on the phone. He gives me a smile before swatting my feet off the desk and with the same motion hangs up.

"Alex Evans! My favorite person without breasts, how have you been? How was Buenos Aires? The girls are out of control, I hear."

"Didn't have much time for *extracurricular activities*." I literally spent more time on the plane and in the airport than I did in that country.

"Sorry, we had to rush you back for Macy's, but I'm sure your bank account is happy and that will soothe your blue balls." He laughs and moves to type on his computer, then looks over at me again. "Now on to the real business. Drumroll please…Next week you're shooting for Calvin Klein again! And this time it's even bigger. You're doing catalog, billboards, PR, the whole nine. So congratulations. In other news, I've decided to elect myself agent of the year."

I sit bolt upright. Now I'm feeling that morning coffee. "Wes, you're the man. That's amazing. What's something like that pay?"

"Don't get too bogged down with pay. It's a stepping stone. The next stop is booking the fragrance campaign. Then you'll be set for life." He's got his game face on, trying to keep things in perspective, but I can see the excitement clearly shining through his eyes. This must be a big deal. "The Klein shoot is a weeklong job, so we're still discussing usage and all that. I'll get back to you on the numbers, but I assure you, you'll be pleased. The concept is a little out there, but the photographer you worked with on Tuesday will be doing the CK shoot. Some kind of urban safari theme."

"You mean Janessa Fields?"

Wes lifts an eyebrow. "You've really got the name game mastered, don't you? I almost never have to prep you like I do everyone else. That skill will come in handy at these upcoming jobs. It gets real political and who-is-in-with-what-photographer is at the top."

The shock is hitting me now. I don't think even Jason or Landon, my agency-assigned roommates, have gotten jobs this big before and they're both at least five years older than me. "I can't believe this."

"Well, you better start believing it, Alex. I told you that you had something special. And not just the hair," Wes says, grinning at me.

I'm blond, and that's not as common with male models. My old agency had no problem booking jobs for me when I was sixteen and seventeen—Abercrombie kids and gigs like that—but she told me I wasn't buff enough and I didn't have the "man look" to keep booking jobs after eighteen. But eighteen happened six months ago, and I'm still going. Not that I didn't take her feedback to heart. I did. I hit the gym hard, and I haven't missed a day since. I also started looking for a new agent. Someone who thought I still had a chance to keep going.

"One more important detail..." Wes whips out a copy of *US Weekly* and spreads open a middle page. I nearly spit my coffee all over the magazine when I read the story headline.

"*Fashion's Newest Teen Couple: On camera, American model, Alex Evans and French native Elana, are headlining for Calvin Klein. Off camera, sources confirm a budding teen romance.*"

So, I guessed right. It *is* a couples thing. "Who made this shit up?"

Wes lifts his eyebrows, leaning back against his seat. "*I* made it up, and you're going to go along with it because it will make you very, very rich, understood?"

No. Fucking. Way.

"Seriously, man? She's fourteen. People aren't usually into that sort of thing."

Wes waves his hand as if I'm so behind on the information chain. "Oh, don't worry about that. We changed Elana's age to eighteen. The designers thought it would reflect poorly on them, promoting such a young model as a sex symbol."

And changing a model's age makes them more ethical?

"This has disaster written all over it," I say.

Wes rests a hand on my arm and gives me his serious, I-know-what-I'm-doing face. "Trust me. It'll be just fine. All you need to do is show up at a few events together, no girls in your apartment for a while, not even the fake girlfriend. We want to keep it all clean and moral. Kara and I have heard that's in right now."

So it's not just his idea. He's conspiring with Kara, Elana's agent.

I sink back into my seat, wishing I could crawl into bed again and give myself a few more hours of sleep before tackling this challenge. "She's just a kid, Wes. What if she gets...*attached* or something?"

He pauses for a second, contemplating his answer. "We'll cross that bridge when we get to it."

I know what he's really saying; it's not his problem if Elana gets emotionally attached. He knows I won't. Still, I don't really like this. Not at all. But Wes is the person who got me a permanent place in New York and full-time work for the most part. Before signing with him, I was only coming to New York a few times a year starting with sophomore year of high school. My parents thought it was something I was doing for fun, like going away to camp. I still don't think my parents get it. But they let me leave and come here, so whatever.

"Be on your best behavior," Wes says. "A one-woman man."

I shake my head, too tired to argue further. "Great. Just great."

"I'll email you the rest of the details for the shoot later today," he says dismissively.

The ringing of the phone is my signal for escape. I head back outside and plan my route to the gym. As tired as I am right now, I should go back to my apartment and fall into bed for at least sixteen hours, but of course, I'm not doing that at all. Instead, I've chosen to beat my body up a little more by rock climbing and possibly some cardio and weights. The second I let myself have a break or a day off, I'm going to wake up with a beer belly and man boobs, and no one will hire me.

After I'm all changed and ready to climb, I see a skinny kid with wild black hair flying up the wall, Spider-Man style.

"Elliot!" I shout from the ground below him. "Don't you ever go to school?"

Elliot's grip slips on one of the holds, and he looks over his shoulder at me. "I'm homeschooled."

That explains why the kid is always here on weekdays around lunchtime. I guess it doesn't make sense for a fifteen-year-old to cut school and hang out at a fancy health club at Chelsea Piers.

Elliot is halfway to the ceiling when I finally hook myself up and start climbing. It takes me a few minutes to catch up, but I manage to without seeming too out of breath.

"So what's new in the world of fifteen-year-olds?" I ask him, reaching for some chalk from my bag.

"How should I know?" Elliot grins at me. "I'm socially challenged, remember?"

"Yeah, you are." He and I came to this conclusion a few weeks ago when I noted that he never got a single pop culture reference I'd made in front of him.

We work in silence for a few minutes and I can't help but wonder what Elliot's parents must be like if they wanted to homeschool their kid. I know my mother went nuts with four kids constantly trashing the house and breaking shit. She never said this, but I bet she was more than happy to see that school bus pull up every morning.

"So what's the deal with the homeschooling?" I ask Elliot when our paths have brought us close enough to talk. Sweat drips from my forehead and my hands shake from gripping the holds so tightly. "Are you, like, really religious or something? Avoiding exposure to the theory of evolution?"

"All Jehovah's Witnesses drop out of school at my age so we can help spread the word of God," Elliot says.

Shit. I nearly slip from the wall, then I swallow hard, digging for something redeeming to say.

"That was way too easy." Elliot snorts out a laugh. "My parents are professors. We move a lot. They've gotten grants and different research projects. I've only been in New York for about eight months. I *was* going to start school, but now my mom's talking about spending a year in Nepal, so I figured I'd wait and see."

"Nepal? That sounds…"

"Odd? Unconventional? Boring?" Elliot suggests.

Maybe. Probably.

"Hey, is that why you're climbing all the time? Thinking of tackling Everest?"

Elliot rolls his eyes. "Sure, why not? I'll just wait until the angst of my teen years overwhelms me, and it'll be an awesome suicide attempt."

If this kid wasn't so geeky, he'd be incredibly cool. "I'm going to do it someday."

"What? Suicide?"

"No, climb Everest." My hand and foot both slip from their holds as I say this, and I end up with a big scrape down the front of my leg.

Elliot cracks up. "Nice. You won't last a day on a real mountain at this rate. What makes you want to take that plunge?"

"My dad got me this book about Everest when I was eight, and I've kind of been obsessed with it ever since. At one point I had memorized the names of at least a hundred people who died climbing it." I've never really admitted this to anyone, so I'm just waiting for Elliot to laugh at me again.

Only he doesn't.

"I saw a Discovery Channel show about this group of people making the climb. Did you know Everest is taller than twenty-one Empire State Buildings stacked on top of each other?"

"Yeah, it's nuts." I'm really straining now, looking for a blue hold within reach of my left foot. I would totally die on a real mountain right now.

"There's, like, more than a hundred dead bodies just lying around the peak," Elliot says, hardly sounding as strained as me. Maybe it's easier if you're lighter. "I wonder why they just leave them there."

"Maybe someone thinks we'll invent a way to revive frozen

dead people in the future," I say, totally joking, but of course Elliot takes it seriously.

"No, the human freezing theories always revolve around being frozen alive, not dead."

"Well, they were alive before they froze to death, right?"

"Huh." Elliot's forehead scrunches up. "Well, that's true…"

The frozen body conversation goes on for a while longer until I finally finish my route and return to the ground.

"I've got to do my real workout now. See you tomorrow?"

It's already evening by the time I get back to my shared apartment in SoHo. I'm looking forward to doing nothing but eating my take-out sushi, showering, and going straight to bed. Jason has tacked two more 11x13 photos of himself on the refrigerator. I debate making some modifications to the photo with a green Sharpie lying on the counter, but I don't have the energy, and some people don't have a sense of humor, unfortunately.

After eating, I flop on my bed and pick up my latest Everest book.

Then I remember something minor mentioned in my meeting with Wes this morning. Janessa Fields is the photographer for the CK shoot.

I snatch my phone from the nightstand and search for Eve Nowakowski's number and send her a text.

ME: Are you by any chance working for Calvin Klein next week?
EVE: Why? Are you?

I feel a tiny surge of something that resembles excitement. She didn't even hesitate to reply. She must have saved my name in her phone. But maybe she saves everyone's name?

ME: Yes. And so is Janessa Fields, so I thought…

EVE: Well, at least I'll have someone with a brain to talk to.

ME: That's a compliment, right?

EVE: Sure.

ME: Remember Finley Belton from the Seventeen shoot?

EVE: The girl with a fortress. I remember.

ME: She's booked CK for two days as well. Another nice person to talk to.

EVE: That's good to know. Do you think Wes will be around at all?

I sit on that question for several seconds, wanting to know whether this is a good or bad thing. Finally I decide to ask.

ME: Is it bad if he is there?

EVE: If by bad you mean awkward, anxiety-filled tension? Then yes.

ME: Ok. I guess things didn't end on good terms with the two of you?

EVE: To be expected when you walk away from a huge Gucci campaign and leave your agency to take the blame.

I don't really want to discuss Eve Castle's last days, and I doubt she wants to hash it out.

ME: Want to talk about running instead?

EVE: Lol. I thought maybe I scared you off with that running group invite.

ME: The Hot College Girls' Running Club? Nope. Not scared at all. Quite the opposite. I had to go to South America the other day and then I did a shoot for Macy's. But I'm ready for your sales pitch now.

EVE: Where do I begin? The really cool route? Or the "really hot college girls"?

ME: All of it. I need all the details. And photos if you have any...

EVE: LOL

This could be an interesting week. Eve texting me and me having fake dates with my fake underage girlfriend. Maybe Wes is right about superstardom being in my future. I'm already acting like a real celebrity.

Chapter 7: Eve

October 9, 4:30 a.m.

New York City is the city that never sleeps. That's a fact. However, at around four thirty in the morning, the city closes its eyes a bit just to rest them. There's a stillness in the air that you can only feel in the wee hours of the morning.

It takes two cups of coffee for me to get up at three thirty in order to aid the other photo assistants at Milk Studios rental office with gathering equipment before heading to the location.

We finally pull up to the designated street right near where *Seventeen* shot the other day and across from Columbus Circle. After a bumpy ride in the back of a van, my head is spinning so bad that I'm nearly positive I'm going to puke from car sickness. Something I've been cursed with my whole life. This is not how I wanted to start off my first day on the job. I have to sit down on the curb for a few seconds, briefly letting my head fall between my knees. I don't get too much of a break before I see Janessa's out-of-place Land Rover pull up. I rush over to help her unload her equipment.

"I hope you're ready for a long week, Eve," Janessa says as she gets out of the truck. She turns to face me and then adds, "Holy shit! You look like hell. Are you hungover?"

I shake my head vigorously as if the movement alone is tangible evidence. "I had a long ride in the back of the equipment truck, but I'm fine. Just a little carsick. It'll pass, I swear."

"Why don't you go sit in the RV, take a few minutes to pull yourself together? I'll have Juan help me unload the rest of the gear."

"Thanks, Janessa," I say, trying to stop the heat from creeping up to my face. This is not how I wanted to start. "I'll grab some water and I'll be fine."

As I enter the RV, Hugo's unmistakable cackle is the first thing I hear. He's in his tight, burgundy man jumpsuit complete with an ascot and his ever-present Gucci man purse. He's holding the rest of the crew hostage as he recalls his antics from the night before. I take a seat on the couch, trying not to listen, but I can't really help it.

"Can you believe she would wear that to a Tom Ford party?" Hugo says, like he's speaking about the military launching a deadly missile or something. I try not to roll my eyes. "Speaking of tom*foolery*. Did you hear that our models today are in a hot-and-heavy relationship?"

Everyone seems to regard this information with interest, though they're all a little too cool to act super excited like Hugo.

"I just saw it in *US Weekly*." Hugo whips the magazine out of his back pocket and holds it up for everyone to see. He clears his throat dramatically, and I do roll my eyes this time. "*Gorgeous up-and-coming fashion models Alex Evans and Elana*—très chic: she's only got one name, like Madonna—*started dating after a chance meeting on the set of* Seventeen *magazine. The fashion couple has been cast to debut their new romance on billboards worldwide courtesy of Mr. Calvin Klein, who just happened to be seeking a real-life romance for his upcoming ads."*

The *Seventeen* magazine shoot—Elana and Alex. Maybe he took her to that One Direction concert after all. Maybe they hit it off during an Auto-Tuned, lip-synched version of *You Don't Know You're Beautiful.* How sweet. I can't help laughing under my breath, but luckily no one notices and Hugo isn't done with his gossip session.

"My hair and makeup is going to be gracing the new up-and-coming fashion couple of the year. You can all bow before the queen!"

As the RV erupts with laughs and conversation, I'm left thinking about the reality of this new piece of gossip. Would Alex really agree to something like this? She's so young. What am I saying? Age didn't stop Wes from hooking up with me. Why would Alex be any different? Even if he does seem different.

But he knew I'd be here and he's been texting back and forth with me over the course of this past weekend. He's even shown hints of flirting. And so have I, to be honest.

I wouldn't put it above Wes to make this relationship happen for the cameras.

I'm already sick of this job. Sick of this world. The push-your-way-to-the-top stuff here makes Columbia look tame. And you know it's bad when a job is more complicated than life at an Ivy League school.

Feeling less nauseated, I get up from the couch and head outside to help Janessa. Maybe if I'm really helpful, we can finish early.

Janessa sees me emerge from the RV and waves me over. She quickly points out the producer, Russ, who's standing a few feet away from us. "Russ did some scouting last night and I want to go with him and check out some of the locations so we have an idea of light and timing and such. You stay here and make sure the equipment gets set up and let us know if there's any problems."

"Sure. I'll hold down the fort."

As I rush over to the equipment van to make sure everything is being unloaded properly, I notice the catering has arrived and I sprint over to clear some room on the preassembled tables that now hold everyone's coats and bags. Walking back to the RV, balancing a huge pile of belongings, I notice Alex arriving in a black town car. I'm caught off guard when he scans the room, his gaze pauses on me, and then he smiles and waves, like I'm the very person he had been looking to see first thing this morning.

Not his supposed girlfriend, Elana.

Chapter 8: Alex

I don't realize I'm grinning at Eve until I hear the car that dropped me off pulling away. Then I remember the conversation I had in Wes's office on Friday.

Be a one-woman man.

I smooth my face into a more neutral, disinterested look and walk toward Eve. "How's it going?"

Eve shrugs and her eyes dart around as if she's still testing the waters to see if anyone remembers her. "Could be better. But also could be worse."

I spot Elana arriving with the round Hispanic woman who is claiming to be her assistant. I carefully conceal myself behind Eve. I'm so not in the mood for this. And what the hell is wrong with Wes? Dropping a bomb like this on me *after* the article is open to public eyes. When had he told *US Weekly*? Obviously before they could write and print that article. What if they had called me asking for a statement? I guess he must have thought of that already. Wes doesn't screw up details like those.

But now I'm looking at this girl, and I know she's not eighteen, and I know I *am* eighteen, and it's weird. I wonder if she had the same conversation with her agent, Kara.

"Look, your girlfriend's here," Eve says, and I hear the disapproval dripping from every word. Or maybe I'm just imagining it.

I hate that she knows about me and Elana already, and Eve and I haven't even gotten started yet. I'm probably going to have to stop texting her. I probably shouldn't have started in the first place. Lindsey, my ex-girlfriend, was right. I wouldn't want to choose a girl over career opportunities. That's what she had said when we decided to break up.

So, if my two-year-long high school relationship had to go, worrying about being able to continue texting another girl just for fun can't exactly be a priority at the moment. I run my fingers through my hair. "Right...*good*. I've been waiting for her to show up."

Eve gives me a weird look. It feels like forever since I've done the girlfriend thing and I have no idea what my next move is. But I decide to man up and break the ice with Elana.

I step right in front of Elana, interrupting her conversation with someone, and grab her by the hand. "Excuse us for a minute," I say, grinning at the woman who's glaring at me like she's a father about to whip out a shotgun. The nanny posing as an assistant.

And I really hope my parents don't pick today to start reading pop culture magazines.

Elana follows me behind the RV and out of sight from anyone else. "So," I say, scratching the back of my head. She looks even younger without makeup on. Maybe I should take her to Chuck E. Cheese's for our first date. "You're cool with this relationship thing? Because if not—"

If not what? I don't know why I presented it that way. Wes didn't give me a choice, so that means probably Elana doesn't have one either.

"Its fine with me," she says with her thick French accent. "I like acting. And maybe it won't be for too long, right?"

"I hope not," I blurt out and then immediately regret it when I see the look on her face. "Sorry. I didn't mean it like that. It's just that I don't really know you. And besides, you're…" *A child. The same age as my little sister.*

"I understand." She flashes me a smile and then both of us are being called over to hair and makeup. "Kara explained it to me. We're both professionals during the shoot, so there's nothing to pretend while we're here."

I let out a breath, relieved that we don't have to look all coupley and in love or something when I'm trying to get through this job. I rest a hand on her shoulder and even that feels awkward and heavy. "Okay, don't worry. Everything will be fine," I tell her because it seems like something I should say. I *am* the adult in this pair. Technically speaking.

The next couple of hours zip by. I hardly have time to breathe. But every time I'm not under the spotlight, I find my gaze drifting to Eve. She looks nervous, but she's also right there on top of things. I watch Janessa go through a series of shots with her, and Eve makes suggestions on the lighting and angles, then Janessa shouts out directions to the crew, making the necessary changes.

When we all get a break to eat, I almost sit by Elana, but she's going through her schedule with the "assistant" and Eve is sitting by herself, picking at a bagel and writing furiously in a notebook that's propped up on her knees. I plop down on the ground next to Eve and wait for her to notice me.

She doesn't look up from her notebook when she says, "So, I guess that One Direction concert worked out pretty well?"

I laugh. "Yeah, sure."

"I love how her nanny looks like she's ready to chop your balls off."

I stare at Eve, trying to rewind the past ten seconds and make sure I heard her correctly. "Did you just say nanny?"

"Assistants don't usually feed their bosses gummy vitamins and force them to open textbooks." Eve sets her notebook down and turns to face me. "I know you're not really dating her."

Uh-oh. Not good. I stuff a big piece of bagel in my mouth. "Yes, I am."

"Let me guess," Eve says. "The designer wanted the two of you as a package deal. It wouldn't be the first time a designer used real-life couples. But surely they aren't telling people she's fourteen, right?"

The bagel congeals itself to the roof of my mouth. How does she know all this? I've only been in a fake relationship for a few days, and we're already being outed by one person. I cough to keep myself from choking, and Eve hands me a bottle of water.

"Forget it," she says. "You don't have to answer that. It's none of my business."

I take a big swallow of water and clear my throat. "It's possible you're right," I admit, though some part of my brain is screaming at me to shut up before I ruin the lie Wes has worked hard to build.

Surprise fills Eve's face and I'm not sure whether she's shocked to be right or shocked that I admitted it. She leans closer and lowers her voice. "Was it your idea?"

"God no," I say without hesitation. "In fact, I got the plan after the story broke."

"So how old is she now?"

I take another swallow of water, keeping my eyes on Elana and her nanny. "Eighteen."

Eve laughs and picks up her notebook again. "It's so typical, isn't it? Goes right with the modeling world. You don't like something, well, go ahead and make it look exactly how you want it to. Whatever amounts of lies and Photoshop that requires."

"Bitter much?" I say and she smiles at me, her nose wrinkling, and I can't help but notice the freckles running across the bridge of her nose and spreading outward.

"I *was* bitter. I'm over it, mostly. I get a flash of it every once in a while, and I have to hold myself back from standing up and giving a big speech."

I kind of want to ask her more about what happened and why she bailed when everything had been going so well for her, but part of me doesn't want to know. I like her like this. Eve, the college girl. The photographer's assistant.

"How are you holding up so far?"

She sits up straighter and smiles again. "You know, it's actually been pretty awesome. I screwed up a couple of things right off the bat and Janessa doesn't like people who have their heads up their asses, but she's also not above listening to my thoughts."

"Or maybe she listens to you because you're actually good,"

I say. "You have a huge advantage in this setting. You've been on both sides—the one taking the direction and now the one giving it."

She beams at me and then it fades to a more skeptical look. "I don't know if I can believe you or not. You could just be sucking up to me because I know all your secrets now."

I roll my eyes. "Fine, don't believe me. But don't act like you know me or something just because I'm in the tabloids this week." What I don't say, though I'm sure she hears it, is *you of all people should know better than to make non-fact-based assumptions about people.*

The skin under her freckles turns pink. "Okay, I don't know you, and I was going to say that I know your type, but that's totally..."

"Hypocritical?" I suggest, then stand up before she can answer. "I should get back to work."

Truth is, she probably does know my type, but maybe I don't want to be *my type* anymore.

Chapter 9: Eve

God. I'm such a bitch sometimes. He was probably trying to be nice. It's just so hard knowing who's putting all those words in Alex's mouth and getting him jobs like this one, and to not lump him together with lying agents like Wes and arrogant models like... well, almost all of the ones I've met.

Not that Alex isn't arrogant. He totally is, and it's the first thing I noticed about him at the last shoot, but today he seems subdued, like he's not in his own skin.

And holy shit. I never expected him to admit to the fake relationship thing. I wasn't even 100 percent sure until I saw his face. He needs to do a little better if he plans to keep up the story for more than a few days.

"Eve?" Janessa calls.

I scramble to my feet and head over to where Alex and Elana will be shot together for the first time today. Elana looks stunning getting out of the safari jeep parked smack dab in the middle of Columbus Circle in her slim cheetah-print minidress and a green linen safari jacket. Elana was made for these clothes. There's no denying that a part of me was happy being in the spotlight. It's intoxicating.

"I'm having trouble getting the positions I want and still have all the clothes showing," Janessa says to me once I'm beside her. "I'm not used to that being an important factor."

I scan the set, looking Alex and Elana over, head to toe. "Do we need shoes in the shot?"

"Apparently it's a must." Janessa nods toward Jacqueline, the stylist.

I almost laugh at Janessa's reaction. I'm sure she thinks that the concept and the angles should be most important. But this is fashion. Shoes *are* essential.

"I have an idea?" I say like a question because I don't want to overstep my boundaries.

She holds her hand out as if to tell me to go ahead. I walk closer to the costars and take Alex's hands, pulling his arms around Elana's waist. When he stiffens, I lift my eyebrows subtly to remind him that everyone is watching, and he really needs to be on. "Elana, put your arms here." I wrap her arms around Alex's neck. "Now, lift her up."

After Alex does as he's told and Elana is off the ground, I grab her fancy boots and lift them up toward her butt so we can see the shoes.

"Don't move," I order. Then I walk back beside Janessa and look them over. "What do you think? We can't see the front of her. That might be a problem."

Janessa lifts her camera and looks through the lens. "It is a problem."

My stomach drops, and I feel like a complete idiot for even opening my mouth.

"But," Janessa continues, "you gave me an idea. We can do three different shots. Back this one up two steps and do a strip of three pictures, like we're getting her walking into his arms."

"Then we've got the outfit, the shoes, and the chemistry between the happy couple," I add.

Janessa nods, her lens still glued to her face. "Not bad, Eve."

I catch Alex listening to Janessa's praise. He smiles at me. I feel guilty all over again and make a promise to apologize later for snapping at him.

While bringing this new vision to life, Janessa quizzes me on the correct ISO, lens use, and sun position. Some of it I answer easily, but most of it, I'm listening intently to her answers. I really do have a lot to learn.

After we're finished for the day, Janessa and I are walking up the steps to the RV when I hear Hugo's loud voice project to New Jersey and back.

"Come on, you have to remember her?" Hugo says. "You mean Wes has never once mentioned her?"

I freeze on the top step, my heart pounding. Janessa sighs and throws me a look that's either angry or sympathetic. I can't tell. But I can tell that she knows. She must have heard Alex at the *Seventeen* shoot. She was right behind me when he made his very loud proclamation, *you're Eve Castle!*

"Look at how tall she is," someone else says. "And gorgeous."

"I think she's put on a few pounds. That's why I didn't recognize her right away. Plus size might be her best option now," another person says, and group laughter follows.

"Are you sure Wes has never brought up the subject?" Hugo says, probably asking Alex.

Great. Just great.

"Wes's former clients are none of my concern," Alex says. "Just so long as he keeps booking jobs like this for me, I don't give a shit who else he's worked with."

"Spoken like a true diva," Hugo says. "You know, I might have done her makeup once, now that I think about it."

Oh God. I'm so not going in there now. No way.

I turn my back to Janessa. "I forgot one of the bags. I'll just go grab it."

Janessa catches my arm before I have a chance to run away. "Come on. Let's get this over with. You can't hide out all week, and frankly, I'm going to get sick of hearing them whisper about you for the next four days."

My eyes must be huge right now, but my feet move in the direction Janessa's tugging me. As soon as we enter the RV, Hugo's voice cuts off. He's standing in the middle of the nearly packed room. Alex and Elana are standing together on the far side of the room, and the producer, Russ, is near the door.

Janessa's hands land on my shoulders, pointing me toward the center of the room before releasing me. "I'd like all of you to meet Eve Nowakowski. My assistant. She's a student at Columbia. She takes decent photos, though her approach is a bit unconventional. She has a lot of technique problems to work out, but I'd say she has potential as a photographer. So whatever else you've heard about her, let's focus on the present, understood?"

Nobody moves or says anything for what feels like ten minutes but is probably only three seconds. My face is so hot it must be red as a tomato.

Finally, Alex claps his hands together. "Sounds like a plan to me. And being the diva that we all know I am…" He crosses the small space, moving toward me. "I'm going to remind you that my contract states the photographer or the photographer's assistant is required to get my approval on the shots for today before you send them on to the designer." He turns me around to face the door. I seem to have lost my ability to move without direction. "I'd like to do that now, if you don't mind."

The air outside of the RV feels so good on my hot face. Alex's hands drop from my shoulders and I spin around to face him. "Nobody's contract allows for that kind of clause."

He shrugs. "I'm sure someone's does."

I'm still in shock, so I don't notice Alex looking slightly nervous until he says, "It wasn't me. I didn't tell them anything."

"What?" I shake my head, mentally catching up to him. "Oh… yeah, I didn't think it was you. It was only a matter of time, right?"

We've put some distance between us and the RV, and now Alex looks like he's fighting laughter. "It was Elana."

I glance at him to see if he's serious. "No way."

"Apparently a handful of models inspired her to leave home and pursue her dream, and one of those people is Eve Castle."

I start laughing so hard I have to lean against the wall to keep myself from falling over. *Talk about ironic.* When Alex and I both stop laughing, I look over at him and hesitate before asking, "Were you lying about Wes? Has he ever mentioned me?"

Any hint of a smile or amusement drops from his face. "No, he hasn't."

I don't know if I should feel glad or upset, but I end up feeling a little of both.

"We're all business," Alex says as if sensing that I might take this personally. "We would never sit around and hash out his past clients. We just don't go there, you know?"

"I know." Needing a change of subject, I point a finger at the RV. "Thanks for getting me out of there. And for what you said earlier. You're not as arrogant and self-involved as I falsely assumed."

Okay, so I never really thought Alex was self-involved, but I don't think he's going to experience an ego decline anytime soon, and there's no need for me to go out of my way and boost him up even higher.

A smug expression fills his face before he turns his back to me. "See you tomorrow, Eve."

I stand there for a long time, watching everyone pack up and leave. A long, black car with tinted windows pulls up for Alex, and then another identical yet separate car arrives for Elana. She glances in my direction and gives me a small wave before sliding in the car.

A rush of emotions I can't quite identify floods over me as I think of her looking at my picture in a magazine all the way from France. I remember doing the same thing at her age. And I also remember getting into dozens of black cars, closing the door, and finding Wes seated in the back, usually on his cell phone waving at the driver to pull away before anyone could see him. At first it was hot and exciting, sitting there waiting for him to hang up, knowing we would be all over each other the second he did.

Then later, the walls between us and the rest of the world were so thick, I could sit right beside him in that car and feel more lonely than I'd ever felt in my life.

In the beginning, if I dropped into my seat, exhausted and frustrated, Wes would rub my shoulders and tell me I was beautiful and that he'd make sure I was a huge star by the time eighteen came around. But after the excitement wore off, he'd start listing off all the things I needed to do to improve my stamina...*stay away from carbs...why do you think so many models smoke...maybe if you hadn't stayed up so late studying for classes that you don't even need to take.*

Wes hated that I wouldn't drop the correspondence courses when I turned sixteen.

"Why do you need to go to college, Evie? You're a professional. You need to focus on your career."

Once, he threw my SAT prep book into the kitchen sink, not knowing it was full of soapy water. I had to buy a new one to replace it. After that, I hid all my books and never studied in front of him. We went a long time without fighting after I made that decision. The break from arguing was such a relief that I almost did drop my classes.

Wes and I were made to do nothing but destroy each other, and love wasn't enough to fix that. Maybe love is never enough. Maybe relationships need to be based on practical matches and common goals.

Or maybe there's something wrong with me. Maybe I'm not compatible with anyone.

I spot Janessa and Russ walking toward me, and I pull myself from the wall. I'm still technically on the unpaid clock.

"Well, that went well," Janessa says and I don't know if she's talking about the drama from a few minutes ago or the day as a whole.

"Sorry about the gossip session earlier," Russ says to me. "We're glad to have you here, Eve. You'll bring a unique perspective for sure. And it's great to hear your recovery went well."

Right. My recovery. From drug addiction.

I suppress a laugh. "Uh…thanks."

Russ leaves me alone with Janessa. We both stand there in silence for a minute, and then she says, "I suppose you could have started next week. I'm doing a series on statues in New York City."

I laugh. "Too late now."

She gives me a hard pat on the arm. "It's good for you. Builds character."

A few minutes later, I'm back in the bumpy van. As we pull away, I get another text from Alex.

ALEX: News has spread to Nebraska.

I have no idea what he's talking about, but I decide to remove his real name from my phone before replying. It takes me a second to label him. Usually, I don't put real names in my phone. Steph is Reese Witherspoon—short, blond, curvy, and outgoing…it fits. The RA for my dorm is Bella Swan because she shakes her head a lot when she talks and she trips over everything.

Alex gets labeled Calvin Klein.

ME: Nebraska?
CALVIN KLEIN: My parents. My hometown.

Alex is from Nebraska? That might be worse than Indiana.

ME: Which news has spread? The fake g/f?

CALVIN KLEIN: Yep. Except not the fake part.

ME: This is bad?

CALVIN KLEIN: Haven't decided yet.

ME: Are you going to tell them it's fake?

CALVIN KLEIN: Too risky. Neighborhood gossip has traveled all the way to NYC before.

ME: But if you told them not to tell…?

CALVIN KLEIN: Doesn't matter. They won't get that it's important to keep it a secret.

ME: You don't have to explain to me. My parents are selfish a-holes too.

CALVIN KLEIN: They aren't assholes. They're normal. Normal people don't get this world.

ME: I get it. You shouldn't tell them. You're right.

CALVIN KLEIN: Where do you take a 14 yr old on a date?

ME: PG-13 Movie? Chuck e cheese?

CALVIN KLEIN: Ha-ha. We think alike.

The van stops, and I tuck my phone away before climbing out. It feels special to be one of only a few people to know Alex's secret. That's probably why he texted me. Who else besides Elana is he going to be able to vent to?

Chapter 10: Alex

October 10, 7:30 a.m.

"I really need a job."

Eve is sitting on the floor beside the makeup area, fiddling with her camera while Hugo works on getting me ready for today's shoot.

"Aren't you working right now?" I ask Eve.

"A paying job," she says. "My phone bill is due, and I don't want to have to cancel my data plan. I'm way too dependent on it."

One of the interns is sitting on Eve's other side, and Finley is beside the intern. She's probably talking to them and not Hugo and me. I've got to learn to butt out and not act like I'm always listening to everything Eve Nowakowski has to say. Even if I am.

"I hear Sears is casting for their spring catalog right now," Hugo says.

Eve looks at him like he's gone completely mad. I can't tell if he's being sarcastic or not. But at least I'm not the only one eavesdropping.

"Don't knock Sears," Finley says, flipping through a magazine.

"I've booked a ton of jobs with them, and the money does add up."

"Not a modeling job," Eve says to Hugo. "A normal college student job."

"I've been babysitting my professor's kids," the intern girl says to Eve. "It works out well, because I don't have to commit to a schedule. It's whenever they need me, and the kids basically never come out of their rooms. I get all my studying done. It's about as cushy as it gets."

"Clearly these kids are much older than my five-year-old brothers," Finley says. "Or they're on heavy sedatives. I can hardly read a recipe when I'm watching them, let alone get any amount of studying done."

Eve straightens up and pulls the camera from her eye. "I can babysit. Do you know any other professors seeking child care?"

The girl shakes her head and stands up. "I'll keep an eye open though."

Eve looks disappointed. "Thanks."

The camera is against her eye again. My gaze travels across the room to see what her current subject might be. Or in this case, *who*.

Elana is lying on her stomach on the floor, books open in front of her. She must be doing schoolwork. Guess no one is concerned about her academic level tipping people off that she's not eighteen?

Hugo has just finished with me, so I walk quietly behind Eve, squatting down to see her pictures. She takes a whole bunch of shots of Elana's hand—the one holding the pencil—and then several more of her profile. With her hair falling forward, you'd never know it was Elana in those pictures.

"You're gonna get in trouble again," I whisper and Eve jumps.

She glances over her shoulder at me and sighs with relief. "No, I won't. I'm supposed to be taking pictures."

"Yeah," I say. "For Calvin Klein."

Eve flashes me a huge fake grin. "Fine, I'll stop. I know you have to look out for your girlfriend. So nice of you."

She walks away from me, camera around her neck, and goes right over to Elana, sitting down beside her. Elana springs up, shutting her book, obviously excited to have Eve chatting with her. I had planned to grab a book from my bag and sit near them, pretending not to listen, but before I can do that, Eve points to Elana's schoolwork and starts speaking to her in French. Like really fast French. Accent and all. I can pick up a few words of French, but this conversation is totally lost on me.

I stare at them, my mouth half-open, watching and hearing their words bounce back and forth. Elana looks very comfortable talking to Eve.

"Are you eavesdropping or does it all sound like gibberish to you too?"

Finley is standing beside me now, watching the same two girls that I'm watching. "Complete gibberish. They're probably going to talk about us in French all week."

Finley laughs. "They might talk about *you*, but I'm usually out of the gossip circle. In fact, I like to remove any trace of rumors and personal information about anyone work-related from my mind."

I turn to her and roll my eyes. "That's so not possible."

"It's mostly possible. But you have to really not care and really not want to know details. Ignorance is bliss." She bounces off to set, flipping her blond hair over her shoulder. Does she know Elana's real age? If she does, it sounds like she's denying it. She doesn't want the responsibility of knowing. Especially if Finley's going to be rooming with her soon.

Someone slings an arm around my shoulders and steers me in the other direction. I turn and look at Wes who has appeared out of nowhere. "Hey…what are you doing here?"

He drops his arm from my shoulders and nods toward the RV to our right. We step inside and Wes shuts the door. "I just got off the phone with a top designer, can't say who yet, but I've snagged an invite for you and your girlfriend to her party tonight. There're a few important people who would love to see the golden couple, maybe get a few pictures."

I sit down on the table and rub my eyes. "Have you checked with my girlfriend's nanny yet?" I'm being a prick. I know I am. But I can't help it.

Wes folds his arms across his chest. "Have I ever steered you wrong? You've done nothing but move up since we've been working together, and I need you to give me a little bit of credit."

I let out a breath, feeling guilty. "Right. Okay, okay. I'll be perfect tonight. Don't worry."

"That's what I like to hear," Wes says. "I'll have some clothes sent to your apartment and a car at eight. The driver can pick up Elana after so the pair of you can arrive and leave together. An hour or so should be good enough."

There's a knock on the door, preventing me from responding. We both watch it open just a little and then Eve pokes her head in. "I'm supposed to tell you that Russ needs you ninety seconds ago."

I grab the doorknob and open it the rest of the way, not even thinking about what I'm doing. Eve gets one look at Wes, and her entire body goes completely rigid. Her eyes are wide, and I can tell she had no idea he was here.

Elana is standing behind Eve. She says something in French and Eve turns around and answers her in French. I've already been given an out from this awkward moment, so I grab Elana's hand and tug her away from the RV. "I think Russ needs us."

When I glance over my shoulder, Eve is still standing in the doorway.

Chapter 11: Eve

"Hi, Evie," Wes says.

When the hell did he get here, and why did Russ have to send me to fetch Alex? "Hi," I manage to say.

Wes walks closer and leans against the door frame right across from me. "How's the shoot going so far? Do you miss being the star yet?"

I ignore the first question because he probably has a better answer to that than I do and jump to the second question. "Does it really matter if I miss it?"

He shrugs, eyes locked on mine. I really wish he would stop with the direct eye contact thing. It's so intense.

"Thought you might miss it, that's all," he says.

My heart is like a wild animal. I think it wants to run away as bad as the rest of me does. "Not really."

Why did he have to pick right now to decide to detach his eyeballs from his BlackBerry?

"I find that hard to believe." Something on the set drops or gets banged and it makes a loud clank. Wes keeps staring at me anyway, his attention not wavering for even a second.

"I've made a few calls. It's not over for you if you don't want it to be."

My voice surfaces and somehow comes out even. "Yeah, I've heard Sears is casting. I'm jumping right on that one."

"Better than hiding out in Indiana," he says. "Better than hiding behind the camera."

"I *like* being behind the camera."

"Have you had lunch yet?" Wes asks. "Let's go out somewhere. Catch up."

Is he insane? Seriously. "I'm working."

He smiles at me in that way that used to turn me into girl-with-a-huge-crush mode. "I think I have enough pull to excuse you for an hour."

"Yeah, that'll go over real well, Wes," I snap. "I'm already dealing with all kinds of shit from everyone. Russ keeps telling me he's so glad my recovery went well. I don't need to add fuel to the fire by walking out the door with you."

"And whose fault is that? Who taught you to be a professional only to have you leave Gucci on the first day of shooting?" He sighs and shakes his head. "You've made your own reputation."

I spin around, turning my back on him. "I shouldn't even be having this conversation here with you."

I make it about three steps before he grasps my arm, turning me around. "Where then, Evie? Where can we have this conversation? Come over to my place later."

He actually looks sincere, and I can't help but think for a split second that this isn't wrong anymore. It's not illegal. I'm an adult and so is he. We don't have a business relationship anymore. I've grown up and I might not piss him off and frustrate him as much as my younger self did.

He must have seen the potential for concession on my face because he steps closer and his hand slides up my arm. "All I want is to give you the same chance you had before everything got screwed up. Five years ago, you were Elana, and I don't think your time is up yet. Everyone deserves a second chance."

Turning him down this time is a little easier than I thought it would be. I'm not sure why, but I don't feel as small as I did last week. "I already told you, Wes, I'm okay. Just let it go. I have."

There's a hint of that old storm in his eyes. It could easily be mistaken for passion. He grips my arm tighter.

"Eve?" Janessa says, appearing on the step of the RV.

Oh God.

Wes releases my arm and leans in to kiss me on the cheek. "It was good to see you again, Evie. I'm glad you're doing well. Let me know if you change your mind about those calls I mentioned making earlier."

He gives Janessa a quick nod and then he's gone. I turn to face my new boss. She lifts her hands up, like she's completely exasperated.

"I'm trying to help you here, Eve, but whatever that was"—she points in the direction Wes exited from—"it's not helping everyone see you as my assistant and not a new rumor to spread."

"I'm sorry. It won't happen again, I promise."

She stares at me for a long moment and then says, "Good."

· · ◆ · ·

October 10, 6:30 p.m.

"So what was Janessa like the rest of the day? Did she seem pissed off?" Steph asks while we're in the dining hall trying to make something healthy out of dorm food.

"No, she was totally normal, like it didn't even happen," I say with a sigh. I've been pushing food around my plate for thirty minutes and haven't taken more than two bites. An old habit already reemerging at the first sign of stress.

"Do you think he'll keep showing up the rest of the week?" Steph asks.

"If he does, I'll deal with it. Today was better than the first time and maybe tomorrow, if it happens, it'll be even easier."

"You're not thinking of letting him help you model again, are you?"

I shake my head. "I think it's a lot more complicated than Wes is letting on. He doesn't even rep girls anymore."

"Promise me you won't let yourself end up alone with him again?" Steph says. "I'm seriously worried about that guy."

"I promise." I stare at my salad and rice and draw in a deep breath before shoving in a few bites, swallowing, but hardly chewing. "Just three more days. Three more days."

"Assuming you survive the week, Friday we are going to celebrate at the frat house again—" I groan and she narrows her eyes at me. I've been to a few frat parties with Steph already and was completely unimpressed. "This party is going to be much better than the last, I promise. It's that annual live music for charity ordeal."

I perk up a little. "I've heard of this and it did sound pretty awesome."

Steph folds her hands over the table and stares at me. "I think you need to have some new experiences, meet some new guys. Promise me, when you finish on Friday, we'll go to that party, get crazy drunk, *and* find you a random guy to hook up with."

I shake my head. "I'm not going to hook up with someone I meet on Friday. That's so not me. Maybe I'll give a guy my number or have an intelligent, mutually enjoyable conversation." *Like the ones I have with Alex.* I think it, but I try not to let myself absorb it. Although, the twenty-minute discussion we had this afternoon on superpowers gained via radioactive spills versus radioactive spiders was far from intelligent and far from relevant to anything we were doing. But it beats some frat boy going on about losing an intramural football game and not caring if I ever got in a word in.

"Fine," she concedes. "One kiss. Just find one guy to kiss and consider it symbolic for you turning over a new leaf, deal?"

"Deal," I say after a long pause. It's a reasonable compromise and might even be fun. And if I have a few more days like today, I'll welcome the getting drunk part on Friday.

My phone goes off, vibrating against the whole table. Steph leans in and reads it. "Calvin Klein? You don't actually know—"

"Seriously? Um, no, I don't." I snatch the phone off the table and laugh at her. My heart flutters a little before I answer it. "Hey... what's up?"

"I have a question for you," Alex says, like it's so normal for him to be calling me.

"Aren't you supposed to be at a party with your costar?" Thank

God for that party, because it created some afternoon gossip during the shoot today that distracted everyone from me and my Wes drama.

Steph has already pushed her tray aside, leaning on her elbows to listen in. I'm starting to realize more and more every day that my roommate is a complete straight shooter; she doesn't hide anything. We're even more opposite than I realized.

"The party's not until later," Alex says. "And you're not supposed to answer a question with a question."

"Okay, what's *your* question?"

"How do you feel about dog walking?"

Um, what? "Personally or in general?"

"Personally," he says. "The reason I'm asking is, I know this guy and he lives near Columbia and needs someone to walk his dog a couple of times a week and you said you needed a job."

This isn't even close to what I'd expected him to say, so it takes me several seconds to catch on and Alex eventually prompts me again. "Eve?"

"Yeah, dogs. Love dogs. I want to have a hundred someday."

Alex laughs. "I don't really care if you like dogs, so no need to impress me. Do you want the job?"

"Yes, totally."

"Okay then, I'll pass your email along to my...*friend*," Alex says.

"Who is this guy?" I ask, though I really don't care. A job is a job and I need one. Badly.

"Oh, you know, just another rich kid on the Upper West Side living on Mom and Dad's money. He dabbled with designing. I walked in his show a few months ago, not my proudest moment.

Hopefully the fact that I'm helping you out will be enough to put a stop to any inquiries."

And yeah, I'm curious but I'd never seek out the evidence because it just feels like an unspoken agreement between the two of us ever since Alex said that he never believes that tabloid shit. "My lips are sealed."

"Cool," he says. "John will email you soon. He's a little strange and mildly obsessed with me, so consider yourself warned."

"Isn't everyone obsessed with you?"

Steph's mouth opens like she wants to say something, but she doesn't.

"If only that were true," Alex laughs. "Then I wouldn't have to work, and I'd be off climbing Everest."

"Why would you be climbing Everest?" The words are out of my mouth before I remember him saying something about the indoor climbing wall and how he wants to try something outside soon.

"No reason," he says quickly. "I just mean, I'd be doing whatever I wanted."

"Okay, well, I'll be sure not to tell John that I'm, in fact, your number one fan."

"A catfight would break out, and you'd be back to your financial crisis."

I laugh. "Thanks, Alex. I really appreciate this."

"No problem," he says. "I have one more question. What were you and Elana talking about today? That was way too much French for me to follow."

I glance at Stephanie and decide to hold off on that talk. "Um, I'll text you later with that information, okay?"

"Sure. See you tomorrow, Eve."

I hang up and Steph returns to eating her dinner, but only for a minute before she starts drilling me.

"So, Alex…the guy you supposedly only gave your number to so he'd join your 5K team," she teases. "Have you been running together and I missed it?"

I shrug. "He's nice. That's all."

Except I'm not 100 percent sure that's true.

Chapter 12: Alex

October 10, 8:30 p.m.

EVE: $300/wk to walk a dog! Is he insane?!

I laugh at Eve's text, glad John contacted her so quickly. I'm not sure what will be required of me as a return favor, and frankly I'm a little scared, but hearing the relief in her voice on the phone earlier made it worth it. I don't know what the fuck is going on with her and Wes, but based on how shaken she looked the rest of the day, I can only assume it wasn't a friendly chat to catch up. Could he still be that pissed at her after all this time? Even though things are going great for him, career-wise.

Man, last time I asked John for a favor, more specifically for World Series tickets, I ended up in his apartment trying on some weird-ass punk version of a Scottish kilt, knee socks included, and a vest with no shirt underneath. I wouldn't let him take any pictures though. But still, I'm pretty much scarred for life.

ME: Yes, he's insane. But its pennies to him.

The car pulls up to Elana's agency apartment, and I stow my phone away and jump out to open the door for her. She walks out alone, wearing half a dress. Or at least it looks like half is missing. It's blue and black, of course, matching my black shirt and blue tie that Wes sent over for me to wear tonight.

Elana looks pretty nervous, even stumbles a little in her heels.

"Hey," I say. "Nice dress."

She smiles at me as I open the door for her. "Thank you. I really don't like it, to be frank. I feel like if I bend to pick up something, it will break open."

I laugh and slide in beside her. "The photographers will love that." Her eyes widen, and I can tell I've made her more nervous. "If you drop something, I'll pick it up for you. How's that sound?"

"Thank you."

My phone buzzes again, and I pull it out to read Eve's reply text.

EVE: John just asked me if I've ever dressed a dog before! Wtf?

I glance at Elana who's watching me carefully and then I think about all the people that might be looking over my shoulder, reading "Eve Nowakowski" on my phone. I quickly delete her name and then hesitate before saving her number with a secret nickname…*Harvard*.

ME: Jamiroquai only wears designer clothes. She's never naked.
HARVARD: The dog's name is Jamiroquai?
ME: Yep. After the singer. Virtual insanity. Canned Heat.

HARVARD: Oh boy…what did u have to wear in that show? I can't even imagine.

ME: No you can't. I still need therapy.

HARVARD: Are you ignoring your date?

ME: Maybe. We're in the car.

HARVARD: Pay attention to her for a while and then I'll tell you what you wanted to know earlier.

ME: Deal.

I tuck my phone away and sit in silence for a minute, twiddling my thumbs. "So, Eve's French is really good, huh? Mine's terrible."

"Yes," Elana nods. "She's very nice. I don't believe anything they say about her."

My eyebrows shoot up. This girl doesn't beat around the bush. "Really?"

Elana angles her body to face me, giving me a clear view of way too much skin in the front. I force my eyes up.

"The agency claimed she was going to rehab, but if a model goes to drug rehab the reports always say, oh she has exhaustion and is dehydrated." She waves a hand around as if mimicking Hugo during one of his gossip sessions. "If they say drugs, it means they're hiding something much worse."

"What's worse than drug addiction?"

I stop thinking about it because Eve is slowly becoming more *Harvard* and less Eve Castle and I don't want that to change.

"I don't know," Elana says slowly, every word laced with her thick French accent. "She looks even more beautiful now, doesn't she?"

I'm not sure how to respond to that since Elana is my fake girl-friend and all, and honestly, I haven't seen many pictures of Eve from her time in the spotlight. "She looks...*healthier*," I say finally.

Elana nods, her dark eyes staring into mine. "I can't wait until I'm an actress. I'll eat bread every day and gain fifteen pounds. Maybe I'll even have curves. I love curves on women."

Me too. At least we have one thing in common.

"Actress, huh?" I say, hiding a smile. She's confident in the way a five-year-old is telling you she wants to be an astronaut. Like it's so easy, it's already a done deal. I think my sister Katie still secretly wants to be a pop star, though she won't say it anymore now that her Hannah Montana phase is long behind her.

Katie who has been giving me hell via text message about the *US Weekly* article. Worse than my parents even. She wants to know every detail about Elana and our relationship. I hate lying to her.

I flip through the family text messages I've acquired and ignored throughout the day.

KATIE: I can't believe Elana has that Prada bag! Do they pay her to walk around with it?

BRAD: Hey little bro, they're gonna get the French chick some implants before she does Victoria's Secret, right? Let me know asap. We've got a bet going at the bar tonight.

MOM: You look bigger. You're not taking steroids like that Twilight werewolf boy, are you? Dr. Weinstein just told me they have long-term side effects. Call me right now!

JARED: Don't worry, I calmed Mom down. Told her if you were taking roids you'd actually be able to grow some facial hair. She's fine now.

KATIE: Think I could pull off a belly button ring? This girl in my gym class says she can do it for me.

I feel my blood boil and I quickly type in a response to that last text.

ME: Great idea. Enjoy the Hepatitis C and the staph infection.

KATIE: Okay, okay. It was just an idea.

I shake my head and stuff my phone away. I can deal with the rest of them later.

"Yes," Elana says, reminding me that I had just asked her a question about the actress thing. "And singer. I've studied dance some too, so Broadway is a possibility."

Right. And I'm going to climb Everest.

We've arrived at the apartment building where the party is being held. I turn to Elana before the driver opens the door. "You're okay with this, right? There's photographers and…it's not real…I don't want it to be real. You understand that?"

I had to ask. What if she does get attached? She's fourteen. Isn't she supposed to get crushes on idiot older boys? Better someone else than me.

Her face turns completely serious and she says, "Yes, and no offense to you, Alex, but I would never be interested in a boy who agrees to something like this."

I should be offended. But coming from this girl, it just makes me laugh. She's not a complete naive princess. "If that's true, then promise you won't date any models, because they'd all probably agree to something like this. Even the girls."

She smiles at me as the door opens, and already I see cameras flashing. "I promise."

I feel about 10 percent better when we step out of the car. I'm comfortable enough to rest my hand on the small of her back and look like a couple. We pose for a few photos and one photographer shouts at us, "What about the language barrier? Do you speak French, Alex? How are you communicating?"

I give my best smirk. "Her English is way better than my French. Hell, her English might be better than my English."

Elana smiles but looks incredibly shy and not willing to speak up. We head inside, refusing any more questions.

With Elana wearing those heels, we're exactly the same height. But she almost looks taller because her legs go on forever. Eve's legs look like that too. (Yes, I've checked out Eve's legs. I am a dude.) In build, Elana is basically a dark-skinned version of Eve. Eve's freckles and the small strands of curly hair that slip out of her messy bun make her a little more like the girl next door, whereas Elana's bone structure and facial features are sharper and more intense.

There are no photographers inside the party, but we do get a few heads turning our way after entering. I'm holding Elana's hand now, but she seems to be a little steadier in her heels and less nervous.

A waiter approaches us with a tray of champagne glasses. Elana picks one up right away. I follow her movement even though I'm not a champagne kind of guy.

Everything about this party is stuffy and formal. I hate it after only two minutes. We make our way around the large main room in this penthouse apartment, stopping to talk and shake hands with various industry people. Elana does a great job, kissing everyone on both cheeks and giving me lots of sideways glances that could be deemed as romantic. I guess. After nearly an hour of this (though it feels like six hours), we end up separated. I'm leaning against a black grand piano, downing a vodka club when I get another text from Eve.

HARVARD: How's the party?

ME: *snore* please tell me you are at a much cooler party. I can live vicariously through you.

HARVARD: Sorry. I'm alone with my calculus book. We've been together for hours. Barely pulling a C in this class. Math is my greatest weakness.

ME: Can't you just find some college boy/math geek to seduce into free tutoring?

HARVARD: You watch too much TV. And clearly overestimate my ability to seduce anyone.

ME: Come on. It's not that hard. You were a model.

HARVARD: I took direction very well. On my own=Epic fail.

ME: Ok. Tell me the big secret with Elana.

HARVARD: It's not big. She's worried about the rest of the week. So far it's been pretty tame and since it's CK…you know…

ME: Foursomes on big billboards over Time Square.

HARVARD: Exactly.

ME: Do you know the concepts for the rest of the shoot?

HARVARD: I heard Russ and Janessa talking today.

ME: And…? Elana's gonna be topless, right? Great.

HARVARD: Probably. But I don't think topless is a problem for her. It's the kissing…that kind of stuff.

ME: Well I'm not really looking forward to that either but I kinda figured there'd be some lovemaking in jeans.

HARVARD: Lol. I'm sure she'll be fine. Speaking of your gf… Where is she?! Are you watching her?!

Shit!

I look up from my phone and the room forms right in front of me. It had dissolved for a little while. Probably due to my strong desire to be anywhere but here. Wishful thinking. I glance around searching for the tall girl in half a dress.

"Looking for your girlfriend?"

"Actually, I am—" My voice cuts off when I come face-to-face with Jennifer, the *GQ* intern I left asleep in my apartment last week. And had not called again since. My eyes widen with panic. "Oh…hey, Jennifer."

Do I get points for remembering her name?

She grins—huge and uninhibited. *Oh boy.* "Awkward, huh? You look so uncomfortable, I'm gonna let you off the hook. This time."

Okay, no more interns. No matter what Wes tells me to do.

She tugs at my tie, holding me in place for a second. "One question?" I nod and swallow hard. I don't think I'm being let off the hook at all. "How far did we—"

Thank you, gods of one-night stands.

I rest my hands on her shoulders. "Nowhere. I swear. You fell asleep, and I crashed on the couch."

"Great." She sighs with relief. "Elana disappeared into the last door on the right about ten minutes ago. She's with Devin Stone."

Fuck almighty. Devin Stone is the scummiest of scummy models and he's beaten me for jobs more times than I can count. Ten minutes is more than enough for that dude to have removed what's left of her dress.

I try not to look too concerned or in a hurry as I'm rushing down the hall, heading toward the last door on the right. I hear laughing right before I turn the doorknob. The first thing I see is a wall covered by a giant painting. Some kind of trendy graffiti thing.

"It's by a street artist in Paris," Devin says. "She had it flown in a few weeks ago. Paid at least a million for it."

"It looks like schoolchildren got in a paint fight," Elana says.

Devin laughs and I try not to scowl as he moves right behind her. Then he notices me, standing in the doorway. "Hey, Alex. Good to see you again."

Yeah. Can't say the same. "You too, man." I reach for Elana's hand, tugging her gently toward me. She's got a glass of red wine in place of the clear champagne. How much could she have drank in the thirty minutes we were separated?

Who cares? Just keep her from looking like someone else's boyfriend and the job is done. She's not my sister. She's not my responsibility. I need to focus on that.

"So..." I say to Elana. "Have you had enough of this party yet?"

I'm glad to be standing close to Devin now. I like the two

inches I have on him. I stand up even straighter, lifting my chin so I can appear to be looking down onto his shiny black hair.

"I'm ready if you are," Elana says.

I was ready an hour ago when we stepped through the doors.

Devin picks up Elana's free hand and kisses it. I fight the urge to gag. He's so phony. I'm not Mr. Honest and genuine or anything, but manipulative and charming beats phony any day. Besides, he's like twenty-two or twenty-three. And she's fourteen. Well, I guess she's eighteen in his eyes, but still…

"Lovely to meet you, Elana," he says. *Gag*. "Nice to see you again, Alex. You're looking a little more…*fit*."

I snort back a snide remark and guide Elana toward the door. "Later, Devin." The second we're outside again, my grip tightens on Elana's hand, my anger at a near boiling point. "God, I hate that stupid prick."

She looks at me, lifts her eyebrows, and plasters on a huge fake smile, discreetly nodding toward the photographers still staked out in front of the building. I let out a breath, trying to relax. I don't look at any of them or respond to their questions. I keep my eyes on Elana while thinking about what Eve said in her text earlier.

Might as well get it out of the way now before it becomes this big thing. And she said she wants to be an actress, so let's act in love.

I lean in closer to Elana and the second my eyes close, I try to imagine someone else, someone older. My mouth makes contact with hers and I can feel her stiffen at first and then she catches up to me.

It's a fairly quick kiss, no tongues involved. But I try to do a good job of making it romantic by putting my hand on her face and then kissing her forehead before opening the door to the car that's just pulled up for us. Once we're moving, I notice her eyes focused on the front of the car, her hands fiddling nervously in her lap.

"Was that okay? I just thought…"

She manages a small sideways glance in my direction. "It was perfect. For the story, anyway."

She's handling everything really well. Maybe we *can* work together on this project. It's impressive, actually. I know I was never this mature at fourteen.

Elana leans back in her seat, and for the first time tonight, she looks like a tired kid. She probably has a bedtime.

"Your friend Devin?" she says. "He's sleeping with the party host."

My head snaps in her direction. "What? How do you know?"

The party host is a big-name new designer Wes is probably trying to get me in with. She's also pushing forty years old.

Elana grins, obviously enjoying the fact that she can get to me through gossip. "He showed me all her artwork and had detailed information on when it was bought and delivered. Obviously he's spending time in her apartment. And I saw her watching him. That's why I let him lead me away, just to see her reaction."

I gape at her. "Who are you? A secret agent undercover as a fourteen-year-old? Are you even French?"

She laughs. "I think if Kara and Wes want us to be this designer's top picks and someone is working against one of us, we should feel free to…*investigate*, do you not agree?"

"Oh, I totally agree. That was super badass." I put my fist out for her and she stares at it for a second, a little bewildered, then eventually bumps her fist into mine. "Next time let me in on your James Bond plans, because I was bored as hell in there."

Suddenly, I remember the buzzing I felt from my pocket while distracted by Devin Stone earlier. I pull my phone out and glance at it.

HARVARD: Did u find her?! Tell me you found her?
ME: She's fine. We're headed home. No worries. How's calculus?
HARVARD: I've just bought three pastries from the coffee shop if that tells you anything.
ME: That bad, huh? Which coffee shop?
HARVARD: Hungarian pastry shop. Near campus.

I look out the window and check our location. Then I turn to Elana. "Want to get some coffee?"

Chapter 13: Eve

I laugh out loud when Alex and Elana walk into the coffee shop decked out in their formal wear. If Alex is this deadly in a tie, I have a feeling the shirtless jeans look in tomorrow's shoot is going to be mighty distracting. And they're such a contrast to me right now. I'm wearing my pink flannel pajama pants, a T-shirt, and a hoodie. My hair is still wet from my post-workout shower a few hours ago.

"You guys look hot," I say, gesturing toward the two empty seats across from me. "I'm not sure we coordinate enough to share a table."

Alex glances out the window in front of the store, eyes darting all over the place. "Just checking for paparazzi. There was a bunch outside the party tonight."

I roll my eyes. "And you don't think someone on your team called them up beforehand?"

Someone like Wes.

Alex shrugs, not committing to an answer. He knows. He has to.

They both sit down across from me, but Alex jumps up quickly, turning to Elana. "What would you like? Coffee? Food?"

He's just remembered he's on a date.

She glances longingly at my plate of pastries and then back at Alex before sighing, "Just tea, please. Herbal tea."

I close my calculus book, knowing I'm as prepared as I'm going to be for tomorrow's quiz. "Love your dress," I say to Elana. "How was the party?"

She yawns and eyes the pastries again. "Oh, tolerable."

Alex is back with tea for Elana and coffee for himself. I slide the plate of two remaining pastries toward Elana. Buying three was a moment of weakness. I haven't even gotten halfway through the first one. "Help yourself," I say.

She shakes her head vigorously. "Lumina would kill me."

Lumina. The assistant (nanny) with the irremovable evil eye.

I'd like to trivialize Elana's concerns, but I know firsthand that those pastries can be the difference between Calvin Klein and Sears catalog. The two of us are living examples of this. I'm Sears now; she's CK. I'm eating an apple strudel; she's not.

I slide the plate toward Alex. "How about you?"

He shakes his head, not even looking a bit conflicted. "No thanks."

"It's better if you eat them than me," I say, thinking he's probably worried about taking food from the poor girl in need of employment. "It's not like you have to worry about fitting into a dress. Aren't you on the bulking-up plan?"

He laughs, his really blue eyes on mine. "I eat plenty. I just make it a point to stay away from anything that doesn't have nutritional value. Or at least that's what I've been doing for the last six months. It's working, so I'm sticking with it."

"Wait, carbs and refined sugar aren't nutritious? How did I not know that?" I say. "Are you really going to get fat from eating junk food every once in a while?"

"No, I won't get fat. That's nearly impossible." He looks away, staring at the wall behind me. "Both of you will murder me if I tell you the truth."

Elana and I are giving him all our attention now. "This I have to hear," I say. "Spill."

"All right, but you've been warned." He looks back and forth between the two of us. "You know how I'm not, like, super buff." We both nod because I guess this is true, though super buff has always been kind of gross to me. "Basically, if I skip one meal, I'll lose five pounds." He snaps his fingers. "Just like that. You should see my dad. He's a stick and he eats three steaks and six potatoes a day. But if I eat garbage, I can't get through my twice-a-day work-outs, and then I shrink back to stick boy. It has to be protein, fruits and veggies, and whole grains…lots of grains. I probably have to eat around three to four thousand calories a day."

"You're right, I hate you," I say.

"Me too," Elana says.

"Beer is my big weakness," Alex admits.

"My parents own a bakery," Elana says. "I spent my childhood smelling bread baking and cakes and pies. Crepes are my weakness though. With strawberries on top. If my mother knew I ever turned down food when I'm hungry, she'd have me back home that day."

"Just don't get too obsessed with resisting," I say. "It can go wrong in a couple of different ways. You either go crazy and eat a dozen crepes in one day, or eventually, you can't stop resisting or feeling guilty. This is temporary and all the diet stuff should be too."

Alex's eyes are wide; this more serious conversation is making him uncomfortable. Or maybe he's one of those people who'd rather not see anyone's dirty laundry because then you have to care and acknowledge it. I can sort of relate to that, but for some reason, since the opportunity presented itself, it feels important to tell Elana what I know.

She smiles at me and then stands up. "You know what? I might go look at the selection. Perhaps there's something small."

Alex and I watch her make her way over to the counter. She stops halfway there and lifts one of her feet, removing her shoe. She does the same thing with the other foot and holds the black heels, dangling them from her finger.

"So, did you talk to her?" I whisper to Alex. "About the shoot tomorrow? She's really nervous."

He takes a sip of his coffee then says, "Didn't talk to her, but I kissed her. Just to get it out of the way. We had a photo op after the party."

I force a neutral expression onto my face. "Okay. Well, that's one method."

He shrugs. "It wasn't bad. She's a cool kid. I think we'll be fine."

I have to admit, I'm a little relieved. Elana seemed like a bundle of nerves when I talked to her this morning. Plus, I've seen all the CK ads. They aren't tame by any means. And I know for a fact that she hasn't—

Oh shit. I bet Alex has no idea. I'm fighting the big giant grin that's about to take shape across my face. His big brother complex isn't going to be able to handle this news at all.

"You know that was her first kiss." I lean in closer to Alex. "Her very first kiss with Alex Evans. She'll remember it forever."

His coffee slips from his hand and he nearly drops it but catches his fingers around the rim of the cup just in time. "What the fuck, Eve? You couldn't have told me that in your text?"

I glance over at Elana, gliding along the floor, checking out every item in the glass case. "Does it really matter? It's not like that would have changed anything between now and tomorrow morning. I think you guys are basically going to be all over each other. Like wild jungle creatures or something. I heard the concepts. They're all very primal."

Alex's serious expression falters and he laughs. "Primal, huh?"

I nod and resume eating my delicious apple pastry. Unlike my two table companions, I will not be photographed in underwear anytime in the near future. "My first kiss was at a shoot for *Teen Vogue*. The guy was at least twenty, and no one gave me any direction. So of course, I did what all my friends told me to do—stuck my tongue in his mouth. I had no clue that people don't use their tongues on TV or in pictures."

Alex bursts out laughing and puts his face in his hands for a second. "Oh man…that sucks. No wonder you don't want to seduce math geeks."

I feel myself blushing, and I drop my eyes to the table for a second. "It was awful. The guy—I can't even remember his name—took it as an invitation for some action after the photo shoot. What about you?"

"My first kiss was in seventh grade," Alex says. "Behind the bleachers during one of my brother's football games. Other than a few instances of teeth bumping, I'd say it went pretty well."

"In seventh grade, no one would have kissed me. I hardly ever talked to boys in middle school because they all stared at my chest instead of my face. Not because I had huge boobs, but because that was eye level for them."

Elana returns to our table, carrying what looks like a container of yogurt with tons of fruit on top. "I'm pretending it's bread," she says.

Alex taps his finger on my calc book. "So this is the devil? Wish I could help you, but I never made it anywhere near calculus." He narrows his eyes at me. "How did you manage to keep up with high school? I'm assuming you didn't drop out and do the GED thing like I did? Columbia doesn't accept GEDs, do they?"

"It wasn't easy," I admit. "I did correspondence courses when I lived in New York, but what really helped me get into Columbia were the classes I took during my two summers in Europe. One of the designers I was working for then was into brainiac models and all for me taking language immersion, art history, photography. It was an amazing experience especially for someone like me, from small-town Indiana. I'm hoping to go back to Paris next summer. Assuming I get the scholarship that I'm working on." I groan out loud, eyeing my evil calc book. "Assuming I pass my quiz tomorrow."

Alex is leaning back in his chair now, coffee cup heading toward his mouth. "I feel extremely inferior to you. Are you trying to accomplish this? Because you've totally succeeded. I pale in comparison to Eve Castle."

I shrug and grin at him, ignoring the casual drop of the name I worked so hard to bury. "Well, you are better dressed."

"I don't know, it's kind of badass to go out in public in your pajama pants like you don't give a shit. That's confidence."

My comeback is halted by Elana's eyes turning into giant saucers. She swears under her breath in French. "Lumina's here."

Alex looks at her, totally confused. "How did she find us?"

"Maybe she called the driver?" Elana says.

The heavyset Hispanic woman stomps into the coffee shop, silencing all three of us. She spins around as if surprised by her surroundings. "Elana! This is where you went?"

"Obviously," Alex mutters under his breath. I catch his eye and start laughing.

Elana sets her yogurt down and looks over at me. "Lumina, you remember Eve, she's Janessa Fields's assistant?"

Lumina turns her evil eye on me. She's like a big scary dog, so I do the first thing I think I'd do with a wild dog—throw food at it. Or in this case, I hold out the plate with a smile. "Pastry?"

The anger fades from her expression, and even her shoulders drop a couple of inches, revealing that she does, in fact, have a neck. Her hand reaches out for the cream cheese pastry on top. "Thank you, Eve."

Then she turns the intense, strict-mom face to Elana. "It's late, very late."

"If she needs to go," Alex says quickly, "take the car. I can catch a cab or the subway."

"Very good," she says with a nod, gesturing for Elana to stand.

Elana turns to both of us. "Thank you for a delightful evening."

"Uh, yeah, you too," Alex says.

"See you tomorrow," I say.

As soon as they're out of sight, both of us start laughing. "Did you have a Lumina?" Alex asks.

"Sort of," I say. "But she was pretty young and I ran circles around her. Only lasted a couple of months, and then I was on my own. Looks like they're taking better care of her."

Alex shakes his head. "Yeah, they've lied about her age and got her into a fake relationship with an eighteen-year-old guy."

"Good point. But at least you aren't taking advantage of her." I check the time and then start to pack my books and laptop into my bag. "They're closing soon. And Steph is probably worried about me by now."

"Steph?"

"My roommate."

He hands me a notebook that had been resting under his elbow. "Roommate, huh? A hot roommate?"

"Yeah, as a matter of fact, she's a total knockout. I'd introduce you, but you already have a girlfriend." I sling my bag over my shoulder and wait for his retort.

"I'm beginning to learn," he says slowly, like he's been thinking about this. "The more hookups I have, the more they come back and bite me in the ass."

"At least you're not actually in a complicated relationship. A hookup you can always come back from," I say bitterly, then just to cover up my own personal investment in that statement, I add, "Just ask Bill Clinton."

He holds the door open for me and I walk through quickly. "You know…" he says, following me outside into the cool night air, "if this were a first date for me and you—hypothetically—I'd say it wasn't an epic fail. So, maybe it's just seduction of men smarter than you that you screw up. Since you mentioned your inability to sexually bribe math geeks for free tutoring."

"Maybe. It helps that you're pretty easy to be around. I don't have to choose College Eve or Model Eve. Same with Elana," I add quickly so he doesn't think I'm openly flirting or something.

Am I flirting? Have I already been flirting the past few days with all the texting?

He looks surprised, like I've said something totally out of left field. But then he smiles and says, "I kind of like that. Just be you. I don't have to try to guess or play any games. Those are exhausting sometimes." He points at the stairs to the subway station. "That's my ride. See you tomorrow?"

"Yep, tomorrow." I turn the corner, heading toward my dorm.

I should have said something nice to him too. Something about how I like that he trusts me with his secrets and trusts my advice. That's not an easy thing for someone like Alex to do. He's so focused on his career, I don't think he ever counts on anyone but himself. Sure, he needs people in his world, but he's in charge when it comes down to it. It's like he's totally carefree and boyish and yet he takes 100 percent responsibility for all his actions. I thought he was predictable, but he might actually be an anomaly.

I almost feel bad for telling him it was Elana's first kiss. He looked really wigged out about that. But if Elana is anything like me, she might not count that as her first kiss. I didn't count my technical first kiss as my actual first kiss. The actual first kiss belongs to Wes Danes. He had been my stand-in agent for a few weeks while we were both in Paris. Wes was brand new to the agency. He was twenty-four and full of charm and hotness, but also super intense when it came to me and work. He wanted everything to go perfectly and nothing to happen to me while on his watch. I got invited to this party thrown by one of the French models and Wes told me not to go alone, but being a stubborn fifteen-year-old, I went anyway.

I couldn't believe how fast this guy managed to get me alone and out of earshot of anyone. But the real shock came when he pinned me against the wall and leaned in to kiss me. The door flew open, and all I could see were hands grasping the back of the guy's jacket, shoving him to the side. Wes stood in front of me, looking so pissed I almost didn't follow him out of the room.

He waited until we were in the hotel elevator, on our way up to my room on the eleventh floor, to say anything. "I specifically told you not to go to that party, Eve! I'm not a babysitter and I'm sure as hell not your parent, so please don't pull this shit again."

My legs were shaking. I'd never heard Wes yell before, and I had no idea what would have happened with that guy if I couldn't get away from him. If Wes hadn't shown up. I was usually a lot smarter than that, but sometimes my independence gave me a big head and I thought I could handle more than I actually could.

"I'm sorry," I managed to squeak out.

Wes stomped out of the elevator and I followed. "You're *sorry?*" he yelled. "Of course you're fucking sorry. You damn near got assaulted in a foreign country. It's probably not even a crime here."

I leaned against the wall beside my hotel room door and turned my head away from Wes, trying and failing to hide the fact that I was crying. I heard Wes sigh, and then he started digging into my purse, looking for the room key. The door finally clicked open, and Wes steered me inside, sitting me down on the end of the bed.

"Look, Evie," he said, squatting down on the floor in front of me. "You have to realize that you're a dime a dozen right now. Everyone is waiting for you to be just like all the other hyped-up teen models they hear about. You girls come and go in a steady stream. But I think you're different, Eve. I really do. But it doesn't matter what I think."

I wiped my face with the bottom of my shirt, and Wes gave me another exasperated sigh, probably hating watching me ruin designer clothes, before grabbing and wetting a towel from the bathroom. I took it from him and started cleaning off my smeared makeup.

"He was really nice," I said, referring to the guy model I had met at an art gallery earlier and the same guy Wes had just yanked off me a few minutes ago. "We were talking about art and music and weird American culture stuff. He didn't seem so...I don't know... *forward*, I guess."

Wes sat beside me and took the wet, messy towel from my hands, tossing it onto the chair next to the bed. "Let me just give you some advice on guys—since I am one. You're going to have to wait a long time before you can really get someone to love you for the right reasons. Because there're too many other factors to influence people. You're beautiful, smart, soon to be famous, and you have money now. Most likely Mr. Art Gallery doesn't care an ounce about you. Trust me."

My heart sank to the pit of my stomach. It wasn't like I'd fallen in love with someone in one day, but it had seemed like a beginning to me, and hearing that I had gotten it all wrong made the situation so hopeless. And I felt like an idiot, in front of Wes. Someone I'd developed a bit of an inappropriate crush on. And now I was sobbing like a fifteen-year-old with a crush. Perfect.

I nodded and more tears spilled down my cheeks. "I get it. I should have listened to you and guys are assholes and none of them are ever going to care about me. Thanks for the advice."

"Except me," Wes said, his voice turning a little more gravelly. "I care about you. I shouldn't, but I do."

My heart pounded, hearing all the intentions in his voice, and I wanted to hear them. I really did. I turned myself to face him and he reached a hand out to smooth my hair down. It had to be a complete mess. I got daring and lifted a hand to touch the fashionable stubble on his cheeks. I thought he'd stop me. I thought he'd yell at me again. I thought he'd stomp out of the room. But in a matter of two seconds, we went from sitting beside each other to kissing. Hard and intense in a way I'd never done before. And it wasn't an equal partnership. It was Wes guiding me through it like he'd guided me away from that guy and into my room. I didn't have to feel like I needed to know what I was doing. He knew I didn't. He *liked* that I didn't.

After what felt like a minute or maybe an hour, he pulled away from me, resting his forehead against mine, breathing hard. "Evie, this can never happen again, understood?"

"Okay," I said, but even an inexperienced teenager like me knew that when anyone says it'll never happen again, that means it most likely will. And I almost smiled at the thought of kissing him again. It felt dark and dangerous, yet very safe all at the same time.

Every time I thought about that first kiss, my mind always drifted to Wes, squeezing my arm until bruises formed. Wes, yelling at me for gaining a couple pounds and jeopardizing a big job he'd gotten me. Wes, shoving me into a wall and then minutes later holding me and telling me he was sorry. Then Wes in his boss's office, glaring at me while denying I ever meant anything to him. And I could almost feel my heart breaking all over again. Where did I screw up with him? Where did it turn so bad? Because that first kiss was everything I'd ever dreamed it could be. Everything.

I wonder if Alex would listen to that story like he listened to the other one? Does he suspect the tension between me and Wes is about anything more than my abrupt departure? He couldn't possibly know it was more than that. No way. Alex would have major issues with that information, and I'd know if he knew.

And what if Wes is right? Maybe I needed to wait until I was a nobody again before someone would truly care about me?

A nobody like College Eve. Like Eve Nowakowski.

Chapter 14: Alex

October 11, 2:30 p.m.

I'm gonna ask Eve out.

Or at least I'm going to try to. Last night, I could have sat there in that coffee shop for hours. And this morning, it occurred to me that all of our accidental run-ins and all of our conversations are directly related to this CK shoot, which is going to end on Friday and it's already Wednesday.

At least if I ask her out, she'll know that I'm not talking to her and hanging out with her just because of the shoot. Okay, I am, but I want to keep doing it after. And I want her to know that.

Of course there's the Wes issue, but he and I don't get personal, so it shouldn't be a problem. And then there's Elana. Even dorky Elliot has heard about the two of us. He mentioned something about my "girlfriend" while we were climbing today.

I keep replaying my last conversation with Eve and thinking I said all the wrong things. Why did I have to mention her pajama pants? It sounded so condescending, but in reality, her attire made me want to take her back to my place for movies and a sleepover.

My ringing phone distracts me from mentally rehearsing asking her out, or at least to hang out. We could do the friend thing. I'd take that over not seeing her at all. Maybe I need to join her running club. That could work.

"Hey, Wes," I say as I'm waiting with dozens of tourists to cross the street on the way to today's location. "What's up?"

"Alex Evans, I fucking love you!"

I pull the phone away from my face for a second to keep my eardrum from bursting. "So it's good news?"

"Yes, good news, as in your genius intuition and a perfectly timed kiss with *the* Elana has popped up on one hundred and seventy-two websites so far," Wes says. "My Google Alerts are going nuts."

Oh. That. "Right. Glad I made it look convincing."

"Convincing?" he says. "I'd say innocent and adorable come to mind. And even better...fragrance campaign."

I freeze right in the middle of crossing a busy street until someone ahead of me yanks me onto the curb, preventing my death by taxicab. "Are you serious?"

"I've had two conference calls already this morning," he says.

I can practically hear the squeak of his chair as he leans back in it and tosses his feet on the desk like he's Superman. As far as I'm concerned, he is fucking Superman. "So, it's a couples thing?"

Fragrance campaigns are the big bucks, and many of the big-name designers have used real-life couples before and made it a big deal to tell everyone about it. Although, given my situation, I'm starting to doubt the validity of any of those couples.

"Yep," he says. "I knew lanky, blond guys would get to have

their day eventually. I knew it the second I saw you. That's what it comes down to. Elana's face is so intense and totally take-charge-I'm-wearing-the-pants. And you've got the innocent, all-American boy look going on. Every woman in America will see those ads and imagine being able to tie you up to their bedpost and have their way with you, like Elana gets to."

I have to work very hard not gag. "Okay, I get it. I look help-less and defenseless and she looks like the independent woman every girl wants to be. It's not all that original of a concept."

"No, probably not," he says. "And you won't look helpless in the ads. You'll come off as a guy who's not afraid to sit in the passenger seat every once in a while."

I can live with that. "So when do we get to break up?"

"You did *not* just say that out loud, did you?" Wes warns.

I glance around the street, squinting into the sun. The smell of exhaust fumes and sewers fill my nostrils, but no one appears to be lurking nearby, waiting to hear that my celebrity relationship is fake. All of this makes me wonder how often this happens. Are any Hollywood relationships real? And how far do they take it? Marriage? Kids? Maybe Brad and Angelina borrowed those kids from a service or something. I rented my trumpet in middle school for three years; maybe you can rent kids for a few years. If there's a way, I can guarantee Wes will figure it out and have me and Elana signed up by next week.

"Sorry. Won't happen again," I tell Wes. "Besides, I don't see anyone who might have been listening in."

"Yeah, well, those tabloid creeps are pretty good at their jobs."

This makes me think about Eve and all the rumors that were

spread about her. According to the tabloids, Eve ended up in drug rehab.

I still don't believe that though. But asking her for details or trolling the Internet for old gossip headlines would risk seeing her in a different light, and I like her like this.

College Eve...*Harvard*. Or Columbia. Whatever. Same thing.

Okay, speaking of Eve.

Chapter 15: Eve

I'm thinking it could be a bad sign that I can spot Alex from nearly two blocks away. Or maybe it's proof that I'm an excellent photographer who studies her subjects diligently. At least I have an excuse. But it's only got a shelf life of three more days.

I start walking toward him, and he hangs up with whoever he's talking to, tucking the phone away in his pocket.

"Hey, Harvard," he says. "How was that calculus quiz?"

I think I'm already smiling. *Damn.* "Harvard is in Boston, Alex."

He shrugs and pulls his sunglasses over his eyes, like he forgot to do this when he got off the subway. "That's what my phone calls you. Can't be too literal or people might find out about our secret affair."

Unfortunately, I know all there is to know about secret affairs. I can feel myself blushing and I'm glad that we've turned and started walking forward again and don't have to stand face-to-face. "Well, my phone calls you Calvin Klein."

He almost looks offended. "That's very literal. You can't do better than that?"

"It's not because of the shoot," I explain. "I was thinking about you and...*Annie*..." I watch Alex's face to see if he's caught on to the code name I've just made up for Elana based on her Broadway aspirations. We can't exactly talk about the fake relationship using real names when we're out in public like this.

He pauses for a second and then nods. "Right, *Annie*. Okay, keep going."

"Have you seen *Back to the Future*?"

His eyebrows go up above his sunglasses. "I have."

"Well, you know when Marty goes back to the fifties? It's a year when his parents were in high school, and his mom thinks his name is Calvin Klein because it's on his underwear?"

"Still very literal, Eve," he says, his gaze fixed on the block in front of us. "I thought you were smart."

"Or you're just too dense to get it." I roll my eyes. "Marty's mom is all over him, totally falling for him, but she doesn't know it's her future son. And he's totally wigged out about it, rightfully so since it's his mom, but he still has to play along and take her to the dance. The thing with him and his mom is like you and *Annie*. Except minus the space-time continuum issue and the fact that *Annie* is also playing along. It's creepy for you and maybe not so creepy for her, I guess."

"Huh." He opens the door that will lead us into the studio and I walk through before him. "Sorry I insulted your intelligence. And skipping over small talk to jump right to space-time continuums is kinda hot. We should do this more often."

If I wasn't sure before, now I'm 100 percent positive he's flirting with me. And I'm 150 percent positive that I like it.

The elevator feels especially warm with both of us confined to a small space. Alex removing his sunglasses and revealing his blue eyes doesn't help my whole blushing situation. *The all-American boy*...that's what Janessa and the producer nicknamed him. The kind of boy who supposedly will get his heart stomped on by a dark-skinned French beauty.

Alex, in real life, seems too strong to let someone walk all over him. And he also seems too decent to stomp on anyone else's heart. But then again, that's what I thought about Wes.

"So," I say, to break the silence. "I met John and Jamiroquai this morning."

I had, in fact, spent a whole fifteen minutes with the weird pseudodesigner this morning for a "meet and greet," as he called it. Luckily, I won't have to run into John very often, because I'll be walking the dog when he isn't home.

Alex laughs. "Sorry you had to start your day with that."

"It's okay. He paid me for a month up front so it was worth the suffering." We're in the studio now and he's about to head to wardrobe. He looks like he wants to say something to me, but the stylist calls him over. I clap him on the back before he heads off. "Good luck. It's gonna be a rough day."

Chapter 16: Alex

When I finally give the rack a closer look, I start to weigh the options. There's a varying array of briefs, boxer briefs, and pseudo-banana hammocks with full backs in every color under the sun—black, neon green, pink, yellow, gold, red, navy, bright fuchsia. As the stylist is looking through the rack and sizing me up, probably trying to match my coloring, I'm silently chanting, *boxer briefs, boxer briefs…*

He's reaching a hand toward the banana hammock rack and I suck in a breath, trying to look cool with whatever.

But seriously. No one is cool with whatever.

Time to start facing the fact that I'm going to be on a billboard in SoHo with my junk pretty much exposed in bright yellow-and-black drawers. The ads will probably come out just as my mom has gotten over the viral Internet spread of Elana/Alex couple photos followed by the Internet spread of breakup photos (fingers crossed), assuming Wes doesn't actually insist on the fake marriage and kids ordeal. Wait, that part was just in my head. He hadn't actually proposed that. *Proposed.* Bad word choice.

"Nah, not these, they're not relatable enough to the G.P." the stylist says.

I let out a sigh of relief. But no sooner do I look back up and he has a pair of black briefs with neon-green micro-polka-dots.

"These are perfect. You're ready to be pounced on by the woman of your dreams," he says.

"Great. Can't wait to…try these suckers on."

"You'll look amazing, right, Amy?" he says to the woman silently following him. "Amy, write down the description and the style number. I'm going to tell Janessa we're almost ready. Then make sure you get Elana started as soon as she's done with hair and makeup. We're way behind with her already."

Yep. A dude just told me I'm gonna look amazing in skimpy underwear.

He leaves without waiting for a response and makes his way to set.

Amy looks up long enough to smile and then blindly searches for a robe on the rack before handing it to me. "Might want to put this on too."

After a quick change and after they've lubed me up with some makeup and self-tanner, I'm off to set. The thing about shooting underwear shots is the light is important. Janessa has two guy assistants as stand-ins testing everything. I resist the urge to go talk to Eve and instead sit down on the couch. I'm not about to ask her out while wearing neon polka dots. That's got failure written all over it.

And I almost did it earlier, right before the stylist interrupted. The timing would have been perfect. Well, perfect if we're not thinking about my current fake relationship.

We would have to make this a low-key date. Somewhere off the beaten path of the paparazzi. Somewhere that appeared innocent, like two coworkers meeting up for coffee or something. Either that or we bring Elana along. But Eve wouldn't want to be photographed with us, I'm sure. Given her history in my world. Plus, Wes would probably flip given *their* history.

As soon as Janessa sees me on the couch, she ushers me over to fill in for one of the assistant stand-in guys. I ditch the robe and feel the awkwardness Richter scale skyrocket. In an attempt to save me from pretending this assistant dude is Elana, Janessa tells him to go adjust one of the other lights in the back of the set. Out of the corner of my eye, I spot Eve standing out of Janessa's line of sight. She's trying not to smile, but she's doing it anyway. At my expense. I decide it's time to look the beast in the eye. I wave dramatically at her, like I'm flagging her down.

Janessa follows my wave all the way to Eve, who turns completely scarlet.

"Eve!" Janessa says. "Step in for Daniel. You're closer to Elana's height."

Her eyes get really big and round, but her voice stays totally even. "Okay."

Well, this should be interesting. Of course it would be much more interesting if she was also wearing neon polka-dot underwear.

"Guess your time in the spotlight isn't over after all," I say when she appears in front of me.

"This is not exactly the spotlight, nor do I have any choice in this matter," she whispers, leaning in close so I get a whiff of her hair and something that smells like cinnamon. "How far along do you think Elana is on hair and makeup?"

I'd already heard from nearly a dozen people during my prep process about how behind they were with Elana. "I'd say we can run through the whole shoot in the time it takes for her to get done."

Janessa interrupts us by shouting some directions. "Stand a little bit more spaced out and pretend like you're throwing something at the other person."

"What exactly are we throwing?" I whisper to Eve.

"The designer said something about neon body paint. We had a meeting yesterday. It goes with the whole safari theme. Which is Janessa's thing."

Janessa cuts in again. "Get really close!" *I can totally do that. Just give me my pants back.* "Alex, dip her down like you're going to kiss her."

I love pants. I will never take them for granted again. When I get the fragrance campaign, I'm donating a bunch of money to a pants-related charity.

But in the meantime, I don't have a fragrance campaign and I'm not about to show any signs of fear. Fashion people can smell it a mile away and then ruin my chances.

"You heard the boss lady," I say to Eve before hooking an arm around her waist and tugging her closer. My fingers brush over a strip of bare skin on her lower back and it sends my pulse racing so fast that I'm sure she can feel my heartbeat. And for a good long second, I don't even care. Let her figure it out if she hasn't already. I hadn't planned on playing hard to get or any other equally frustrating mind games.

I move my hand up to the back of her neck before I lean her backward. My eyes are still locked with hers. I'm fighting the urge to undo her ponytail and run my fingers through her hair.

For the cameras. Of course.

"That looks good. Got everything I needed," Janessa says. "Eve, do the pose you came up with. Haven't tested the lights for that one yet."

I pull Eve upright again. Her face is bright pink. "Wow, we're doing an Eve Castle original pose."

Now she looks embarrassed. Maybe because I called her the wrong name.

"I'm sure this one won't end up on the billboard or anything. Janessa needed a couple more ideas so we could give the designer lots of options. She told me to come up with something weird."

I take a small step back and hold my arms out. "Okay, well, direct me, then."

She's lost her ability to make eye contact with me. Quickly, she turns around and holds her hands out above her shoulders. "Come closer."

I step right behind her, lining up my toes with the heel of her boots.

"Closer," she says, lowering her voice. I have to move my feet inside of hers to get the front of my body pressed against the back of hers. "Now give me your hands."

I'm beginning to understand this whole passenger seat meta-phor. I think she could keep talking and I would just keep doing. Anything. My hands land in hers and she pulls my arms around her. I throw a sideways glance in Janessa's direction just to see if she's planning on breaking us apart anytime soon. She's got camera pieces on the floor and she appears to be deep into a lens selection session.

"So," Eve continues. "We need to make our arms twist around each other."

My right arm is suddenly tangled with her right arm, like a twisty straw. And then she does the same with the left arms. Then she pulls them in to her chest and it's like this mass of arms and hands so intertwined I can barely tell whose is whose. And I have no clue if I'm holding on to her or if she's holding on to me. And I know she can feel my heart pounding against her back because her voice wavers when she speaks again.

"Elana's skin is much darker, so with her, it'll look amazing. Like a chocolate and vanilla twist cone," she says. "This shot is just for her bikini bottoms. She won't have a top on so we're relying on your arms to cover her up. We're going to cut the image down the middle. Probably do some from the side and then some vertical but just the right half of the body. So we'll get two legs, but your skin tone and hers contrasting, kind of like how the panties come in different colors. It gives that whole 'anything is possible' subliminal message." She laughs a little, sounding more comfortable than she did a minute ago.

I'm too distracted, being wrapped around Eve, to really process what she's saying, even though I'm listening to every word. Too much of her body is touching my skin. The good kind of too much.

"I saw Elana's hairstyle," I say, speaking into Eve's light-brown ponytail. "It's big. She'll end up taller than me. Might look weird with my head hiding behind her?"

"Oh, right." She shifts her head so it falls onto my shoulder. "Forgot that part. We don't want to be able to see your face in this one. So, can you—"

My eyes are already focused on the skin on the side of Eve's neck, predicting her next direction. I lean down until my ear rests on her shoulder and I'm suddenly wishing her shoulders were bare like Elana's will be. "Like this?"

"Uh-huh." Her voice catches on the last syllable, when the tip of my nose makes contact with her skin. "Just keep your face out of the picture and look like you're kissing her neck, or you can actually kiss her neck, but I wanted to leave your options open since I know you have issues."

I laugh against her skin, and since Janessa hasn't told us she's gotten what she needs, I lean in a bit more and touch my mouth to her neck. *She said I had options, right?*

I hear her sharp intake of air, a short gasp that she cuts off immediately, and then instead of stiffening, like I thought she might, I feel her muscles relax against me. I move my mouth a couple of inches and kiss a new patch of skin. There's a lot of surface area to cover. I wish everyone would leave and we could—

Oh shit. Not good. *Remember the tight briefs.* They hide nothing. I draw in a deep breath, squeezing my eyes shut and focusing on the image of my mom staring at a billboard of me in these boy-panties, as she would call them. My rock-solid work mode has obviously shut off.

I'm so not used to this happening.

Eve releases one of my hands, covers her face with her free hand, and starts laughing. *She knows. She totally knows.* I press my forehead against her shoulder and keep breathing in. "Ask her if we're done?" I plead with Eve, whispering so quietly I'm not even sure if she heard me.

"Got everything, Janessa?" Eve calls, still covering her face.

"Five seconds," Janessa says. "Don't move."

Eve is still laughing, but she surprises me by whispering, "I'm sorry. This is my fault."

I've pulled my shit together and returned to normal professional Alex so I can finally raise my head from her shoulder. "Yes, this is completely your fault."

"Done!" Janessa shouts. "I think I'm gonna like that one, Eve."

We both release each other at the same time and Eve manages to scoop my robe off the floor without hardly moving or bending over. She turns around, tossing it over my shoulders and then tying it in the front.

"Don't want you to get cold," she says, still laughing.

"Cold would be good." Some of my makeup has transferred onto her. I rub the side of her neck with my fingertips, trying to remove it. She looks worried, so I give her a smile. "I'm fine now, I swear, momentary lapse of focus. Won't happen again."

She looks down at her hands. "Sorry."

New subject. Like now. "I have a question to ask you…"

She steps back and swipes at her own neck, checking for more makeup. "Okay?"

"I won't ask you today. Tomorrow. When I have jeans on."

She frowns. "Actually, I'm only here in the afternoon tomorrow, with the other models. I have a couple of classes I can't miss, and I think your call time is in the morning."

A whole day without Eve. Not cool. "Oh, well, then Friday."

"Friday." She rushes over to help Janessa, and I decide to step out of the lights for a few minutes and get my act together. As much as I enjoyed being tangled up together, it would probably be better for my career if Daniel did the future stand-in jobs instead of Eve.

"Okay, Alex, Elana is on set," Janessa says.

I ditch my robe once again, waiting for a hair and makeup touch-up. After it's done, I walk out and Elana is nowhere to be found. Neither is Janessa. I turn to one of the assistants and open my mouth to ask what's going on, but I never finish my sentence. Something smacks me in the chest with a loud *splat*. I look down and neon yellow paint now covers my chest. Then I see topless Elana and her big hair and black panties, followed closely by Janessa. Elana is hurling paint like an Olympic softball pitcher.

"Did you play softball in high school or something?" I ask her. I praise myself silently for thinking to say high school instead of middle school or elementary school.

"Nope. Cricket," she says with a smile.

As she chucks another glob of paint, I leap out of the way. Janessa is behind the camera now, snapping picture after picture.

Elana's managed to stay almost clean while I'm a complete mess. "I need a bucket to even the odds," I say, looking around for more paint.

"Janessa said it's time for the girls to carry the big guns," Elana says.

I shake my head at her, avoiding looking at her bare breasts. "So I've heard."

Wild intertwining, twisting, jumping, and running ensues while globs of paint are thrown haphazardly around the studio. When I finally get close enough to grab the paint jar with the tip of my finger, Janessa tells us to stop.

The paint stays on my fingertips as I halt mid-windup. "It was just getting good. Elana's not nearly as painted as me."

"I told you, Alex, it's a ladies' world and you're just living in it," Janessa says.

There's not really anything to do except laugh. I thought this was going to be a glamorous job. And here I am in briefs looking like Swamp Thing.

"That was so fun," Elana says, moving to stand beside me. "Maybe they'll clean it up and we can do it all over again. It was just like a food fight. I've always wanted to be in a food fight."

"The pictures look great, guys." Janessa has a big smile on her face. "Seeing Alex drenched in paint with that smug look on his face…good stuff."

I fold my arms across my chest, staring down at the photographer and then Elana. "I'm just soaking it in, guys. Just soaking it in, waiting for my turn."

Janessa points to a spot on the set. "Let's do the pose Eve rehearsed with you earlier."

Elana and I work together to get ourselves tangled up. Eve was right. It does look cool with her dark skin and my lighter skin.

But I can't bring myself to let any part of my face touch her neck and I try my best to make sure her arms are the ones making contact with her breasts and not mine.

"Beautiful," Janessa says. "Now, dip Elana the same way you dipped Eve in the same spot, same expression on your face, as if you're just about to kiss."

Elana cuts in. "But we're not actually going to kiss?"

Janessa just waves a hand as if she doesn't care either way.

As we get in our places, I whisper to Elana, "You okay?"

"Yeah," she says, looking nervous, then she glances sideways at Eve, who is close by, adjusting a light, then back at me. "Just do it…like last night. People will expect that."

More underage kissing. Fun.

"Just barely touch your lips," Janessa directs from a distance.

My body tenses as I lean in closer, my lips meeting hers. Last night it was quick and impulsive. Now it's slower and I have way too much time to look like I don't want to be here.

"Alex, a little more desire," Janessa says.

This is where the acting comes in handy. As I'm looking at Elana, her black hair is fading to brown and her tan skin turns creamy. She's Eve and I'm kissing her and she's kissing me back.

Janessa's voice breaks through the fog of girls shape-shifting in front of me. "Perfect, guys. We got it. You can get cleaned up. Great job."

I pull away from Elana quickly but without dropping her on the floor. I'm watching her face, waiting to see if I've done any damage. The kind that can only be done to a fourteen-year-old girl who's in a fake relationship with an eighteen-year-old guy.

She's already laughing though, and wiping her mouth with the back of her hand. Eve is standing close by, her eyebrows raised all the way up. "You guys look like a five-hour clean-up job each," she says. "Yet another reason I love being behind the camera."

Elana and I are standing side by side now, and I notice several things all at once. First, Eve isn't holding a camera. Second, she's wearing a very old sweatshirt inside out and beaten-up holey jeans and old boots. She knew it would get messy today. I glance sideways at Elana and nod toward Eve.

"I think somebody missed all the fun today," I say. "Such a shame."

Elana is already smiling and nodding. Eve's hands go up in the air and she backs away slowly. "No…no way…"

Both of us dive for her at the same time and wrap our arms around Eve, making sure to rub plenty of paint all over her. Then Elana and I let go and turn around, leaving Eve standing there sputtering.

"Nice work," I say, giving Elana a fist bump, which she's actually ready for this time.

"At least she doesn't have it in her hair," Elana says, plucking at a long dark strand full of multicolored paint.

"We should have gotten her hair. She was mocking us. No one gets to mock us and keep their perfectly white sweatshirt clean."

When I glance over my shoulder, Eve is staring at me.

Chapter 17: Eve

I'm totally into him.

I'm so into him that I'm staring at the back of Alex's retreating form, and Janessa has to say my name three times before I can allow my brain to figure out that this requires an action on my part.

She's standing behind me with Russ beside her. "Let's go over the pictures."

I glance down at my newly painted sweatshirt. I'm a complete mess. But so is she. I head over in Janessa's direction and sit on the floor beside her, keeping myself carefully positioned on the giant drop cloth.

The weirdest part of figuring out that I'm into Alex is that it's not actually weird at all. I like him. I'm pretty sure he likes me. We're both eighteen. Is it really possible that I've managed to have a normal experience?

Okay, my ex *is* his agent and he *is* in a fake relationship with a fourteen-year-old future supermodel, so maybe that takes things out of the normal category. But even with that, it's the closest I've been to ordinary.

I hope he's not too humiliated by his "momentary lapse in focus" to talk to me. I'd been just as turned on as he had, but fortunately, I don't have to wear those feelings for the entire crew to see.

"Eve?" Janessa asks. I shake my head, focusing on the monitor in front of us. "Here's your pose."

I stare at the tangible creation of the vision I'd had in my head. Elana looks gorgeous and Alex looks completely at her mercy. I laugh under my breath. I guess he sort of is.

"What do you think?" I ask Janessa. I'm already biting my nails. It's one thing to be her assistant, a totally different thing to have her use my idea and compare it directly to her own.

Janessa concentrates on the monitor for a long time, her expression completely blank. "I think it's the anti–*Fifty Shades* image."

I sit perfectly still, waiting for her to explain.

"If I had to do it over," she says, "I would bring their arms lower, covering her belly button, and have their hands be the top of the picture and continue the image from the waist down."

I'm already nodding and cursing myself for not thinking of that. "That would have been so much better."

Janessa shrugs. "But it's not a bad picture, Eve. In fact, it's a good picture, and a pose that I wouldn't have thought up on my own. But there's always something to be learned, right?"

"Right."

"However," she says, flipping back to a previous image, "I might like this one better."

I'm expecting another Alex/Elana photo, but it's not. It's me and Alex testing the lights, which weren't quite perfect yet, but seeing our arms twisted together and Alex's face buried in my neck, it's so good it makes me blush.

"You're best when you don't overthink," Janessa says. "When you were in the pose, you were feeling your way through it. But when you placed Elana and Alex, you were under the gun, and everybody was watching. You got caught up in the exactness and forgot to make it look natural. Taking a random photo and directing someone are two different skills. But both are very important skills."

"Yeah, totally." I can't tear my eyes from the picture, but I'm listening and she's making a lot of sense.

"You have a roommate, right?" Janessa asks and I nod. "Use her or another student or two and take some practice photos this weekend. Give them direction and see what you can learn."

"Sure, great idea. Thanks." I glance up and see Alex walking my way, dressed in jeans and a T-shirt. I reach over and turn off the monitor, getting rid of the picture of us. Janessa's moved on to discussing the photos with Russ, so I tell her I'll see her tomorrow and then meet Alex in the middle.

He's got a towel in his hand. He raises it to my face and wipes off the paint that he'd rubbed all over my cheek earlier. He's still got paint in his hair and on his ear and neck.

"I'm going home to shower," he says. "Most likely a few times."

"Me too. I'm hoping wet paint will get me a seat on the subway." I look right at Alex and try to imagine being somewhere else with him. Like at the coffee shop last night.

And then I know I'm going to do something Stephanie would be very proud of. A huge giant leap for Eve Nowakowski. I open my mouth, and the words tumble out. "My roommate and I—"

"Hot roommate." He grins at me. "I like where this is going."

I snatch the towel from him and start rubbing paint from my

arms. "We're going to this frat party on Friday and…do you want to go?" I blurt out.

He opens his mouth and then closes it quickly. His forehead is all scrunched up. "I was gonna ask you out."

I stand there trying not to laugh. "Should I take it back?"

He leans in closer, lowering his voice. "A frat party, huh? Think it'll be free of tabloid spies, or should I bring the old lady?"

Wait, did he just say yes? "No tabloid spies. Guaranteed. But not a good place for a high school freshman."

My eyes follow his hand as he frantically digs for his phone in his pocket. "Shit." He lifts his eyes to meet mine. "Sorry, I have to answer this…but yes, Friday. Party. With Stephanie."

He gives me another smile and then turns around to answer his phone. He remembered my roommate's name? I only mentioned it once last night.

I decide to leave before anything can go wrong because that went a little too perfectly.

Once I'm out of the studio, I pull out my phone and send a text to Reese Witherspoon (a.k.a. Steph).

ME: I have a date for the party on Friday.

REESE WITHERSPOON: Who?!

ME: Alex

REESE WITHERSPOON: The CK model? Omg. Best roommate ever. Does he have a friend?

ME: Don't know about the friend, but remember Wes?

REESE WITHERSPOON: Of course! He's not coming too, is he? If so, I might have to remove his balls.

ME: No, Wes is not coming!!! But he's Alex's agent, remember?

Okay, so maybe the perfect moment had to end right now with me prepping Steph for Friday night, but at least I'll get it out of the way sooner rather than later. Alex might know that Wes and I have some tension between us, but unlike Steph, he has no idea about our real past.

REESE WITHERSPOON: Oh boy.
ME: I don't want him to know about me and Wes.
REESE WITHERSPOON: Gotcha. Consider me prepped.

Where was Stephanie two years ago when I could have really used a friend? My phone buzzes again, distracting me.

REESE WITHERSPOON: Don't forget, you promised me drunkenness and kissing.
ME: Yeah. I know. Remind me to tell you a funny story later. It involves underwear…

Before I can put any distance between me and the studio, I spot Elana outside alone, eyes darting around like she's waiting for someone.

"Hey," I say. "Where's Lumina? I haven't seen her all day."

Elana glances at me and smiles. "Her grandmother died early this morning. She's flying home for a few days."

It doesn't seem right, leaving her alone out here in New York City.

"Are you waiting for a car? Or do you need a cab?" Before she can answer, I spot a black town car pulling into the only available space nearly half a block away.

And then I see him climbing out of the car. Wes. Coming to pick her up. Just like he did so many times with me.

A sick feeling washes over me, but Elana looks relieved to see Wes. Her relief doesn't stop my heart from pounding, my palms sticky with sweat. Why do I have to be the one to see this? Why do I have to carry this information when I'm trying so hard to let go of the past?

Calm down, Eve. You're jumping to conclusions.

I stand there like an idiot while Wes rests his hands on Elana's arms and then kisses both of her cheeks. "So sorry to make you wait out here. Kara had a meeting and couldn't make it."

"It's okay," Elana says, glancing from Wes to me, then back to Wes.

"Evie, look"—his eyes move up and down me—"messy."

My mouth falls open to respond, but nothing comes out. I'm surprised I can even hear over the thud of my heart. I don't know what I'm doing, just that I can't let her get in that car with Wes alone.

"Actually," I manage to stutter, looking right at Elana, "I was going to ask you if you wanted to…to grab some food, maybe see a movie? Go shopping?" *Fly to the Caribbean, rob a bank, file our taxes for next year?*

Wes flashes me his smug professional grin. "She's got castings all evening, Evie. That's why I'm here. To accompany her."

It's like my brain snaps back to reality. *This isn't a fucking Lifetime movie, Eve. Get a grip.*

Elana looks disappointed and even lets out a little sigh of protest, showing her real age. "Another time?"

"Yeah, of course."

Wes says nothing, only raises an eyebrow as if silently asking me what I'm up to, when I really want to ask him what *he's* up to. He could have sent anyone to accompany Elana. Or just sent the car without a chaperone.

I stand there and watch as he rests a hand on the small of her back and guides her to the car. I can't shake the feeling that I know something I shouldn't. But why is it my responsibility to act? Two years ago, I finally mustered up the courage to tell someone about me and Wes, and that person humiliated me and accused me of lying. No one will believe me now either. No one will care.

Besides, it's probably all in my head. Maybe Wes wasn't even as bad as I remembered. Maybe that's all in my head too.

I almost text Alex to ask him if he knew Wes was picking up Elana today and see what his reaction is, but selfish me is really looking forward to our date and I want to be normal and not throw this into the mix of our weird drama.

Is that awful of me?

· · ◆ · ·

My brain is still clouded with Elana and Alex stuff when I get off the subway near Columbia and pull my ringing phone from my bag.

It's Jeff, my fellow hometown outcast and the guy I shared an apartment with during most of the gap between leaving New York and coming back this past August.

"Hey, Jeff!" I try to sound excited to talk to him. I like Jeff a lot. He basically saved me from being forced to stay with my parents in their trailer after they squandered almost all of my modeling income on God knows what. But talking to him reminds me that I'm not quite as together as I like people to think. And the longer I go without these reminders-of-my-past phone calls, the more I begin to feel free of those chains. Free to choose my own path.

"Eve, the Ivy League Diva," he says in his famous girlie voice that is so endearing. "How's New York? Are you really working for Calvin Klein? I assumed you were bullshitting me in that email."

I laugh. "It's true, but I wish I weren't working for CK. Although today wasn't too bad."

"I need phone numbers, Eve," he says. "You owe me at least a couple of digits belonging to some hot boys in tight jeans."

"I'll give you two digits and you can guess the rest."

"Smartass." I hear a sigh that's significant enough to get my stomach churning. The real reason he's calling is coming. "I thought you should know that your dad was in the ER last night."

I stop in the middle of the sidewalk, dread sweeping over me. "What for?"

"He ran his truck into a stop sign, smashed the front end in. Hit his head pretty hard on the dash," Jeff says. "I tried to avoid him, but he pissed off all the other nurses, and they had to send me in. And I had to test him. There wasn't any way to get around it. His blood alcohol was point two—"

"Jesus." I let out a breath, trying to calm my anxiety. "Was he conscious? Did he say anything to you?" Jeff is silent for three long beats so I prompt him again. "Jeff?"

"He said, aren't you that fag sleeping with my daughter," he finally admits. I close my eyes and shake my head. *Fucking unbelievable.* "Does he even realize how many things are wrong with that statement?"

"God, Jeff, I'm so sorry."

"His head is fine. Mild concussion," he continues. "But I don't know if he's going to be able to post bail, and the cop that came to pick him up said that it's his third DUI in twelve months."

"Uh-uh," I say, anger building in me. "I'm not helping him. Let him stay there. The entire town is probably safer that way." Besides, I can't bail him out. My parents took most of my money, and I handed what was left over to the Columbia bursar's office.

"You know me, Eve, I don't like to get involved in your family business, and I'd never judge you for keeping that asshole locked up," he says. "I just thought you should know what happened in case you hear it from someone else or if your mom calls sobbing and makes up the details to work in her favor."

"Thanks." I take a few breaths of fresh October air and release them slowly like the yoga instructor taught us when Steph dragged me to class last week. "Jeff, you gotta get out of that town. Seriously. It's never going to get any better for people like you or me."

"It just so happens that I applied for a job in Indianapolis," he says. "And I have an interview next week."

"That's great! Really great. I'm so happy for you."

After he tells me a little about the job and the area, we hang up and I find a bench to sit down on. My feelings drift from elation for the fact that I'm not thirty-two like Jeff and still trying to get out of our town, to guilt and anger as I stare at my mom's name in my phone, trying to decide if I should call her to see what she's going to do about Dad.

Reluctantly, I hit call and put the phone against my ear. The miles between us now give me a bit of confidence, especially knowing that I literally can't run home to help.

"Mom, it's me, Eve," I say after she picks up.

"Let me guess, you're home again, aren't you?"

The condescending "you think you're so much better than me, but you aren't" tone grates at my last nerve. "No, Mom, I'm in New York."

"Oh," she says. "Well I'm on my way to Florida to stay with Betty. She's got a place near Miami now."

Betty is my mom's sister and she's an evil-eyed, bitter lady pothead. "I thought Dad wrecked the truck?"

"You heard about that, did you?" She sounds nervous, maybe because she's abandoning her husband while he's in jail. "Well, I told him not to go out after he'd been drinking. He's done it to himself. I got Grandpa's truck. He can't drive no more anyway."

There's so much to absorb all at once that I'm speechless for a good thirty seconds. Growing up, I'd always felt like I had a lot in common with Matilda. I guess it helps a tad to know my mom is just as likely to neglect Dad as she was me. All this time, I'd thought it was just me.

"I'm not going to go home, Mom," I say firmly. "I'm not gonna bail him out or even talk to him if he calls me for help. Maybe if I had money left I could do something more." Probably not bail him out though. Rehab, maybe. *Since I'm an expert on rehab.*

I don't wait for her to reply. I've said what I needed to say. All that's left to do is hang up the phone and tuck it back into my bag.

I wish I could say this is all done without guilt because I know I'm right, but that would be a lie. They're still my parents. Writing them off has not been easy; I'm not sure it ever will be. Maybe someday I can bring them back into my life. But right now, they're a sinking ship, and I'm barely treading water. If all three of us end up drowning, what would that accomplish? Nothing. Absolutely nothing.

Chapter 18: Alex

October 13, 6:30 p.m.

Eve approaches a really big old building and slides a key into the door.

"Is this the party house?" I ask. I have no idea where we are and where we're going. The words *John Jay* are written on the building. Doesn't sound like a frat house, but what the hell do I know?

"This," she says, pushing open the big front door, "is where I live."

I follow her inside and glance around the halls and the dining room as we walk through.

So this is a college dorm.

She smiles at me before pushing the button on the elevator. "I need to change before we go anywhere, and Steph is at a study session for her poetry class so she's not back yet. Is that okay?"

"Totally okay." I lean against the wall beside the elevator, watching her face carefully. "So I get to see your room?"

She rolls her eyes, probably at the implied innuendos. "Yes."

After we get off on the eleventh floor and walk down a long

hallway, Eve unlocks the door to a very tiny room. There's a twin bed pushed against each side of the room and a desk at the end of the bed. One side of the room is purple and white and the other is brown and teal. The wall on the purple and white side is covered with band posters, ticket stubs, receipts, and random labels. The teal side has dozens of photos taped to the wall. The back wall has built-in dressers and a small closet. No TV or game systems or couch. Just a minifridge with a microwave on top.

I walk through the doorway and sit on the brown and teal bed. "It's very…*quaint.*"

Eve's already sifting through the closet. "This dorm is supposed to be all singles and all freshmen, but the housing waitlist was so long this year that they took corner rooms and turned them into doubles. Supposedly they're bigger. I don't really believe it. Anyway, a few sophomores got thrown in here too. Like my roommate."

"That sucks," I say. "But it's probably helpful to have a sophomore for a roommate your first year."

She shrugs and pulls a pink long-sleeve top from the closet. "We got a big price break since we're sharing, so I really don't mind."

I decide to kneel on her bed and study her photos just in case she's planning on changing in here. I'm going to need something to look at besides her. Although, it *would* even the score. She's already seen me in underwear.

I start with the far side of the photos and study them from top to bottom. I can tell most of the images were taken outside somewhere in New York City. But none of them are complete objects or people. She's found a hundred ways to slice an image in half and still have it be symmetrical.

From the corner of my eye, I can see Eve sliding her jacket off. I keep my eyes trained on the wall. "Want me to leave?"

"No, I'll be done in like ten seconds. I'm afraid to leave you alone in the hall." She laughs and then her voice gets muffled from the shirt she's probably pulling over her head. "There are girls *and boys* on this floor that wouldn't be above kidnapping you for the night."

My eyes rest on several pictures of Elana. I remember Eve taking these earlier this week. "She looks so young."

"I know. It's weird how when you shoot her from the front and get her entire face, she ages like six years. Something about her bone structure."

It helps that Elana's not standing up in any of the photos. She's either lying on her stomach with her pink cell phone, or tapping her pencil against a textbook.

And then I see me. The pictures she took and pretended to be capturing shots of the view out the window. It's just my profile and there's a shadow over my face so you can't really tell it's me. I'm also hunched over like I've forgotten to stand up straight.

Eve catches me staring at myself. She's now wearing jeans and the pink shirt she yanked from the closet a minute ago. She's morphed back into College Eve. "Is it weird that I have pictures of you on my wall?"

"You can't really tell it's me," I say, but it is a little surprising. Not weird, just surprising. I don't have pictures of anyone, including myself, in my room or in my shared apartment at all.

Eve moves beside me and taps the picture I'm looking at. "I like this one a lot. You look human."

I laugh. "As opposed to alien?"

"As opposed to supermodel."

"I get it. You're against Photoshopped models and all that," I say. It's a tired argument—though I'd willingly have it with Eve—but it's not like I can change the world or anything. It's not like I have any say in what's done to my pictures.

She pulls two rubber bands out of her long wavy hair, letting it fall loose from the tight bun. I immediately smell her shampoo. "It's not Photoshop that makes me hate fashion pictures. I edit too. I'm just not as intrigued by images where the subject knows they're being photographed. It's like being on trial. You're going to hide all your vulnerability, all the raw emotion that you get in a real image."

"So what you're saying is, if I were to replicate this pose..." I tap the picture in question. "But this time I knew you were taking a picture, I couldn't make it look the same?"

She's still staring at the image. "I don't know. Maybe I'm too biased to answer that since I'm the one who took the photo. Maybe it would only look different to me."

Just hearing her say that makes me realize how much of her goes into her pictures, and how little of me is actually in a photo from any professional shoot I've ever done.

"I think I get it." I scan all her photos again. "If you don't include the entire subject in the picture, then people are free to fill in their own blanks."

I'm not even sure where that came from. It sounded like a fucking Freudian analysis or something. The air must be different on a college campus than in the rest of New York City, and it's gone to my head.

Eve turns her eyes from the picture and stares at me. "Maybe."

Her proximity to me becomes the only thing my mind is able to focus on. I didn't come on this date just so I could kiss her, and I didn't come into her room for that reason either. Which is why I know for sure, the second her head turns and her eyes meet mine, that it's exactly what I *should* do.

I only have to lean in a few inches before my mouth is on hers and her eyes are closing. And there's nothing to look at or think about, nobody watching us or taking our picture. It's as easy and natural as taking my next breath, and I know I'm already addicted to kissing Eve before my tongue has even moved past her lips. My hands are going to insist on living in her hair forever, even if it's really hard to walk around anywhere. And I'm pretty sure my heart is going to beat at this much faster pace for good.

I should have done this five days ago. *And every day since.*

And I was wrong about my hands; they decide on their own to drift under the back of Eve's shirt. I tug her closer until she's pressed against me, her arms tight around my neck. Somebody will have to carve a statue of us just like this.

After a few seconds or a few minutes—I'm not sure—she pulls away, then drops her arms before sitting back on her heels. She's smiling but also biting one of her nails, so I'm not sure what her "after" reaction is yet. I know the "during" reaction had a positive charge to it.

I'm about to say something, but I'm still breathing like I just sprinted fifty yards to catch a bus.

"Do you think this is okay?" she asks. "You know, with Elana and all?"

Elana who?

Oh right. *Elana my almost supermodel girlfriend.* "I don't think Elana's going to tell anyone if she does find out," I say. "We just have to be careful. There're so many places to go that aren't going to bring on any tabloid people or anyone in the fashion industry at all."

I think I just turned date into dates. Which is something I haven't done since my high school girlfriend, Lindsey.

"Are you going to tell Wes?" she asks.

I snort out a laugh. "God no."

Her face relaxes and I decide to tuck that subject far away. "It's gonna be weird for you, right? Seeing pictures of me and Elana together?" I stop and refill my lungs with university air. "Of course it's weird. It's probably been weird watching us at the CK shoot all week."

She rubs her hands over her face and then starts laughing. "We haven't even officially started our date. Maybe we should forget about those details for the moment."

"Good plan." I stand up and pull her off the bed beside me before kissing her again.

The sound of someone about to open the door breaks us apart and we look almost innocent by the time a short blond girl bounces into the room.

"Stephanie, right?"

She looks me over, shaking her head back and forth. "Oh no. You can't go out like this," she says.

"Like what?" I look down at my outfit. Maybe it's a little too designer? Wes is pretty much a stickler for me looking photo ready at all times.

"Yeah, that Dolce & Gabbana blazer, while classy as hell, won't blend in well with the Sig Pi guys. They're a little like... what's the word? Neanderthals," Stephanie says.

Eve throws a weary glance in my direction. "I told her you're avoiding the crazy tabloid people tonight."

"So you're not spotted cheating on your fake girlfriend," Stephanie adds.

Okay, I guess college roommates don't keep secrets from each other. Which is so weird to me. I hardly tell my roommates anything.

I pull my backpack off the floor and set it on the bed, opening it up. "I've got a T-shirt and gym shoes?"

"Perfect," both of them say.

"Where's the bathroom?" I ask, trying to peek inside the closet to search for the secret door.

"Down the hall," Eve says. "We can check it first before you go in. It's the girls' side of the floor."

After I switch to my blend-in clothes and use the bathroom, Eve takes a turn and comes out five minutes later with her hair brushed and makeup on. I can't stop myself from staring a few seconds too long. Even without having changed, I would do a much better job of blending in than she will.

Before we head back outside, Stephanie tosses a Green Bay Packers hat on my head. "I don't like the Packers," I tell her.

She holds the bill firmly in place, not allowing me to remove it. "It's key to the disguise."

I roll my eyes before adjusting it to my size. I'll have to come up with an excuse for this one. I'm not about to be accused of being a fan.

Eve stops when we get outside. Digging in her purse, she removes her cell phone and glances at an email. "Oh my God! Look what Janessa just sent me."

Stephanie and I both lean in to read.

Just talked to CK marketing. This photo will be on a billboard in SoHo. Congrats, Eve. Keep it up and you'll be doing my job.

—Janessa

She scrolls down, revealing a photo of Elana and I from yesterday's shoot when Eve had classes she couldn't miss. "An Eve Nowakowski original on a giant billboard," I say, grinning at her. "Not too bad for a freshman."

Eve looks like she just won the lottery. "I didn't even know you guys reshot this pose. And I like it much better with the jeans, and Janessa fixed your hands...it looks beautiful."

"It looks hot," Stephanie says. "Those jeans hug you in all the right places, Alex."

Normally, I'd respond with a snappy retort, but looking at this photo makes me think of being tangled with Eve in an almost identical fashion. She must be thinking the same thing because pink creeps up from her neck when she glances sideways at me, smiling a little before tucking her phone away. "Another excuse to celebrate tonight," she says.

"A damn good excuse," I add. "That's a pretty big item to add to your résumé."

She's still beaming. "You think?"

"Yeah," Stephanie and I say together. Not that I know anything about photographer résumés, but when you've done something that just about any random person would consider cool, it's a huge asset. It has to be.

When we finally start walking in the direction of our destination, Eve's arm brushes against mine, and I immediately reach for her hand. It feels important, doing this off camera just because.

Chapter 19: Eve

October 13, 11:45 p.m.

"Why did I have to pay five bucks for my beer and you didn't?" Alex shouts into my ear as we elbow our way through the herd of students.

This frat house event is actually pretty cool. The music is amazing and live, which is better than the last party I attended.

"Because I have boobs and you don't," I shout back to him. "Want to go outside?"

I can't hear his answer but I can see that he's following me, so we won't lose each other in the crowd. It's cold outside, but I'm already sweating after the first two acts—both groups who played lots of thrashing, jumping-up-and-down music.

"Feels good out here," Alex says as the cool air hits us from the yard in front of the frat house.

Steph waves us over and we join her group of two guys and a girl who I think are also journalism students like her. I can't remember their names though.

"Okay, so," Alex says, turning to me and taking a big drink from his cup. "What if I send you in there to get my next drink? Will it be free?"

"If she's getting two drinks," Steph answers, "then no, ten bucks."

"Sexist pigs," Alex mutters under his breath and we all laugh.

One of the guys points at Alex's head and says, "Dude, Packers? Seriously?"

He rolls his eyes. "I lost a bet."

"You live on campus?" the guy asks Alex. Steph and I both stare at Alex, having no clue what he should say in response.

"No, I'm not a student here," he says smoothly. "I'm at Hunter College."

"He lives in Jersey," Steph chimes in.

"I see," the guy says. "So you just come here to steal all the hot Ivy League girls who have spent their school years studying and are ready to unleash their sexual prowess on you."

Alex smirks. "You got it, man."

I let out a sigh of relief. He's good at this. It's almost like he wants to be this person tonight.

Forty-five minutes later, while Alex is in the middle of an animated discussion about the first band with Ben or Bill or Bob (can't remember his name), my roommate tips over and falls asleep in my lap. At least one of us kept up the crazy drunk plan for tonight.

"I'm impressed that her head didn't hit the table," the guy with the B name says.

Alex leans around me to look at Stephanie. "Time to go?"

I push the hair off her face and pat her cheek gently. "Steph?"

When she doesn't respond, Alex laughs, stands up, and then says, "Yep, time to go. Want me to throw her over my shoulder?"

Steph ends up walking most of the way back to the dorm, but

she leans on me the whole time, her eyes opening and closing. I get her onto her bed and pull her shoes off, then grab Alex's bag for him.

He tosses it over his shoulder and leans against the door frame before hooking an arm around my waist, tugging me closer. "So, what are you doing tomorrow?"

I feel myself smiling. I'm kind of done acting cool in front of him. "Probably some studying, some picture taking, some running with my 5K team."

His eyebrows lift. "Running? Let's do that. What time should I be here?"

Many different comebacks and smartass remarks surface about him not being invited or him being a little too eager, but none of them leave my mouth because they're all things you say when you don't want someone to know how you really feel. "We meet at ten."

"I'll be back at ten, then." He smiles then brings my face closer so he can kiss me again.

Kissing Alex is like getting the chance to be a kid again. It's light and uncomplicated and exhilarating and completely consuming in a way that isn't even a little bit scary. All I can feel are his lips on mine and his hands touching my cheeks and my neck and my hair and my body leaning against his. The way his legs shift to fit one of mine between them and the way our feet line up...if we were a picture, I'd never be able to decide which half to show.

His eyes are still closed when he whispers, "I should probably go."

I give him one more quick kiss on the mouth before backing away. "It's no big deal if you change your mind about tomorrow considering it is tomorrow and already after one."

He stands up straight and grins. "I won't change my mind."

After he leaves, I lock the door and turn on my reading light so I can check on Stephanie and then I fall into bed with my clothes still on and start mentally replaying all my favorite parts of the evening.

Chapter 20: Alex

November 20, 1:30 p.m.

"What happens if I let go?"

So, it's not Chuck E. Cheese's, but it's my idea of an appropriate date with a fourteen-year-old. Plus, I get to work out. Kill two birds with one stone. After six weeks, I've gotten pretty good at this fake girlfriend thing and I'm not too bad at the real girlfriend thing either.

"It's totally foolproof, I swear," Elliot says to her.

My phone beeps, and I fish it out of my pocket to check the incoming text.

> **WES**: Someone just tweeted pics of you and the gf having lunch. Very cozy. Nice work! Keep it up.
>
> **HARVARD**: Elana's salad looked really good. Was that avocado?

I laugh to myself. Wes isn't the only one who's seen the tweeted photos already. And we just had lunch, like, an hour ago. That's insane.

ME: Yes, it had avocado. Maybe I'll bring you one later.

"Are you texting?" Elana says, looking over her shoulder. "You're going to drop me, aren't you?"

It's amazing to me how quickly Elana's accent is fading.

I stuff my phone into my pocket. "I'm a hundred percent focused on you. Just don't, you know, go crazy or anything. You can stop a few feet up if you want."

That comment wasn't intended as a challenge, but when Elana glances over her shoulder at me, I know that's exactly how she takes it. *Oh boy.*

By the time Elana climbs (to the very top, of course) and then figures out how to rappel off the wall, she's addicted and wants to go again. I'd been hoping to get in some weights and cardio since I finally landed that big *GQ* spread Wes has been pining for. And we start the week after next. Right after Thanksgiving.

The way things have been going with the fragrance campaign and the *GQ* spread, I have a feeling I'm going to have to add "and I owe everything to Wes Danes" on my tombstone.

"The treadmills are really cool. They have satellite TV," I say, trying to entice Elana into helping me finish my daily to-do list. I might not be the best boyfriend, but I'm an excellent multitasker.

"If you want to go work out, I can help her climb," Elliot suggests.

I can tell he doesn't really think I'll go for that, given the fact that I'm supposed to want to be around my one true love every waking hour. Before I blurt out a yes, I stop myself and glance at Elana, who's a whole head taller than Elliot and a whole year younger (though he thinks she's eighteen).

Elana gives me one of her famous smiles and says, "Go, we'll be fine."

I pat Elliot on the shoulder. "Don't let her go anywhere or get hurt or anything."

Elana rolls her eyes and then I take off before I can change my mind. If I can finish my workout and get Elana back to her crazy-ass nanny in time, then I might have enough time to pick up an avocado salad before I meet Eve on campus.

It takes me an hour to get back to Elana and Elliot. Neither of them are wearing a harness anymore. They're sitting on the bench across from the women's locker room, both with some handheld game device—a device that looks much too large to have fit into Elana's tiny designer handbag.

"How's it going?" I say.

Neither of them look up, but Elana says, "We're playing Words with Friends. Have you played before? It's so addicting."

Yep. Chuck E. Cheese's would have been just fine. I do love Skee-ball.

"You just got this game," Elliot says to Elana. "How are you so good already?"

She shrugs and gives him a smile before tucking her toy into the pocket of her long dress coat. "Beginner's luck."

"Ready?" When she nods, I toss my gym bag over my shoulder and stick out a hand to help Elana up.

"Nice meeting you, Elliot," she says.

He waves and says, "See you later, Elana. 'Bye, Alex."

"Later, man." I wait until we're out the door before throwing an arm around Elana's shoulder and trying to look madly in love with her.

"I like him," she says right away. "He's so normal. Very American, but not like you."

I laugh and give her shoulders a squeeze. "Thanks. Wouldn't want you to like anyone that's like me."

She rolls her eyes. "That's not what I meant. He's more of an outsider...what is that word? I can't think of it now."

"Loner?" I suggest.

"Yes! That's it. Loner." She waves down a cab before I even get a chance to. "It's like that for me too. I'm not around people my age."

I open the car door for her and wait until she gets in before sliding beside her. I never thought about what it might be like for Elana. "Maybe you can find a group or a club or something with girls your age?" I suggest because I don't know what else to say. Seriously, like what? Girl Scouts?

She stares out the window, keeping her head turned away from me. "It would be just like school. I scare people away. My mother and Lumina and everyone always tell me girls are just jealous and boys are intimidated. I don't know if that's true or not, but it doesn't matter. The outcome is still the same. They don't like me."

I sink further into my seat, staring at the back of her head. Her tone put a note of finality on the subject that keeps me from asking questions or making more lame suggestions. But it doesn't keep me from feeling a tiny bit responsible.

Maybe I've spent too much time freaked out about the age issue and haven't paid attention to the fact that I could be a better friend to Elana. We are coworkers, whether I agree with that choice or not.

Chapter 21: Eve

"I would like you to choose three images to turn in to me, and each one must have a human subject," Professor Larson says to our class. "It's always the people thrown into the mix that make you all want to go screwing with nature."

Screwing with nature. *God, I love this man.* In the most unromantic way possible.

After Larson dismisses us, I stroll up to his desk to ask the same question that I asked last week and the week before. "Any word on the interview schedules for the Mason Scholarship finalists?"

He's shuffling papers on his desk, preparing to stuff them in his briefcase, but he glances up and smiles at me. "Your lucky day, Miss Nowakowski."

I watch as he sifts through pages and then pulls out a single white sheet of paper with my name on the top. I scan it and see that my interview with the selection committee is scheduled for January twelfth.

January twelfth seems so far away and yet way too close. Will Janessa have had enough time to make gushing comments about

my skills and responsibility in letter form for the selection committee? Will Larson?

"I'll have my letter of recommendation ready for you before
final exams," Larson says as if reading my mind. "How is your job
with Janessa going?"

I tuck the paper into my camera bag. "It's been great. We're
shooting a lookbook for Ralph Lauren now. Before that, we did
a spread on New York City statues that I think you'll love when
it's published. The angles are brilliant. I've never seen anything
quite like it."

He snaps his briefcase closed and gives me another grin.
"Fantastic. I'm sure you have some wonderful stories to tell everyone back home over the holiday."

"Actually, I decided to stick around here." I shrug and try to act
like I actually considered going back to Indiana. As far as I know,
my mom's still in Florida and my dad is still in jail or court-assigned
rehab. "Flights are so expensive this time of year, you know?"

He frowns and then grabs a pen and a scrap of paper before scribbling something on it. "My wife is famous for her Thanksgiving
spread. She'd love to have a couple more guests at the house. She's
trying to hide the fact that she's down about our daughter not
making it home this year. Come over around noon."

The way he says it, it sounds like an assignment instead of a polite
suggestion that people make when they feel sorry for you. Which is
why I find myself taking the paper from his hand where he's scrib-
bled the address of an apartment building on the Upper West Side.

"Okay," I say.

"And you're welcome to bring someone if you'd like."

He disappears into his office before I can back out. When I look down at the paper, I realize he hasn't included his phone number, only the address. He's going to tell his wife that I might come and bring a plus one and then she'll cook more food and it would be awful if I didn't show. I've heard that's how normal families operate.

I shake my head, trying to figure out how I went up to ask a question and suddenly had holiday plans that involved a family dinner, something I have zero experience with. When I finally head outside, Alex is waiting for me, his skateboard tucked under his arm.

And he's brought food.

I smile and take the salad container from his hand. "You didn't have to bring me this."

"It's only fair," he says. "Have to give all my girlfriends equal treatment. Besides, Elana and I got our lunch for free."

"Model perks," I say with a sigh. "I do miss some of those extras, like free food and drinks just because."

A little while later, I'm sitting at one of the outdoor tables behind my dorm, eating the delicious salad, and Alex is riding his skateboard along the ledge and trying to make it flip in the air. It's cold out, but in the sun it's tolerable.

"What would happen if you broke your arm before the *GQ* shoot?"

"Wes would murder me in my sleep," he says and then he continues to attempt the crazy trick, which makes me laugh.

"My professor invited me to Thanksgiving dinner at his apartment."

Alex spins the skateboard to a stop. "Kinda creepy. Isn't that breaking some university rule?"

I laugh at the idea of Professor Larson being a perv. "He invited me to dinner with his family. His wife and a kid or two and grand-kids, I think. He's old and not even a little bit creepy."

The concern drops from Alex's face and he goes back to balancing on the ledge. "That's cool."

I shove the salad container aside and pull out my camera. He's engrossed in trying to get the skateboard to rotate once in the air and then land upright on the ground and not the ledge. I think he's eventually planning to land on top of the board. I take several shots of him deep in concentration.

"Remind me again why you're not going home for Thanksgiving?" I ask Alex, hoping maybe I can lead into him being my plus one at Larson's.

"My mom would flip out if I missed Christmas and I don't want to fly home for both." He picks up the skateboard and sits down in the chair beside me, turning to face me. "Part of me wants to stay here because I don't want to have to deal with questions about my girlfriend and another part of me wants to buy two plane tickets and drag you to Nebraska with me just so I can be the Evans kid with the hottest girlfriend."

That gets me to smile. "Your brothers don't have hot girlfriends?"

He laughs. "Let's just say they roam around a lot. Although my mom did say that Jared is dating someone and they live together now. Or maybe he's just staying with her? Mooching off her, probably. High school football gods tend to get very spoiled."

"You could bring Elana," I suggest.

He shakes his head. "It's one thing to have my family reading tabloids about us and mentioning her on the phone every once in awhile, but to bring her into my house and completely lie to them, I can't do that."

Every time he says something like that, it feels like the half images of him plastered on my wall get filled in a little bit more.

"I get it." I place my camera back in the bag and scoot my chair until he's close enough for our legs to touch.

He immediately starts moving his hands back and forth over my thighs, like he's trying to keep my legs warm through my jeans. Which, of course, works perfectly because there's no other way to be except very warm whenever Alex has his hands on me. For a second, I forget that we're outside and debate crawling in his lap and putting more body parts within his reach.

"What do you and Elana talk about?" Alex asks, shifting subjects on me. "Like grown up stuff or kid stuff, or normal girl stuff?"

"I don't know what you mean. Like things besides work and modeling?"

"Yeah, I guess."

Okay, what's going on with Elana? It's times like this when I think it could be helpful to tell Alex about me and Wes, but then I can't because I'm pretty sure it would change everything. And why should I have to have my past following me around like an unwanted shadow? I've already had to live it. Isn't that enough?

"We talk about modeling and college and the subjects she's studying now, how hot you look in Calvin Klein boxer briefs. Stuff like that."

He laughs and then closes the gap between us, kissing me in a way that makes me forget it's November and that we're outside in thirty-degree weather. "Steph is still around, right?"

"Yeah," I say with a sigh. I love my roommate, but there are moments like this one when a single room would be quite useful. "She's not going home next week either. She has a relative in Jersey she's spending Thanksgiving Day with."

His face brightens. "Oh, so she'll be gone for what? A few hours?"

"Probably, but I pretty much had no say in the matter of joining my professor on Thanksgiving. So I'll be gone too."

He hides the disappointment well. Alex can be very patient when he wants to be. He doesn't seem to mind that our time together almost always involves being outside or at a public place like the campus bookstore. Last week, he even sat in the library with me for three hours, helping to make flash cards for my chemistry class. Of course we did explore the consistently abandoned rare books section.

"You should invite Elana," Alex says suddenly. "To your professor's place."

I smile. "I was hoping to talk you into going with me. He said to bring someone."

He looks excited by this suggestion. "You think we can do that?"

"I don't see why not. Professor Larson isn't going to have any idea who you are or even care."

"I'm in," Alex says. "But maybe you should take Elana instead. Something's up with her. I think she's homesick or just...*lonely*."

This surprises me because I didn't think Alex had allowed himself to look at Elana long enough to see something like that in her. And now I'm worried all over again. "What makes you think that?"

"She met Elliot today," he says.

"Okay?"

"I left her alone with him." He diverts his eyes from mine like he might be in trouble for this. "Elliot volunteered. She wanted to climb again and I wanted to work out. When I came back, they were playing video games and then on the way to drop her off, she said she really liked him because he seemed normal, but nothing like me."

"Not like you, huh?" I can't help teasing him. "Maybe you're right. Let's bring her too. I don't think Professor Larson will have a problem with it and besides, you know she's not going to eat much. Thanksgiving is practically a carb fest."

Alex picks up my hands and holds them to his face. "You're cold. We should go get coffee."

We both stand up and then he tosses my bag over his shoulder. Instead of walking toward warmer places, I decide to kiss him again, which ends up lasting for several minutes. "Elana is very lucky to have you for a fake boyfriend."

He takes my hand in his and starts walking. "I could probably be a better friend than I've been. I treat her like another bratty sister I'm forced to drive around. It's not like she isn't helping my career a ton."

I can't make it to the coffee shop without throwing at least a dozen sideways glances in Alex's direction. Sometimes, I have to look to make sure he's real and other times I'm convinced he's the most real person I've ever known. There's no way to keep myself from comparing this to being with Wes, which was so heavy and dramatic. It's like comparing Advil to a narcotic that does the job but drags you into this alternate reality and it takes so long to find your way back. I don't feel lost or pulled under one bit right now.

My fingers lace through his, and I inhale a slow deep breath, closing my eyes for a second and memorizing this feeling. No matter what happens between me and Alex, no matter how long we get to be us, I need to remember what this version of falling in love feels like. I really thought there was only one way to do this, and that way is absolutely frightening to imagine now.

Chapter 22: Alex

November 26, 12:05 p.m.

An old man in dress pants and a Bill Cosby sweater greets us at the door. The place looks cozy, but not tiny like most New York City apartments. He's definitely not broke from teaching all those classes at Columbia, that's for sure.

"These are my friends, Alex and Elana," Eve says, pointing to each of us.

"Tom Larson." The man reaches out to shake our hands. "My wife will be thrilled to have you. Looks like she's cooking for a hundred." He disappears with all our coats and then, after returning, ushers us into the living room.

There's a fireplace and a grand piano and at least five floor-to-ceiling bookshelves. Eve is already taking it in, probably debating scanning every title one at a time.

"Thanks so much for having us," I say on my and Elana's behalf. Elana's pressed herself into Eve's side and gone completely quiet.

A door swings open and the scent of onions and celery wafts toward us. A petite older woman with a mix of gray and brown hair enters the room. She smiles at the three of us. "Which one of you is Eve?"

Eve lifts her hand a bit. "Me."

"So glad you came," Mrs. Larson says. "Who are your friends? Are they students too?"

"Alex and Elana." Eve points to each of us again. "And they're not students, they're, well…"

I decide to intervene again. "We met Eve at a photo shoot for Calvin Klein. She was assisting the photographer."

She looks us over and takes in my designer shirt and jeans and Elana's Armani pantsuit. Then she turns to her husband. "Wasn't Janessa working for Calvin Klein?"

Professor Larson scratches the top of his head, where his hair is the thinnest. "Well, that would make perfect sense, then, since Eve is working with Janessa."

We all laugh and Mrs. Larson claps her hands together. "Okay then, mystery solved. Small world, isn't it? And we're so happy to have you. Hope you don't mind, but I'm going to have to return to the kitchen."

The way Eve is biting her nails and shuffling her feet around, I get the impression she's nervous. It could be because it's a holiday and this isn't her family. I don't know much about Eve's family other than when she told me her parents are assholes. She doesn't bring them up, so I've left the subject alone.

Maybe her nerves have to do with a weird academic thing since we are at her professor's house. Maybe she thinks she's being graded or something. I could totally see Eve worrying about shit like that.

"Do you need any help?" I ask Mrs. Larson.

Her eyebrows shoot up. "You'll have to roll up those sleeves."

I grin and begin unfastening the button at my wrist. "I can do that."

Eve jumps to attention. "I'll help too."

We leave Elana with Professor Larson and follow his wife into the kitchen. I'm already at the sink washing my hands when Mrs. Larson pulls out a cutting board and top-grade chef's knife.

"Have you ever used one of these?" she asks both of us, holding up the knife.

Eve shakes her head.

"Only when my mother wasn't looking," I say.

"Alex will be chopping, then. And I won't tell your mother." After digging through the fridge, she tosses several clear plastic bags of veggies onto the cutting board and hands me a towel to dry my hands. "And Eve gets to peel."

Eve follows my lead and washes her hands. "What am I peeling?"

"Potatoes?" I say, guessing. "Maybe sweet potatoes?"

Mrs. Larson smiles. "You've done this before. Willingly or by force?"

I laugh, thinking of my brothers shoving me into the kitchen with Mom while they watched football all day. When I was really young, my job in the kitchen was to give Katie pointless tasks and make her think she was actually helping while keeping her out of my mom's way. "Well, it's willingly today. That's all that matters, right?"

"Good answer," she says.

Eve is wide-eyed, like she has no idea what to do with the potato peeler she's just been handed along with the big sack of Idaho potatoes. Mrs. Larson laughs at her expression. "Go on. Just give it a whirl. No one's grading you."

I have to snort back a laugh, and Eve rolls her eyes in my direction. Mrs. Larson sets up a pot of water on the stove to get it boiling and I begin chopping zucchini.

A buzz comes through the kitchen intercom system, and our cohost rushes out to answer the door.

"I feel like I'm doing this completely wrong," Eve says from her spot over the garbage disposal. "I don't think there'll be much potato left by the time I get done with it."

I smile at her and set down my knife. I take the mostly peeled potato from her hand and rinse off the gritty brown substance. "There. Now you can see what you actually need to shave off."

She stares at me and then takes the potato back. "That's much better. Thanks."

"I take it you haven't been subjected to eighteen years of family Thanksgiving dinners?" I ask.

She shakes her head. "I think my grandmother cooked once when I was very young. Before she died. And another year, my dad took us to this diner in town and they had turkey and stuffing. And of course we did the First Thanksgiving lessons in grade school."

"Funny that you had to come to New York City to do this holiday the normal way," I say, making light of, not for the first time, the obvious differences in our families. "I didn't think there were actual New Yorkers who did the traditional kind of thing. I thought it'd be too trendy or something."

"Is that why you wanted to come with me?" she asks, flashing me a smile, then her grin fades and her eyes focus on the vegetable in her hand. "I forgot one…a few years ago I had Thanksgiving dinner with the designer working for Calvin Klein."

The knife almost slips in my hand. "Seriously?"

Chapter 23: Eve

Looking at Alex's face right now, the openness, the acceptance, I almost want to tell him all the details of that incredibly stressful holiday. One that ended with me losing my virginity. I remember every detail like it happened hours ago.

Wes had given me almost no advance notice about this party. I'd been looking forward to a few days off and maybe some quality time with my secret older boyfriend despite the gradual shakiness of our relationship.

"Why are you dressed like a prostitute?" Wes had said the moment I opened the door to let him into the agency apartment. "I specifically said conservative attire."

"Hannah said to not wear any major labels. This is all I had." I followed him as he rushed in and headed straight for my closet. Hannah was Wes's assistant. She'd sent me an email with very basic instructions less than twelve hours earlier.

Wes was fuming as he shifted clothes to one side of the rack in my closet. "Hannah obviously doesn't know what happens when you're allowed to think for yourself."

My insides recoiled at his hurtful words. They were coming

more and more frequently and I was beginning to wonder if I really was clueless.

"Lucky for everyone, you have me." He removed a knee-length dress and a brown sweater. "Stockings, black heels, hair down, not too much makeup," he rattled off. "You've got fifteen minutes."

I stood there, biting my nails, waiting for him to leave the bedroom. He pulled my hand from my face, examining my nails before letting out a long sigh. "You have to stop that. And you want me to leave, I assume?"

"No," I said, even though I really wasn't sure if I could handle stripping down in front of Wes. We hadn't gotten that far yet. Underwear, sure, but I hadn't been completely naked in front of him before.

He rolled his eyes and moved toward the door. "Time to grow up, Evie."

I let out a huge breath and hurried to change my clothes. Ten minutes later Wes pronounced me decent looking, but the tension continued on the car ride to the party.

"There are three girls in line for this CK campaign," Wes said. "You've got at least five pounds on all of them. I've already promised the client that you would lose the weight—"

I turned around in my seat to face him. "Wait…what? I have to lose five pounds?"

Was this the reason for the knee-length dress and the long-sleeved sweater? He wanted to cover my trouble spots. I only weighed 120 pounds and at five eleven, that wasn't much.

Wes let out a frustrated breath. "God, it's only five pounds, Evie. And it's just for this job."

I stared straight ahead. "So you're trying to tell me not to eat anything at the party?"

"Lean protein, raw vegetables, and you can have all the vodka you can handle, got it?"

"Got it." I closed my eyes for a second, wishing for a few moments of calm to balance out this constant storm of tension.

"This job is yours to screw up," Wes said. "You have to show some maturity. And the nail-biting has to go. And do *not* fidget with your hands."

I didn't say anything more, because it was easier to weather Wes's mood swings with silence.

At the party, I put plain turkey breast slices and carrot sticks on my plate and nothing else, even though my stomach growled the second I smelled the freshly baked rolls. When I sat down at the table, Wes sat beside me and discreetly moved half the turkey from my plate to his and placed what looked like vodka and a few ice cubes in front of me. I stiffened under the weight of his glare and cut my meat into tiny pieces before eating only a small portion of it.

I was almost too nervous to answer the questions that the other guests happened to ask me. I'd have an answer ready and then panic, analyzing each word from Wes's perspective, and end up with my mouth hanging open like an idiot. Then Wes would pinch me hard in the side, and I'd come up with something to say. I downed enough vodka in three hours to last me for the next five parties in an effort to ease my nerves.

Eventually, the drinks and lack of sustenance caught up to me. When I stumbled into a middle-aged man who looked like he might be someone important, Wes grabbed me by the arm and said a quick good-bye, steering me out of there.

He was quiet in the car, but the second we walked into my empty apartment, he shut the door and started shouting at me. "What the hell was wrong with you tonight? Have you lost the ability to answer simple questions?"

My eyes could barely focus on the wall in front of me, let alone his storming face. "I don't know. I was so nervous."

He swept his hand quickly over the coffee table, flinging papers and remote controls across the living room. "Do you want to blow this opportunity? Is that what you want, Eve? To go back to Indiana and live with your parents again?"

I fought off the tears that threatened to fall. "No."

"Then why the fuck did you transform into some robot savant?" He moved in my direction, but before he could reach me, I ran for the bathroom and puked up gallons of vodka and carrot sticks.

Wes found me minutes later, leaning over the sink, fumbling with my toothbrush. He released one of his famous frustrated sighs and spread a gob of toothpaste across my toothbrush.

"I recall telling you to drink all the vodka you could *handle*." The anger had dropped from his tone. Like maybe he'd figured out that at sixteen, I might not know how much I could handle. "Just so you know, this isn't the method of weight loss I'd recommend."

I had finished brushing my teeth and felt about 20 percent less drunk, which basically meant I wasn't wasted enough to pass out, but plenty drunk enough to start crying. "I can't lose five pounds. It's impossible. I know they're going to pick someone else."

Wes led me into my room and began removing my party clothes

and replacing them with a T-shirt and shorts. "I want you to get everything you deserve, and I'm not sure that's possible without me intervening. You're so fucking hardheaded. If you'd just listen to me, we wouldn't have these problems."

There was so much emptiness inside of me, so much rejection, I could hardly stand it. How many times had my own father called me fucking hardheaded? Too many to count. And then eventually he stopped calling me anything, which was even worse. "I should quit. Go to college a year early. I'm just going to disappoint you over and over again."

"Damn it, Eve!" Wes yelled, startling me out of my tears. "Cut that shit out right now. I swear you act like a five-year-old sometimes." He gripped the top of my arms, squeezing so tight it brought tears to my eyes again.

I tried to fight his grip and back away, but then he started shaking me, and dozens more tears tumbled down my cheeks. "Stop it. Please, Wes."

His eyes widened, and his face filled with alarm. And then he released me. I fell back on my bed and pressed my nose into the pillow, sobbing as quietly as possible. I'd expected to hear him storm out and slam the front door, but he didn't.

Thirty seconds later, Wes lay down beside me. He placed a hand onto my back and put his mouth close to my ear. "I'm sorry, Evie. I'm so sorry. Look at me, please?"

On command, I turned my head and saw all the regret and vulnerability on his face, the kind of emotion that made me feel like maybe I wasn't all alone in my world. Then he touched my cheek and said, "This is so hard sometimes because…because I love you."

My whole body was frozen for a long second. And then we were kissing. Like two people desperate for air, drowning underwater. Later, when he asked me if I wanted to stop, it was the first time I told him no. I was tired of the barriers between us, and him saying he loved me seemed to make this event more important somehow.

·· ◆ ··

"Hey, you okay?"

My heart is racing, just thinking about the intensity of that holiday with Wes. I shake my head and attempt to smile at Alex. "Yeah. I'm fine."

At least I know Elana's here with us and not being forced into some awkward meal with a designer. Not within Wes Danes's grasp.

Alex must have sensed something unpleasant going through my head because he looks concerned. He sets the knife down and places both hands on my shoulders and rubs them gently before planting a kiss on my cheek.

I close my eyes and try to imagine these same hands squeezing my arms until they left tiny bruises. Bruises that shined black and blue and then eventually faded to yellow after several days. It doesn't seem possible for Alex to do this. But how long will it be before I manage to piss Alex off to that point? Maybe I *have* grown up. Maybe back then, I'd been too young to handle Wes and the friction between us.

Alex holds one of the five peeled potatoes up to the light above the sink. "It's perfect. I've never seen such a smoothly peeled vegetable in my entire life."

"I so needed to hear that." I turn my head to kiss him, but just as my lips touch his, the kitchen door swings open.

And in walks Janessa Fields.

Chapter 24: Alex

Of course Janessa Fields is here. Of course my elation with the idea of spending a carefree day with Eve while fulfilling my duties to Elana would have some kind of glitch.

Eve and I both freeze, staring at each other and still standing way too close to be just friends. From the corner of my eye, I see Janessa shaking her head and then she laughs.

"I want nothing to do with this phony relationship story, do you understand?" Janessa's gaze bounces from Eve to me.

Eve nods and finally whispers, "Okay."

Janessa helps herself to a carrot stick from the veggie tray and dunks it in the dip before taking a big bite. "Does the French teen know?"

Does Elana know? Good question. She has to know.

Eve looks at me and I take a step back and clear my throat. "Yeah, I think she does."

"Good. Then consider this"—she waves her arms around as if drawing boundary lines on the apartment—"a safe space. But I want nothing to do with the story. I'll deny ever knowing anything. I'm taking pictures, not selling my soul. Is that clear?"

Relief washes over me. "Very clear."

Janessa smiles and snatches another carrot before heading out and calling over her shoulder, "Happy Thanksgiving, by the way."

"I had no idea she would be here," Eve says.

"She seems cool with it." I pick up the knife again and resume cutting vegetables.

After a couple of minutes, Eve starts laughing really hard, and I look over at her. "What's the joke?"

She shakes her head, still laughing. "I'm just trying to figure out how we ended up here. Having Thanksgiving with Elana and Janessa. Also, I'm cooking, which I pretty much have never done in my entire life."

"Correction, you're peeling, not cooking." I toss a slice of zucchini in my mouth and chew it quickly. "Holidays can get pretty fucked up. Probably why some of the best comedy movies take place on a holiday."

"We have odd dates, don't we?" Eve says.

"Very odd."

But this revelation only makes me more excited for future dates. I love that we have no plan and there's always this possibility of crazy awesomeness around every corner. I wouldn't mind if some of the craziness involved fewer people and possibly less clothing. I would totally be down with that. But for now, I'll take whatever I can get of Eve Nowakowski.

Chapter 25: Eve

I can feel the aches in my muscles and the chills and sneezing that come with the first signs of a cold.

And yet I'm outside, in SoHo to be exact, jogging with Alex.

My toes are numb inside my running shoes. The high-tech running tights I borrowed from a girl in my dorm are not keeping my legs as warm as they claim to.

"I think I might have considered college if I knew there were teachers like Professor Larson," Alex says. "He seems like the kind of dude who would be above giving grades or some liberal artistic move like that."

I laugh. "Yeah, right. He grades tough. I'll be lucky to get an A in his class. Actually, I got an A minus in my independent study course."

"Well, I guess it is Ivy League. They're all about grades."

We get to a street corner and have to wait at the crosswalk. I bend over to catch my breath and then spend thirty seconds coughing into my elbow, like a good citizen.

"You caught that kid's cold, didn't you?" Alex says, eyeing

me. "I saw the runny nose and knew we were in for some germ exposure."

"I'm in denial." He's talking about Olivia, Professor Larson's three-year-old granddaughter who was at Thanksgiving dinner. I'd seen the runny nose too and I was worried about it. I probably mentally contracted the virus just from worrying about it. The only cold I got last winter turned into pneumonia. I don't have time for pneumonia right now.

We cross the street and Alex pauses again and touches my red nose. "We should stop. Let's go have breakfast somewhere."

"We've only gone two miles." My protest is weak, because my body is weak at the moment. Then it's like the world is trying to stop us, or actually give me pneumonia, because the sky opens up and pours icy cold rain on top of us.

Alex covers his head with both arms. "Shit!"

It only takes about thirty seconds for my shoes to get soaked through and my teeth to start chattering. He looks over at me and points in a different direction than the one we were originally headed in. "Change of plans."

After running another four blocks with shoes that weigh an extra twenty pounds from water, Alex pulls me under the awning of a tall apartment building. His gaze darts around the street, then he removes a pair of sunglasses from his coat pocket and puts them on my face. He pulls the cold, wet hood of my jacket over my head.

"What are we doing?" I ask.

"Going inside." He's still looking around as he leads me through a door, nudging me in front of him. He walks in the lobby and bypasses the elevators. "We'll take the stairs, just to be on the safe side."

I stop at the first landing. "Is this where you live?"

"No, I like to hang out in stairwells of random apartment buildings." He's already charging up the next flight.

I have no choice but to plunge ahead after him. "I thought your place was off limits?"

"Desperate times." He glances over his shoulder and grins. "I didn't see anyone outside, did you?"

"I don't know. I wasn't paying attention. What about your roommates?"

"Gone." He finally stops at the fifth floor. "They're both in Brazil doing some summer catalog shoot. We can leave separately, later, after we dry off and regain feeling in our toes."

He's right, I can't feel my toes, but I *can* feel my heart speeding up when he unlocks the door and allows me to walk through first. It's a good-sized place, not all that different from the agency apartment I used to live in. I move to take my shoes off at the door, but Alex nods for me to follow him.

"Don't bother," he says. "Let's leave all the wet stuff in the bathroom."

On the way to his room, I peek into the two roommates' personal space. Both have unmade beds and clothes on the floor, but nothing too disgusting like I'd imagined there'd be from a trio of single guys.

Alex's queen-sized bed *is* made and the only thing on the floor is a laundry basket of neatly folded clothes sitting beside the desk. He's also got a fancy-looking speaker system and a big flat-screen TV mounted on the wall. Throw in a microfridge and I could live in here for weeks.

"You make your bed?" I shift around, trying to find a spot where I'm not going to drip on anything electronic.

"My mom forced me to for eighteen years," he says. "Old habits die hard, right?"

"Eighteen years? I'm sure your infant self didn't know how to make a bed."

"Okay, maybe like thirteen years." He opens the door to the bathroom, and I'm surprised that he has his own and doesn't have to share the one I saw in the hallway with his roommates.

Yes, I could definitely live in here.

"How did you swing this?" I ask, pointing inside the bathroom.

"I got it after the last guy moved into his own place. Jason and Landon came after me, so they were stuck with the other rooms. I'm sure there'll be bloodshed over this room if I ever move out."

I walk tentatively into the bathroom and put the toilet seat down before sitting on it and beginning the process of removing my soggy shoes and socks. My teeth are chattering so hard now, I probably won't be able to talk. Still in the bedroom, Alex closes and locks the door, then digs in the laundry basket. His hair looks much darker wet and drops of water keep falling into his eyes while he sifts through clothing. When he enters the bathroom, he hands me what looks like two folded towels and a T-shirt and boxers.

"You want me to wear your underwear? That seems serious," I say as I'm pulling the rubber band from my hair and watching the water get squeegeed out of my ponytail and onto the tile floor.

"You're more than welcome to hang out naked while we wait for your clothes to dry." He grins and then reaches into the shower, twisting the metal knob and turning it on. "Give it a good five minutes to warm up, and be careful, because the hot water heater is set at like a thousand degrees."

He's already turned around and is reaching for the doorknob to close the door behind him.

"Are you leaving?" I blurt out. I'd figured he'd at least try to make the most of this situation.

He spins slowly to face me again. "I don't have to."

I stare at his feet, feeling warmth return to my face. My heart is now an Olympic sprinter. Six weeks may have passed, but we haven't had this moment yet. We haven't ever been alone like this. "Aren't you going to take off your shoes?"

His eyes stay on mine as he kicks off one shoe at a time.

After, he reaches down to pull off his socks.

Then his shirt.

My teeth are still chattering, making my move a lot less sexy, not to mention the fact that removing a skintight long-sleeved shirt that's soaking wet is much harder than it looks. Alex steps closer and takes the hem of my shirt in his hands and slowly raises it over my head. He has that deep look of concentration I've seen on him when he tries to flip his skateboard in the air and land on it. His hands skim the length of my sides and then he wiggles my soaking wet sports bra down my body until it lands around my ankles.

My gaze travels down his body. I'd seen him shirtless so many times during the week of the CK shoot, but the only time I've really let myself look is when I'm studying the picture on my wall of him from that first *Seventeen* shoot.

And of course that photo is only half of the reality.

I place my palms flat against his chest and rest them there, feeling the thud of his heart pulsing through my fingers. Then my fingers curl around his sides, my thumbs trailing down his stomach. I could spend hours covering every inch of his skin just like this. I hear his quick intake of air when my thumbs land on the waistband of his shorts.

Steam rises from over the shower doors. Alex glances at the shower and then quickly slides off his shorts and steps into the shower. I go through the process of tugging the tights off my legs before he reaches a hand out and pulls me under the stream of hot water. My skin is so cold it stings at first, but then Alex kisses me and I don't feel the sting anymore.

Chapter 26: Alex

The water suddenly shifts from lukewarm to icy cold. I have no idea how much time has passed or how many kisses we've racked up or whether it all just counts as one long kiss, because that's what it feels like.

Eve and I jump apart and I fumble around for the knobs, quickly twisting them, shutting the water off. She's out of the shower before my eyes open again, a towel wrapped around her body and a folded one in her outstretched hand.

I take the towel from her, dry my face, wrap it around my waist, and then try to read something in her actions. She's quickly turned her back to me and is already sliding into the boxers and T-shirt I gave her.

I'm not sure I had a specific post-shower agenda for us, but I know whatever it was, it didn't include getting dressed. We were so close, pressed together the whole time in the shower, that I didn't really get to look at her and now all I want to do is lay her across my bed and study all the parts I have yet to see.

I stand there like an idiot for several seconds while she towel dries her hair, and then because I don't know what else to do,

I scoop all our wet clothes from the floor and gather them in my arms.

"I'm gonna toss these in the washer." After I get the clothes started on their twenty-eight-minute cycle, I return to my room and lock the door again, drop my towel to the floor, and grab a pair of boxers from the basket for myself.

Maybe I went too fast? But we were just kissing. *Naked kissing.* Some roaming hands. But still, I'd been ready to walk out of that bathroom before she stopped me. Okay, 90 percent ready.

I snatch my towel off the floor and walk back into the bathroom to hang it up. Eve stops squeezing water from her long hair and looks at me in the mirror.

"I'm confusing you, aren't I?" she says. "Mixed signals or whatever."

"A little," I admit.

She turns around and I take the towel from her hands and hang it beside mine. She looks embarrassed. "I'm sorry. I think I've kinda let myself forget how this all goes. It's been a while."

The giant ball of confusion in my head finally unwinds itself. *Eve is nervous.* I let out a sigh of relief and lean back against the shower door. "There's no script to follow here and certainly nothing to apologize for. In fact, I'm starting to wonder how I've gone all these years showering solo. Such a mundane activity all alone."

She laughs and rests her forehead against my shoulder. Already the dread and panic I had a couple of minutes ago fades.

"Isn't there a really nasty word for girls who get naked and then put their clothes on before...before..."

"Maybe," I jump in to rescue her from searching for the coolest way to say the word sex. "But I think you're exempt from that word if you put *my* clothes on." I pull her out of the bathroom and toward my bed. "We've got seventy-two minutes before your clothes are ready. What do you want to do?"

It's not a loaded question. I'm honestly asking her because me setting the pace probably isn't the best idea right now. If she says she wants to watch CNN, I'll watch CNN. Whatever keeps the awkward moments away because those don't really go with *us*.

She lifts her eyes to meet mine, but I'm focusing on her teeth sinking into her lower lip. That sense of dread returns. I know I'm going to say or do the wrong thing and send her running out of here in my underwear.

"I'm not sure I want to…you know…" she says, braving the eye contact but not the use of the word. "But that's all. Everything else is—"

More relief washes over me. I lean in to give her a quick kiss on the mouth. "Okay."

The confidence we had ten minutes ago under the stream of hot water returns. She lets me pull her down onto the bed and tug the borrowed T-shirt off her and onto the floor. The rain is still hitting the pavement outside, creating this entrancing sound, like we're on an island with no other humans in sight. Like we have an infinite number of hours, even if we don't. It makes me want to slow everything down so I can stow it into my memory frame by frame.

It's been a while since I've done this in-between stuff.

Chapter 27: Eve

The loud buzz of the washer startles both of us. My eyes fly open and I'm suddenly aware of how heavily I'm breathing and how it feels like there're four hands all over me but it's really only two; they just keep leaving a trail of heat between their previous location and the current one.

"I'm sorry," Alex says, his mouth pressed against my neck. "It'll just keep buzzing like that until I at least open the lid. Something's wrong with it."

He pushes himself up and rolls off the side of the bed, onto his feet. "I'll be right back."

The fog begins to clear from my head and I still can't believe how easy this has been. For a while there, I thought we were gonna be stuck with all that awkwardness. The shower had been easy because subconsciously, I knew what we *wouldn't* be doing in there and I hadn't really thought about after. I know guys aren't supposed to make a girl go too far if she doesn't want to, but I had totally dangled everything in front of him and then slammed the door shut, so it's not like I expected anything that resembled patience from Alex.

"Uh-oh," Alex says after flopping down beside me again. "You look contemplative. Is that a word?"

I laugh. "I think it is. I'm just wondering..." I roll on my side to face him. "Well, you didn't ask me why I don't want to and I thought—"

"Should I have asked you that?" He places his hand against my stomach and slides it up toward my breasts. "It doesn't really matter to me why. I mean you can tell me if you want, but I'm not going to talk you out of it, or into it, technically speaking. It'd be like dragging someone to a movie I've been dying to see but know they'll hate. Not really fun for anyone. And I'm kind of having fun right now, aren't you?"

"Yes." I can feel myself smiling as I lean down to kiss him. "That's actually what I'm worried about. I haven't really liked it before."

"What? Sex?"

I nod and stay propped up on my elbow, hovering over him. "I didn't hate it or anything. It was just so-so, you know?"

"Oh." His eyebrows shoot upward. "I guess I don't know personally. I'm a guy so it's usually not so-so, as you put it, but I'm sure it happens. So what specifically were you disappointed with?"

How do I put this into words for him? I didn't feel the connection I thought I'd feel. It didn't solve my problems with Wes. It didn't make him want to be with me forever. I'm glad about that last item, but now I'm wondering if my naive girl fantasies ruined the experience. Honestly, I don't even know what would be considered realistic expectations for this particular experience with Alex. I want to ask him this, but I'm too afraid. Too embarrassed. Those kinds of questions seem like such a buzzkill.

"I'm sure it's totally me," I say in a rush. "I'm probably dysfunctional or something."

Now he looks like he's fighting laughter. He brushes my hair back behind my ears so it doesn't keep falling into his eyes. "I highly doubt that, Eve."

He sits up and then he's standing on the gray carpet again, reaching down to grab jeans and a T-shirt.

"See? I've already scared you away, haven't I?" I stretch out on the bed again, pulling two of the pillows under my head. "You're getting mental images of what dysfunctional Eve looks like, aren't you?"

"Not even close." He grins and squeezes my ankle. "But I promised you breakfast and it's almost noon. If I starve you, I'm pretty sure you'll leave before you have to."

"When do I have to leave?"

He opens a desk drawer and tosses a white, folded piece of paper at me. "I'd say we have enough supplies to last at least forty-eight hours, when the roommates return."

I hold up the paper. "And Thai delivery until midnight on weekends."

"It's just across the street," he says. "Tell me what you want and I'll run and get it."

I barely gaze over the menu before pointing to a random item. My appetite seems to have vanished and my head is throbbing. *Damn cold.*

As soon as Alex is out the door, I realize how incredibly freezing I am. I peel back the covers on his bed and slide under, curling myself into a ball, waiting for heat to fill the empty space.

Chapter 28: Alex

November 28, 4:30 p.m.

Eve's been asleep for nearly three hours. I figured she'd wake up when I sat beside her on the bed and opened a carton of very strong-smelling Thai food or even when I turned on the TV after fifteen minutes of being bored with the silence, but she didn't.

It wasn't until she rolled over in her sleep and started coughing that I remembered her coughing earlier and our discussion about the cold she most likely acquired from Professor Larson's granddaughter two days ago. After moving the hair off her face, I felt her forehead and decided to make a run to the drugstore for some supplies. Other than a giant first aid kit from my mom and a giant box of condoms my dad got me for my birthday (because he's obviously under the impression that all people do in New York City is have sex), this apartment is pretty devoid of cold and flu season items that are always available in bulk at my house.

I've been back for an hour now and she's still asleep. I decide to wake her up. She hasn't had anything to eat or drink today that I'm aware of and that seems like it might override the need for sleep at some point.

"Eve?" I shake her shoulders gently and wait.

She sits up, squinting from the bright sunlight that's decided to emerge right before it's time to set again. "It's still Saturday, right?"

"Yeah." I laugh. "I'm not *that* patient."

"God, I'm sorry," she says. "I don't even remember falling asleep."

I give her a weary smile. "I hate to say this, since you're in denial and all, but I'm pretty sure you have a fever."

She slides out of bed and finds the T-shirt I loaned her earlier and pulls it over her head, inside out. "I should go. I'm going to get you sick."

"It's too late to worry about that." I reach across the bed and tug her back in and toss the covers over her again. "You should have something to drink. Water, orange juice, tea, soda?"

"Orange juice sounds good," she mumbles with her face half against the pillow.

I return five minutes later with a glass of juice, a bottle of water, a bag of drugstore supplies, and reheated chicken soup from the deli across the street. I picked it up on my way back from Rite Aid.

Eve is sitting up, taking tiny sips of the juice, when I dump the contents of the bag onto the bed. "Okay, you totally didn't have to go shopping for my cold."

I shrug and hold up the box of tissues and the nighttime cold medicine. "I've never done this for anyone before, but I highly recommend these two items, and the soup is fantastic. I go there and get it sometimes even when I'm not sick."

"Thanks Alex," she says with a grin, picking up the spoon and soup container.

I flip through the channels while Eve finishes her soup and her juice and then downs the cold medicine. When I hold up the new toothbrush I bought today, she laughs and says, "You really don't want me to leave, do you?"

"Keeping a sick girl prisoner in my apartment is a longtime fantasy of mine."

She smiles at me before getting up to use the bathroom and the new toothbrush. When she comes back, I get under the covers with her and turn on an episode of *The Office* waiting for me on my DVR.

I have a feeling that Eve curling up to me in my own bed is going to be a lot like the shower. It won't ever be the same, lying here by myself. And what if this opportunity doesn't come again for months? What if Elana and I have to be a couple for two years or longer and this is the only time Eve and I can be alone together? Could I survive the relationship without this now that I've had it? Maybe we could both take a separate flight to some remote tropical island that doesn't allow people with cameras and we could spend the weekend there every month or so.

Maybe I should just enjoy this right now and quit obsessing about tomorrow and the next day.

Chapter 29: Eve

November 29, 1:00 a.m.

It's dark when I wake up again. The cold medicine has kicked in and brought my fever down. I raise my head and glance around the room, my eyes still adjusting to the dark. Alex has cleaned up the dozen wadded-up tissues I tossed on the nightstand and removed the empty soup container and refilled my glass of orange juice. I reach over and snatch the water bottle, taking a big swig and returning it before allowing myself to take in Alex's sleeping figure.

A wave of emotion hits me when I finally stare at him. He's lying on his back, hair messy, his mouth half open and his chest rising and falling slowly. I keep picturing him walking to the drugstore and thinking about me with every one of the dozen items he bought today. There's so much good in him that I'm desperate to find a way to unzip him and crawl inside and let myself be even closer.

There's really no reason for me to not get as close as possible. I may have had some reluctance earlier, but it's faded little by little throughout the day.

Maybe that was all part of his plan, but that doesn't change how I feel.

I lean closer to Alex and touch my mouth to his. His eyes are still shut but he lifts a hand to my hip, skimming his fingers up my side, under my borrowed T-shirt. I smile against his mouth, my heart speeding up. Is he in the middle of some hot dream and that's why his hands are in motion while his mind is still asleep? In that case, I might as well lure him awake properly. I sit up and remove my shirt, tossing it onto the floor before hovering over him again.

When I kiss him this time, there's a brand-new kind of heat filling the space between us as my bare skin presses against his. This is the first time I've ever felt this urgency, this completely self-involved need to have someone inside of me. To be that close for the sake of being that close and no other objective except that it needs to be Alex. Maybe that's the answer I was looking for earlier about expectations? Maybe I just needed to want it so much that the outcome would be inevitable.

Alex's mouth starts moving against mine, his fingertips gliding up my sides again. The more of my bare skin he comes in contact with, the more he seems to wake up until he finally pulls his mouth from mine, staring up at me wide-eyed.

"You would make a great alarm clock, Eve."

Two entire seconds pass, both of us frozen, him feeling the tension radiating off me. And then he flips me over onto my back, his mouth trailing kisses all along my neck before moving lower.

By the time his lips reach my stomach I can hardly breathe, let alone speak, but I manage to stutter out a few words. "Do you have—"

"Condoms," he finishes for me. "Yeah, but if you want to wait…"

I shake my head. "No…no waiting."

His fingers trail lightly over my inner thighs and my hands land in his hair, gripping fistfuls of it.

It's like I'm on some two-day staycation from my regular life. The Alex Evans resort in SoHo, complete with clean towels, laundry service, cold and flu supplies, and all the key ingredients for falling in love.

Chapter 30: Alex

"Do you think we'll be able to come here again?" Eve asks.

I'm still waiting for my heart to slow down and my breathing to return to normal, so I don't answer her right away. My mind is lingering on the feel of her fingers pressed into the skin on my back, her hands tangled in my hair. I guess I've learned my lesson. Just accept that I'm not going to get what I want and then maybe it'll happen anyway. But that's not entirely true. I really did just want her to stay. Okay, so maybe the getting naked part was subconsciously on my list. We were all wet when we got here. Stripping was a necessity.

Eve's head is on my chest now and her body is halfway on top of mine and I can feel her relaxing into me, preparing to drift off. I rub the back of her neck with one hand and rest the other hand on her thigh.

"We will. I'll figure something out," I say finally then I switch subjects. "So, what's the verdict? Have you changed your mind about the whole not liking sex thing?"

She laughs and I can feel her face heating up. I love that she's completely naked with me and there's still a way for me to make her blush.

"In this case," she says, "yes I've completely changed my mind."

Okay, so I'm not too arrogant to enjoy hearing that. "Maybe it's that long absence you mentioned earlier. How long are we talking about?"

She's quiet for a while and I can practically hear her contemplating something. "Since I left New York the first time."

The question is hanging in the air. She knows I want to know why she left, but I'd never push the issue. I've kept the door open and somehow, I can tell she's about to walk through.

"If I told you that I left because of a guy," she whispers finally, "would you think less of me?"

"You ditched Gucci because of a guy?" She stiffens in my arms. I lift her chin and kiss her, long and slow, before saying, "Forget I said that. No, I don't think less of you."

"Well, I am much wiser than I was two years ago, if that helps at all." Her fingers glide over my chest, and she turns her head to kiss my shoulder. "When do you do the fragrance campaign?"

"Next month."

"What happens after?" I can hear her carefully hiding the hope in her voice, trying to sound like it doesn't matter.

I tighten my arms around Eve as if my subconscious is telling me to hold on to her just in case. "I don't know. Maybe by then people will be over Elana and I being a couple."

Mentally, I'm calculating what I'll get for this fragrance campaign. They're still negotiating, but it'll be somewhere between a hundred thousand and five hundred thousand depending on how many years it runs for. It's two thousand a month for this apartment, plus another two thousand for additional monthly expenses. On that, I can't even make it to twenty-five, let alone to retirement, assuming I actually start a retirement fund, on that one job. I've got a decent amount saved up already, but it's only savings if I have other income.

Eve lifts her head to look at me, pulling me from my mental math. "It's not just the couple thing that people are latching on to. You had jobs before Elana came along. You were on the rise. I had a couple of meetings with the CK designers, so I heard them talk about you. They love you. Trust me."

I don't really know how to respond to that. Eve saying those things carries even more weight than Wes's pep talks because she doesn't bullshit about stuff like this.

"Let me ask you this, then," she says after my long silence. "What do you *want* to do after the fragrance campaign? If you could pick any job or anything?"

Have my real girlfriend over whenever I want. Introduce her to my roommates. Take her somewhere that's not a library, bookstore, coffee shop, or jogging route.

"Honestly?" I say and Eve nods, waiting. I gently press her head until her cheek is resting against my chest again. "I wouldn't mind being able to call my mom and maybe my sister and tell them I'm dating this really hot, really smart photography student from Columbia. They'd be pretty damn impressed."

She finds my hand and squeezes it. "Where were you three years ago? I really could have used a nice boyfriend then."

"As opposed to a not-nice boyfriend?" I can't help asking. Seriously, what does she mean by that?

"Something like that," she mumbles and then drifts off to sleep before I can ask anything else.

Chapter 31: Alex

November 29, 8:30 a.m.

"I can hear your stomach growling," I say to Eve when I'm sure she's awake. "Does that mean you're feeling better?"

"A little." She stands up, giving me a full view of her naked body. She catches me looking and smiles before tossing on my boxers and T-shirt. "I'm going to get the clothes from the dryer."

My first instinct is to grab her and pull her back onto the bed and have a repeat performance of last night's activities, but people do have to eat sometimes. I get up too and put on gym shorts. "I'll see what I can scrounge up in the kitchen for breakfast. We might have eggs that haven't expired yet."

"You know eggs take forever to expire. Those dates are totally bogus," she says. "After a certain amount of time, they might not be good for baking, but they don't actually spoil like in a food poisoning way."

I guide her out the door in front of me. "How do you know all this stuff? You don't even cook."

She shrugs. "It's science. I like science."

"Unlike calculus—" My voice is completely cut off after Eve's loud gasp fills the apartment and we both see the man sitting at the kitchen table, drumming his fingers against the wood surface.

My heart begins to sprint. "What the hell, Wes? How did you get in here?"

His face is tight and composed. "It's an agency apartment. I have a key."

I watch his gaze travel from me to Eve and it's like everything is in slow motion, dozens of pieces clicking together all at once. The business face Wes always wears drops and his eyes widen. "Evie, what…?"

My gaze goes back and forth between the two of them, Eve's expression of both dread and shock and Wes's expression of complete shock. Like someone has pulled the rug out from under him.

As far as I know, Wes has only been in this apartment one other time since I've lived here. There's only one explanation for why he's here. He knew I brought someone up here; he just didn't know who. And the who seems to have changed this whole event from a PR related issue to something personal.

A knot forms in the pit of my stomach; panic and nausea are feeding it and making it grow in a matter of seconds. I know with such certainty that something happened with them. God, I can't even form the words in my head because I don't want the mental image. *Wes…Eve…and she was what? Fifteen? Sixteen?*

Fuck, I can't even…please tell me they didn't—

Stop! Think about something else. Anything else.

Wes pulls his shit together quickly and stands up, gripping the metal chair so hard his knuckles turn white. "It's all over the Internet. Alex Evans cheats on his girlfriend with mystery girl. I've called, emailed, left you at least seven messages. Where the hell is your phone?!"

Okay, work. I can focus on work.

It's on my dresser. I don't know why it didn't go off. I've been too distracted by Eve to even consider looking at it since yesterday. "I was in the rain. Maybe it got wet and I didn't realize—"

"Doesn't matter." He shakes his head, drawing in a deep angry breath. "I didn't come here to lecture you, Alex. I came to save your ass, and you're going to do everything I tell you, understood?"

I can't take my eyes off Eve, but I sink into a chair and slowly begin to feel the weight of what I've done. If I'm cheating, CK isn't going to want me and Elana for this fragrance campaign. They wanted a happy couple in love. CK could even pull my photos from the campaign we already shot and reshot. Depends on what side of the scandal they want to be on.

And what the fuck is up with Eve and Wes?

My chest tightens, and I'm getting a little dizzy. This is too much. Way too much.

Wes is in front of me in no time. "Calm down. It's gonna be fine, I promise. I want you to go get dressed, put on whatever you wear to the gym, get your gym bag, and walk out of here. *Alone.* And go work out like you normally do on Sunday."

"What about...?" I nod toward Eve, who is still wide-eyed and frozen.

Wes glances at her, locks eyes with her. "I don't think Eve wants to be responsible for ruining your career, do you, Evie?"

She shakes her head and whispers, "No."

Wes nods and turns back to me. "She and I will wait a while and we'll walk out of here together."

Oh no. No fucking way. "Uh-uh. I'm not throwing Eve under the bus just to save my ass."

"Alex—" Eve starts to say but Wes cuts her off.

"This isn't going to hurt her at all," Wes says.

But it's going to kill me. I don't want to see pictures of them together. I don't want to think about the fact that she might have slept in his bed and he might have done with her what I just did with her.

She basically said as much last night. The last time she'd been with anyone was before she left New York. *She left because of a guy.* Because of Wes.

I feel sick. Really sick. In the dark last night, I told Eve I wouldn't think less of her, but now I'm not so sure. And I think I only said that because it kept me from seeing everything I didn't want to see. I don't want to see it now, and I don't ever want to hear Wes calling her Evie again, like it's a nickname with a long history. A very personal history.

Eve folds her arms across her chest, hugging herself. Why does she look so guilty? I'm the one who brought her up here. It's my fault we're in this mess. Unless there's something going on between them right now? God, I can't even begin to process that.

"Just go, Alex," she says so firmly it pulls me to my feet.

Wes grips both my arms, looking me over. "Gym clothes, gym bag, don't show any sign of apprehension when you leave the building, okay?"

I nod and then I do exactly that. I'm too hurt and shocked and disgusted to do anything else.

Chapter 32: Eve

The second the apartment door closes behind Alex, Wes places his hands gently on my shoulders, guiding me over to the couch and forcing me to sit down. He takes a seat on the coffee table across from me.

"Are you okay?" he asks. "I'm sorry you had to be dragged into this. I had a feeling Alex was doing some on-the-side fooling around, but he should have known better than to bring you here."

I close my eyes and try to rewind the past twenty-four hours and fix this whole mess.

"I can't blame him completely," Wes says like I've jumped into this conversation or something. "He's just a kid and I've put a lot of pressure on him."

It's a little funny that Alex is eighteen and Wes is forgiving his screwups like he's a Labrador puppy who can't help humping the houseguests and peeing on their shoes, but he expected me to act like a professional, mature adult at fifteen years old.

"He's not like you, Evie. He's got both eyes focused on the prize, and I know him well enough to know that his priorities are always going to be work first."

So that's where I screwed up. I fell in love with you. And you were the professional one because you threw me under the bus to save your ass and then sent me to fictional drug rehab and let your boss declare me mentally unstable to the New York Times. *Thanks for clearing that up, Wes.*

I can't fight the tears that roll down my cheeks as I keep all these thoughts locked inside my head. Wes leans back, taking in my expression and recent show of emotion.

"How long has this been going on? You and Alex?"

I wipe my eyes with the sleeve of Alex's shirt. It smells like him. And the way he looked at me before he left, a mixture of hurt and disgust. He knows. I know he knows. "That's not really any of your business. You already said Alex is focused on work, so why does it even matter when it started? Obviously he's just fooling around. Nothing serious."

He rests his hands on my knees. "Okay, maybe I was wrong. Maybe this is more than I thought he was capable of."

Even though he tries to hide it, I can see the hurt flicker in his eyes. Something gives inside me and I find myself answering his question. "Since the CK shoot."

He exhales and then focuses on my face. "Okay then. If you really care about him, Eve, you'll stop this, whatever it is. Alex isn't like you. He's not going to be able to go to an Ivy League college. He doesn't have a plan B. He's a good kid, don't get me wrong. He's very smart when it comes to this industry, but I don't know what else he'd do with his life. If he loses this campaign, it's going to be a hard, fast, downward spiral. Is that what you want?"

He makes it sound like Alex is an invalid or something. He's not, but there's enough truth in Wes's words to keep me from arguing.

And I doubt a six-week relationship is going to be enough for Alex to ditch his career for love. That's the last thing I'd ever want.

I swallow the lump in my throat. "No, I don't want that."

"Good." Wes pulls me up to a stand and sighs. "You have no idea how hard it is for me to see you here, wearing his underwear."

He leans in closer, his nose inching toward mine. Instincts kick in, and I immediately lean away from him. He drops his hands from mine and lets out a frustrated groan. "God, Eve! You act like I'm a stranger or something. I know you a hell of a lot better than Alex Evans does."

"You *knew* me, Wes," I correct. "Past tense."

I step around him and go looking for the dryer so I can put my own clothes on. When we finally get to exit the building, Wes grabs my hand and before I can stop him, he tugs me closer and kisses me right in front of the building. I'm stung by old feelings that emerge because they're so different than with Alex. They're a betrayal of my much more aware, emotionally stronger mind. I don't want to be that girl again.

I can't be that girl again.

I have to work hard not to push him away, but luckily he breaks it off quickly, and I swear I see him give a tiny nod to some random dude across the street. I'm squinting to see if the guy is holding a camera, but before I can get my answer, Wes drags me into a black town car with him.

I sit as far away from him as possible and press my cheek against the cool window.

The only positive today is the fact that I never got a chance to tell Wes that I have a cold.

Chapter 33: Alex

November 29, 11:00 a.m.

I can't work out. I can't do anything except pace the men's locker room for an hour until it's been long enough for me to go back home. I don't want to appear out of my usual routine so I have to take the subway instead of a cab.

The thoughts going through my head are failing to form anything coherent. All I know is that I have to talk to her. Like now. Without Wes. I send her a quick text once I'm back in my apartment.

ME: I'm coming over.
HARVARD: No! Too risky.
ME: Okay, I'm calling you now. If you don't answer, I'm coming over.

She answers on the first ring. I can hear the congestion in her voice and the cold that still lingers.

"I really don't want to do this on the phone, but whatever," I say right after she says hello. "First, I have to know. Is the Wes thing past tense?"

There's a long pause. Maybe I've surprised her by figuring out her secret. *Their secret.*

"Yes, it's past tense," she says finally. "Until the *Seventeen* shoot back in October, I hadn't spoken to Wes since the day I left New York."

"Eve, how did that happen? It's illegal, really illegal. Did he... did he, like, force you or something?"

She coughs for several seconds before responding. "I should have told you. I almost did a few times. Maybe if I had explained..."

"What exactly should you have explained?" I make sure to sit myself on the couch just in case I get nauseous or dizzy again.

I hear her take a deep breath and I do the same, anticipating the worst. "We were together for a long time before I quit modeling. He didn't force me. It wasn't like that. I wanted to be with him. He tried to say no to me like so many times and I just kept making sure I was in the same places as him and making sure he knew how I felt."

Maybe I don't know Eve as well as I thought I did.

I feel like hurling, but I haven't eaten anything today.

"So you guys had a...a *relationship.*" I stop for a second, finding my voice again. "For how long?"

"It started when I was fifteen," she says.

The chunks, or lack of, are rising to my throat. How old was he? Twenty-three, maybe twenty-four. That's fucked up.

"But if he didn't force you and you wanted to be with him, why did you leave? I know you didn't really go to rehab."

"It's complicated. Wes and I just had too much friction. Maybe because he was my agent and we were dating. It got to be too much, and I couldn't deal anymore. Gucci wanted me to lose weight and so did the next gig and my schoolwork was piling up and I just…I couldn't deal." The emotion has dropped from her voice. She's in numb mechanical mode and I wish I could do the same, but I can't seem to do anything but feel all of this as it knocks me down from a dozen different directions.

"You should have told me. If I had known about you and Wes…" I'm squeezing the TV remote now; it's about to shatter to pieces any second.

"What, Alex? What would have happened if you had known?" she says.

It's obvious what she's trying to get me to say: *I wouldn't have even considered dating you*.

"I don't know," I finally reply.

"I don't want to be with him anymore. I haven't for a long time," she says.

She isn't exactly pleading or anything, but I feel defensive all of a sudden. My guard is up because I don't know her like I thought I did and who knows what this will do to me? And I'm not about to tell her I'm scared of getting hurt and that maybe it's too hard to be with her and know that she was with Wes. So I take a different angle, one that's comfortable and familiar. Most of all it makes sense, and I need things to make sense right now. "I can't lose this job, Eve."

She goes completely silent again and then eventually whispers, "Okay."

And I know she gets it. She gets that I can't take the risk that I took last night. I can't be around her. I can't screw up my fake relationship with someone who's already been a tabloid writer's wet dream. It feels like I'm being punched right in the gut.

"Maybe," I say slowly, digging for an ounce of the hope I had a little while ago, pacing in that locker room. "Maybe it doesn't have to be forever. Things change and…"

"Yeah, maybe." She doesn't sound hopeful though.

It sounds like good-bye. So that's exactly what I say next: "'Bye, Eve."

After I hang up, more reality kicks in and I pick up my phone again, my hands still shaking, and call my fake girlfriend to update her before she gets infected by the tabloids.

Chapter 34: Eve

November 29, 2:30 p.m.

The pictures are online by noon. Steph is lying beside me in my bed, her laptop open, a mask carefully placed on her face for fear of catching my cold. Her free hand is positioned beside the tissue box, handing me one every few minutes. I still can't believe Alex knows about my history with Wes. He just figured it out by looking at Wes's shock from seeing us together, yet two years ago, I couldn't get anyone to believe me. I should feel lighter, free of these secrets I've been holding in for so long, but I just feel trapped by them.

"Oh boy." She lets out a low whistle. "*Former crackhead teen model returns to her roots and has taken up sleeping with agents to get work—too bad she's going to have to look for plus-sized opportunities.*"

I blow my nose and toss the tissue into the garbage across the room, sinking it on the first try. "That might be the worst one yet. What's crack again? Is that cocaine?"

"I think it's the cheaper version of cocaine," Steph says. "For the people in the ghetto."

"Great." I continue to stare at the ceiling while Steph searches the web.

"God, what the fuck? You are so not plus-sized. What is wrong with these people? Size four jeans practically fall off of you."

"Actually, size four could be plus-sized. Six totally is. There's a lot of money in those jobs." I find myself laughing because that's what Stephanie has found most offensive in that article. "Is Alex in the clear yet?"

"Still looking," she says. "Oh! Here we go. *Apparently, Alex Evans isn't cheating on new girlfriend, French model Elana. A source close to the rising star says he met Eve Castle while on a shoot for Calvin Klein. Apparently she's trying to worm her way back into the industry by taking nonpaying internships. 'Alex is a decent guy,' a publicist for the agency tells us. 'He's always willing to offer advice and he's too polite to turn down an invitation for coffee.' Of course, photos reveal that Eve is now sharing intimate moments with her former agent, Wes Danes, who happens to be Alex's current agent and the man who tried to help Eve through her past drug addiction. Hopefully, it's past.*"

"Wow," is all I can say.

"This is so wrong," Steph says. "You wanted nothing to do with that industry. You're a fucking Ivy League student! Are you fucking telling me none of them were able to find out that you go to Columbia? You have to counter this with something. You have to find your own tabloid person to schmooze."

I laugh, but there's no humor in it. Steph is a journalism student. It's about time she learns the truth about her future profession. "That never works. Ever. Nobody will read an article full of hard facts with no commercial appeal. The bad stuff is always easier to believe."

"Are you intentionally quoting *Pretty Woman*?"

"Yes, I am. That's what I feel like at the moment. A prostitute who's falling for a nice successful guy and—"

"Wait," Steph interrupts. "Wouldn't Elana be the prostitute? She's the one posing as his girlfriend."

I shoot a glare in her direction and she shuts up. "What do you think are the odds that Janessa is reading the fashion and model industry gossip this weekend?"

Steph's face turns weary. "Oh shit. I didn't even think about that."

"I hate that they called me an intern," I say. "I'm a fucking assistant. It's insulting."

"Actually, Eve Castle isn't an intern or an assistant. Eve Nowakowski is," Steph corrects.

And that's why they don't know that I'm a student. That's why they don't know that I'm not interested in the least in modeling again.

"You should have seen how he looked at me," I say.

Steph sets her laptop aside and gives me a sympathetic look through her mask. "Is it the age thing? How did you explain it to Alex?"

"I told him what I had with Wes was my choice and I wasn't sleeping with him to get jobs or being forced into it." A lump forms in my throat just thinking about the past few days and how easy it was to be with Alex and how I'd hoped we'd be able to find a way to be together like that again.

Steph eyes me suspiciously. "You didn't tell him how Wes treated you, did you? That he hit you?"

I divert my gaze away from her. "I don't see any reason to explain that. It didn't have anything to do with age, and honestly I think I've built it up to be something worse in my head. And what is Alex going to do about it? Wes hasn't done anything but help him. He won't have any reason to believe me. Then what? He'll stay with me because he feels bad that Wes wasn't nice to me when I was sixteen?"

Stephanie's face is more serious than I've ever seen it before. "Promise me you won't go back to that guy again, Eve?"

"Who? Wes?" She nods. "Not a chance in hell."

But I'm pretty sure Eve Castle is dating him now.

Chapter 35: Alex

November 30, 8:00 a.m.

Wes pulls up in front of my building when I'm heading out for the *GQ* shoot. I'm not starting a fight with him today, but I can't look him in the eye without having the urge to throw a punch. My legs are heavy as I climb into the back of the car and sit across from him.

The last thing I ever expected Wes to do is start talking about Eve.

"I just want you to know," he says, while I'm staring out the window, "I really loved her. I know what you're probably thinking. I know the issues you have with Elana's age, but this was different and I truly loved her."

That gets me to look in his direction, but I don't have anything to say. To me, it isn't different.

"There's a lot you don't know about Eve," he says.

I turn back to the window. It's killing me to think about her and killing me five more times to think about them together.

"Eve is messed up, Alex. It's not her fault. She's got shitty parents who sold their daughter away for cash. I was naive and I wanted to be there for her. She needed someone to look out for her. She had no one. At fifteen she had no one."

"I get it," I snap without taking my eyes off the car window.

"I was stupid enough to think that I could actually rescue her from herself, but I didn't know shit about dealing with girls who had major daddy issues, negligent parents, abuse. She was so insecure it started bleeding into her work." He pauses and takes a breath like he's overcome with emotions. I totally can't look now. There's no way I'm doing the dudes-sharing-our-feelings game with Wes. "I think she panicked. She thought I'd dump her back then, and that's why she experimented with drugs. That's why she let me find the evidence. I didn't tell the agency. I just wanted her to be okay. I should have known she'd take it that far and I should have known that I was in over my head. But I loved her, and that screws with your mind sometimes. Eve is very easy to love, and I just don't want to see you get pulled under like I did. You have so much poten-tial, Alex."

My heart is racing, trying to process everything. It mostly goes with Eve's story. She said she left because of a guy and because it got too hard, but maybe she doesn't even know she's screwed up. How can I blame her for being fucked up if she's got shitty parents and her only help came from an agent who isn't above sleeping with underage girls? But would I be any better than Wes at helping her? And the Eve I know can stand on her own, can't she? I've never felt like us being together was an issue of depen-dency. Or codependency. It was like we made each other better. And I'm already talking about her in the past tense.

It's only been six weeks. It's only going to feel this intense for a little while, and then I'll be able to let it go. To let her go.

"I can see that this is hard for you," Wes says. "I don't want to tell you what to do or who to date, but being with someone like Eve takes so much out of you. It's draining and heavy and you get sucked down this hole that's hard to get out of. I don't want that for you. I want something better for you."

"It doesn't matter," I say to him finally. "I ended it."

"I'm sorry." He sounds like he means it, but I don't know for sure. I don't know anything for sure anymore.

·· ◆ ··

After the *GQ* shoot finishes up, I see Wes has decided to pick me up once again. Maybe he's worried that I'll run off and see Eve if he lets me out of his sight. I almost turn down the ride, but I'm starting to feel like shit—feverish and achy from the inevitable cold brewing in my immune system.

I thought he'd just drop me off, but that would be good luck, and I seemed to have run out of that. And now he's opening the car door, allowing a middle-aged woman to slide in between us.

A reporter. Great.

"When we scheduled this, I had no idea there would be so much drama over the weekend," the lady says, giving me this fake laugh.

Wes lifts his eyebrows, conversing with me silently. And as much disgust as I feel toward him right now, I can't deny the fact that I screwed up big-time this weekend and he saved my ass. Totally saved it. I have to keep going along with his plan because he's very good at damage control.

"You're from Nebraska, correct?"

"Correct."

"And you finished high school or dropped out?"

"I got my GED. My parents insisted on it if I wanted to move to New York." I have to look at her. It would be rude not to.

"And did you know Eve Castle before you moved to New York? Did you guys date before Elana?"

"What?" I'm caught off guard by the quick shift, but I should have anticipated this, considering the way she opened the conversation. "I met Eve the same day I met Elana. She was observing the *Seventeen* shoot I did with Elana back in early October."

Wes gives me a small nod behind the reporter's head.

"But you knew who she was?"

"Yeah, I'd heard of her."

"Did you help get her the internship? Is she still addicted to drugs or trying to make a comeback? It would be nice if she had parents to make her get her GED like yours did. Poor girl doesn't stand a chance surviving in New York without an agency behind her and jobs booked."

Do they even do any fucking research before making up these questions? I close my eyes and rub my temples, trying to rid myself of the throbbing headache that is most likely the beginning of a cold I caught from Eve.

"I'd rather not answer any questions about Eve, if that's all right with you."

She glances at Wes, who shrugs like I'm too big of a star for him to be able to tell me what to do. Yeah, right.

"Okay, sure," she says.

"And you seriously need to fire your information source. Besides the Nebraska part, I don't think you've said one true thing yet."

Wes coughs loudly.

But the reporter lady just gives me a sly grin. "All right then, the diva emerges. I suppose it's justified, considering the campaign you've just landed."

I roll my eyes. Whatever. I'm a fucking diva. Put that in your fucking magazine.

"So, Elana," she says, leaning in closer. "She's great, isn't she?"

"Yeah, she's great. I just love her to death." I give her a grin to rival the one she just gave me.

"That's so sweet!" She glances at Wes again and then back at me. "Want to add some expert sex tips? I'm sure the male readers will appreciate it, especially if they get to imagine themselves with The Elana."

What magazine is this? US Weekly?

I smile at her again. "We're waiting."

Wes flashes me a thumbs-up. What a fucking hypocrite.

The reporter lady rolls her eyes. "Of course you are."

The rest of the questions are focused on my early jobs and the beginning of my career and how lucky I am, blah, blah, blah…

I'm so ready to get the hell out of this car and go home and start being sick.

Chapter 36: Eve

December 1, 3:00 P.M.

I can sense something is off the minute I walk into Janessa's office, and it's not just the raging 104-degree fever I'm attempting to keep down with both Advil and Tylenol.

She doesn't spit instructions at me like usual, with her back turned, eyes on the computer screen. Instead, she spins in her chair to face me, and even worse, points to a chair for me to sit in. Janessa never lets me sit.

I sink down in the seat, solely fueled on adrenaline.

"I told you, Eve," she says, blowing out a frustrated breath. "I told you I was on your side but I needed you to help me out and not feed this gossip-driven industry anything new."

My heart sinks to the pit of my stomach. "Oh. That."

"What happened?"

I shake my head, fighting tears. "Does it matter? It only matters what people think happened, right?"

"The designers saw your name on the call sheet and told me no way, find a new assistant," she says, giving it to me straight and direct. I expect nothing less from Janessa. "I can still use you here in the office, editing and doing the preshoot work, but I can't have you on set right now. Not for this job."

"But it's a really long job." I'm trying not to cry, but it isn't working. "My interview is in January. What if this happens again with the next job? How are you supposed to review me if I haven't actually been assisting?"

"I can't make them allow you on set, Eve," she says. "I can't bail on this job either. I'm right in the middle of it. I have a contract."

I quickly wipe my face, feeling nothing but defeat. "I know. I'm sorry. It's not your fault."

"Listen, you'll be gone for semester break soon, right? Maybe next semester, everything will have faded and you can jump in and help me."

God. Semester break. This is getting worse and worse by the minute. The dorms close for a month, my mom's in Florida, my dad's still in jail as far as I know, and Jeff would probably be cool with me staying at his place again, but I'm not even sure I can afford to fly home. Where the hell am I supposed to stay?

None of this is Janessa's problem. She's put up with enough of my shit already. "You're right. Semester break should help."

"You sound like hell," she says. "Why don't you get some rest and call me tomorrow and I'll set up some times for you to do edits."

"Okay…thanks."

Once I'm outside, heading toward the subway, I get the sense that someone is following me, and I have to work very hard not to break down and cry or else I'm going to get a Google Alert telling me about my latest crisis. *Well, Eve Castle's latest crisis.* Maybe I'll be homeless this time or fired from my unpaid internships for sleeping with agents. 'Cause everyone knows I sleep with all of them. As many as I can get my hands on.

·····

"You've got to be kidding." I stare at the papers in front of me then up at the middle-aged woman behind the desk in her tiny Student Aid office cubicle.

Steph is seated beside me, and she leans in to get a closer look. "What is this stuff? I didn't know you owned a car?"

I swallow the dryness in the back of my throat. "I don't."

My eyes meet Steph's and she says, "Your parents did all this?"

I can't do anything but nod.

"Because of your credit score being so low, getting loans for next year is going to be impossible," the woman says, looking both uncomfortable and sympathetic.

"But it's fraudulent," Steph argues. "That stuff can be erased."

The woman nods. "True. But in this case, if it is your parents using your name and Social Security number while you were still technically under their care, it's very difficult to contest."

After leaving Janessa's, I headed right back to my room to tell Stephanie what had happened, and after an hour of talking through the logic with her, I had come into this meeting ready to bite the bullet and start the process of student loans that would take me a hundred years to pay off. And now, thanks to my parents, I couldn't even do that.

"She's emancipated. Why doesn't she qualify for loans again?" Steph asks.

"Because in the last tax year, I technically had a hundred grand in my bank account." This possibility had already been explored many times over. Hence the need for a scholarship.

"But," the woman says, trying to inject some amount of hope into the conversation, "this time next year, you'll have a much different financial status and I imagine you'll qualify for some grant money then."

I sat there feeling sick as a dog, nodding as she went on about a few options for much smaller scholarships that could help for next year, and then finally Steph and I left the office carrying a dozen pamphlets on student aid and a copy of my very flawed credit history.

It seemed fitting that my life in the tabloids mimicked that of my credit report: lots of experiences I never had but that my name has been attached to.

"Look," Steph says. "This semester and spring semester are paid for. It's just a matter of next year. And you heard that woman, even the year after next will be easier. One year, Eve. Two semesters."

"Right," I say, nodding, trying to catch her logic, her hopeful energy. There's got to be a way. There's always a way. I should know. I've dug myself out of some very deep holes.

"Worst case," she adds. "You find some rich family on the Upper East and become their live-in nanny for a year. People do that."

"That's a good plan B to replace the student loan plan." I'm shivering from the fever, talking through chattering teeth. "The Mason Scholarship was always a long shot."

"But just being a finalist will look great on your résumé," Steph says.

After we walk into our building and I've breathed in enough warm air to stop my teeth from chattering, I say, "There's one other much less appealing, but technically possible, option to explore."

Steph hits the button of the elevator before looking at my face, her eyes wide with comprehension. "Oh no, you're aren't actually thinking about—"

I let out a breath. "I'm just saying it's an option."

"Why does this feel like one of those one last jobs, gotta help your gang brothers or Soprano family deals?" Steph asks. "Like you'll go in, but never come out again."

I shake my head. "It doesn't have to be like that."

But really I'm not sure what it would be like to model again. Or if the Sears catalog is even hiring still.

Chapter 37: Alex

December 3, 10:00 p.m.

"Why are we here again?" I ask Elana.

Unfortunately, I'm feeling well enough today to be forced into another party with my "girlfriend."

"New collection of Gucci watches, remember?" she says, quiet so no one will hear. "Are you okay?"

No, not really. My tie is strangling me, probably because my glands are still swollen. But my fever is gone and my nose isn't dripping like a faucet anymore.

I miss Eve. I miss texting her. I miss libraries and coffee shops and her and her camera. I wait until we're alone at the bar before responding to Elana's question. "Have you talked to her?"

Elana nods, knowing exactly who the her is I'm referring to. "I think she's still sick. We didn't get to talk for long."

A pang of guilt hits me hard. *She's still sick.* "What else? The tabloids have been publishing the worst kind of lies I've ever seen in my life."

Elana looks down at her hands, currently gripping the edge of the bar. "She can't assist Janessa right now. The designers don't want her on set."

I press my face into my hands. "Fuck. This wasn't supposed to affect her."

Elana leans down so our heads are practically pressed together. It's very cozy for a "couple" photo. *Smart girl.*

"What do you think about Eve?" I ask Elana. "Do you think she's messed up?" I hate to even ask, but maybe I *was* in over my head. "She's had a hard life."

What the hell am I doing consulting a fourteen-year-old for advice?

"She's had a hard life," Elana agrees, looking like she's really thinking her answer through. "She told me a little about it, but she's not trying to give a sob story. I think she just wants to move on."

And now I've made that impossible for her because she's lost her job with Janessa.

Wes interrupts our private moment. "Elana, honey, I've got someone I want you to meet."

Elana set her glass down on the bar without hesitation. I zoom in on Wes's hand resting on her arm as he guides her away. The nausea from the other day returns, and I set my own drink down, pushing it away. I watch them walk across the room.

Is this why Eve was always asking me about Elana? Where she was and who she was with?

I'm so deep in thought that I hardly notice Elana's agent, Kara, sliding beside me at the bar, watching the same two people that I'm currently staring at. "Here we go again, right?" she says, low enough so only I hear it.

I snap around to look at her. "What do you mean?"

"Nothing." She shakes her head, looking extremely pissed off about something, then the anger drops from her face, and she fakes a smile. "I forgot why I came over here, not for alcohol. I'm supposed to tell you that you're allowed to leave. Wes said he wants you healthy and rested up for tomorrow. Just sneak out when no one's looking."

"What about Elana?" I ask. "Are you taking her home?"

Now I sound like Eve. But Finley, that girl from my agency, was right about the plan for Elana. December first came and Lumina was gone. Finley moved in with Elana and her other roommate, so maybe I can talk to her about keeping an eye on Elana.

Kara sighs and points to my glass of wine, signaling for the bartender to bring her one. "Wes will take care of it; just go. You're free, unlike the rest of us."

My palms are sweating and my stomach is queasy. I slide off the bar stool and instead of sneaking out, as I've been instructed, I walk over to where Elana and Wes are talking to a Gucci designer I recognize from the last party. Before anyone can say anything to me or reintroduce me, I lean close to Elana and whisper, "Wes said we should make up an excuse to leave. He wants us healthy for the fragrance shoot."

I can see confusion and then nerves reflected in her expression, but she hides it quickly and turns to the designer, "Excuse me," she says. "My parents are trying to get ahold of me. I need to give them a call. Really lovely to meet you."

I try not to groan out loud. It's the middle of the night in France, but I guess if it's an emergency people call in the middle of the night. Whatever. She can work on her lying skills later. I pull her away and toward the exit before Wes can stop us. He's probably got a car for me, but I'm not going to stick around long enough to ask. We grab our coats and then a cab. If he gets pissed at me for taking Elana away from an important conversation, I'll just tell him I must have misunderstood Kara and thought we were both supposed to sneak out.

"That was really nice of Wes to let us go early." Elana settles into her seat. "Maybe I can watch Letterman."

I don't think I've ever been this nervous or stressed out in my entire life, and she is the epitome of calm and relaxed.

"Elana," I say slowly, trying not to sound like something is really wrong. But of course she looks at me with alarm. "You can't—I mean—just stick with me, okay?"

She turns to look at me. "What do you mean?"

My phone buzzes in my pocket. I know it's Wes so I don't look at the text. "It's just...there're people who do really bad stuff...take advantage of children—"

She glares at me and scoots further away. "I'm not a child!"

Okay, this isn't going well. "I know you're not a child. I didn't mean it that way. Fourteen is old, really old."

"I'm fifteen." She won't look at me now, but there's a shake in her voice like she's about to cry. "Yesterday was my birthday."

"Oh." I let out a breath. How did we go from preventing statutory rape to birthdays? "Well, happy late birthday."

"Thanks."

I can tell we've hit a wall, and this birthday thing is a big deal to her. I probably jumped into the more serious topic too fast.

I suck at this. "Let's go somewhere and have some cake. Have you had cake yet?"

"Wes and Kara brought me a cake yesterday," she says.

Wes actually gave cake to a model? That's a shocker. I bet he laced it with laxatives. That would explain her moodiness. "Then we can do something else. You are my girlfriend after all, right? We have to celebrate your birthday."

Elana's too polite to not at least smile at my sorry attempt at a joke. "I feel like going home."

"You would tell me if you, you know...*liked someone*? Maybe wanted to date them secretly?" I spit out the words with a great deal of effort. "Like if you had a real boyfriend, you'd tell me, right?"

She finally turns to face me again. "Like how you told me about you and Eve?"

"Oh, come on, you knew."

"Not because you told me, and not because Eve told me," she challenges.

I'm currently at a loss for words, and the cab has now pulled up in front of Elana's building. She rests a hand on the door handle. "Just admit it, Alex. You hate being around me. You hate this whole situation, and if you didn't feel so guilty about lying to everyone, you wouldn't care about me at all. And Eve is only nice to me because of you. She'd do anything for you."

"That's not true," I say, trying to sound as firm as possible. At least the part about Eve isn't true. She worries about Elana all on her own. But what she said about me, that's mostly true. I don't hate her. I really don't. I hate the situation.

"Good night, Alex." She's out of the cab so fast, I don't even have a chance to check the outside of the building for weirdos or potential murderers, but I make the driver wait for her to go inside before I give him my address.

I instinctively reach for my phone, preparing to send Eve a text before I stop myself and remember that she and I are over. And the text I got earlier surprisingly wasn't from Wes. It was from Katie.

KATIE: You are all over the Internet. What's the real story?

ME: Trust me. It's not nearly as interesting as anything you've read.

KATIE: You can tell me the truth. I won't tell anyone.

ME: It's complicated and your life should stay as simple as possible. Just promise me something?

KATIE: What?

ME: Don't become a model.

KATIE: Yeah right. Want to talk?

I let out another long sigh. Talking to Katie about all her high school angst actually sounds kind of nice, but I know she'll want to know what's going on in my life, and avoiding the truth is one thing. Lying is a completely different thing.

ME: I'm beat. Maybe tomorrow?

KATIE: Sure.

More guilt is invading me. She probably thinks I don't want

to listen to her current life's drama, or that I'm too cool for my family and my little sister.

As an afterthought, I send one last text to her, because there are two people I'd like to say this to but only one who I'll actually allow myself tell.

ME: I miss you.

Chapter 38: Eve

December 5, 1:20 a.m.

I'm coughing up blood. And possibly a lung. At least that's what it feels like. "This is bad," I say to Steph, who has just shot up out of her bed.

"You need to go to a doctor, seriously."

I can hardly move, let alone contemplate the idea of getting somewhere like a hospital. I know what this is and it's not going away without some strong antibiotics. Or at least I hope that's the worst-case scenario.

"I'll go with you," Steph says.

"No, you've got an exam in a few hours. I could be there all night. I'm not dying, so who knows how long the wait will be?" She looks reluctant to agree, so I add, "Just help me bundle up and maybe get a cab."

Steph loans me her extra thick ski jacket, scarf, and hat and then comes downstairs with me to hail a cab. I feel like I'm only half in reality, like my brain is fogged up and I can't get a grip on anything but surviving.

· · ◆ · ·

"You have pneumonia," the ER doc says.

"What's the treatment?"

He's already scribbling on his prescription pad. "First off, you have to push fluids. You're dehydrated. I'm giving you an antibiotic and you should take it with food. Also a cough syrup with codeine so you can sleep, and an inhaler to get your airways open."

"Which ones do I absolutely need? Like if I can only afford one or two?" I have the bare minimum of insurance policies that the university requires and it doesn't cover prescriptions.

The doctor opens his mouth to protest, but a nurse walks in, followed by Wes.

Wes is here in the emergency room. Lovely.

"What are you doing here?" I say, not hiding the whine or the frustration in my voice. "And how the hell did you know I was here?"

"Twitter." He holds his phone up. "I think you have someone following you."

"Oh great, I'm probably pregnant, overdosed on crack that I bought from the ghetto dealers, and I bet I have an STD too." I glance up and see that I've scared both the doctor and the nurse. "Not really," I say quickly.

"Well then." The doctor taps the stack of prescriptions. "To answer your question, you need all of these. You've got finals coming up, right? You need all the help you can get."

I don't even realize I'm crying until the tears start landing on my hand. *Finals*. No place to stay for winter break. I'm sick as a dog. I can't work with Janessa. And Wes is here.

The doctor sits beside me and pats my hand. "We can keep you overnight if you want? IV fluids can do wonders."

"No!" I wipe my eyes with my sleeve. The co-pay for a hospital stay is something like a thousand dollars. I mean at this point, a thousand might as well be a million.

Wes snatches the prescriptions off the bed and turns to the doctor. "Where can we get these filled tonight?"

The doctor looks relieved. "Pharmacy right across from the information desk."

"Come on, Evie." Wes holds out a hand for me.

I don't know why, but I follow him even though it's a really bad idea, but what the hell am I supposed to do? While we're waiting at the pharmacy, I curl up in a chair and doze off. I barely notice Wes pulling my purse from my hands and spouting off my address, phone number, birthday. My ears perk up when I hear them say it's nearly two hundred dollars for the prescriptions. I peel my eyes open to see Wes remove his own wallet and hand over a credit card.

When Wes comes back over, I manage to open my eyes long enough to say, "I'll pay you back."

"Don't worry about it." He leads me out the doors and into a cab.

My head bobs around as I fight to stay awake, but I'm aware enough after about ten minutes to realize we're not headed back to my dorm. "Where are we going?"

"My place," Wes says.

"No! I can't. My roommate is expecting me." I look over and he's got my phone in his hands, then he hands it to me.

"Text her. You can't go to class when you're this sick, Eve. Just sleep on the couch tonight," he says. "You only have to walk about three feet to get to both the bathroom and the kitchen. Let me help you. It's the least I can do."

So now he feels guilty for letting everyone think that I was a druggie at sixteen. That's nice. We're already dating online. I guess I might as well get something out of this nightmare. "Fine. Whatever."

He's moved since when I dated him. This place is bigger and full of black and gray electronics, and of course it's neat as a pin, with everything perfectly in place.

Wes gives me a very fluffy pillow and a very soft, warm blanket, and I'm already curled under it, ready to drift off, when he lines up the prescription bottles on the coffee table.

"God, Evie, what have you done to yourself? This is a lot of drugs," he says, examining each bottle.

"Well, I decided it might be fun to put bacteria into my lungs and see what happens." *Didn't he say he wanted to help?* "Who doesn't want to cough up blood and have a hundred and five fever?"

"I just mean you're working too hard, putting too much pressure on yourself, not getting to the doctor soon enough."

Thanks. I'll remember that when I find a time machine and jump back a few weeks.

I sift through the bottles and find the antibiotics. "I need to take this one with food."

Wes walks to the kitchen and opens up the fridge. "Sushi?"

I groan way too loud for him not to hear. "Maybe just crackers or something?"

He returns with two packages of saltine crackers that must have come with takeout from somewhere. Wes doesn't cook or buy groceries. I stuff them in my mouth along with some water from the glass Wes gets for me after I ask for it. I take the antibiotic first, then I move onto the cough syrup with codeine, which tastes horrible. He watches as I go down the list and follow all the directions.

"You've done this before?" he asks.

I nod and return my head to the pillow. "Had pneumonia last year too. Apparently once you've had it, you're ten times more likely to get it again."

He stares at me for a long moment, then says, "Why do you hate me so much, Evie?"

"I don't hate you. I just hate my life right now."

He sits on the coffee table and folds his hands in his lap. "What can I do to help you?"

"Ask the designers that Janessa Fields is working for to let me back on set," I say.

"Which designer?" he says.

"Ralph Lauren."

He's thinking, the wheels are churning, but if I know Wes like I think I do, he'll choose work over helping me. "I can't do that."

I let out a short laugh. No surprise. I lie there for several minutes with my eyes open, watching Wes move around the living room, putting every item back into place and fixing himself a drink.

The way I see it, I have two options right now:

1) Continue to cry and be depressed about Alex and my scholarship and hope that things fix themselves so I don't have to quit

school after freshman year or be left hanging by a thread while I scramble to find another scholarship; or

2) Do something I hate just long enough to put school and tuition completely in my control and spend the final three years of college focusing on photography and not freaking out constantly about paying the next semester of tuition.

I don't want to be the kind of person who sits back and lets her life get ruined by other people. If it's going to be ruined, I should get to do the ruining myself. "Wes?"

He sets down his bottle of whiskey and caps it before looking over at me. "Yeah, Evie?"

"If I did want to book some jobs, what would I need to do before you'll send me on any castings?"

His face is completely businesslike when he says, "Lose ten pounds."

I swallow the lump in my throat. *I'm such a sellout.* "Is that all?"

He walks across the room and sits on the love seat. "Lose the superior, Ivy League attitude. No one likes a snob."

Before I can open my mouth to respond to his bullshit, Wes leans over, so close I'm worried he's going to kiss me, and I have nowhere to move since I'm lying on the couch.

"You don't have any new piercings or tattoos, do you?" he asks, grinning before backing away again.

"No, but I have stretch marks from that crack baby I gave birth to in a crack den." I sink into the pillow, closing my eyes again. "You know, after my post-rehab relapse."

"Good thing for Photoshop," he says. "I forgot how funny you are when you're not ridden with insecurity."

Asshole.

My eyes fly open as I remember something really important I probably should have brought up earlier. "I need a place to stay for winter break."

He stands up and moves toward the kitchen to place his glass into the proper slot on the top rack of the dishwasher. "You can stay here."

"No."

Wes laughs. He knew I'd say that. "I'll give you a key to one of our agency apartments. The girls sharing it are gone until February, but it's just between you and me, all right? At least until you actually book something."

If I book something.

The codeine kicks in, sending me into a deep sleep before I can worry anymore.

Chapter 39: Alex

December 15, 11:30 a.m.

I've done more appearances with my "girlfriend" in the past two weeks than I can even begin to count. The plan was to defuse the cheating rumors by starting rumors about how inseparable we are. The only problem is, Elana's not speaking to me.

And this isn't like the silent game where one person refuses to talk to you, waiting out the inevitable blowup that will be followed by making up. My high school girlfriend, Lindsey, used to play that game with me sometimes and it would always end in some pretty hot makeup/make-out sessions.

But with Elana, it's different. She's talking to me. But it's only polite distant words you'd say to a stranger forced to sit beside you on a transatlantic flight. It's like she's decided that she can't trust me, and winning back that trust isn't an option. She's being careful.

And it sucks.

Especially right now because there's a very pissed-off photographer in the studio with us, begging for some small drop of chemistry, and we don't have it today.

I'm thinking about Eve and how she would be able to say the perfect thing that would drag me out of this slump. Classes are over for the semester at Columbia. I know this because I looked it up online last night and I have no idea where she is right now. Surely she didn't go back to her shitty family in Indiana? One tabloid mentioned something about her dad being in jail, but I'm not stupid enough to trust that source.

"Alex!" Graham, the photographer, lets out a frustrated groan, rubbing his temples and closing his eyes briefly. Graham is British, but not the polite kind of British. This dude is hardcore. Way more blunt than Janessa Fields could ever be. In fact, I doubt he has any holiday cards waiting for him in his mailbox today. Or ever. "You've got the sex appeal of a seventy-year-old man right now. We're selling sex here, people, and Elana..."

Elana's supposed to be straddling my lap while we're seated in a chair, looking lovingly into each other's eyes. She's sort of doing that, at least the sitting on me part, which is why I feel her entire body stiffen in preparation for the criticism about to be dished out.

"Your body language could pass for thirteen years old, tops," he snaps. *Not a bad guess.* "And with your boyfriend here and his inability to do anything remotely sexy, these photos are going to be lovely. Every old man suffering from ED will buy CK perfume so they can get their own thirteen-year-old to sit on their lap. It's bloody brilliant."

I've been insulted and criticized enough to let it bounce right off me, but Elana hasn't. She stumbles off my lap, onto her feet. Even with her dark skin, I can see her face is bright red and her eyes are filling with tears. She turns around and walks off at a quick pace, sniffling the whole way to the restroom.

Graham throws his hands up in the air. "Great, just great."

The entire crew seems to be scrambling around to accommodate his tantrum. His assistant brings him a bottle of imported spring water and a small hand towel. I'm debating going into the women's restroom to lure Elana back when I see Wes walking into the studio.

"Finally!" Graham says, rushing over to Wes. Did he have someone call him because we're so awful today? "I can't work with them," Graham tells him loud enough for everyone to hear.

Wes holds up his hands in front of him, nodding. "Just give me a minute to talk to them. I promise, we'll get the pictures you want."

Graham turns around and shouts to everyone. "Lunch break! And then we'll see if there's actually any talent in these well-paid children."

I'm still standing in the center of the set, right behind the chair, so I decide it's a good idea to step out of the lights and lurk in the shadows for now. Wes moves quickly toward me, looking calm, but I can see the intensity is there, based on the way his hands squeeze open and closed.

"I'm going to go fix her," Wes says in a low voice, nodding toward the restroom. "And you're going to get your shit together and quit pissing off this photographer, understood?"

"I can talk to Elana," I say quickly.

Wes shakes his head. "She doesn't want anything to do with

you. I don't know what you did to her, but she's just texted me and Kara both to say she can't finish this job today because you don't like her."

"Where's Kara?" I glance around, hoping she's here.

"Barbados," Wes says before walking off.

My heart is hammering. I have to do something. I have to keep an eye on her. I skim the table with the catered lunch and grab some fruit and a sandwich just to keep from looking too obvious. Then after Wes goes in the bathroom, I head that way, leaning against the wall beside the bathroom door. I lodge my foot in the door crack just enough to hear voices emerging.

"I think he'd rather have you sitting on his lap than me," Elana says. "He would rather touch anyone but me."

"In a few years, he'll probably feel very different," Wes says, using the complete opposite tone he used with me a minute ago. "Just because Alex doesn't realize how special you are doesn't mean other people don't see it. This is a really big job, if you haven't noticed."

He sounds kind and warm and full of caring thoughts. Like the ultimate manipulator.

"What can I do to make this better?" Wes says.

"Don't tell Kara that I ran off set to cry in the bathroom."

"It'll be our secret. Cry all you want, then turn on that actress charm, put your game face on, and go back out there ready to work, okay?" Wes says.

"What if I still can't do what Graham wants? He's awful."

"I'll tell you what," Wes says. "You figure out how to make that guy happy, and I'll personally accompany you to that Broadway show you want to see. Kara told me about that. You and Alex have been so overbooked lately, not much free time."

"Really? You'll go with me to see *Jersey Boys*," Elana says.

"At this point, I'll do just about anything to keep you two from losing this job, even if that includes show tunes and choreography."

I hear water running and someone walking around, but so far, the steps haven't moved toward the door. I could interrupt, walk in and say I wanted to check on her…

"They should have casted Eve in this campaign," Elana says. "Her and Alex wouldn't have any trouble finding chemistry."

Wes lets out a short laugh. "I think Eve is a long way from a Calvin Klein fragrance campaign. I've sent her on ten different castings, and she hasn't booked anything yet."

What?

Footsteps move closer to the door, so I slide over toward the men's restroom and dive inside. I immediately toss the food that had been hanging limply in my hand into the garbage. I lean over the sink, drawing in a deep breath, trying to process everything.

Eve's modeling again.

And Wes is the one sending her out on castings.

I pull myself together and glance in the mirror, checking my face for signs of distress before exiting the bathroom.

Work. Focus on work. Climb that really big ladder. A ladder Wes has built for me. I can see the back of him now, scanning the studio for me, most likely. I walk up beside him.

"You're welcome," he says when he sees me. "Now please try not to screw this up any more, all right?"

"All right."

He nods like we're okay and he's not pissed at me anymore, but when he starts to leave, something takes over and I can't stop myself. I grab his arm and he turns around to face me.

"Eve's modeling again?"

His eyebrows lift. "You were listening."

"So it's true?"

He shakes his arm from my grip and shrugs. "You tell me, Alex. I thought you knew her so well."

I'm careful to lower my voice. "I told you we broke up. I haven't talked to her since that day in my apartment."

Wes is fiddling with his phone now, like this isn't a conversation that's important enough to warrant his full attention. "I felt bad for her. She's broke, and, let's face it, she was never going to get that scholarship. Evie's always had an issue with thinking realistically. She asked me to help her make some money, and I agreed. She'll never make enough in one semester to pay a year's tuition at Columbia, let alone three years, not if she's still hanging on to that assistant's job. But she's stubborn and won't believe me until she's standing in front of the much cheaper state school, like the rest of us." Wes looks up at me for a second. "Well, maybe not you. You were smart and knew your limits."

"My limits?" I ask, confused.

"You know, college, a different career. I've been telling Eve since she was fifteen to put the books away and make the most of these crucial years before her body isn't worth anything. I've always felt like you understood that."

He's leaving me and heading over to Graham before I can get another word out and I don't think I could anyway. Wes just spouted off my exact plan and philosophy for my life and my career, but it sounded horrible hearing it from someone else. And hearing it applied to Eve and her life.

By the time Elana emerges from the bathroom, my stomach is in knots, mirroring the web of lies and manipulation I'm currently tangled in. It's so big and twisted, I'm not even sure I'll ever find my way out.

"Elana." I reach for her hand, but she pulls it back and turns to me with a huge smile on her face.

"I'm fine now. Sorry about everything."

"All right!" Graham says, clapping his hands together and standing in front of us. He takes a slow deep breath as if counting to ten in his head. Maybe it's some kind of anger management technique. "It's been brought to my attention that perhaps the concept for this shoot needs a little...*epic twist*."

"Epic twist?" Elana and I say together. What the hell does that mean? Is he going to kill us and then pose our dead bodies himself, *Romeo and Juliet* style? I wouldn't put it past this guy.

"I'm thinking something more distant. Like you're reaching for her, trying to lure her back, and there's this barrier between you. It's very *Hunger Games*."

I glance at Elana and then we both speak in unison for the second time. "Sounds perfect."

Chapter 40: Eve

December 20, 1:45 p.m.

"I told you, I'm fine."

Steph has called me every day since leaving New York last week. She's worried about me taking these jobs, losing ten pounds (I've actually lost twelve without even trying thanks to a lengthy bout of pneumonia), and being anywhere near Wes.

"You can stay with my aunt in New Jersey," Steph says for the hundredth time. "I've already asked her. She's totally cool with it."

I'm rushing to get to a casting by two and my phone rang the second I got off the subway. It's freezing, but I can't put on a hat and screw up my hair, so I have to let my ears sting from the cold. "Nobody is in the apartment I'm staying in. It's in a really nice neighborhood, and I can come and go as I please. It's fine, I swear."

"Yeah, but Wes has a key," she protests. "Doesn't he?"

I don't know how to get her to stop worrying. "Yes, I'm sure he has a key, but he's not going to show up and let himself in. He's not like that. It's more about manipulation with Wes, and my guard is up."

"Okay," she concedes. "Call me tonight if you want to talk?"

"Sure, thanks, Steph."

I could have really used her a few years ago.

"And don't forget! Final grades will be online in five minutes," Steph adds before hanging up.

My stomach immediately twists in knots. I think I did okay, but I'm not sure. I need a 3.8 GPA this semester to continue to be eligible for the Mason Scholarship. Long shot or not, I can't help but still want it. And I had a 3.95 at midterm.

When I get to the casting, I have a couple of minutes to rush into the restroom and fix my hair and makeup before giving my name to the casting director. I've done so many of these in the past couple of weeks, I can't even remember what jobs I'm trying to land. Now that I've survived finals, I have more time to be present at the castings and be a little more charming. I'd love to spend some of this extra time helping Janessa with her current job. I can't bring myself to tell her that Eve Castle is modeling again, but I might have to soon.

The second I exit the bathroom and enter the waiting area, I pick up cell reception again. I quickly pull up the student website and scramble to type in my login info. My eyes zip through the first part of the grades listed:

PHOTO 1 (LARSON) A

ART HISTORY (LARSON) A

INDEPENDENT PROJECT (LARSON) A

AMERICAN LITERATURE (ROWLING) A

"Eve."

I glance up from my seat in the waiting area and see Alex standing in front of me. My heart skips a beat and then I'm on my

JULIE CROSS AND MARK PERINI

feet before I realize it, stuffing my phone into my pocket, walking down the hallway and around the corner.

He's followed me, just like I'd hoped. "Hey," I say, faking calm.

"What are you doing here?" He's not trying to hide the surprise from his face or his voice. He's not trying to hide the emotions either, or to look distant and uninterested.

And I know I've got to be the tough one today. For both of us. "Just at a casting for…I don't actually remember what it's for, I've done so many recently."

He's wearing a black leather jacket, gray scarf, and jeans that fit just right. He looks perfect and important and like someone who belongs here. I could never be the reason for taking that from him.

Alex glances briefly down one side of the hall and then the other before leaning in closer. "Are you…are you okay? Elana said you were sick for a long time." He scans up my entire body and then his gaze lands back on my face. I know he can tell I've lost weight but he doesn't bring it up. "I thought the dorms closed. Where are you staying?"

I look right at him and lie. "At Stephanie's aunt's place in New Jersey."

I don't want him to be tempted to come and see me. Though after the last time we talked, I thought he'd be too disgusted to even think about seeing me again. Or hurt. Or both.

"You're staying there for Christmas?" he asks like this is hard to believe. I just shrug and don't give a verbal response, then he adds, "Elana's leaving for France tonight."

"She told me. She seems to be in a better mood lately."

Before they shot the fragrance campaign, I got this weird vibe from Elana's texts and finally broke down and called her. She spilled about her and Alex not getting along and I was so afraid of her not being under his watch that I worked hard to redeem him and told her about his sister, Katie, and how he's protective of her. That seemed to help.

Alex gives me a tiny smile. "She's speaking to me again. That's something. She didn't give me a Christmas card or anything, but she did give me a Prada bag full of makeup for Katie. A sixteen-hundred-dollar Prada bag for a girl she's never met."

Elana's probably been given more than one sixteen-hundred-dollar Prada bag, as hot as she is right now. Model perks. And this conversation is too friendly. It's killing me.

"What about you?" I ask. "Where are you headed for Christmas?" I know the answer but it helps a little to pretend like I don't know him well enough to have this information already.

"Nebraska," he says. "I fly out on the twenty-third."

I nod toward the waiting area. "I should get back in there. They'll probably be calling for me soon. I wouldn't want anyone to see us talking. Wes will be really pissed if we end up with another photo op."

He takes a step back and his face turns completely impassive, like I've just reminded him of everything. "Right."

I move past him and head toward the waiting area, but his voice stops me again.

"Eve, wait."

I turn around and face him. My defenses fall for a few seconds, and I'm hit with the feelings I'd stuffed away these past few weeks. I miss the person I could be with him, the way he looked at me, like I was important and special and interesting just for being me and not Eve Castle. *I miss him*. There, I said it. Or at least I thought it. Now I need to get away from him before I break down and tell him all this. I need my life to stay in order.

"I'm fine, Alex. Just let it go." I watch his face to see any signs of him backing off and when he doesn't, I take one last stab, right in the gut. "You know what? I've already done the secret relationship thing and you know how that turned out. So this—you and me—it was a bad idea from the beginning. I don't know what I was thinking. If I had just…" I cover my face for a second, digging for that last ounce of courage. "If I had just let things end when the CK shoot ended, I wouldn't be here. I'd be on set with Janessa."

His eyes drop to his feet, and he starts buttoning up his jacket, adding a forceful edge to his movements. "That's fine. I get it. You have Wes to figure everything out for you now."

"Just like you," I remind him before spinning around to leave. This time he doesn't stop me.

I only get to sit in the waiting area for about one minute before my fake name, Eve Castle, is being called by the nineteen-year-old intern who is acting as the receptionist.

"Please bring in your portfolio and two comp cards. You can leave your purse and your jacket and everything else out here."

I take off my jacket and put my purse down on the chair I'd been sitting in and follow the intern down the hallway into the casting studio. As she opens the door, all eyes are on me. The familiar scent of judgment fills the air. In my previous modeling years, I'd developed the ability to guess if that judgment had a positive or negative charge to it.

In this case it's the latter.

I do my best to ignore instincts and smile anyway.

"How are you guys? My name is Eve Nowa…Castle." *Shit*. I take a breath and close my eyes for a second. "Eve Castle."

"Hello, Eve *Nowa* Castle." The malicious sarcasm seeps out through her smirk and monotone speech. "If you *could*, could you leave your book with us, take a comp card up with you, and step on the middle line."

"Gary, please take a picture of Miss Castle."

Standing on the line, I notice that the whole panel of people supposedly casting are otherwise engaged with some form of technology—iPhone or laptop. While I'm frowning at the lack of social courtesy, Gary says, "three."

Damn. I totally wasn't ready. I'll have to wow them on the rest of the shots. As the picture comes up on the screen facing the client table, Mrs. Bossy Pants says, "Okay, I think we have everything we need! Thanks."

Seriously? One picture?

As I walk out, no one says anything else, which infuriates me even more. Maybe it's these people setting me off or maybe it's the combination of them and seeing Alex again, but I'm so pissed I can't even think straight and I end up shouting, "THANKS FOR YOUR TIME, EVERYONE!" and slamming the door.

I'm 100 percent sure I won't be booking *that* job.

I give the cold December air a second to cool me off before digging for my phone and looking at the rest of my grades. My heart is still racing from Alex and the casting and my hands shake as I scroll down to view my final grade:

CALCULUS 220 (SIMON) C

FALL SEMESTER GPA: 3.6

My vision blurs from shock and tears. I got a C in calculus…I got a C in calculus…*oh my God*…how did this happen? I know I missed classes when I was sick, and that final was a struggle, but I thought I'd pulled off a B.

That's it. It's over.

I needed a 3.8 to be eligible to win the Mason Scholarship. I'm out of the running. No interview. Nothing. I don't even need to be Janessa's assistant anymore. I mean what's the point? And yeah, I knew it was a long shot, but getting kicked when I'm already down hurts like hell. The GPA had never been my biggest concern. Not even close.

I lift my sleeve to wipe tears from my cheeks before they freeze against my skin. My entire body is hit with pain that has everything to do with failure. I can't keep moving down the busy sidewalk, so I lean against a building, closing my eyes and trying to breathe without breaking into sobs.

I'm not even close to calm when my phone, still clutched in my hand, buzzes. I wipe my eyes again and groan.

"What?" I snap.

"Jesus, Evie," Wes says. "Hello to you too."

I start walking down the sidewalk, clueless as to where I want to go. "If this is about the casting I just finished, can we discuss it later?"

I'm about to hang up on him without hearing his response, but before I can, he says, "Nope, it's about some of the castings you've been on the past few days. You booked two jobs. An editorial and a small catalog, so congrats."

My feet slow down automatically as I process this information. I glance up at the sky for a second. Maybe there *is* some higher being that doesn't get a kick out of watching me drown. And maybe it's only a pinky toe reaching out to pull me up, but it's something.

"I'm not getting a scholarship," I blurt out to Wes. "My GPA isn't high enough, so I'm out."

"I'm sorry," he says. "But honestly, Evie, it was a long shot, right? Stick with what you know you can do and you won't have to deal with that level of disappointment again."

"Yeah, it was a long shot," I admit. "Email me the job details and send me out on whatever castings you've got. I'll take all of them. I'm going to tell Janessa I quit. There's no point in keeping that up, right?"

"No point at all," Wes says. "Schedule's on its way to you."

"Thanks, Wes."

I hang up the phone and realize my life must be complete shit right now if I'm thanking Wes Danes.

Chapter 41: Alex

December 23, 6:30 p.m.

"There's a party tonight at Jenna Phillips's house," Katie says, looking right at my mom from across the table. "It's a pre-holiday thing. Soda and board games and all that."

"I don't know, sweetie." Mom's voice emerges from the dining room where I'm about to enter. "Will her parents be home?"

"I think they'll be right across the street at a different party," Katie says.

Just as I sit down, my dad gives his one-word answer. "No."

An odd and uncomfortable quiet fills the walls of my parents' four-bedroom tri-level home, and it has nothing to do with the tuna casserole topped with crushed potato chips that my mom is famous for.

My dad is seated at the end of our dining-room table, reading the sports page. I'm sure he already read it first thing this morning. I'm also pretty sure my mom hasn't changed her rules of no newspapers at the table, which is why she's busy glaring at my dad. Katie's sulking and is now completely invested in picking the peas out of her casserole and sliding them to the far side of her plate.

My brother Bradley is shoveling food into his mouth and watching Katie make designs with her peas. My oldest brother, Jared, and his girlfriend, Leslie, who I met for the first time today, are busy looking at each other as if silently conversing about how weird my family is.

"Leslie's a vegetarian," Mom says out of the blue, breaking the full four minutes of silence. Everyone, including me, looks up at her. "But she eats fish."

I guess this is supposed to be an explanation for why we're having this meal instead of steak, but tuna casserole has been on my mom's weekly menu since I graduated from Gerber baby food. I don't think she changed anything for Leslie's sake.

"So, Leslie," I say to break the awkward silence. "My mom said you're a teacher?"

"It's my first year teaching. I'm at St. Mary's. Second grade."

"Cool. Where did you go to college?"

The whole family seems to be hanging on to this conversation as a lifeline. I don't know exactly what is up with all the weird silence and everyone behaving themselves, because I got the impression from Mom that Leslie's been around my family enough. She spent Thanksgiving with them. So it must not be her presence that's causing the shift, even though Jared having a girlfriend *is* quite a shocker for me.

"University of Nebraska in Lincoln," she says.

"So, you're a Cornhusker?"

She just smiles and doesn't give another reply, because it isn't really a question. And the conversation has died.

I think I've pissed Jared off or something, because he sets down his fork and looks over at me. Maybe he feels inferior because his girlfriend actually graduated from college and his college career ended with his football career.

"So, Alex," Jared says. "Where's your girlfriend? Emma, right?"

I force down a mouth full of noodles and mushroom soup concoction and then clear my throat. "Elana. And she's in France with her family for Christmas, then she's doing a runway show in Paris after New Year's."

My dad snorts back a laugh and opens his paper to the middle section, completely hiding his face. In the five hours since I arrived home, I've started to get the feeling that my dad thinks I'm gay. And it might be easier to just admit to it then to try to convince him otherwise.

"Aren't you worried about her hooking up with some French dude," Jared says.

My mom moves her glare from Dad to Jared. I don't know if she's glaring because she doesn't want my feelings hurt or because the term "hooking up" isn't on her list of polite dinner conversation words.

"I'm sure she'll be fine. We'll be fine," I add as an afterthought just to keep the hoax alive.

Bradley decides to speak up for the first time tonight. "Does she even speak English or is it all physical—"

Mom slams her fork against her plate. "Bradley!"

Katie starts laughing. I kick her in the shin from under the table. "Yes, it's all physical," I say, rolling my eyes. "Just hours upon hours of making out and sex. Lots of sex, thanks to the giant box of condoms Dad bought me." Dad drops the paper below his eyes and raises an eyebrow. "And despite the language barrier, I have picked up a few French words, but none of them are appropriate for the dinner table."

Leslie's face turns bright red, probably due to her second-grade mind-set. My mom still looks pissed at Brad for starting this whole conversation.

"Oh, come on," Brad says. "Don't tell me all of you weren't dying to ask him that. She was like topless and all over him in those Calvin Klein pictures. And then he was hooking up with that other model, the hot brunette who's sleeping with his agent to get work."

My eyes are probably massive right now. I look from Brad to Katie, and Katie gives me a weary smile and says, "He's on Twitter."

I stare at my older brother in disbelief. Both of my brothers are the polar opposite of me—dark hair, stocky build, just under six feet—and then there's Katie and me, the scrawny blond kids. It's always been us against them, so it's not like I ever expected any amount of acceptance from them, but this is worse. They're embarrassed by me. I can tell. That's why no one is saying anything. That's why the usual texts teasing me about various industry items have stopped these past few weeks.

I pick up my plate and carry it to the kitchen sink. I walk past the table again, muttering, "I'm tired. I think I'm gonna take a nap." Then I head down the basement steps to my old bedroom.

·····

It's nearly eleven at night when I wake up again. I'm starving, because my tuna casserole went half untouched. I walk up the steps and hear Brad and Jared's voices. They're playing cards at the dining room table and drinking Dad's beer. I can also just make out the soft muffled sound of my parents' upstairs bedroom TV telling me they're already in bed, watching the evening news, like always. It's a little weird that Jared is still here and Leslie isn't, considering they have an apartment about ten minutes from here.

"Hey," I mumble as I walk past them, into the kitchen.

"What? No suitcase?" Jared calls from the dining room as I'm pulling random items from the fridge in preparation for making a monster sandwich.

"We figured you'd be tired of us by now," Bradley adds.

"Just getting a snack." I continue to pile cold cuts and cheese onto a slice of bread, topping it with spicy mustard and another piece of bread. I return everything to the fridge and then join them in the dining room, standing against the wall. "Jared, I thought you lived at Leslie's place?"

"Not at the moment." He doesn't look up at me, his eyes on the cards spread across the table. "Her parents are visiting for the holidays. She doesn't want them to know we live together."

"Won't the smell give it away?" Brad says.

Jared half stands up in his chair and reaches across the table and slugs him in the shoulder. "She's fucking Catholic. You know how they are."

They both crack up and relax back into their chairs. Brad glances at me and then back at his cards. "Alex knows all about

270

that. He's waiting for marriage, right? What was that magazine we read that in…*GQ* or maybe it was *US Weekly*?"

I set my sandwich down and grip the back of my dad's chair at the head of the table. "All right, Brad, what do you want to know? Let's just throw it all out there so you can quit getting your information from Twitter."

He tosses a card onto the table and looks over at me. "You don't tell us shit. Where else are we supposed to get information from? I got tired of running into people around here and having them tell me what's going on with my own brother."

My knuckles are white from squeezing the chair so hard. "What do you want to know?" I repeat, emphasizing each word.

He and Jared shake their heads and go back to their game.

"I'm sorry, I didn't realize that it was my responsibility to warn you before any fashion gossip popped up on the Internet," I snap. "I'm sorry that Mrs. Hensley next door saw me on a billboard in underwear before you did."

I'd heard this one from my mom last week. I figured it had come up in a family discussion.

Brad pushes his chair back and lets out a frustrated sigh before turning to Jared. "I'm getting another beer. You want one?"

"No, I'm good."

He's got the top off the new bottle of beer before he responds to me. "I think the underwear was probably the easiest to deal with."

Sarcasm drips from his voice, and I know he's about to really let loose on me. "Have you seen the picture of this Eve Castle chick making out with your agent?" He's flipping through his phone, scrolling through Twitter and then holding up a picture of Eve kissing Wes. I'd read that there was photographic evidence a while back, but I'm relieved to see that Eve's wearing the clothes I recognize from our last rainy run. Wes had said they would be leaving my building together. This was part of his plan to save me. And even though them kissing might have happened more than once, so far I hadn't been given any proof of that.

I have to look away from the picture after only two seconds. It feels like the worst punch in the gut I've ever gotten in my life. How did Eve stand looking at pictures of me and Elana?

Brad is scrolling again, pulling up another photo. "Look at this one. This @fashion_gossip81 chick got another picture of her a few days ago. I think she's hittin' the crack again. She's melting away."

"She had pneumonia, you asswipe!" He's hit a big giant nerve, which doesn't happen too often with me. And before I even realize what I'm doing, my hands are gripping the front of Brad's shirt and I've just slammed his back against the wall. I don't even remember walking across the room.

Brad lifts one eyebrow, reminding me of Dad, and gives me a split second to realize what I've started. I might have acquired a little more muscle power from my hours in the gym these past several months, but I had nothing on either of my brothers.

Shit.

With almost no effort at all, Brad lifts an arm, and his fist makes contact with the side of my face. My grip loosens on his shirt as I stumble backward a few steps. But one hit isn't nearly enough to stifle my anger. Before I can stop myself, I'm diving forward, tackling my brother to the floor. He lands on his back, a loud thud echoing through the entire house.

"Boys! Knock it off!" Dad shouts from upstairs, probably thinking this is just another indoor wrestling match.

Brad and I freeze for a second and the hesitation is enough for me to get a good swing in, hitting his cheekbone just like he hit mine. And he looks pissed. So pissed I can tell he's about to break my nose, but before he gets the chance, Jared, who is twice as strong as Brad, is yanking me to my feet.

"Cut that shit out before Mom comes down here." He shoves me across the dining room, positioning himself between Brad and me. He looks completely calm, like he's already bored with this activity.

Brad scrambles to his feet, straightening his shirt. I'm surprised to see a grin spread across his face. "Little bro's learned how to throw a punch. One that's actually got some force behind it."

Jared rolls his eyes. "Yeah, all those years of beating on him paid off."

Brad shrugs. "I don't know about you, Jare, but I'm quite proud."

I'm rubbing my face. I can't help it. There's already a lump forming on my right cheekbone, and my eye feels puffy. Now that the adrenaline rush is fading, it hurts like hell.

Jared, at twenty-two, seems to be so much more mature than Brad and me, because he ruins the potential for another fistfight by turning to me and saying, "Personally, I don't give a shit if you take a million pictures in banana hammocks or whatever the fuck they're called. I don't care if you want to hook up with a dozen girls. But what pisses me off, and obviously Brad too, is that we know most of that is bullshit, and you don't trust your own brothers with the truth. I'm not talking about Mom or Dad. Hell, I don't tell them my personal shit, but Brad, he knows it all."

I plop down in a chair, running my hands over my eyes. "Trust me, you don't want to know. You're not going to get it. I don't get it half the time."

"Right." Brad takes his seat again, taking a long swig of his beer. "Us small-minded folk don't understand complicated matters."

"That's all right. He doesn't have to tell us anything. Let's just have a nice Christmas together, make Mom happy." Jared has uncapped another bottle of beer. He hands it to me and sits down again, across from Brad. "Wanna play? We can deal you in."

I stare at them for several seconds, trying to figure out what the hell just happened and then I let out a short laugh, shaking my head. "Sure, I'll play."

"Good, it's much better with three," Brad says.

It feels like I'm in an alternate reality right now. If only I could punch a few people in New York and fix all the drama in my life.

"How's it going with Dad?" I ask Jared after a few hands of Texas hold 'em. "Work and all?"

"It's all right." Jared shrugs. "I wish he'd quit being so hard-headed and admit that he can't work the hours he used to. His back is shit right now."

"I thought that surgery helped him?" After throwing out his back a dozen times, my dad finally went to see a doctor last summer who said he needed surgery to repair a ruptured disk.

"It did," Brad says, "But he's not exactly a teenager any-more, and Jared's got everything under control, got the books all squared away and the staff managed. He doesn't need to be on-site lifting shit every day."

Huh. Jared must be doing more of a manager thing then. I don't think my mom ever said anything about that on the phone. I figured he was just getting by, helping out enough to count as an employee. High school football stars like Jared tend to get a lot of things handed to them. Not that he's an asshole or anything, but I've never thought of him as the responsible, manager type.

"Dad's done manual labor all his life." Jared steals a drink of my beer even though he said he didn't want any more. "If he's not working, I don't think he knows what to do with himself."

My dad is not a man of many words. He's quiet and calculat-ing and would rather get his hands into a project as a method of getting to know someone or catching up with his sons than sitting down to a card game and a few beers.

Brad suddenly straightens up in his chair. "I think I heard the TV go off upstairs."

Jared gets up and tiptoes over to the back door that's right behind me. He turns the vertical blinds just enough to get a partial view of the deck my dad built himself. It surrounds our aboveground pool.

I glance back and forth between the two of them. "What? Is there an eclipse that I didn't hear about or something? A new hot neighbor that rakes leaves naked at midnight?"

Brad shuffles the cards and then starts to deal a new hand. "Didn't you hear Katie ask Mom about Jenna Phillips's party?"

"Yeah, but Dad told her no—" I snap my head to look outside. "You think she'll sneak out?"

"I'd bet my Mustang on it," Jared says.

"Jenna Phillips's party." I let out a sigh, hating how old Katie is getting. "I was there last year."

Jenna Phillips is the youngest of three hot, popular sisters in my high school. She's a senior this year, and her older sister, Ally, was a year older than me, and Ruby is the same age as Brad. I was lucky enough to get sandwiched between two of them age-wise and thus had four years of the best high school parties. And the best part was that they only live two blocks away.

But Katie...no way should she be anywhere near one of those drunken, lust-filled celebrations.

Sure enough, after two more hands of cards, a pair of pink and blue Nikes dangle down from the second floor into view.

Brad snorts really loud. "Leave it to our dorky jock sister to wear gym shoes to a party."

I can now see the strap of the Prada bag I gave her in secret earlier today also dangling down. "I bet she's got some tall shoes tucked into that bag."

Both Brad and Jared turn to stare at me, like they can't figure out how I might have guessed that. "I don't keep high heels in a purse, if that's what you're wondering. It's a New York thing. Everybody walks a lot. You swap shoes right before you get where you're going."

"Okay then." Brad shakes his head. "Maybe she's smarter than we thought."

Jared whips out a flashlight. We wait until Katie's feet hit the deck and she's got her back to the door before the three of us get up from our chairs and move toward the sliding glass door. She's already in the grass crunching leaves under her shoes, so she doesn't hear us carefully slipping out into the cold.

The flashlight is clicked on and aimed right at her. Jared whispers loudly into the dark, "Where you headed, little sis?"

Katie turns slowly, revealing her panicked face and her heavy makeup and carefully styled hair. "Just going out for a run. Can't believe cross-country's over already. Don't want to get out of shape."

"Wait...do you hear that?" Brad says dramatically. "I think that's music coming from the Phillips's house. I bet they've got a mean game of Monopoly going on over there. What do you think, Alex?"

I look over at Brad before saying, "I'd put my money on Twister."

Katie folds her arms across her chest, glaring at us. "Fine! Tell Mom and Dad. Go in and tell them right now. I'm going anyway, and I'll deal with the consequences later."

"If we do that, you won't be driving until you're thirty," Jared says. "Consider us catching you, instead of Mom or Dad, a gift." He nods toward the door. "Now get your ass inside."

I look over at Jared and realize he's telling the truth. He'll never tell our parents about Katie sneaking out if she gives up without a fight. I wonder how many secrets he's keeping of mine. If I searched my memories long enough, I could probably find dozens, between him and Brad.

The only problem is, Katie's not budging. I can tell she really wants to go to that party. Hell, I went to that party freshman year, so who am I to say she can't go? Now, I'm looking at Brad, who seems to be reading my mind. I didn't go there alone freshman year. I went with my much cooler senior brother who got crazy drunk but somehow still managed to keep me out of trouble.

Brad looks at Jared. "She'll just try to do it again when we're not here. We can't play dining room patrol officer forever. I don't even like playing cards."

So they planned this stakeout all along. What else had they been doing to keep Katie out of trouble that I didn't know about? I always thought it was me who looked out for her. I guess that's kind of hard to do from across the country.

Jared lets out a breath, obviously conceding. He nods to Brad and says, "Leave a note in case Mom gets up. Just say we went to Benny's for ice cream."

We cross the yard together as Katie removes a pair of black ankle boots from her bag and slides them on. If she ditched the glasses and the braces, she'd actually be on her way to looking like a high school girl. That's a revelation that I hate even more than her going to this party.

Jared stops at the end of the driveway to the Phillips house. "I think I'm gonna wait outside."

"It's fucking cold out here," Brad says. "Come on, free beer and loud music. What's there to think about?"

Jared shrugs. "I'll probably freak those kids out. They'll think I'm someone's dad showing up to bust everyone."

Katie rolls her eyes. "No one is going to think that."

He's still deliberating when Katie bounces toward the door.

Finally Jared sighs and says, "Let me call Leslie first, just so she doesn't hear from someone else that I was hanging out with high school girls." He shudders like the thought is so absurd.

Brad and I leave him alone and enter the party house. We're hit with loud country music the second we open the front door. It's hot as hell in here from the dozens and dozens of bodies bouncing around all over the house.

Brad elbows me in the side, nodding toward the door. "He wants to marry her."

"Who? Leslie?" I can't fathom the idea of any of my siblings getting married.

"Yeah, he's saving up for a ring."

"Maybe he should get his own place first before worrying about jewelry." It slips out before I can stop it. I know right away that I sound like a judgmental prick.

Brad glares at me. "He has a place. He pays more than half of the rent at Leslie's apartment. She needed help with the bills. Her teaching salary isn't much, and she's got a ton of student loans. Jared's not gonna jump into this wedding thing until he knows he can afford it. Leslie's parents are nice and all, but they're broke as hell, and you know Mom and Dad aren't exactly debt free either."

No, I didn't know that, actually. But I can't respond because Jenna and Ally Phillips have just spotted us.

"Oh my God!" Jenna says. "Alex and Bradley Evans at my party."

Ally laughs at her. "Oh, it's your party now?"

"Just keepin' an eye on Baby Evans." Brad points at Katie, who appears to have found some friends to talk to. Two of them are male, which distracts me even more from my conversation with Brad. These guys appear to have the mannerisms of awkward freshmen.

"I always forget that Katie's your sister," Jenna says, looking right at me. "She looks a lot more like you than Bradley though."

Ally hands us each a red Solo cup of beer. "Let's toast to being done with high school, shall we?"

I raise my glass and stop when I see a short blond girl. Lindsey, my ex-girlfriend. Brad's gaze follows mine and he spots her too, across the room. He elbows me in the side again. "Go say hi, break the ice, and get the awkward shit out of the way."

I down my entire cup of beer and get a refill before mustering up the courage to face Lindsey. I can tell by her expression that she'd already spotted me in the last few minutes.

"Hey, Alex," she says. "How's it going?"

I scratch the back of my head, trying to make eye contact. "Good. Just came here with Katie and my brothers. We're doing the chaperone thing."

I look down at my cup, feeling the weight of a big wall between me and this person I used to know very well, maybe better than anyone else. "So how's school?"

She smiles like she knows I'm working hard at this conversation. "It's good. How's New York? I heard you've got yourself a hot French model for a girlfriend."

My pulse speeds up a bit, anticipating more tension, but Lindsey looks amused. "It's kind of crazy right now, so I'm glad to be home for a little while. What about you? Any new boyfriends?"

"Yeah," she says, watching my face carefully. "Simon Wallace."

Okay, I was expecting some college boy *not* from our hometown or our circle of friends from high school, but whatever. I take another drink, finishing off my second cup of beer. "That's cool. Simon's a good guy."

She looks relieved, like maybe she thought my feelings would be hurt. I don't think of Lindsey like that anymore, but I'm not sure when it stopped. Before Eve, would I have felt a twinge of jealousy hearing about Lindsey and Simon? Possibly. *Probably.*

Both of us are quiet now, staring at these two kids making out. They look like freshmen, maybe sophomores.

"It's weird, isn't it?" Lindsay says. "How you can really think you're in love until the next person comes along and then it's like, okay, this is actually love. I'm sure it's the same way for you and Elana."

I keep my eyes on the kids swapping spit and let my mind drift to a couple of years ago when Lindsey and I stood not far from that spot, having our own make-out session. And yeah, there was a time when I thought I loved her, but eventually I started to wonder if maybe I wasn't built for that sort of thing.

Until Eve.

For the first time since Wes interrupted our perfect weekend together, I let myself think about her without the logic and the work stuff getting in the way. I've never in my life been so content to do anything and nothing at all with one person. I can't imagine ever feeling that way with anyone else again. And I've had an entire month to get over her. Do I need another month or will I be stuck like this forever?

Simon Wallace walks through the front door right then, and Lindsey's face perks up. She turns to me and gives me a quick hug. "It was good to see you, Alex."

"Yeah, you too." She walks over to Simon, and he throws a wary glance in my direction, but I smile and wave before turning my back on them and scanning the room for Brad, Jared, or Katie.

Both my brothers come up behind me, offering up more beer. I'm already getting pretty buzzed, but at least the party was close enough for us to walk.

"How'd it go?" Brad asks. "Nobody threw a punch. That's always a good sign."

"So you knew about her and Simon?" I ask him and he nods. "It's no big deal. Simon's cool."

"What about this punk Katie's talking to?" Jared says, pointing to her, not even attempting to be discreet. "Do we know anything about this kid?"

Katie glances in our direction, using her eyes to try and tell us to back off. Brad grabs the back of the shirt of a puny kid who walks past him. "Hey dude, who's that kid over there by the kitchen door?"

Brad turns the kid to face Katie, who looks absolutely mortified.

"The one talking to the blond chick with the black boots?" the kid squeaks out.

"Don't ever refer to her as a blond chick, got it?" Brad says. Jared rolls his eyes. "What's his name?"

"Dave…Dave Mackler," the kid says, turning red in the face.

"And do you know Dave Mackler?" I ask.

Brad releases him and the kid slowly turns to face us. "Uh, yeah, we're sort of friends, but I've never talked to Katie before, I swear."

"Does Little Davie Mackler have any outstanding qualities?" Brad asks.

I think Brad is enjoying this most of all, but I can't say that I'm not getting a kick out of this kid who's about to piss his pants.

"Well, he's in advanced math, and so am I. And he runs cross-country, but he's not as fast as Katie."

"Of course he's not," Jared says. "She's an Evans."

The three of us look over at Dave Mackler, who is extremely skinny but on the tall side for a freshman. His skin is clear, and his clothes are fashionable enough to blend in, but he doesn't reek of popular kid or anything. He doesn't look extremely uncomfortable talking to a girl, but he's not trying to make a move or anything. He's basically me, four years ago. Which honestly isn't too scary of a thought.

"Let's go out back for a while," I say to Jared and Brad. "Katie's fine."

We get more beer before heading out and I can already tell that I'm going to be way more drunk than my brothers due to the size difference. I toss my hat on and button up my jacket when the cold air hits me. Jared got stuck inside talking to Ruby Phillips, so I hit Brad up for more details on our earlier conversation.

"So Mom and Dad have a bunch of debt?" I ask. "Because of the business?"

Brad seats himself on the rail of the deck, looking out at the woods behind the Phillips house. As a kid, I always wished we lived a few blocks over so we could have the woods in our back-yard too. But we had a pool instead. Something you could only use a couple of months out of the year.

"They *had* a bunch of debt," Brad clarifies. "Before Jared stepped in and started doing all Dad's books and snagging him a few bigger commercial contracts."

"Jared did that?" I lean on the railing beside Brad, watching the trees move in front of me as a result of my beer buzz.

Brad glances over his shoulder and then lowers his voice. "If you ever tell Mom or Dad this, I'll come to New York and kick your ass."

"Tell them what?" What could Jared possibly be hiding from my parents that's big enough to get Brad this worked up? Does he have a criminal record or several illegitimate children in other counties?

He lets out a breath, giving one more glance over his shoulder. "Jared never hurt his knee. He didn't even want to quit school. But he only had a partial scholarship, and when he heard Dad was on the verge of losing his business and filing for bankruptcy—"

"How is that possible?" I interrupt. "How could I not have known all this?"

Brad shakes his head. "How could *you* not have known? What about me? I didn't know until last spring, and I was an adult in college two years ago. They should have at least told me, maybe you, but at least me."

"So Jared dropped out to save them money?"

"That and he figured if he worked full time for Dad without pay, he'd help cut down on staff expense." Brad stops for a minute, drinking more beer. "Turns out he's pretty good at the business stuff. He started working sixteen-hour days, taking over the accounting, letting more employees go, getting Dad twice as many contracts. And you know Dad, how good he is with people once he's got the contract. He doesn't go home until it's perfect. Dad always did okay on his own before the recession, but Jared and Dad…I wouldn't be surprised if they start making some good money soon."

"Wow, I had no idea." I don't know what else to say.

"That's because you were a kid. You didn't need to know," Brad says. "I'm pissed as hell they didn't tell me and let me drop out of school. It's not like I had a football scholarship like Jared, not like I was going to college for any reason other than avoiding the grown-up world."

Both of us shut up when the sliding door opens, and Jared emerges and leans against the rail beside me, offering me yet another drink. Yes, I'm getting trashed tonight.

"Little Davie's still got his hands in his pockets," Jared reports.

Brad nods his approval. "Smart boy."

"And I checked both their cups. They're drinking root beer," Jared adds.

I polish off my current drink and move on to the next one, waiting a second before blurting out, "Elana's only fourteen. Wait, she's fifteen now. She just turned fifteen."

My hands are wrapped around the red Solo cup and my eyes are focused on the liquid sloshing around inside, but I can feel their stares.

"Everything I read said she's eighteen," Brad says.

"Well, that's a lie."

"No way." Brad's staring like he's waiting for the punch line. "You're serious?"

"That's illegal," Jared says. "You could get arrested."

"Not true." Brad swings his legs around and leaps down from the railing, leaning beside me rather than sitting on the edge. "The age of consent law in New York states that if there's less than a five-year gap and the minor consents to the sexual act, you'd have an affirmative defense."

I groan. "There's no sexual act—"

"How the hell do you know that?" Jared asks Brad.

"I'm sort of studying for the LSATs," Brad says. "I know I never declared a major, and the *Guide to Taking The LSATs* book is bigger than anything I've ever read in my life, but I took two criminal justice classes this semester, and I really liked them."

"Good for you, man." Jared gives Brad a fist bump. "Sounds like we could use a lawyer in the family with our little brother running around hooking up with foreign underage girls."

"I'm not hooking up with her!" It feels so good to say the truth out loud. "It's just a stupid marketing scheme my agent came up with to pitch us as a couple to Calvin Klein. The relationship is completely fake."

"But you've kissed her. I've seen pictures," Brad points out. "And she's been topless and on top of you."

"Yeah, for the cameras, for work." I let out a frustrated groan. It's so hard to compete against these tabloid stories and ads that look so real. "And she's French. Topless is not a big deal to Elana. Trust me."

"Seriously, Alex, it's kind of lame, isn't it?" Jared says. "How much could this relationship be worth?"

"So far," I say, "about a half a million, and there's a lot more to come depending on how long the fragrance campaign lasts and what we're offered next. I've heard rumors of a Gucci watch campaign."

Brad lets out a low whistle. "Shit. Never mind. I'd fake it with a French teen for that kind of cash. How hard can it be?"

"You really want to know?" I look back and forth between them. "My role is very similar to what we're doing tonight, only worse, because it's just me keeping an eye on her and there're a lot bigger creeps in the fashion industry than at a high school party."

"Wow," Jared says.

I'm on a roll now, not able to stop myself. "And then there's Eve."

"Eve Castle?" Brad asks.

"Yeah." I rub my eyes, ridding them of the blurriness from too much beer. "It's my fault she even has to be Eve Castle again."

·· ◆ ··

December 24, 1:45 a.m.

"I think we should all fly to New York tomorrow and beat this Wes Danes's ass," Brad says after I've finally finished telling them the entire story.

"Eve doesn't seem like the type to get back with him," Jared says. "I bet all that is fake and now I'm doubting the validity of every notable relationship I've learned about from the Internet."

"No kidding," I add.

Brad suppresses a shudder. "I feel like a sick bastard for spending a good ten seconds staring at your fake girlfriend's picture."

"That's exactly the attitude I've had," I admit. "And it got me on Elana's bad side. She thinks I hate her. And we nearly got booted from our fragrance campaign because of a lack of chemistry."

"Can't you just break up with her and tell everyone you're in love with Eve?" Brad suggests.

I never said I'm in love with Eve. Is it that obvious? "Not before Calvin Klein releases those pictures and pays me. They could still pull the job out from under us."

Jared looks at me. "Then you man up, tell everyone the truth, and if that ruins your modeling career, you'll come home to your family—who are a lot more accepting than you think—and you'll figure out what the hell you want to do with your life, just like the rest of us."

"Would you quit working with Dad for Leslie?" I ask him, challenging his advice.

"No, because he's my dad and he needs me," Jared said without pause. "Would I have given up my football scholarship to keep Leslie's life from going to shit, like Eve's has? Yes, absolutely. Not only because I love her, but because that's the honorable thing to do."

"But how does ditching Wes Danes and telling the world he's lied about Elana help Eve pay for school without modeling again and get her out of every tabloid?" Brad says. "How does it actually help anyone?"

"I don't know," Jared says finally. "But if I were you, Alex, I'd look into what made her walk away from all these things you're not willing to give up. Especially if she didn't have our parents and our family to come home to. There's a piece missing from this story."

"What do you mean there's a piece missing?" I ask.

"Think about it," he offers. "A fifteen-year-old in a relationship with someone my age. She needed him. She needed an adult figure in her life. It's sick to think about, but I just don't see the motivation for her to give that up if it was all her decision and not his. You said she disappeared without telling him, right? She gave up a big-money job?"

I'm pretty trashed now, but I hear his words through the fog in my brain, and theories spin through my head. I have trouble thinking of Eve as younger. Since she told me on the phone that day I found out about her and Wes that it was her choice, that he didn't force her or manipulate her into anything, I haven't been able to get past the hurt and jealousy I'd felt in that moment. I haven't allowed myself to think about what motivations she might have had to get into that relationship in the first place. What motivation would any fifteen-year-old girl have in that situation? Wes is controlling in a way that offers a certain amount of security for someone like me and Eve. There's a lot of shit Wes takes care of that I never have to worry about. He makes sure I'm prepared for every casting and every job.

Jared pulls out his cell phone and glances at the time. "It's late. Let's collect our delinquent sister and get home."

In nearly two hours of talking, Dave Mackler has managed to move closer to Katie but still has his hands stuffed in his pockets.

"Amateur," Brad snorts.

"Katherine Marie Evans," Jared says. "Time to go home."

Katie turns to us, looking us up and down. "Are you guys drunk?"

"Yes." I steer her away from Dave, not giving her a chance to say good-bye or exchange phone numbers. She can do that at the next party. Like next December.

"I thought you were here to supervise me, not get trashed," Katie says as we're heading down the street toward home.

"We're gifted," Brad says. "We can do both."

Katie swings her Prada bag in front of me, flashing me a smile. "Do I really get to keep this? It's amazing. But the money I could get selling it on eBay is enough to pay for wakeboarding camp next summer."

"I'll tell you what." I throw an arm around my sister, leaning on her a bit for balance. "You do my taxes this year, and I'll pay for wakeboarding camp."

"Are you serious? I have to ask you again when you're not drunk, don't I?" She sighs but gives me another smile. "That was really nice of Elana to give me the bag, regardless. She seems pretty cool."

"I bet you guys would have a lot in common," Jared says, leaning on Brad and trying not to burst out laughing.

Brad snorts into the cup of beer he filled before leaving the party. "Yeah, like algebra."

I kick Brad in the back of the leg to shut him up.

"Maybe Mom and Dad will let me come to New York soon and I can meet her," Katie says.

"Maybe her nanny can arrange a playdate." Brad is laughing hard now, and I'm left with no choice but to join him.

"So, Davie Mackler, huh?" I say to her.

"Dave, his name is Dave."

"Don't worry, Katie. We know his name," Jared says. "We've already interrogated his friends."

Katie sighs again. "Why can't I be an only child?"

When we get back into the house, our note is untouched, Katie makes it upstairs without having to climb through the window, and Mom and Dad remain completely in the dark about their only daughter's first high school party.

I'm too keyed up to sleep once I'm alone in my bed again, which is why I find myself playing with my phone, staring at "Harvard's" number, until I finally, on impulse, hit call.

Chapter 42: Eve

December 26, 1:20 a.m.

I'm pacing this empty agency apartment, biting my nails. I can't stop. I've been this way for a good hour. Ever since I got off the phone with Elana.

She had called me to ask how my Christmas was, and I could hear the shift in her voice from the last time we talked three weeks ago. She had been very standoffish that day and cut the conversation short. But not today. She was bubbly and excited. I tried to convince myself it's because she's home with her family, but then she said his name.

"*Jersey Boys* was so good, Eve. Have you seen it?"

"No, I haven't," I said. "When did you go?"

"Wes took me last week. Don't tell Alex. He's so weird about that stuff. Anyway, I can't wait to get back to New York now. I want to see every Broadway show one at a time."

Despite the shock and growing weariness, I somehow managed to sputter a reply. "Wes took you to a Broadway show?"

"Yes, he's so much easier to talk to than Kara, especially about jobs," Elana said. "And she's got so much going on. I feel like I'm just a check mark on her daily task list."

At this point, my stomach had started twisting into knots. I should have seen this coming. I should have let myself guess it a long time ago and then stayed the hell out of Elana's life.

Now, I'm pacing and I'm stuck being the only person who's able to read between her words. I need to tell someone else, let it be their burden. Janessa, maybe? But after quitting a few days ago, I'm embarrassed to even run into her, let alone have a serious conversation. Besides, Janessa made it clear at Professor Larson's place on Thanksgiving that she did not want to be inside any circles of secrets.

And I have no proof that this is anything more than Elana crushing on Wes and Wes sucking up to her, taking her places so he can keep her happy and keep the Elana/Alex jobs flowing in.

I stop in front of the couch, staring at the blank TV screen. That's right, I have no proof. No one is going to believe my story from two years ago, which means they won't believe there's anything to worry about with Wes and Elana.

Then I'm off the hook, right?

My other question is what would Alex do if he knew what I know? And that message he left me the other day, I've listened to it so much I've memorized it, *"Hey Eve, sorry to call so late. I just…I just wanted to hear your voice. Call me back whenever. I'm in Nebraska visiting my family so I'm not busy or anything."* He had paused for a good three seconds before adding, *"And I miss you."*

I had almost hung up without hearing that last part. He sounded so genuine. Just hearing his voice reminded me of how safe I'd felt with him.

I dive for my phone, which is lying on the coffee table, and pull up the voice mail to listen to it again and see if I can get my heart to stop pounding and my hands to stop sweating. But instead of listening to Alex's message, I see a text that he sent twenty minutes ago. My mind must have been elsewhere, because I never heard a sound from the phone.

> **CALVIN KLEIN:** I interrogated an agency intern. I know you're staying in Elana's building, I don't know which apartment, but I'm sitting by her door on the eleventh floor.

My heart starts pounding in a completely different way. He's back from Nebraska? Did he come back to see me? Why else would he leave on Christmas Day? And how did he find out where I'm staying? I'm sure Wes didn't tell any interns. I had lied to Alex and told him I'd be at Stephanie's aunt's place in New Jersey.

As I'm going through these questions in my mind, I'm already putting on my flip-flops and heading to the door even though I know I shouldn't. But I just spent Christmas alone and besides, he texted twenty minutes ago. He's probably gone by now.

I'm on the eleventh floor too. I'm surprised Alex couldn't figure that out. But there are a few agency apartments in this building. I only have to step out the door and turn the corner and I see him right away. He's sitting on the floor beside Elana's door with his back resting on the wall, his head hanging a little like maybe he's falling asleep.

I stop before I reach him, wanting to keep some distance between us. He lifts his head and locks eyes with me.

"You didn't call me back," he says, as if that is enough to explain why he's not in Nebraska anymore and why he's here in this build-ing at one thirty in the morning.

I open my mouth to respond, but the door beside Alex flies open and a blond-haired girl wearing glasses, flannel pajamas, and a very pissed-off expression stumbles out.

Finley Belton.

The only nice person from the *Seventeen* shoot. I feel a wave of panic. Elana's in France, and neither Alex or me have any reason to be in this building, considering no one is supposed to know about the key Wes gave me to the agency apartment.

I freeze in my spot. It's too late to hide. She stops in front of the door, her eyes going back and forth between the two of us, Alex on the floor and me standing in the hallway.

"Finley," Alex says, looking up at her. "How's it going? We were just—"

She lifts a hand to stop him. "Save it. I don't want to know." She turns to me. "Since you're secretly occupying Kylie and Preston's place, think you could water that plant in the kitchen? I was sup-posed to do it and I keep forgetting."

"Um, sure," I say, holding my breath. "No problem."

"Am I the only one who's being driven crazy by those loud fucking guys upstairs?" she asks, but it seems rhetorical, so Alex and I both keep our lips sealed. "I swear they're trying to break furniture in half by jumping on it hard enough."

She spins around and heads for the staircase in her PJs and bare feet. "Good to see you guys again, by the way," she calls over her shoulder.

Alex looks up at me. "I had no idea she was here."

Every defense I've been holding on to crumbles right at my feet. I can't convince the logical part of my brain that he shouldn't be near me or the other way around. Truth is, I know he's not Wes. He's in an entirely different universe than Wes.

I watch as he scrambles to his feet, his mouth opening and the words falling out quickly as if they'd been waiting to be used. "I just…I have some things I need to say in person, okay?"

"Not out here." I nod down the hall and Alex follows me and then closes the apartment door behind us.

"Is anyone else here?" he asks.

I shake my head and give him a full thirty seconds to grow more nervous, but he doesn't. He looks really determined, but for what, I don't know. And I don't let him tell me because I'm thinking about that night in his apartment. I'm thinking about the shower and waking up with him the next morning. I close the space between us and press my mouth to his just as he opens it to speak.

He stiffens for a brief second, like I've startled him, and then he's pulling me into his arms, his fingers in my hair. And oh my God, kissing Alex is even better than I remember. There're weeks of intensity built into this kiss, and there's a resolve on Alex's end, one I can feel right away, and it scares me. He's come to some conclusion that's going to shift the world all over again and I don't know if I want to hear it. So I push those thoughts away and let myself escape.

After his coat falls to the floor, I reach for the bottom of his shirt, backing away from him briefly so I can tug it over his head and toss it toward the couch. His hands slide gently under the back of my shirt and I'm so caught up in the feel of it, I don't notice right away that he's stopped kissing me.

"Eve." His voice is somewhat strained as he tries to catch his breath. "We should…we should talk."

I pull away and open my eyes, then rest my hands on his face. "I miss you too. I'm sorry I didn't call you back to tell you that. I listened to your message so many times."

He stares at me for a long time, and I see it again something's changed since I ran into him at that casting. He doesn't look scared anymore. But I am.

I'm petrified of losing what little grip I have on my life at the moment. That doesn't change the fact that I really do miss him and he's right here in front of me. I drop my hands from his face and press my cheek against his chest, squeezing him around the middle.

Alex's arms are tight around me and he whispers into my hair, "If I had known you were by yourself, I would have stayed here."

A few tears gather in the corners of my eyes, so I keep my face pressed against his skin and hidden. Maybe I'm not as unlucky as I thought. *Alex misses me.* Some people don't have anyone to miss them.

He lifts my chin so I'm forced to look at him and, oh my God, the second I see his face, I know he's going to say it. I'm starting to panic because this internal battle has taken shape inside my head. I desperately want to hear it, but I know I can't handle it. My hand is shaking when I lift it to cover his mouth.

"Don't. Please don't say it," I whisper.

I expect him to look hurt. A guy like Alex Evans probably doesn't throw around the "L" word too often, but instead, his eyes get wide for a second, then he peels my hand from his mouth. And just like that, we're kissing again.

Kissing and moving closer to the couch and removing more clothes.

⋯◆⋯

An hour later, we're sprawled out on the living room floor and I'm close to dozing off. The couch pillows are under our heads and the comforter from the bed I'm sleeping in is wrapped around us. Clothes are scattered all over the living room. It's a complete disaster, but I'm too comfortable and too exhausted to clean up right now.

Alex rolls on his side, leaning over me and brushing the hair off my face. "Eve?"

I fight to keep my eyes open but manage to focus on the swirling blur around his black pupils. "Yeah?"

"Do you trust me?"

The question jolts me awake. "Uh-oh."

His forehead wrinkles and he leans in to kiss me quickly on the mouth. "You're already panicking. You don't trust me, do you?"

"It's not that—"

He gives me another kiss and shakes his head. "I understand if you don't. It's okay. I mean why would you? It's my fault we got caught together and that you can't work for Janessa."

Elana must have spilled that piece of information. "But you didn't do it on purpose. It's not like you were trying to mess things up for me."

"I know." He closes his eyes briefly and then opens them again. "But that doesn't mean you aren't going to tread cautiously around me."

"I tread cautiously around everyone, Alex."

"I know that too. And I also know that there's nothing going on between you and Wes. I can't believe I even let my mind go there for a second. Even with the photos, I of all people should know better."

My stomach twists into knots again. Just the mention of Wes makes me think of him and Elana and I should tell Alex. I really should tell him. But that means I'd have to own it. The whole responsibility of knowing something I don't want to know.

And then it occurs to me that I've done the same thing to Alex. I've told him about my scholarship, and now he knows that I've lost that opportunity and that I'm modeling again even though I don't really want to. I've dumped all my shit on him, and he's stuck with the responsibility of helping me, or at least feeling guilty about it.

I never wanted to make Alex feel stuck with me.

I sit up and pull the blanket up under my arms. "Listen, I've just gotten everything in my life to a manageable level, and I really can't rock the boat or be caught in another tabloid scandal—"

"I'm breaking up with Elana," he blurts out, sitting up beside me.

Chapter 43: Alex

Eve is looking at me like I'm crazy. Like she's wondering if really good sex does strange things to my head. And I'm not gonna lie, it does, especially with her. But I've had two days to think about this, and I know it has to be done. I don't have to expose every detail, but I just have to be me again.

"I'm calling Wes tomorrow to tell him, and he's gonna be pissed as hell, but he'll get over it and figure out a solution both of us can live with," I say.

"You'll lose the fragrance campaign," Eve whispers. "They'll reshoot it with someone else."

I nod. "I realize that. I'm willing to take that risk. I'll still get enough jobs and income on my own, and you know Elana won't have any problem absorbing this setback. She's way hotter than me right now."

Eve's just sitting there frozen and panicked.

"And now, if you want," I say, because she's not responding, "you can get away from the rumors about you and Wes. I know plenty of people in the industry if you need to work. I'll help you get hooked up with another agency and another agent, and it would be like a fresh start for you. Bury all those demons."

I know for a fact she hasn't officially signed with Wes or the agency yet. The intern I strategically conned for information told me that, along with unintentionally revealing Eve's location by telling me that Wes requested an extra key for an apartment in this building. I put two and two together after talking to Stephanie and hearing that Eve wasn't at her aunt's place in Jersey. Plus, Eve's only booked two jobs and hasn't even done them yet. No reason to sign anything.

Eve shakes her head, looking royally pissed off. "Don't you get it, Alex? No one else is going to sign me. Wes is doing this out of guilt. He feels sorry for me. I bet he's bribed these people into giving me the two jobs I've managed to get. They probably owe him a favor or he promised them a bigger client in return."

I drop my hand from her face and try to process why she looks so panicked and angry. And then I remember Jared's words from the other day,

If I were you, Alex, I'd look into what made her walk away. There's a piece missing from this story. Think about it? A fifteen-year-old in a relationship with someone my age. She needed him. She needed an adult figure in her life.

Then I think about all the things Wes has said about Eve...*Eve is really messed up...she needed someone to look out for her...she was so insecure it started bleeding into her work...Evie's always had an issue with thinking realistically.*

"Why are you letting him set these limits for you? I don't get it," I say. "It doesn't seem like something you'd do."

Eve scoots away from me. "What are you talking about?"

I reach for her again, but she moves back farther. "**Wes.** I'm talking about Wes. He's making you think no one can help you except him. That without him, you're a hopeless cause."

She jumps up from the floor and starts rifling around for her clothes. Not a good sign.

"Unfortunately, right now, that's probably true," she snaps as she tosses her sweatshirt over her head.

Since I don't want to sit on the floor naked while she's pissed off and fully dressed, I reach for my boxers and slide them on before standing up to retrieve my jeans.

I'm fastening my belt while she's pulling on her sweatpants, her back to me. "If he can't have you, he doesn't want anyone else to have you. He wants you to need him."

She spins around, her face twisted with anger. "Don't fucking psychoanalyze me! You make my life sound like the plot of a Lifetime movie. Yes, a messed-up fifteen-year-old version of me needed someone like Wes, but I'm not that person anymore. I need him for completely different reasons now. He can tell me whatever bullshit he wants to as long he keeps booking jobs for me."

I move closer to her, carefully noting the way she's squeezing her hands into fists. "What are you not telling me, Eve? Why would you give up all of that money and fame to go back to struggling? Did you catch him cheating? Did you love someone else and you couldn't tell him?"

She closes her eyes, letting out a frustrated breath. "Trust me, you don't want to know."

I try to rest my hands on her arms, but she jerks away from me. How did we go from rolling around naked to this distant, don't-touch-me situation? "I do want to know. I really do."

Her eyes fly open, and she looks right at me, resolve filling her expression. "Fine. Just remember that you asked for it."

I hold my breath and wait for her to fill in this big blank that's been hanging over my head ever since Jared brought things to light for me.

"He scared me. He'd get really pissed off and then...and then throw things or sometimes hit me." Her voice is shaking, but she looks sure and confident with the idea of telling me now. "When words weren't enough to bring me down, Wes got physical. I wasn't the compliant, obedient client that you are. I pissed him off, a lot. I screwed up a lot. The more I loved him, the more desperate we got to cling to each other. And I never expected that leaving, my threat to try and get him to go back to being nice again, would ruin my career. I thought he'd fix it like he'd fixed everything before that. But he didn't. And it was too late." She takes a breath and then goes in for one last hit. "And just so you know, Elana is into Wes, really into him. But I don't know if it's been reciprocated or not. I don't know if it's just a crush."

I feel like the wind has been knocked out of me, and instinctively, I back up a couple of steps as if the space will help me think or react or something.

Eve nods expectantly. "That's what I thought. You don't want to deal with this any more than I do. You just want me to get a new agent and for you to break up with Elana and then everything with you and me will be just fine. But the truth is, right now, everything is just fine for you, Alex, and you're an idiot for even thinking about screwing that up."

I open my mouth to protest while Eve sinks into the couch, putting her head in her hands. "I told you the truth, so can you leave now?"

It's not really a question, and her voice is so cold I can't bring myself to move closer again. I pick up my shirt from the floor and throw it over my head and then put on my shoes.

"Eve," I start.

"Just go, Alex!" she snaps.

And then she gets up and locks herself in one of the bedrooms, giving me no choice but to head back to my place. It's probably best that I leave now anyway. It's hard to think about talking to Eve right when I'm filled with two very conflicting, yet completely dominating thoughts: (1) I'm in way over my head, and (2) I need to punch someone, and Wes Danes is at the top of my list.

On the walk home, I call Brad even though it's the middle of the night. I don't know what else to do with this bomb that Eve has dropped on me.

It takes a few tries to get him to answer, and I'm already rounding the final block, almost at my place, by the time his groggy voice interrupts the rings.

"Okay, shithead, you better be in jail and needing bail or on your deathbed to call me at this hour," Brad says.

"I'm contemplating murder and need you to talk me out of it or into it. I'm not sure which."

"I'm listening."

I enter my building and head for the stairs up to my apartment, checking Jason and Landon's empty rooms before locking myself into mine. I take my time giving Brad all the details I've recently acquired, and he surprises me by taking the logical route, which seems to be more of Jared's approach lately. I think subconsciously, I chose to call Brad over Jared because I didn't feel like being rational.

"So what are you planning on doing?" Brad says. "Showing up at Wes's place and beating the shit out of him for hitting Eve two years ago?"

"Sounds like a plan to me."

"Sounds like a good way to go to jail, ruin your life, and in the process leave Wes alone with Eve *and* Elana," Brad says. "And let me help cancel out some of your other predictable options in advance. Like telling someone what Eve told you with the hope of getting Wes arrested?"

"That's reasonable, right?" I'm not able to think even a little bit clearly at the moment so I'm relying 100 percent on my brother, who has been known to read summaries of SparkNotes instead of reading the entire SparkNotes or actually reading a required book.

"This is how it will go down, Alex. You'll tell Wes's boss or someone above him and then they'll ask Eve if it's true. She'll say no, because she's trying to make money and she's trying to get the drama out of her life. In reality, there was no risk in her telling you the truth." He pauses, giving me a second to catch up. "The only reason she didn't tell you everything already is probably for her own pride. Girls who have been through what Eve has tend to blame themselves and they tend to be ashamed of it and think it makes them look weak or stupid or not worthy of someone who wouldn't hurt them."

I can't get past the fact that he hit her. He hit her and he needs to pay for that, but I get what Brad is saying about Eve finally telling me the truth. She had a clear objective. "She's trying to push me away. That's why she told me."

"Yeah, she was banking on the truth being way too much for you to handle," he says. "Even if Wes isn't going to hit her ever again, he's got her wrapped around this manipulative cycle of verbal and mental abuse, giving her just enough of what she needs to keep her around."

"So what now? I can't pretend she didn't tell me what she told me."

He lets out a long sigh. "I hate to say it, but there's not much you can do at the moment. Eve is an adult. It's up to her to decide if she wants to speak up. Elana, on the other hand, is not an adult, but she's in France right now, and Wes is in New York, correct?"

"Yeah." I rub my temple with my free hand and close my eyes, trying to calm myself. I hate doing nothing. I think it's the hardest plan for me to follow.

"Do what you had planned already," Brad says. "Tell Wes you want to break up with Elana and ditch that fake relationship. Wes isn't her agent, so maybe he won't have any reason to be around her anymore. And as far as Eve goes, she just needs to know that you're there for her. What exactly happened tonight, by the way? You guys didn't…"

My very long moment of silence answers Brad's question.

"Oh man, Alex. Bad idea. Very bad."

"I know," I groan. "That's not why I went over there. I tried to talk first..."

"Believe me, I get it. It's just that her and Wes, it sounds like it was all drama and sex and fighting, right?" he says.

"Right." I blow out a frustrated breath. "And I just gave her a very similar memory with me. Sex, drama, and fighting. God, I suck at this."

"I don't blame you, little bro. She's hot," Brad says, and I let out a short laugh. "But don't sell Eve short. She left him once when she was in a much worse place. She's stronger than you think. And if I were you, I'd have that conversation with Wes about the breakup over the phone. If you show up at his office in a few hours, I doubt you'll be able to exhibit any amount of self-control."

"Right. Good call." I flop back onto my back, staring up at the ceiling. "How do you know all this stuff?"

"Psych 302," he says right away. "And the two criminal justice courses I took this fall. Look, common sense is something you don't have right now, because you're way too emotionally invested, which is why you need to take it slow. Don't do anything crazy."

"Were Mom and Dad upset that I left early?" I need a change of topics before my head explodes, and Eve's radio silence is what drove me to come back to New York before New Year's, when I had originally planned to return.

"Nah, they're cool with it."

"Oh come on, don't bullshit me. I left before Christmas dinner. Mom's obsessed with Christmas dinner."

"Jared told them about Elana and Eve," Brad says. "They needed to know, and you can be pissed off if you want, but it was stupid not to tell them."

I should be furious, but after everything that happened at home the past few days, I trust Jared. "How'd they take it?"

Brad cracks up. "I think Dad's secretly relieved that you're not gay."

This gets me to laugh again. I totally called that one. "And Katie?"

"She knew something was up when you left early, but Jared just told her not to believe everything she reads online."

"Thanks, Brad, seriously. I think I was on the verge of doing something really stupid."

"And don't get me wrong," Brad adds. "I didn't say you shouldn't ever consider killing that fucker. Just say the word, and Jared and I will be there to back you up. You gotta plan that shit, you know? Cover your tracks, remove the foren- sic evidence…"

Now *that* sounds like my brother. "I'll keep that in mind."

After I get off the phone with Brad, I take a quick shower, reluctantly washing off the scent of Eve still lingering on my skin— her fruity lotion, her Chapstick. It felt so good to be that close to her again, but Brad's right. It was a bad idea. I need to prove to her that I'm not Wes Danes. That I'm here in whatever form she wants me to be.

Before I fall asleep, I set my alarm to wake me up in a couple of hours so that I can get this damn breakup over with as soon as possible.

Chapter 44: Eve

December 26, 8:30 a.m.

I'm tapping my fingers on the cold surface of the desk. My legs are shaking and my eyes are glued to the open door, waiting for Wes to appear. It's exactly eight thirty and he's never late. Ever.

I don't know what Alex did after he left last night. I hope he was too shocked and too disappointed and overwhelmed to do anything. But the way he looked at me last night, like he was willing to take this big giant leap regardless of the consequences, makes me think a confrontation is possible. As in he might have shown up at Wes's place at three in the morning to... to what? I don't really know.

Before my cell phone turns to eight thirty-one, I spot Wes coming down the hall, his peacoat and scarf perfectly in place, dress shoes shiny, and dark jeans carefully broken in. He grins when he sees me, showing no signs of having had an intense middle-of-the-night visit from Alex Evans. I hold my breath as he sets his leather bag on the desk and takes the seat across from me. I've already gotten coffee for both of us from the shop down the street.

He lifts his cup and takes a sip. "Thanks, Evie."

"So I just wanted to say"—I take a deep breath, forcing out

the anxious and desperate vibe from my voice—"I wanted to say thanks for everything you've done for me so far."

He meets my gaze intently. He slowly removes a folder from his briefcase, spreading several photos out across the table. "These are your new portfolio pictures. I'd say they turned out pretty amazing."

My gaze travels from Wes to the pictures lying on the table. Wes arranged this shoot, and I haven't even signed with the agency yet. He probably paid for it out of his own pocket, which is why all the pictures are natural, no wild clothes or extravagant hair and makeup.

My face looks hollow and my arms way too skinny. I can't believe I've become this. I mean, the pictures are amazing, don't get me wrong, but knowing what it took to get me to look that thin, I feel like the world's biggest sellout. I know for a fact there are plenty of female models who can eat normally and still look like that on their own, but I've had to take extreme measures to fit this mold, and my immune system is shot. I'm weak and fatigued. I'm not exercising as much as I used to for fear of the muscle showing too much.

"I sent these out to some of my contacts," Wes says. "An editor at *Cosmo* said you look amazing and she loved the concept, having you look natural and stripped bare, like a fresh start."

"Right," I say bitterly. "After my time in the crack den and then rehab."

"Everyone loves a good comeback story." Wes shrugs. "Having said that, I've confirmed a gig with *Cosmo* and a few other jobs, but first—"

"I need to sign with the agency," I say, relieved that we are getting to this today like I'd hoped. The money has got to start coming in soon if I want to have enough to cover next year's tuition. Maybe I can work like crazy this summer too, when I won't have classes. *And won't be in Paris*, I can't help thinking. I wanted that scholarship as much for the educational opportunity this summer as I did for the tuition money.

I spend nearly an hour down the hall with an intern, filling out paperwork before I'm allowed to return to Wes's office. I peek in his door to make sure he's not in another meeting before sitting across from him again. "So, *Cosmo*, huh?"

He nods. "Yes. It's a very grown-up job. Think you can handle it?"

"I'll be fine."

"Good. In that case, you're all set."

Wes retrieves my coat from the back of his office door and holds it out for me to put my arms through. When I do, he turns me around and we're practically nose to nose. My heart is already speeding up. His eyes are so intense and full of emotion. I search my thoughts for something to say that will lead to my polite departure.

"Thanks again, Wes," I mumble. "I really appreciate you helping with the photos and all."

He sucks in a breath. "As much as it goes against my nature to admit this," he says, "there's not much that I wouldn't do for you, Evie. Sometimes I wish that weren't true."

Sometimes I wish I could 100 percent stop loving you.

I close my eyes and think about Alex last night, what he almost said to me. I had to stop him because those words are so powerful in a way that's scary and dangerous, and I knew if he'd said it, I would have lost all my resolve to take the logical path.

"You and Alex," Wes says finally. "It's over, right?"

A huge pain moves through my chest and stomach as I force myself to say the words out loud. "Yeah. It's over." I ended it by screaming at him to leave. The scene was so familiar to me in a way that made it easy to get rid of him. Now, I'm struggling with the aftermath.

Wes's hands are on my arms and he leans forward, barely pressing his mouth to mine. He pulls away before I can stop him or even process it, but tears spring to my eyes anyway.

This isn't the man I want close to me. For the longest time, especially in the six great weeks I had with Alex, I think secretly I thought that guys like Alex—boyish, fun, and never too serious—would be the only ones I'd ever be brave enough to date after being with Wes, a very self-reliant man. But last night, when Alex showed up, looking like he'd spent forever coming up with a plan and a solution and the certainty on his face, in his words—he was a man.

And I'm afraid of that particular man for completely different reasons.

Wes releases me and steps back, his eyes moving up and down my body. "Someone like him could never be right for you, Evie. You need a strong guy who can handle your ups and downs, be straight with you. He's lost without an adviser, and sometimes you are too. It would have never worked."

I bite back the words and the tears, reminding myself that I need to be on Wes's good side. "Probably not."

Wes opens the door for me and tells me to call him if I want to get together or talk. I walk away as quickly as possible, not able to breathe until I'm hit with the late December air.

Truth is, Wes is probably right about one thing. Alex and I wouldn't have worked. Alex deserves stability and sanity and someone who will allow him to take that leap of faith and say *I love you*. Somewhere there's a girl who's about to give up on the idea of love. Maybe she's been burned a few times, or maybe she's intelligent and can't seem to meet any guys who can hold a decent conversation. She's okay with who she is but somewhat unconvinced that there's a soul mate for her. And just when she's decided being single is perfectly fine, she'll be on the subway or in Starbucks getting a latte on a Sunday morning when she has time to actually notice the world around her and Alex Evans will pick up the wallet or cell phone she drops and hand it to her. Their eyes will meet; he'll look familiar to her, so she'll say, "Where do I know you from?"

And he'll give her one of his classic sheepish grins and say, "Probably that big billboard in Times Square, the guy wearing the…uh…half-pair of neon micro-polka-dot underwear." And after a reveal like that, who wouldn't want to ask this guy some more questions and then maybe sit down at a table and talk about climbing walls and running 5K races, because after all, it is Sunday and she doesn't have anything better to do and neither does he. At first she'll expect shallowness but be both surprised and intrigued by Alex's self-deprecating humor and under-the-surface humility. And then the carefully concealed intelligence will emerge on Alex's end when she mentions her art history class. Alex will describe seeing the painting up close in Paris last summer. He'll crack a joke about how it looks like children got into their mother's makeup, but she won't be fooled. She'll see that he saw more to it than that but doesn't feel the need to show off. The rest is just a beautiful success story to be told many, many times over at friends' houses, and possibly their wedding.

Alex Evans deserves nothing less than a perfect moment like that. With my million pounds of baggage, I can't give him that.

Chapter 45: Alex

December 26, 10:30 a.m.

I dive for the phone the second I hear the first notes of my ringtone. I've been waiting for what seemed like forever for Wes to return my call. I block out everything I've learned in the past twelve hours and focus on the goal at hand.

"I need to break up with Elana," I blurt out after the short greetings are finished.

"You need to break up with Elana," he repeats, calm and slow.

"Yes."

There's a long pause, and then he says, "Okay. I'll take care of it."

My brain is rushing to catch up. "Okay?"

"That's what I said, Alex." I hear him sigh. "I've been biding my time, coming up with the best plan, ever since the fragrance shoot when it was obvious your chemistry had started going downhill."

"So, I'm out of that job, right? They'll reshoot with a new model?"

"I doubt it."

Wait, what? "Then why couldn't we break up sooner?" I'm

pissed now and trying to get a grip on my anger, afraid all the other stuff I shoved down will quickly resurface.

"A breakup story is a lot easier to digest and accept than a fake relationship story," Wes says, almost sounding bored with this conversation. I'm practically having heart palpitations. "You needed to put the weeks in first. That's just common sense. And then if you appear perfect and happy for too long, people start making assumptions that maybe it's manufactured. Besides, doesn't everyone fall in love with their first costar? And it lasts until the box office buzz dies down."

"So we're breaking up?" I repeat just to be clear.

"I'll have the story to the press by this afternoon. Check tomorrow morning's tabloids."

"Great." Since I'm afraid to move on to other topics with Wes, I hang up quickly and grab the first thing in my reach (a tennis shoe) and wing it at the back of my bedroom door, pretending the door is Wes.

"Dude? What the hell?" Landon, one of my roommates, shouts from the other side.

I let out a breath, trying to slow my pulse as I open the door, deciding to let the story break right here, right now. "Sorry, I just got dumped."

Landon's carting a bowl of cereal, his mouth half full, but he gives me a sympathetic look and says, "Sorry, man, that sucks," before walking to his room. We don't do the roommate thing like Eve and Stephanie.

Eve.

I want to call her so bad, but I know without a doubt it's crucial

I stay far away from her right now so no one has the opportunity to jump to conclusions about Eve being the reason I spilt with Elana. If there was ever a best time to exhibit a high level of self-control and avoid any and all contact with Eve Nowakowski, it would be right now. I can't screw up what little she's managed to scrounge together of her life.

Right now, I need to think of something proactive to do. I need to keep my distance from Wes (so I don't kill him), and from Eve (so I don't screw up her life even more) and all I want to do is find a way to get through to her.

There's a copy of *Seventeen* magazine in the stack of mail on my desk and just seeing the cover reminds me of something and then I'm diving for my laptop, whipping it open, and stretching out on my stomach across the bed. Action via computer isn't much better than action via phone, but there's something I need to see.

The first time I Googled Eve Castle, at the *Seventeen* shoot ironically, I remember seeing one search result that wasn't about her abrupt departure from modeling. It had been a "before" story for *Seventeen*.

It takes me no time at all to find the same search result and luckily the interview has been archived and is online.

A ONE-ON-ONE WITH TEEN MODEL SENSATION EVE CASTLE

…She's only fifteen years old but already she's managed to snag the attention of designers like Prada, Calvin Klein,

Ralph Lauren…Seventeen *editor Jillian Martin sat down to talk to the young star about how she got started and what she's experienced so far in the world of fashion…Jillian even talked her into sharing some of her photos from her summer in Europe and* Seventeen *was so impressed we've included them in this issue along with Eve Castle's candid and enlightening responses.*

JM: *So what's it like to be Eve Castle? Are you a normal fifteen-year-old? Or is that just what you're supposed to say?*
EC: *That's exactly what I was told to say. You've got that right. Unfortunately, I've never really been normal so now's probably not the time to start.*
JM: *What do you mean, you haven't been normal? You were an outsider?*
EC: *I guess you could call it that…I was too tall to be the girl all the boys liked, too skinny to fit into the latest Aeropostale jeans, not that I could afford them…a little too smart to be cool…and my teeth were crooked but braces were too expensive.*
JM: *Your teeth? Really? They look fine to me.*
EC: *That's because I did the Invisalign thing at the recommendation of the agency that signed me at the open calls in Chicago. They covered it upfront and then took it out of my early checks in installments. My teeth were pretty bad. I had a huge overbite.*
JM: *Well, you could have kept it a secret and we'd never have known. Why the open reveal?*

EC: *I didn't sign a contract saying I'd keep it quiet, so I'm not violating anything, but I've seen so many blog comments about me with girls going on about how perfect I am and how they'll never make it as a model because they aren't perfect. Well...I'm not either. I spent years not smiling because I was so self-conscious about my teeth, and add that to me almost never wanting to stand up straight and reveal my full height and you've got a pretty awkward girl.*

JM: *I think many of our young readers will probably throw a party after hearing that you aren't perfect. Kudos to you for admitting it. What do you hope to gain from modeling? What have you gained so far?*

EC: *Until I went to Chicago, I'd never been out of Indiana... actually, I'd been to Kentucky a few times...and Central Illinois. But in the last year or so, I've been to New York City, obviously...also Brazil, Mexico, Canada, Florida, France, Italy, England...I studied in Europe all summer taking language immersion classes. My French is now fluent. I took art courses and photography, not to mention learning about all the cultures. I've met dozens of famous designers and eaten some amazing food all over the world...and wine. I got to drink all the wine I wanted in Europe and it's completely legal.*

JM: *That's incredible, and you've acquired quite a résumé thus far. Are you worried about it ending someday? Being the outcast once again? It's a pretty unforgiving and relentlessly critical industry.*

EC: *I think everyone is using everyone in the fashion world.*

It's not personal, it's business, right? You have to be able to handle that. My goal is to book the best jobs I can, get as much money saved up as possible, travel at every opportunity I'm given, and keep up with my school work so that I can get into a good college.

JM: *College, huh? So that will be the end of the road for you?*

EC: *Or the beginning, depends on how you look at it. And I'm not sure if I'll keep working while I'm in college. That depends on where I get in and whether I'm over the hill yet.*

JM: *I heard a rumor that you've already taken your SATs and got a pretty good score...2100, I believe? That's in the 90th percentile, or at least that's what my research revealed.*

EC: *I did. And I'm going to take them again soon, study some more, and try to do a little better, maybe the 95th percentile.*

JM: *What advice would you offer to young girls wanting to follow in your footsteps? Maybe wanting to reap the travel and educational benefits as you have?*

EC: *Honestly, if you're not even out of high school yet and if you have a good family and a happy enough home, I'd say find another way to travel the world and learn things. One of the reasons I can handle the criticism of the industry and the diets and the body image issues is because I've never really gotten to be a child. I came already prepared for the brutal adult world. If you come into this expecting to be treated differently because you're only fourteen or fifteen, then you're going to get eaten alive. And I think it's a bunch of crap when people call it child abuse. We all get fair and equal treatment in this industry, and by that I mean we're all treated like models. Regardless of age.*

So if you aren't ready to be treated like a model, if you're okay with being a kid for a little while longer, then that's exactly what you should do.

I can't believe she spoke so candidly at fifteen. I bet Wes had a complete shit fit. I would never have the balls to say some of the stuff she admitted. I'd have gone with the standard media answers.

And this article, this is Eve Nowakowski, the Eve I know. Everything Wes has said about her contradicts the person in this interview and maybe she needs to remember. Maybe that's one thing I can do to help Eve.

So I place an order for two copies of this issue and then I send one to Eve's dorm address and one to Elana, because I have a feeling that this might have been the story that made Elana an early Eve Castle fan.

Chapter 46: Eve

January 10, 10:30 a.m.

I've been staring at the magazine I pulled from the mailbox Stephanie and I share for so long I'm about to be late for Larson's class. I only have one course with him this semester and today's the first day.

Alex sent me the issue of *Seventeen* with me on the cover. Technically, it doesn't say anywhere that it's from him, but I know it is. I haven't heard so much as a peep out of Alex since he left the agency apartment on Christmas night. I still can't believe he went through with the breakup with Elana. I wonder how Wes took it? I wonder if Alex is doing okay with work and everything.

Steph did all the online patrolling for me again when the story broke, and no one could get a single comment out of Alex, like he went into hiding or something. Maybe he went back to Nebraska? It's not like he'd call me up to tell me if he did. Not after what I told him and how I reacted to his reaction.

When I get to Professor Larson's class, I slide into the back, wary because I was two minutes late and I dreaded his reaction to seeing me, knowing I failed him completely after everything he did. I spend the first half of the class flipping through the issue of *Seventeen* Alex sent me and rereading the interview I did years ago. I really liked that editor. I felt like she got me and she talked to me like an adult, not the model kind of adult, but the kind with goals and a future and possibilities that had nothing to do with fashion.

After class, I've already decided to man up and face the music with Larson, but he starts walking toward my desk, a huge grin on his face.

"Miss Nowakowski, how was your break? I assume you're all set and totally prepared for your interview in two days?"

My mouth falls open. He doesn't know. And now I get to relive it all over again. "I thought you would have heard by now," I sputter, keeping my eyes on my notebook. "I quit working for Janessa. I didn't get the GPA for first semester, and I'm not eligible for the Mason Scholarship anymore…I wasn't even planning on going to the interview."

Professor Larson's forehead wrinkles. "I see. Well, I can't say I'm not disappointed, but there's always next year."

Disappointing Professor Larson after all he's done for me is probably worse than the feeling I got after seeing the C in calc last month.

Chapter 47: Alex

January 11, 2:00 p.m.

"That's what I'm wearing?" I say to the wardrobe guy.

He looks worried and glances at the article of clothing dangling on the hanger and then back at me. "Is that a problem?"

I laugh. "Just plain old, blue-and-white-striped boxers? No, not a problem at all. In fact, I think I love *Cosmo*."

The guy smiles and shrugs. "Well, it's not a high-fashion piece. We just want you to look like you could be someone's boyfriend or husband. A better-looking version, of course, but still accessible."

Accessible. I can live with that. So far, since the breakup story broke, work has remained steady, though I'm doing smaller jobs, and I doubt Wes is turning anything down, but still, I haven't had any time to add more work to my schedule. It's booked and I'm making money.

Once I'm dressed in my very comfortable (and roomy) boxers, I head over to hair and makeup and immediately spot Eve.

Eve Castle is shooting *Cosmo* today. Had I read the full call sheet beyond the basic info at the time, I might have known that.

But I'm pretty sure I was a last minute add-in, because I just got the details this morning and had to haul ass to get here on time.

I want to walk over and talk to her. She's spotted me. I know she has, but she's trying to look unaffected. I'm staring at Eve across the room in her lacy black bra and panties, when some-one plops down beside me.

"Hey man…didn't know you were going to be here."

Jason, my other roommate, and his girlfriend are seated next to me, taking their turn with hair and makeup. "Oh hey, yeah, this was kind of last minute I guess…"

"You must be the youngest dude here," he says, glanc-ing around.

There are ten models at this shoot, and almost everyone looks like they're in their twenties or thirties. And *Cosmo* usually uses couples for the bedroom shoots, which is obviously what we're doing today given all the underwear and the big bed in the middle of the studio. However, at least two of us aren't a couple. I know that for a fact.

Just when I can't sit still a second longer, the photographer grabs Eve and some dude who looks about thirty and I'm forced to stand there and watch this guy put his hands all over her. And then instead of giving verbal directions, the photographer dude keeps stepping in and finding a million excuses to put his hands all over Eve and physically move her around.

I squeeze my eyes shut, taking lots of slow deep breaths until I can stop myself from wanting to punch someone. That violent rage seems to be happening to me a lot lately, and I'm not sure why. Maybe I need anger management classes or something.

"What are you doing here?"

I open my eyes and see Eve standing in front of me, leaning close. "Working, like you."

Her hair is falling in her eyes, so I reach over and move it out of the way. I can't help it and this whole accidentally working together feels like a temporary free pass to be close to Eve.

"So you and Elana, you really did it, huh?" she says, lowering her voice.

"I told you I was going to." My fingers land on her hip, and I find myself tugging her closer, keeping our conversation as private as possible.

"I thought you left and went back to Nebraska," Eve whispers.

"I was giving you space. I just don't want—"

Her eyes lift up to meet mine. "Yeah, I know."

"You two!" the photographer shouts. Eve and I both jump and then turn around to see him pointing at us. Then he turns to the assistant and says, "Cute, right?"

The assistant stares at us too. "Very middle America, friendly neighbors, high school sweethearts. It should work."

The assistant waves us over and calls the hair girl over, and she starts messing with Eve's hair. Then a wardrobe person puts a long-sleeved, men's dress shirt on Eve, leaving it unbuttoned. And instead of the bed, we get to sit on the long brown leather couch. Actually, we're lying on it, stretched out with our limbs tangled together.

Eve and I are left alone for a minute while lights and cameras are adjusted. I wiggle around to move my arm, which is smashed under both of us and starting to turn numb. Finally, my hand is free and I rest it on Eve's upper arm. "How are you? I mean with school and everything?"

She looks up at me and there are so many words stuck in her expression but she just says, "Good."

I lean in and touch my forehead to hers. "I miss you."

Her eyes widen like she had expected me to play it cool, but I'm kind of done with that.

The photographer stands above and says, "This is a foreplay story. Just do whatever you want."

Foreplay. That explains the shirt and the couch.

Eve lowers her head and at first I think she's getting started on the current job at hand by kissing my neck, but instead she whispers, "I miss you too."

My gaze locks with hers again and then I'm kissing her. My hand slides inside her shirt, tugging her closer. The rest of the shoot becomes the easiest work I've ever done in my entire life.

After we finish our couch make-out scene, Eve and I stand together watching my roommate Jason get tied to the metal bedposts by his girlfriend, who's using two designer neckties to do the job. She has trouble keeping a straight face and it takes a while to shoot.

The whole time we're waiting to be done, I'm racking my brain for a plan. I've given the Elana breakup a couple of weeks to cool down and become old news. I've thought about Eve and Wes from a million different angles, and I know that she doesn't see the same level of severity in that relationship that I see. And I know that getting her to be with me outside of this photo shoot is going to require getting her to see things the way I see them.

But what can I say that will be even remotely enlightening to someone as smart as Eve?

By the time we're all dressed and ready to go, I've made my decision. *Screw the tabloids, screw Wes Danes.* I catch Eve before she gets into the elevator, grabbing her by the hand and pulling her into an empty office.

Chapter 48: Eve

When Alex yanks me into the empty office, I'm positive that we're about to finish our make-out session, and even though everything is complicated as hell right now, I can't say I'm not happy with this idea.

Except he doesn't kiss me or even touch me at all. He's got that serious, grown-up face again, and I back away from him, taking a seat on the edge of an old wooden desk.

"We need to talk," he says right away. "And if you ask me to leave you alone this time, I'm not going to, just so you know."

"Is this about Elana?" My heart is already pounding. I've been worried about her. She was insanely happy on the phone on Christmas and then I've hardly heard from her.

"It's not about Elana, not yet anyway." Alex pauses for a second, taking a deep breath. He looks nervous. "I've been thinking about everything you told me, about you and Wes. And Eve, the more I think about it, the more I know that we need to get him fired."

I suck in a breath. I can't help my shocked reaction, but playing it cool would have been my first choice. "Look, Alex—"

"He needs to be out of your life and out of Elana's," he says.

I close my eyes, drawing in a cleansing breath before opening them again. "Wes is not in my life. He's just my agent. It's not like before."

Alex shakes his head. "Doesn't matter. He's about five steps away from being in the exact same place he was with you two years ago. You just can't see it like I can. It isn't only about him hitting you or about you guys being together like you were. It's about possessiveness. He's controlling and manipulating you."

"If you're jealous or worried about me getting back with Wes," I say, "you seriously don't have anything to worry about. It's not happening. We were a mess together, and yeah, sometimes it's hard getting rid of that part of me that used to be in love with him, but I know it wasn't good and I don't want that again."

I hope that helps clarify things enough for him, because the last thing I want is for Alex to think I'd choose Wes over him. Right now, I'm choosing no one. Obviously the having a boyfriend thing isn't one of my strengths.

Alex's breathing changes, and I can see he's angry or frustrated, but I just feel exhausted and don't know how else to ease his mind.

"This isn't about us," he says finally.

"Is it about guilt? You feel guilty for everything that happened since that day Wes found us in your apartment? It's not your responsibility to fix this, if that's what you think."

"It's not about guilt!" He steps closer. "It's about love. I love you. There. I said it. And there's nothing I can do to change that now. So if you think I'm capable of sitting around watching all this shit happen to you, then, well…then you're wrong."

My heart thuds twice as fast now and tears build up in the

corners of my eyes, but I'm not letting them fall. Not even one. And I can't open my mouth to say anything because my voice will come out all shaky.

Alex scrubs his hands over his face and then drops them, looking completely defeated. "I didn't want to play that card. I told myself I wasn't going to."

I sit there frozen, waiting for Alex to say whatever else he needs to say. All I can do is keep repeating those words over and over in my head...*Alex loves me*...and trying to wrap my brain around this concept.

"Wes should be in jail," he says. "He was twenty-four and he slept with a fifteen-year-old. Can't you see the wrong in that?"

I sigh. "Yeah, it's technically illegal, but I wanted him to, he didn't force me. It wasn't his idea. Things aren't always the way they are on paper."

Alex throws his hands up in the air. "It was his job to stop you! He should have gotten away. He should have told someone and then reassigned you to a new agent. He shouldn't have reciprocated any of your feelings."

"Great. Thanks, Alex." I roll my eyes. "I really needed a reminder of what a crazy seductive fuckup I was a few years ago. Thanks a lot."

He focuses on the wall above my head. "Okay, forget that. Forget the whole age thing. You keep saying how bad you two were for each other, but it had nothing to do with you, Eve. Abusive relationships are not the fault of both parties. And maybe you didn't have bruises and black eyes all the time. It comes in cycles, so you probably had months where everything was perfect and he probably did a lot more threatening than acting on it. A lot more mental hits than physical ones. But it's all the same. I've been doing some research lately. Tell me if any of this sounds familiar."

"Any of what—?" I try to interrupt, but he lifts his hand to stop me.

"Any of the signs that you're in an abusive relationship," Alex says, holding up one finger. "Dominance. Did he tell you what to do? Tell you what to wear, what to eat? Who to talk to?"

I lock eyes with Alex, holding his gaze firmly. "He was my agent. Of course he gave me those directions. Are you telling me he doesn't ever advise you on what to wear and on your diet?"

Alex lifts an eyebrow. "Not outside of work or work-related events. And he advises, not demands or enforces. What about humiliation? Did he belittle you? Criticize you? Tell you that you're a worthless cause or that you're not able to function without him?"

My eyes squeeze shut before I can stop them. My breath is quickening, like something is trying to claw its way out of my chest. I try to stop my mind from traveling to those dark places, but I can't. I keep hearing him—Wes—his words.

Hannah obviously doesn't know what happens when you're allowed to think for yourself.

I want you to get everything you deserve, and I'm not sure that's possible without me intervening.

You're so fucking hardheaded. If you'd just listen to me, we wouldn't have these problems.

You need a strong guy who can handle your ups and downs.

"And we already know that he isolated you," Alex says. "You

couldn't tell anyone you were with him and if you wanted to spend time with him, it had to be just the two of you."

I'm blinking back tears and trying to find my voice again. "Okay, you can stop now."

He just shakes his head. "What about intimidation? Did he smash things in front of you? Break stuff? Let you know that he wasn't above violence?"

How does he know all this? My hands are shaking and my eyes are squeezed shut again. I can't stop the tears from falling down my cheeks. Whatever is caught in my chest is about to come loose. Whether it's words or a sob, I'm not sure yet and it's out of my hands.

"Then he blamed you, right? He made excuses about how unreasonable you were and how difficult you were to be with, and he was probably very sorry and he probably loved you so much that he just got carried away sometimes. Does that sound familiar, Eve?"

I shake my head, unable to open my eyes or lift a hand to wipe my face off. "Stop, please."

Alex places one hand on either side of me, leaning in so close his forehead almost touches mine. My eyes open the second I feel the heat radiating off his body and hitting mine.

"Listen to me," he says, softer and more confident. "It wasn't your fault. Wes is such a master manipulator, Eve. He did it to me too. He told me this sob story about you and how you needed him and you were so messed up and I believed him. For a little while, I believed him. Then I read that interview that you did in *Seventeen*, and I knew someone had sucked the life out of you after that."

I'm fighting the urge to break down so much that I can hardly breathe. Alex lifts a hand and rests it on my cheek, wiping away some of the tears with his thumb. "It doesn't matter how often he hurt you or why he did it or what you did to provoke him. There's no excuse that's acceptable. None. I don't think you've ever let yourself believe that."

I swallow the lump in my throat and shake my head again. "You don't get it. You weren't there. Not everything is black and white."

His mouth forms a tight line like he's biting back an angry retort. He drops his hand from my face and returns it to the desk beside me. "Okay, I wasn't there. But you were. Think about it, Eve. Look at everything that happened between you and Wes as an outsider. What if it were Stephanie or Elana explaining this to you? What if Elana said she deserved to have Wes hit her because she was being a huge brat? What would you tell her?"

My whole body is shaking as Alex's words hit me like the biggest realization of my life. What if it was Elana? It's so much easier to deal with this my way, the way I'd rationalized it for years. Things got bad between us and I had to leave. We loved each other too much to function—this is what I repeated in my head over and over again, and somehow it drowned out the bruises Wes left on my arms, the shattered glass that pierced the side of my neck, requiring stitches, the words that bypassed my skin and went straight for my heart. Wes Danes screwed with my head so bad I can't even see things for what they are.

"It's not your fault," Alex whispers again. "You have to believe me."

Finally, I give him a small nod, and then I let myself break down. I can't really stop it. Alex's arms go around me, and my face is buried in his shirt, and my life is rewinding itself inside my head and showing me colors I've never seen before and none of it is pleasant. It's so ugly I feel sick to my stomach and completely unable to draw in enough air to my lungs.

Alex just stands there, squeezing me and rubbing his hands over my back, like he's not planning on letting go anytime soon. And I'm so tired I can hardly keep myself from slumping over.

Chapter 49: Alex

I don't know how long I stand there letting Eve cry and listening to her breathing, making sure she's not hyperventilating. I'm completely weak with relief. I saw it on her face, that lightbulb of realization hitting, and I knew that I'd somehow managed to get through to her despite all the idiotic things I'd accidentally said.

I want to just let her keep crying and then take her back to her place and make sure she's okay, but I have one more important subject to broach. I keep my arms tight around her, squeezing her to my chest so she can't run away.

"I need you to tell Elana," I say as soon as her breathing returns normal. "Tell her what happened between you and Wes and put a stop to whatever she's trying to have with him before anything can even start."

She lifts her head and wipes her face on the sleeve of her shirt before looking up at me. "Okay, I'll do that."

"You will?" I try to hide the shock from my voice, but it's hard, considering the resistance I got from her earlier.

She stands up and straightens my shirt, trying to rub off the tears and snot with her sleeve. I gently push her hand away. I could care less about my shirt. Her arms go around my neck, and she hugs me tight. "I'm sorry you couldn't meet a nice normal girl with a lot less baggage. Like someone who goes to Starbucks on Sunday and hates boys who are stupid and only talk about sports."

I laugh. "I've met plenty of normal girls, believe me."

She lets go of me and tries harder to remove evidence of her crying by smearing mascara all over her shirtsleeve. "Do you think I'm stupid?"

I stare at her in disbelief. "Why would I think that?"

"For being with Wes at fifteen? For letting him do what he did? For believing that maybe now, after two years, he's actually different?"

I shake my head. "I know what you're thinking, the issues I have with Elana and me being falsely together, my opinions. But I'm not you and you're so different. I could see how a fifteen-year-old version of you would have connected more with someone older. It's not the age thing. You said so yourself in that *Seventeen* interview; being a model means living in the grown-up world and being treated that way. The real problem is Wes, not the age gap between the two of you. And no, I don't think you're stupid for letting him hurt you. He's an amazing manipulator, Eve. I fell for all kinds of his shit."

She lets out a breath, relieved. "So what now?"

"You mean with you and me?" She nods and then I remember that I told her I loved her even though I wasn't planning on doing that today. "Well, you already know how I feel."

She rolls her eyes. "Okay, but what about—?"

I grab her hand and squeeze it. "What about what? The way I see it, we've got nothing to lose now. There's no fake relationship on the line or scholarship for you."

Dread fills Eve's face. "Yeah, I know, but Wes."

"Right, Wes." I take a deep breath. "Let's not let him find out about us until we have a plan. You talk to Elana and I'll figure out the rest, okay?"

"Okay." She looks nervous. Really nervous. I don't know what else to say to ease her mind. To let her know that no matter what happens, we are doing exactly what we should be doing.

"You leave first, and I'll hang back a while so we're not seen together."

She looks a little lost but nods. "Sure, that's a good plan."

"Eve?" I catch her hand before she opens the door. I place my hands on her face and lean in and kiss her. "I'm not going anywhere. We'll figure this out together, and I won't do anything without talking to you first. I know it's hard for you, but you *can* trust me."

She gives me another quick kiss on the mouth. "Thank you."

I take Eve's spot sitting on the desk in the empty office and wait ten agonizing minutes before heading out, to come up with this great plan that I just promised her even though I currently have nothing to work with.

Chapter 50: Eve

January 12, 8:00 a.m.

"How are you this morning?"

I toss my towel, pajamas, and bathroom supplies onto my desk and glance at Steph, who's tangled up in her covers and barely awake. She stayed up until three this morning listening to me talk and cry and basically tell her everything that surfaced after Alex talked to me yesterday. I honestly don't think I could have picked a better roommate and I don't think I've ever, in my entire life, been surrounded by such supportive people. But the fact that I can't change the past, that I can't help seeing myself as the stupid girl who spent two years blaming herself for what happened with Wes, means it's going to take more than one night to fix me.

"I'm doing okay," I tell Steph finally. "I'm going for a walk. I haven't taken a picture of anything since before finals, and I need to get back on the horse, you know?"

She rolls out of bed and digs through the bottom drawer of her dresser, handing me a bag from Macy's. "It's your Christmas present. I didn't get a chance to get it before I went home."

I open the shopping bag and find a gray knit scarf, gloves, and hat that match my gray and black coat perfectly. I've been relying on stuffing my hands in my pockets and wearing my hair down to keep my ears warm.

"Thanks, Steph. I needed these."

She looks extremely pleased with herself as I remove the tags and bundle up for my walk outside.

It's cold, but the sun is out and it helps me tolerate the temperature. I wander through a few sections of Central Park before settling on Belvedere Castle. My camera is around my neck, but I don't pick it up yet; instead I watch for inspiration. There's a group of middle-school-aged kids in uniforms and another group of elementary-school-aged kids in regular clothes. I spot a few older people, some middle-aged adults taking dozens of pictures and wearing their tourist staples.

My gaze ends up following a little girl with a curly, blond ponytail, ribbons in her hair, and a brown-and-pink jacket. She looks about four or five years old, and she's tugging the hand of a man who's probably in his mid-thirties. Like the little girl, he's extremely well dressed—polished shoes and dress pants. They aren't poor and they don't look like tourists, possibly Upper East Siders.

I lean against the castle wall and start watching the girl and the man through my camera lens.

"Daddy, look! The top is where the princess gets locked up by the evil queen," the girl says, pointing up at the highest part of the castle.

I zoom in on the man's face and see him grin broadly when the little girl turns to see his reaction to her statement about the

princess and the queen. The second she turns back around, his smile fades. It's like he's aged ten years.

I snap a few shots of the girl. Her nose is red from the cold, and after she wipes it several times on her sleeve, Dad pulls a Kleenex from his pocket and wipes her runny nose despite the fact that she tries to wiggle away. He keeps smiling at her, and when she takes off running to see over the other side, his face falls again.

My lens is now zoomed in on him, and, at the same time, I'm trying to remember being four or five years old. Even with my trailer park home and negligent parents, there was always a game to be played or a show to watch or something to make life fun. I didn't have knowledge of grown-up problems. Not until maybe third or fourth grade when I started to figure things out.

I shift my camera to the teachers leading the field trips, and even though they are both a similar age to the little girl's dad, they don't look nearly as troubled. I turn back to him and snap some pictures from several different angles. And then I'm wondering what kind of life event could happen to this man that he couldn't explain to a four- or five-year-old. And he had to wear a mask every time she turned to look at him. Did he get caught cheating on his wife and now the girl's mom is going to leave him and take custody of the child? Did Grandma die and he hasn't figured out how to tell her yet? Did he lose his job? Is the girl's mom sick?

Whatever his story is, he doesn't want to tell her because she'll age ten years too. Events in my life made me feel twenty-five at fifteen, and no girl should have to miss those years. But I did. And I think how I'd love to go back and fix everything, not let myself fall in love with Wes Danes. He's left so many scars on me, a few

I didn't even realize I had until yesterday. But the girl I was when I came to Columbia, when I first met Alex, that girl was good enough to cause someone like Alex Evans to make all kinds of sacrifices to help. I gave him an easy out and he wouldn't take it.

The things in my past are awful things, but would I still be me if I hadn't experienced that life? Without that life, would I be someone who could take photographs good enough to catch the attention of Janessa Fields and the Mason Scholarship committee? Would I be someone with enough drive and motivation to get into Columbia?

I'm honestly not sure that I would have any of that. Maybe the only way forward is to simply move forward, one half-step at a time. Maybe the struggles I'm going to face trying to keep myself in school and trust Alex enough to let him into my life will take me further up that ladder and I'll look back on those hardships and figure out how to appreciate them as well.

I head back outside toward my dorm. I feel lighter and so relieved to have that over and to focus on what to do next. To keep myself here at this beautiful campus.

I cross through the middle of two buildings and stop right in my tracks. For the first time in years, I let myself truly breathe, stop thinking and worrying, because it's going to be okay. Even if I have to transfer somewhere cheaper or take classes part time and work part time, the hole isn't so big I can't dig my way out. It's manageable. My life is manageable.

It's not until I get back to my room and pull the photos up on my laptop that I realize nearly every picture I took this morning is a whole image.

Chapter 51: Alex

January 12, 12:30 p.m.

Janessa Fields just stares at me, completely shocked, and I wonder if this is the first time she's ever been speechless. From what I've seen of Janessa, she seems to have an opinion on just about everything.

I'm in her office, and I've just finished telling her the entire, and I do mean *entire*, Eve Castle/Wes Danes story. Eve will probably never speak to me again after finding this out, but I promised her I'd figure out how to get Wes fired. I have no idea what Janessa will do with this information, but who else can I trust in the industry?

Janessa rubs her eyes and sighs. "I had no idea, honestly. I thought she was doing well and then…and I can't believe I didn't see the signs after the way he cornered her at the CK shoot. But I thought she changed her mind about school and her career and wanted to use Wes to get back into modeling."

"Well, she did want to use Wes, but that was only because—" I stop before saying the truth out loud. It was only because she wasn't allowed on set at Janessa's jobs and that started the chain reaction of her losing her chance at the scholarship and all the other shit that went down.

Janessa seems to pull herself together, not wanting to dwell on what has already happened. "And you think something is going on with Wes and Elana?"

"I don't know what, but something has happened. And he has no reason to be spending time one-on-one with her. He's not even Elana's agent." I let out a breath. "I know this is probably not something you want to get involved with, and I know you've got contracts and bridges into the fashion industry that you don't want to burn, but I didn't know who else to talk to and I feel like Eve's counting on me. And if I can't help her, then she isn't going to trust me, and what if she goes back to thinking that the Wes thing was partially her fault—"

Janessa holds up her hand to stop me. "Alex, I'm not like everyone else in this industry. Yes, I'm here to make money. But I have many, many lines I'm not willing to cross, and if they want me bad enough, which they usually do, then I get to do things my way. First off, don't worry about Eve's school next year. I can give her a paying assistantship. Had I known it was such a dire situation, I would have done that sooner, but I wanted to treat her like a student. She's proven herself worthy of getting an assistant's salary. Her idea for a picture is going on the giant Calvin Klein billboard. She's good. She's incredibly talented."

I let out a breath, so relieved already. "Okay, so no worries about school, then?"

"It's only January, Alex," Janessa says. "She's got plenty of time to figure out a plan for next fall. Eve has some good people in her life. All she has to do is let them help her."

"And Wes?" I ask wearily.

"Get me one piece of evidence or a statement from Elana saying that Wes acted inappropriately and I'll have him fired," Janessa says, causing my heart to sink all the way down to my stomach. There might not even be any evidence to get, and if there is, why would Elana give it to me?

Then she starts to explain her plan, and for the first time since cornering Eve after that *Cosmo* shoot yesterday, I'm thinking that maybe, just maybe, this might actually work.

After I leave Janessa's office, I pull out my phone and call Eve. "Hey, have you talked to Elana yet?"

Eve lets out a sigh that I can hear so clearly through the phone, I know the answer already.

"No, I've thought about it—"

"It's okay," I interrupt. "I've been thinking about it too, and I think we should do it together. You know, because we've both heard different things from her and gotten different hints."

"That would be great," Eve says, sounding relieved, which makes me equally relieved. "I don't want to team up on her or anything, but I could really use the support, to be honest."

"Are you busy now? I'll text her and see where she's at and then let you know where to meet, okay?"

"I'm not busy now, but I have a shoot at two," she says.

"Where?" I ask. She tells me the shoot location. "Perfect. That's not too far from Elana's building."

After hanging up with Eve, I text Elana and ask her if she's working. She replies right away, saying she's at home, so I tell Eve to meet me there in thirty minutes.

·· ♦ ··

January 12, 2:00 p.m.

"Eve!" Elana says when she opens the door. "I didn't know both of you were coming over."

Eve gives her a tight smile and then glances at me, waiting for my brilliant explanation. Eve already looks pale, like she's ready to barf any second. I don't blame her. We basically had this same chat with each other yesterday and who wants to rehash their horrible past two days in a row?

I wait until Elana lets us in and shuts the door before answering her silent question about why we're both here. "We have something we want to talk to you about. It's kind of important." I glance around. "Is anyone else here?"

Elana's eyes are wide with alarm, but she shakes her head.

My fingers fumble for my phone in my pocket. I know Eve would never approve of what I'm about to do, but I'm willing to take that risk.

I carefully place my cell phone on the table along with my keys before sitting down on the couch, trying to make it look like my pockets were just overfilled. Elana warily takes a seat at the opposite end of the couch and Eve is on the love seat, angling herself toward Elana.

Eve opens her mouth to start speaking, and I'm already

predicting her slow, graceful maneuvering into the topic at hand and I just know that it's not going to work.

"We know about you and Wes," I blurt out, cutting Eve off.

Eve narrows her eyes at me like she's afraid I might have ruined everything.

Elana's gaze darts from Eve to me, then back to Eve. "How—I mean, what do you mean?"

Eve swallows hard and lifts a shaking hand to tuck her hair behind her ears. "We know that you have feelings for Wes, and it's just that Alex and I really don't think you should pursue this. We're worried about you."

"You're worried about me?" Elana folds her arms across her chest, defensive mode clearly turned on. "I don't think either of you would ever understand how much Wes has helped me. I almost quit modeling until he stepped in and gave me the confidence to keep going." She turns to me, practically glaring. "I know how you think, Alex. I'm a child to you. You don't get it."

Nausea rolls over me. It's true. I had a feeling, but hearing her practically just admit it comes with a surprising punch.

"Neither of us thinks you're a child," Eve says gently. I glance at Eve and lift an eyebrow. Now's the time to speak up. Eve takes a deep breath and continues. "And honestly, Elana, I do understand, a lot more than you realize."

It's not easy for me to sit there and listen to Eve tell Elana about hooking up with Wes when she was fifteen or how he was nice and helpful and took care of her and then slowly he turned more controlling and angry and abusive. I can't look at Eve while she's talking, so I watch Elana's face. She sits there not moving or speaking. I can tell she's surprised but also unwilling to admit it.

When Eve's voice gets shaky as she tells the worst parts, I have to close my eyes and take a slow deep breath to force the images of me strangling Wes from my mind.

"I should have told you sooner," Eve says, finally reaching the end of her story. "But there were so many things I hadn't even figured out for myself until recently."

Elana looks near tears, but she's shaking her head. "He's not like that anymore. Maybe he just went through a rough time or something, or maybe it's different with me."

"He's twenty-seven, Elana. You're fifteen," Eve points out, keeping her voice gentle and not at all critical.

A tear escapes Elana's eye and rolls down her cheek. She wipes it away quickly. "In France it's different. The culture is different. We don't have the same age stigmas that you have in America."

Eve nods like she's trying to be understanding and patient. And I'm literally getting more anxious and impatient by the second.

"I get that it might be different for you, but even with the age thing aside, Wes has a track record of being abusive, and those kinds of behaviors don't just go away," I say, trying to get to the point quicker.

"How do I even know you're telling the truth?" Elana snaps at Eve. "What if you made up that stuff about him just to keep me away, or make it sound worse than it is?"

Eve flinches like Elana just slapped her. I think having someone not believe her story has always been a fear of Eve's.

I decide it's time for me to intervene again and take over. "In America, it's illegal, assuming you've slept with him already."

Eve glares in my direction, her mouth practically hanging open.

"I knew you wouldn't get it!" More tears fall down Elana's face, and she stands up like she's about to run from the room. "It's not like that and, no, I haven't slept with him, if that makes you feel better."

It does a little, actually. "But you've gone out with him on a date, right?" I press. "You've kissed him?"

Elana turns her entire body to face me and she looks so pissed off. "I've kissed *you*! I've gone on dates with *you*! You and I aren't the same age."

"True," I say, digging for the facts Brad spouted off to me last month. "But technically it's not illegal for us to be together like that, even if everyone knew you're only fifteen. There's not more than four years difference between us."

I give her a second to argue with me and then I continue. "And you knew what you were getting into with me. I made it clear that I didn't feel that way about you. I made it clear that we were just acting."

"Exactly," Elana says. "And Wes isn't acting. He actually cares about me, as a friend and more."

"Elana," Eve says. "Believe me when I say that I understand how you feel and I'm absolutely the last person to judge you—"

I let out a frustrated breath. This isn't going anywhere. "So he did kiss you?" I ask again. "When you went to see that Broadway show, right?"

"I hate you. You were lying when you said we could be

friends." Elana turns to face me. "Yes. He kissed me, and yes, we went to a show together and you can call that a date and tell whoever you want, because to the world, I'm eighteen and it's not illegal and there's nothing either of you can do about that."

With that, Elana takes off for her bedroom and slams the door.

"What the hell was that, Alex?" Eve hisses at me. "I thought the goal was to help her."

"Change of plans." I snatch my phone and keys off the table.

"Are we on different planets right now? How the fuck was that even remotely helpful?"

I glance at my phone, checking to see if I got what I needed. "We weren't getting anywhere with her. It was obvious she'd just keep defending herself."

"What the hell is so important on your phone, Alex? God, I thought you were worried about Elana. I never thought talking to her would involve making her hate us."

"I don't care if she hates me," I admit.

"Well, I do!" Eve says, standing up and quickly putting her coat back on. "She might need me, and now she's going to lump the two of us together. This was a bad idea."

I look at Eve and then rest a hand on her arm. "You're going to be really pissed at me in a few minutes, but all I ask is that you let me explain before you take off, okay?"

"You mean more pissed than I already am?"

"I didn't plan on convincing Elana of anything today," I say. "I just needed to get her to admit that something is going on with her and Wes."

Comprehension reaches Eve's face and she snatches my

phone from my hand, looking it over quickly. "You recorded us? I can't believe you did that? She trusted you. I trusted you!"

I place both hands gently on her arms, hoping she won't try to run off. "Look, Eve, I'd never, ever give your story and your past to anyone without your permission. That's not why I did this. I'll edit out your part. And I don't care if Elana trusts me or not; she's fucking fifteen. The last thing she needs is for us to treat her like an adult. She has a crush on Wes, and it's so serious that nothing we say would ever convince her that he's bad news. Nothing. And I refuse to watch her learn that for herself. If she were five years older, this would be a completely different story. I don't care how mature you think Elana is, she has no fucking clue what the hell is best for her. If we really care about her, we'll use whatever method we have to make sure she's okay. Even if she never likes us again."

Eve is shaking her head, not even close to being on the same page as me.

"My sister is Elana's age. I'd rather she hated me for the rest of her life then let her fall into a relationship where someone is going to hurt her and manipulate her. It sucks, but what choice do we have?"

"Anything but tricking her!"

"Listen—"

"No. Not now." She slams the phone back into my hand and takes a deep breath. "I can't do this right now. I have a job that I desperately need to keep, and I'm going to be late."

Eve takes off, and I don't stop her because the last thing I want is for her to miss a call time and get fired from a job. As much as I hate to leave Elana alone, the better solution is to get this evidence to Janessa as soon as possible. I head out a couple of minutes after Eve and walk the few blocks to my building. When I'm safely in my room, I upload the recording I made at Elana's to my laptop and then email it to Janessa, just like she told me to do earlier. An agonizing hour later, a number listed as *Unknown* pops up on my cell phone, and I pick it up right away, assuming it's Janessa.

It's not.

"What the hell are you trying to pull, Alex?" Wes asks, anger seeping into every word.

Does news travel that quickly? Maybe Janessa uploaded the recording on the Internet or something? That doesn't seem like she's using the proper channels though.

My heart pounds. Wes is on the phone accusing me of something and I need to respond. "I have no idea what you're talking about."

"Right," he snaps. "I don't think you have any idea who you're dealing with. I could ruin you in minutes. A couple of calls to some close friends is all it would take."

The words he's saying aren't absorbing into my brain. All I can do is listen to the sounds of traffic in the background, as if I know New York City well enough to pinpoint location based on the outside noise. I don't. But I know he's heading somewhere. I'm already on my feet, sliding my gym shoes on halfway before flying down the stairs.

"Forget it," Wes says. "You're not the person I really need to talk to right now."

He hangs up, and the second I step outside into the frigid air with shoes barely on and no coat, it hits me.

Eve.

That's who he blames. Elana called him and told him everything she said. He probably doesn't even know about the recording I sent to Janessa.

I'd worried about leaving Elana alone earlier. I may have worried about the wrong girl.

And he has Eve's schedule on his BlackBerry. He knows exactly where she is.

But what if I'm wrong? It's best if I make sure someone is with both of them. This all started to help Elana. I can't let my concern for Eve cause me to forget all about Elana.

While I'm darting around pedestrians and crossing streets with the *Don't Walk* sign flashing, I sift through numbers until I find what I'm looking for.

Finley Belton.

"Finley," I say when she picks up.

"Hey, Alex. What's up?"

"Where are you right now?"

"In the lobby of my building," she says. "About to get into the elevator."

"Great." I let out a breath, tapping my foot as cars zip by, waiting to cross the street. "I need a favor. Elana—"

"Look, Alex, I like you. You're cool. But I can't get in the middle of your girlfriend drama. It's just not how I roll."

I groan in frustration. Why is everything so difficult? "This has nothing to do with girlfriends. If Wes Danes shows up there, I need you to call the police."

"Why?" I hear the skepticism in her voice, and it makes me

wonder if I'm heading to the wrong place. Checking on the wrong girl.

"He can't be around Elana," I explain. "He's dangerous and really angry right now."

But I doubt he's angry with Elana. That's why I'm making the right choice.

"Oh no. I'm so not getting involved in some domestic spat. Call the cops yourself."

"She's your fucking roommate!" I close my eyes, forcing back the anger. I weave through crowds of pedestrians, all bundled up for January. Despite my lack of coat, I can't even feel the cold. "Domestic spat is a term you'd use for people who are of legal age. Elana's not eighteen. She's fifteen. And let's just say he's got a track record for inappropriate relationships with clients much younger than him."

"Jesus, I didn't know she was so young, Alex. I swear," she says, alarm finally ringing through her voice. "He's been here. They've been together here."

"Did you tell anyone?" I drill.

"No."

I can't believe she sat there and watched this happen, that she's had evidence all along and never said a word. She's got my number. She could have told me.

It doesn't matter. Not right now, anyway. "Just do what I asked, okay?"

"Okay," she says without hesitation.

Now please, please let Eve be okay.

Chapter 52: Eve

January 12, 4:10 p.m.

I can hardly sit still through my hair and makeup session. It's like my body really wants to run back to Elana's place and talk to her, but my brain knows I'm supposed to be here and they can't seem to work together.

My toes have just been stuffed into a pair of heels a half size too small. The skirt I'm wearing is so tight, all the way down to my knees, causing me to walk like a duck as I head from set back to wardrobe. I need to get out of here and figure this shit out. I need to deal with the mess Alex just made. I know he's not intentionally trying to hurt me, but what the hell was he thinking?

"There's a guy here to see you," the wardrobe lady whispers to me before nodding toward a stairwell on the other side of the room.

Alex.

I can't really afford to be distracted, but maybe he was able to talk to Elana and everything is okay now. Just hearing that would clear my head for the rest of the day.

Quickly, I shuffle across the room as best I can in this wardrobe and open the large brown door leading to the stairs. The door closes behind me just before I take in Wes's figure.

He's leaning against the wall, arms folded across his chest.

My heart races, and my hand fumbles around behind my back, landing on the doorknob. But Wes is fast. He slides himself beside me, pressing his back against the door.

"What the hell are you doing, Evie?"

The dark storm in his eyes freezes me in place. The low near-whisper of his voice is all too familiar. I swallow hard, looking down at the stairs. Maybe if I'm calm, I can calm him and get the hell away.

Again, my reaction comes too late. Wes grabs my arms and slams my back against the wall behind the door. My breath comes out in quick gasps, and I can't think clearly.

Get away, Eve. Now.

"I don't know what kind of shit you're trying to pull." He leans closer, his forehead almost hitting mine. "But you're gonna fix this, Evie. You're going to undo all the damage you did."

Does he know about Alex's recording? Or did he talk to Elana?

The familiar squeeze against my arms triggers a dozen of memories. I close my eyes and get hit with a year's worth fear and anxiousness. Pain and heartbreak. I try to wish myself anywhere but here, because for the first time ever, Wes might be on his last option for saving his own ass and that's utterly frightening.

But I'm not fifteen anymore. There's got to be a way out.

"Are you jealous of Elana?" he says. "Is that why you made up all that shit about me?"

I open my eyes and stare into his. "She's not even your client, Wes. What *are* you doing with her?"

"She'll be my client soon enough. I'm the one who's helped her career take off, just like I did to yours and Alex's," he says. "It's my word against yours."

"I didn't make up anything about you, Wes," I say, trying to force back the tremble in my voice. My legs are shaking. "I told her the truth. That's all."

"Then untell her." He pulls me forward, toward him, and then slams my back into the wall again.

Adrenaline kicks in, and I wiggle side to side, trying to escape his grip, until I'm finally able to dart to the right. The stairs zoom into focus. I reach for the rail, my foot landing on the first step, when his arm hooks around my waist, the other in my hair, yanking my hair and jerking my neck.

I see his face again, and that crazed look is there. It's an expression I've only seen on Wes a couple of times. He's lost control. His movements are no longer careful and calculated.

He's going to push me down the stairs. I'm gonna be lying in a heap at the bottom by the time anyone finds me.

I open my mouth to scream, but he clamps a hand over it. Blood pounds in my ears, drowning out any outside noise. I lift my knee, hoping to nail him in the balls but end up hitting his stomach instead. He loosens his grip and groans, giving me just enough opening to reach for the rail again, making it down two steps this time before he's pulling me back again, this time with much more force.

Everything moves in slow motion as my feet come out from underneath me and the side of my head slams so hard into the wall, everything goes black for several seconds, pain shooting between my eyes. My back hits the concrete floor with a clank. More pain shoots through my head. Then I look up, vision spotty, as Wes's brown shoes take two steps closer and he bends over, reaching for me, grasping the borrowed jacket I'm wearing in tight fists.

My head is pounding, my stomach churning, and my vision blurred, but I hear the door flying open and I see large hands grab Wes from behind.

Alex.

Two uniformed building security guards race in after him.

I try to stand but end up falling back into the wall and sliding down until I'm sitting on the floor, nauseous and throbbing everywhere.

Stars form in front of my eyes and sound is blocked, but I do catch the look on Alex's face. An expression of complete and utter rage. Something I never thought I'd see on him.

He's got Wes off me in half a second. Wes snaps around to see who's grabbed him. Alex punches Wes square in the jaw, causing him to stumble into the security guards. I watch through the haziness in my head as Alex makes a move to swing at Wes again and then realizes that Wes is already being restrained by the guards.

One of the security guys presses a hand on Alex's chest, holding him back. "That's enough."

The pain between my eyes reaches an all-time high. I press my forehead into the heel of my hands and try to breathe in and out in even intervals.

"Eve?" I hear Alex say. Seconds later, he's beside me, his arms around me, his face in my hair. "Are you okay? Please tell me you're okay."

I give a tiny nod, and this seems to be enough. I must be okay if I can nod.

"I'm so sorry," he says. "This is all my fault. If I hadn't set off Elana earlier, he never would have come here."

My cheeks are wet, but I don't remember crying or any tears filling my eyes. I lift my head for a second, my gaze landing right on Wes. His eyes are huge, like he's just woken up from a bad dream. I can see his muscles visibly relax as he stops fighting the security guards. He's not stupid.

They're talking to him, leading him out the door, but I can't understand what they're saying. I look over at Alex after they're gone. "How did you know where I was?"

"I didn't. Not exactly." He looks up at the ceiling, pointing to something above the door. "Security cameras."

I wince and then lean against Alex, my cheek resting on the soft material of his shirt. "My head is killing me."

His hand gently touches the back of my hair. "What happened to your head? Did you hit it against the wall?" The worry in his voice is undeniable, but I'm too out of it to panic.

Footsteps emerge from all directions, coming up the stairs and through the brown door.

"She hit her head," I hear Alex say and I feel another cold hand against my scalp.

"What's your name?" a voice asks and I answer. I think.

"What's today's date?"

There are at least two paramedics and two cops crammed into

the stairwell now, and all I can focus on is the image I've created in my own mind of Wes leaving the building and walking outside free as a bird. Surely, he's gotten away with this somehow. He always does.

Chapter 53: Alex

January 12, 10:30 p.m.

"Are you sure Stephanie is okay? She's not freaking out or any-thing?" Eve asks as we walk into my apartment. "And what about Elana? Who's with her right now?"

My hands are full with take-out deli sandwiches, concussion treatment instructions from the ER, ice packs, prescription pain-killers, and the pair of pink high heels Eve accidentally stole from today's photo shoot.

"Stephanie is done freaking out. I promised to take good care of you. And Elana is with Finley and Kara. Her parents are on their way from France, remember?" *And we aren't exactly her favorite people right now*, I don't add. It's not the time. I mean we've just gotten her boyfriend arrested for assault, so, yeah, she's not happy with us. Eve will be worried and upset, knowing Elana specifically said that she doesn't want to see us. Me, on the other hand, I'm perfectly content with this, because Wes is in custody and can't go near her. Elana is smart enough and tough enough to deal with all the other monsters of the world without our help if it comes to that. If she continues to hate us.

Eve and I both freeze in the doorway of my apartment. After a few hours in the ER and then a couple more at the police station, the last thing either of us wanted was to be welcomed home with one of my roommates' parties.

It's not a full-blown bash, which is good, but even the ten or twelve people gathered in the living room seem like way too many. I steer Eve toward my bedroom and shut the door behind us. I lay all the junk in my arms onto the bed and then grab a pair of sweatpants and a T-shirt from my dresser. Eve sits down on the side of the bed, watching me move around the room.

My legs have been shaking for hours, and it feels like the second I stop moving, I'm going to fall apart. I set the clothes on her lap. "You can change into these."

"Thanks," she says, staring down at the black Shins shirt resting on top.

"I'm going to get some drinks and stuff so you can eat," I say. "Will you be okay for a few minutes?"

"Sure." She's already removing her jacket as I step into the hallway and shut the door behind me.

Jason and Landon both catch me in the kitchen.

"What's going on?" Landon asks. "Is that the chick from the *Cosmo* shoot? What happened to her?"

I reach into the fridge for two water bottles and then start making a bag of ice from the freezer. "Yes, it's the girl from the *Cosmo* shoot and she has a concussion."

"Seriously?" Jason says. "Is she okay?"

I'm suddenly so exhausted I can barely keep my eyes open. "Yeah, she's okay. Banged up, but okay."

Unfortunately, there's no way to keep at least today's isolated event out of the tabloids. So I decide to give them a quick version. While I'm talking, the number of people in the living room reduces from ten to two. A couple of girls who appear to be cleaning up and fluffing the couch cushions are the only ones left.

"Dude, that's fucked up," Landon says. "Are we getting a new agent or what?"

Both my roommates are also under Wes's rule, though he does have an assistant who does a lot of communication with the nonstar models. I know this because that's how it was for me last summer. Up until about a month before that *Seventeen* shoot where Eve Nowakowski stumbled into my life.

I shake my head. "I don't know." I haven't gotten that far in my thought process yet.

"Well, we're clearing out of the apartment," Landon says. "So Eve can get some sleep."

When I get back in my room, Eve's still sitting in the same spot on the bed. I squat down in front of her and hold the ice to the back of her head.

"Sorry it took so long."

I'm about to stand up, but Eve rests her hands on my cheeks and holds me in place. "What's going on with you? You've been wearing this look for the past six hours, like you're waiting for me to start screaming at you or something."

My legs are finally ready to give out and my knees drop to the floor in response. I swallow the lump in my throat and then shake my head.

"What?" Eve prods, taking the bag of ice out of my hands. "Tell me what's going through your head."

I lean forward until my forehead touches her lap. "I just keep seeing him banging you against the wall or shoving you down those stairs. What if I had gotten there a couple of minutes later? I set all of this in motion. I set off Elana and then she called Wes."

She runs her fingers through my hair. "It's not your fault Wes is Wes, Alex. I know I was pissed at you about what happened with Elana, but you're right. You did the right thing. It doesn't matter if she hates us. I wish someone had done the same for me a few years ago."

I stand up and then climb onto the bed, pulling Eve down beside me. "This isn't how I wanted to deal with everything. Maybe I was in over my head."

She lays her head on my chest. "I can't believe he's in jail. I thought he'd figure out a way to get out of it. Or even to make it my fault and get me in trouble."

"He'll probably get out," I say, trying to hold back my anger. "He'll post bail, but he won't have his job anymore. And you heard the police officer. There's gonna be a trial eventually."

"What about me and you?" she says.

I shake my head. "I don't know, Eve. It's not like I had some hidden agenda or anything. I don't expect anything specific from you. I'm not like Wes, you know that, right? I'm not built that way. I can't even fathom trying to tell you what to do or how to live or ever physically hurting you. But I'm eighteen, and you're eighteen, and there're a million other reasons why we might not work."

She lifts her head and there are tears running down her cheeks. I brush them away with my fingertips.

"I'm pretty screwed up right now," she says. "I don't think I'll be that way forever, but maybe it's not fair to you if I—"

"I don't have any expectations. I really don't." I lean in and kiss her much longer and slower than I'd done earlier today when I thought she was mad at me. "I just want you to stay with me tonight so I can wake you up every fifteen minutes and make sure you have all cognitive abilities intact," I say, reciting the concussion material we got from the ER.

She hesitates before leaning in to kiss me again. "I just want everything to be perfect, Alex."

I pull her closer, laughing a little. "Eve, when has love ever been perfect?"

She kisses me hard. "I love you."

"I love you too."

Yeah, we totally have no expectations for *us. Right.*

Chapter 54: Eve

May 15, 11:10 a.m.

The sound of the wheels emerging underneath my seat jolts me awake. My ears are full of pressure, so I can barely hear the flight attendants prepping the cabin for landing. I yawn and stretch one arm over my head. After carefully reaching into my bag for a piece of gum, I lift the shade up on the window and watch the clouds move from below me to above me and the green patches of land appear in their place.

For the first time in I don't know how many years, I let myself look without thinking or worrying about the future. It's taken a lot to get to this point and who knows what's ahead, so I might as well enjoy it while I can.

In exactly five days I'm shooting a huge campaign for Gucci, the job I walked away from years ago. After hearing the full story about Wes and me and why I left (thanks to a very truthful *New York Times* article written by a good friend of Janessa Fields), Gucci decided that a model who had overcome a difficult past and gone on to become an Ivy League student was exactly who they needed to star in their Fall/Winter catalog. I think it helped that they wanted Janessa so bad and she told them she'd do it if they cast me. Janessa knew this one job would be enough to nearly cover my tuition for next year. Of course she still expects me to assist her as much as possible, which means I may be editing my own photos. Weird.

I laugh a little under my breath at the sight of cornfields on the ground below. This isn't New York, that's for sure. The wheels finally grind against the runway, bumping the passengers around a bit. I glance to my left, staring in disbelief at Alex's head still lying limply against my shoulder. How does he sleep through a plane landing?

"Hey." I pat his cheek lightly. "We're here."

He finally raises his head, flashing me a sleepy smile before kissing me. There's an imprint down one side of his face from the zipper of my hoodie. I snort back a laugh and try to rub it away as the plane pulls into the gate.

He grabs onto my hand and pulls it away from his face. "It's fine. Just don't take my picture."

"How can you sleep like that? Did you drug yourself or something?" I barely dozed off for twenty minutes before hearing the sounds of landing prep.

Alex squeezes my hand as if sensing my nerves. "I guess my head was nice and clear. Makes sleeping easy."

I lift an eyebrow. "Oh, and what exactly is your head usually full of? With your booming career, heavy bank account, and, of course, a kick-ass girlfriend, what can you possibly have to worry about?"

He gives me one of his shameless grins that reminds me of that first day we met. He's different now in my eyes, but still the same guy in all the ways that make him Alex. The biggest difference in him, I think, is that last October he saw only one path for his life, one solution—do whatever it takes to get to the top of the modeling chain. To him, he believed wholeheartedly that he had no choice but to follow Wes's orders.

But there is always a choice.

I've learned this too.

Alex stands up to open the overhead compartment and pulls down both of our carry-ons. "I bet you wish you'd gotten that scholarship so you'd be deboarding in Paris instead of Nebraska right now."

I shrug. Yeah, I'd love to be in Paris for the summer, but it would mean leaving Alex for three months, and it would also mean leaving Janessa for three months, and I've learned so much from her.

Plus there's always next summer.

Alex sets the second suitcase down in front of him, and while we wait for the passengers in front of us to exit the plane, he hooks an arm around my waist and brings me closer. "Have I told you thanks for coming with me yet? If not, I totally meant to."

I laugh. "Only about two dozen times."

"You're saving me from hearing so much shit from my brothers. They'll have to be polite if you're around." He leans in and kisses me. "We can go to Paris for fun if you want. Keep an eye on Priceline and wait for a cheap flight, bring our backpacks, roam around France like nomads."

"Or we can stay with Elana's family," I say. "Her mom loves me. She'll call up the aunts and uncles and get them to put us up for a week or so."

"Sounds like a plan."

Elana's mom gave her and the agency an ultimatum. If she wants to continue modeling in New York City, Momma would need to bunk up with her fifteen-year-old daughter, and the agency would need to foot the bill.

They all reluctantly agreed. And Elana's slowly allowing me back into her life. Alex isn't getting the same courtesy, but I really do think it's more an issue of embarrassment and shame than anything she has against Alex. She and I have fallen into the same trap called Wes Danes. It makes sense that we can join forces so easily.

When we finally make it outside to the airport curb, where all the cars are pulling up, Alex's eyes get wide after spotting a black minivan not too far from the doors. "Oh no."

"What?" I ask, squinting into the sun to see what he's looking at.

"Katie," he says. "She's driving."

"Didn't she just turn fifteen?" That's when I see the tall, very thin man step out of the passenger seat. He's exactly like I pictured from Alex's only description of his dad months ago. "So she's a student driver?"

"Apparently."

Alex's dad says a quick hello and then loads our luggage into the back of the van. He tells me to call him Robert and not Mr. Evans but doesn't say much else.

I get in behind Robert, but Alex stands outside, arms folded across his chest.

"Does Katie have to drive home?"

Katie glares at him. "Get a cab."

She looks too small and young to be in the driver's seat, but

I'm not going to open my mouth. Alex reluctantly climbs in and buckles his seat belt, checking it three times before tugging on mine. He leans close and stage-whispers, "Maybe we should say something important just in case? You know, last words and all."

"Don't be a dipshit, Alex," Katie snaps. "I had to sit in the car when you were driving. We could tell Eve that story about the cow and the baby ducks that were only visible to you."

Alex glares back at her but doesn't say another word. Katie glances over her shoulder and smiles at me. "Nice to meet you, Eve, by the way. And it's so nice of my brother to properly introduce you."

Alex rolls his eyes "Katie, this is Eve. Eve, this is Katie, my annoying little sister."

"Nice to meet you," I say.

The next twenty-five minutes *are* a bit scary. Alex wasn't totally blowing smoke with his reluctance to let Katie drive. I try to focus on his dad and the quiet, calm way he directed his daughter. Like he'd already anticipated and prepared for every mistake she made. And maybe he had if he'd been the one to teach all three boys to drive. There's so much stability and commitment in that task alone. It's obvious how different my family is from Alex's.

We don't even make it inside the house before we're bombarded by Alex's brothers. They're huge compared to Alex, but shorter. Brad walks right up to me and hugs me, lifting me off the ground.

"Eve Nowakowski, the girl who's made our family the most famous people in town," Brad says "I haven't had to pay for a meal since your story broke in the *New York Times*."

He sets me down finally and I can feel myself blushing. "Um, you're welcome?"

Katie smacks him in the back of the head and rolls her eyes in my direction. "Oh my God, Brad, you're such a douche."

Brad shrugs. "I'm just breaking the ice so it won't be weird."

Alex's mom joins us in the front yard and starts handing out jobs. "Put Eve's stuff in Katie's room," she says to her husband before turning to face me. "Is that all right, Eve?"

"Mom, I don't think—" Alex starts to say, but I clap a hand over his mouth.

"Sounds great."

Jared catches my eye and mouths, *good answer*, giving me a thumbs-up. I don't want to pretend with his family, but I'd like to try and make a good impression even if it means three nights of slumber parties in Katie's room. Somehow, I have a feeling she and I will have plenty in common. At the very least, I'll get the cow and baby duck story out of her.

Alex takes my hand and leads me through the house, which smells like Toll House cookies and spaghetti and old family photos and years of all those feet running around. It's beautiful. The back-yard has an aboveground pool and has been carefully picked up and decorated for Brad's graduation party tomorrow. I lean against the rail of the deck and scan the yard and the neighborhood on the other side of the wooden fence. It feels important to be here with him, somewhere outside New York City. Like it's symbolic of our ability to adapt and stick together. We need that.

Alex wraps his arms around me from behind and plants kisses up and down my neck. I shake off the goose bumps he's just given me and turn my head to smile at him. "You look especially happy, which is surprising because I'm rooming with your sister tonight."

"I think maybe I've been looking forward to this a lot more than I let on," he admits.

My thoughts drift back to that first night we spent together at his apartment and what he said after I asked him what he wanted to do beyond the CK fragrance campaign had finished and he'd fulfilled his obligations with Elana.

I wouldn't mind being able to call my mom and maybe my sister and tell them I'm dating this really hot, really smart photography student from Columbia. They'd be pretty damn impressed.

"So I'm only here to make you look good?" I tease.

"It's not only that." He kisses my cheek and then my neck again. "You don't just make me look good; you've actually made me better. More like you've made me *want* to be a better person, which might be even more important than actually being a better person. It changes the way I make decisions, you know?"

I close my eyes and take in a deep breath of Midwest air and chlorine. "Again, where were you a few years ago, Alex Evans?"

"I'm sorry," he says. "But I'm here now."

And I hear what he doesn't say because they're exactly the same words in my head. I'm here for good. Alex is the one thing in my life that I'm completely sure of. Everything else will work itself out.

Everything else is unwritten.

Acknowledgments

We would both like to thank our agent, Nicole Resciniti, for her early dedication and love of this story. We'd also like to thank the Sourcebooks team for all of their hard work and guidance through this process.

FROM JULIE:
I'd like to thank my husband and family. Mark Perini, for being sane and inviting me into this odd, intriguing, and compelling world of fashion and modeling. I've learned so much writing this book.

FROM MARK:
I'd like to thank Julie Cross for believing in me and for being my guiding light throughout this literary journey. I'd also like to thank my parents for their unwavering love and support. Sorry Mom, I'll never be Dr. Perini, but I hope you're still proud!

About the Authors

Julie Cross is the international bestselling author of the Tempest series, a young adult science-fiction trilogy. Julie lives in Central Illinois with her husband and three children. Her knowledge of the modeling and fashion world comes from viewings of the movies *The Devil Wears Prada* and *Zoolander* and her unwavering devotion to the first three seasons of *Ugly Betty*. On a recent trip to NYC, she also took the time to walk past both the Gucci and Prada stores, spending at least fifteen seconds viewing items through the windows.

Mark Perini began his career as an international fashion model ten years ago, while simultaneously obtaining a business degree from Seton Hall University. Turns out fashion's hurry-up-and-wait mentality lends itself quite well to writing. Mark is now a New York City–based author, and *Halfway Perfect* is his first young adult novel. He is also a featured author in the New Adult anthology, *Fifty First Times*.

When he's not working, Mark's traveling the world. He's made a blood pact with friends to see all seven ancient wonders of the world before he's thirty. Four down, three to go.

FALL IN LOVE WITH THE HUNDRED OAKS SERIES FROM

Miranda Kenneally

For more about Miranda Kenneally, visit:

mirandakenneally.com

THE SUMMER AFTER YOU AND ME

Jennifer Salvato Doktorski

WILL IT BE A SUMMER OF FRESH STARTS OR SECOND CHANCES?

For Lucy, the Jersey Shore isn't just the perfect summer escape, it's home. As a local girl, she knows not to get attached to the tourists. They breeze in during Memorial Day weekend, crowding her coastal town and stealing moonlit kisses, only to pack up their beach umbrellas and empty promises on Labor Day. Still, she can't help but crush on charming Connor Malloy. His family spends every summer next door, and she longs for their friendship to turn into something deeper.

Then Superstorm Sandy sweeps up the coast, bringing Lucy and Connor together for a few intense hours. Except nothing is the same in the wake of the storm, and Lucy is left to pick up the pieces of her broken heart and her broken home. Time may heal all wounds, but with Memorial Day approaching and Connor returning, Lucy's summer is sure to be filled with fireworks.

JULIANA STONE

USA TODAY BESTSELLING AUTHOR

"The classic miscommunication, the emotional pushing and pulling, the 'will she?' and 'won't he?' of the destined-to-be-in-love. Readers of Miranda Kenneally, Jenny Han, and Susane Colasanti will enjoy Stone."

—*VOYA* on *Boys Like You*

For more about Juliana Stone, visit:

julianastone.com